Lamekis

also translated by Michael Shreve:

André Laurie: *Spiridon*

John-Antoine Nau: *Enemy Force*

Lamekis

by
Charles de Fieux,
Chevalier de Mouhy

translated by
Michael Shreve

A Black Coat Press Book

Acknowledgements: I should like to thank Paul Wessels for his generous and extensive help in the final preparation of this text and Suzanna Tamminen and Patrick Cline at the Wesleyan University Press.

Visit our website at www.blackcoatpress.com

Table of Contents

Introduction

Charles Fieux or de Fieux, Chevalier de Mouhy, was born on May 9, 1701 in Metz, France, or in Bourgogne if we believe some of his works where he says his family came from that province. According to his title, he was a cavalry officer, which is hard to believe since the *Chronique Scandaleuse* of 1785 described him as hunchbacked and lame—but that is the title he took and the costume he wore for his portrait by Fessard. He was a nephew of the Baron of Longepierre, a pensioner of the King, a member of the Academy of Dijon, an "applauder" and audience leader in the theater, a spy, pen pusher, satirist, blackmailer and professor of morality and religion toward the end of his life; he was a journalist, gazetteer, novelist and playwright, as well as writing about the theater, and one of the hardy libertines of the time. He was a colorful, mysterious, multivalent character and a puzzling, prolific writer who left behind a fog of misinformation making it hard to understand him today.

He arrived in Paris at a young age with nothing but his pen to support himself. The meager pay for his books did not satisfy his needs, so he did whatever he could to supplement them. He first pawned himself off on Voltaire as a literary agent and lawyer and a hired "applauder" for his plays—a common practice since classical times. It seems that de Mouhy sought out Voltaire perhaps to ask him for a loan. Voltaire wrote to Abbé Moussinot, agreeing to meet him, but promising nothing. As it turned out, the meeting went well and de Mouhy started working for Voltaire, but no letters exist between the two, so the exact nature of their relationship remains obscure. At the start, however, Voltaire did give him a loan because he thought he was a promising writer and that his first publications would pay it back.

It is likely that de Mouhy became Voltaire's literary agent in 1736 because only later did he deal with his legal matters. In 1738, Voltaire asked Abbé Moussinot to ask de Mouhy about his work and expenses and to keep everything discreet and secret. At the time, Voltaire was working to tarnish Pierre Desfontaines' reputation,[1] and de Mouhy became his champion. *Le Préservatif, ou Critique des Observations sur les écrits modernes* [The Prophylactic, or Criticism of Observations on modern writing] appeared anonymously in 1738, but was managed and sold under de Mouhy's name to keep Voltaire's own name out of it. When Desfontaines answered with *La Voltairomanie*, a libel suit followed, which was resolved a year later, although the war between the two continued for a long time. In 1738-39, Voltaire needed de Mouhy's help and support. Afterward, he continued working for Voltaire as a literary agent, but became more and more demanding, financially and otherwise.

For four years, between 1736 and 1740, Voltaire found de Mouhy to be a good secretary, better than as a writer, and he appreciated his work as an agent and applauder. For his

---

[1] A jesuit, the Abbé Desfontaines (1685-1745) can be regarded as the founder of a new approach to literary criticism in France at the time, relying on aesthetic and moral judgments as opposed to mere story summaries.

part, de Mouhy did anything he could to make himself worthy in Voltaire's eyes: writing, talking, visiting, selling, influencing, lying, scandalizing, etc. But de Mouhy was small, ugly and poor, so poor that he had to pawn his watch at one point. Voltaire continually loaned him money or just outright gave it to him, but never too much—it was a well-earned honorarium and the work de Mouhy had to do for Voltaire became infamous. On June 3 or 4, 1740, Voltaire gave de Mouhy his last commission. Ten years later, in 1750, he said de Mouhy was libeling him in the newspapers—which is unlikely—and called him a traitor and ingrate, but considering the reputation de Mouhy earned while in Voltaire's employ, perhaps that accusation should be leveled against Voltaire himself.

After leaving Voltaire, de Mouhy joined the service of the Maréchal de Belle-Isle, the Minister of War, doing all kinds of "dirty work" for which he was well paid. That's all de Mouhy wanted, since he really needed money and was not shy about how to get it. But after Maréchal's death, he was left with little if any respect in the world, and all the efforts he made to get some through his writings did not turn out too well for him.

De Mouhy began writing in 1735, launching his productive career with the first chapters of five different novels, including *La Paysanne parvenue*, *La Mouche* and *Lamekis*. Although he did not become rich and famous as a writer, he did earn a living. He wrote because he was hard up for money more than because he was inspired by genius—his works were meant to be appreciated by his contemporaries, not admired by posterity. And indeed, many of his works did have some kind of ephemeral success, especially his earlier ones, which earned him a reputation among novelists. But, generally, his books were not much valued. He gave them titles similar to famous works of the time to attract public attention, and imitated the popular works of writers such as Marivaux and Prévost to take advantage of contemporary trends, which earned him the sobriquet of "opportunist."

He went to cafés and people's homes, listened to everyone and then went back home and wrote a novel with the anecdotes he had heard. When the books came out, advertisements were posted everywhere on the street, and he himself, his pockets full of books, made the rounds of the cafés where people would buy them from him just to get rid of him or (some critics say) he even went to people's houses to give them away just so he could hear them applaud or whistle.

De Mouhy has also been criticized for writing carelessly and negligently, knocking out works of boring nonsense just to pay off his monthly debts. It is true he had the habit of writing as he published and working on several novels at the same time, as if his books wrote themselves (see Part 5, *The book writes itself*).

His admirers, however, talk about his fearless imagination, his mixing of genres, and his talent as a storyteller, writing simply and naturally. And in his compilation of the history of French theater (*Tablettes dramatiques*, later called *Le Dictionnaire*), he was the first to introduce an alphabetical list of all the plays put on in France, with the names of the authors and actors. But whatever was thought of his talent, de Mouhy was unanimously regarded as one of the most prolific authors of his time.

So, even if he wasn't blessed with genius, at least he had talent and an unbridled imagination; if he was only a second-rate writer, he was one of the best, and occasionally produced first-rate work. Unfortunately, he produced too many works early in his career and may have worn himself out in the end. By the time of his death, de Mouhy had penned more than 80 volumes of novels of various types, all vivid, but most of them were written before 1750. Today, his works are extremely hard to find—if anybody is looking—except for *La paysanne parvenue*, about a young country girl introduced into high society, *La Mouche ou les aventures de M. Bigand*, a colorful, comical, fantastic novel about a snitch, and *Le Masque de fer*—The Man in the Iron Mask—about the famous prisoner in the Bastille, which have recently been reprinted in France.

Lamekis, subtitled *Les Voyages extraordinaires d'un Égyptien dans la Terre Intérieure avec la Découverte de l'Île des Sylphides* [Lamekis, or The Extraordinary Voyages of an Egyptian in the Inner Earth with the Discovery of the Sylphides' Island] stands out as different from de Mouhy's other works.[2] It partakes of the then-current trend for imaginary voyages, satirical and didactic works, travel logs, etc., but is not really like any of them. Jacques Bosquet called it the "typical unknown masterpiece." Pierre Versins, in his *Encyclopédie de l'Utopie et de la Science-Fiction*, labels the work "a remote ancestor of Abraham Merritt—especially *The Moon Pool*—and H.P. Lovecraft." There is no real moral or didactic purpose to *Lamekis*, just an author reveling in his wild, explosive, frenetic imagination, perhaps too strange for his time and better understood from a modern point of view. Like *Force Ennemie* of John Antoine Nau, another, later "unknown masterpiece,"[3] de Mouhy plays with both narrative and typographical strangeness—the adjective "extraordinary" in the title is no empty promise. The different physical mazes of the Inner Earth mirror his labyrinthine story structure and state of mind. His use of an invented language, confused and unusual references, fake notes, parentheses, ellipses, etc. have fun with the literature of his age.

---

[2] The first part was published in Paris in 1735 by Dupuis; the second part came out the following year. Parts 3 and 4 came out in 1737 in Paris, but were published by Poilly. The final four parts, 5-8, were all published in 1738 in The Hague, Netherlands, by Neaulme. In 1788, *Lamekis* was reprinted in Volumes 20-21 of Charles Georges Thomas Garnier's ground-breaking imprint, *Voyages imaginaires, songes et visions et romans cabalistiques*, Amsterdam—the reprint did not include de Mouhy's prefaces to parts 3, 5 and 8 from the original edition, which are included here in the Appendix. No other editions of *Lamekis* have been published since then. In this first English edition, the spelling and names have been normalized and section titles given to facilitate reading.
[3] Available in a Black Coat Press edition as *Enemy Force*, ISBN 9781935558491.

De Mouhy was not afraid of parodying his own work in 1752 with *Opuscule d'un célébre auteur egyptien. Contenant l'histoire d'Orphée, par laquelle on pourroit soupçonner qu'il est peu de femmes fidele* [Opuscule of a famous Egyptian writer, containing the history of Orpheus in which one might suspect that there are few faithful women]. But *Lamekis* stands today as his greatest, maybe his only, legacy, one that we would be all the poorer without.

Charles de Fieux died in Paris at 83 years of age on February 29, 1784.

Michael Shreve

LAMEKIS

Author's Preface

On my way back from a long business trip on which I had to stay "incognito," I met an Armenian who was moving to Paris. His conversations were pleasant enough to make up for the boredom of the trip and they made me feel in less of a hurry to get home. One evening while we were walking under a beautiful full moon on the banks of a river that watered the village where we were staying, we began talking to pass the time. It was on that night that this work I offer to the public was born. The Armenian was fascinated by the beauty of nature and he told me all kinds of stories about it. The story of Lamekis fascinated me and I made him repeat it every day so I could take notes. At the end of our trip I found I had enough material for three parts.

It is up to the readers to decide if I was wrong to think that this story is entertaining. It is so new and so full of strange and extraordinary events that I am convinced that I will not disappoint the public by bringing it out.

Now I only have to respond to the concerns of a few people who say that it is impossible for me to have completed all the works that appear under my name and that it would be more probable and even more logical that I got hold of them just to polish them off rather than contribute anything original. I assure the public that I have always worked hard and meticulously to satisfy them and I have always tried to be as entertaining as possible since I find nothing more flattering than to achieve that.

Part 1

The mighty north winds had been tossing us around in a terrible storm for three days and had thrown us on death's doorstep in the raging chaos of our blasted sails, when they suddenly stopped. As the sea slowly calmed and the waves, which seemed to want to smash our ship to pieces, started dying down, we recovered our courage that had been wrested away by our uncertain fate. We made a sacrifice to the god Serapis on the upper deck and sprinkled the ship with precious liquor to purify it of the impurity of our tears. Everyone congratulated one another for escaping what seemed an inevitable death. The fear of danger, which had kept us from minding our natural needs, had vanished and we ran to the food and drink that beguiles care. The present made us forget the horrors of the past—pleasure is never as intense as when it follows woe. The whole crew took part and after the feast, where Bacchus held sway, all of them, even the helmsmen, were charmed into a deep sleep.

I was the only one who did not give myself up to either debauchery or rest. After a light meal I sat on the poop and looked out over the vastness of the sea with my head full of cruel notions about the harsh fate that persecuted me. I was sunk in these sad thoughts when Sinouis roused me.

"What am I seeing?" he said to me. "Lamekis is shedding tears and I don't know why! His great soul is not prone to the fear of death. It's too lofty to stoop so low. Oh Lamekis! Will my friendship for you ever get to the bottom of your heart? Will you always fend off my thoughtfulness? Since I've known you, since melancholy has tainted your thoughts, I haven't been able to earn your trust. If my devotion is worth anything to you, tell me your secrets. Whatever they are, they will be safe in the bosom of a friend who is not only discreet and sympathetic, but who is also willing to lose his life to prove to you his mettle."

"Oh Sinouis!" I sighed, "You don't know what you're asking. How can I give an account of such an extraordinary life? Aren't you afraid that I will make you part of my constant misfortune?"

"No, No," my true friend continued, "nothing could ever sever me from you. It is by following your destiny that I can prove to you the strength of my feelings. Real friends are proven only in adversity. We shouldn't rely on their assurances of zeal until they've been purified in the fire of disaster."

He said a few other things like that and I was so touched that I could not refuse his insistence. For myself I assured him that I appreciated his zeal and to prove it I began to tell him the story of my life as follows.

Lamekis the Elder, High Priest of Egypt, and Semiramis the Queen

My father, Lamekis, was the High Priest of the god whom they worship in Egypt. Everyone respected him for his honesty, his religion and his kindness. The grandeur of all his actions seemed, if I may say so, to be the very image of the divinity they worshipped in the temple. When he pronounced the oracles, they were spoken so honorably that everyone who heard them felt the holiest of emotions. The veneration they had for this minister made him almost as powerful in the state as Semiramis, who was on the throne at the time. The Queen was very attached to my father and nothing could be decided in the counsels without calling him.

One day she summoned him to her chamber. It was the first time that she was alone with him. She had been attracted to him for a long time and the wisdom of his advice had always made less of an impression on her than his handsome face did.

"Lamekis," she said, "I know the laws of the inner temple, but my way of thinking is above vulgar fears. For many years now I have desired to be initiated in the mysteries of Serapis. You have to satisfy me: any opposition to my resolution will be useless. I want the entrance to the catacombs opened for me. I am Queen and in my realm only my sovereign power commands."

"Oh Princess!" the High Priest cried. "What are you asking of me? Do you know the price you will have to pay?"

"It doesn't matter," the impetuous Queen replied. "I want it to happen in three days. Tomorrow I will wait for you to prepare me as you need. Go now and don't answer. Just consider that Semiramis must really appreciate you to honor you with such a grace."

The High Priest was upset by this command. He knew the fury of the Princess when she was hampered in her desires. His predecessor became food for the Sacred Leopard[4] when he refused to let her take part in the feast of the golden horn.[5] It is true that she got revenge for what had got in the way of her desire, but she did not disturb the mysteries by showing up; or maybe also she had heard some of the rumors caused by the death and she did not want to worsen them by being stubborn. But it was no less certain that her power had increased lately and nothing could oppose it.

The High Priest was bewildered and upset. So, being the devoted minister, he ran to his divinity. He invoked it, but was surprised to find it deaf to his voice. "Oh Heavens!" he cried, "Apis refuses to give his eternal orders to his slave! What am I to do? Shall I open the fateful flank?[6] Oh Queen, what have you asked? And you, God, whom I have served for so long, does your silence smile or frown upon an order that is so contrary to the laws of the temple? Semiramis represents your

---

[4] The Leopard was highly venerated. It had traveled with the bull Apis and kept him from danger. It was held in a Catacomb and fed on the bodies of criminals.

[5] This mysterious feast took place on the 1st of Cubai, i.e. May.

[6] The belly of the statue contained the key to the underground.

supreme power; she is its image. But does this extend all the way to your sanctuary?"

He spoke, but the adamant statue made no sign. He opened the sacred flank, took out the golden key and went down into the catacombs where they kept the eternal fire. The flame, which usually rose up in his presence, remained still. He was flabbergasted. He wanted to speak to the minister of the divine worship who was under his authority, but the law of silence, which had been imposed since the creation of the mysteries, forbade it. He groaned inside. The priests were surprised at his visit and shuddered at the danger it foretold. They knew that their superior should not descend into the catacombs except with the King, only for his consecration, and (except for this) he should not appear unless there was a revolution in the state or some unimaginable event. Lamekis bowed down before the sacred tripod and was purified by the fire. His confidence and strength came back to him and when he went back to the upper temple, he was resolved to defend the integrity of the mysteries. He spent the night at the foot of the altar. The vaults trembled; at the break of day thunder roared. The statue groaned. The horns of the divine bull turned black and from its holy mouth these words came out clearly: "Semiramis is Queen and you are her subject."

Lamekis, who was used to explaining the oracles, had a hard time finding the meaning of this one. He spent the rest of the day trying to fathom the sovereign will. It seemed to him that on the one hand it was declaring to him the authority of the ruler and on the other the obedience of a subject. He worshipped the divinity, prayed that it would inspire him and, filled with an inner comfort, he went to see Semiramis.

"Well now!" she said when she saw him. "Is the statue of Serapis open to me? Am I going to penetrate at last into the heart of the mysteries?"

"Semiramis is Queen and Lamekis is her subject," the High Priest replied. "It is for me to obey, but I have to tell you and warn you of the consequences of your dangerous curiosity. Ah, Madame," he continued, "master this desire that can

Semiramis trembled at his speech, which was pronounced with such grandeur that it seemed at that moment that the god was speaking through his mouth. Her mind wandered for a few minutes, but her heart (though warned) set her above all fear. "Ah!" she sighed, "what does it matter if I die, as long as I'm with the one I love! Yes, Lamekis," she saw him shrink back from her declaration, "I love you. I am carried away by an invincible power. The crown cannot protect my heart from the weakness of love. I fought against this relentless flame in vain—nothing will ever be able to extinguish it. My only hope is to invoke Apis in the heart of the mysteries. There I will be healed or find relief for my pain. It's no use scaring me or opposing my will. I have to go into the sacred caves and bury my passion and shame in their silence. Go!" She did not want to give him time to answer. "At sunrise I will be at the temple gate. And remember, if you resist, I will raze it to the ground."

Lamekis still tried to use all the eloquence at his disposal to bring the impetuous Princess back to her senses. He argued in vain because she was used to following no law but her own will. Resistance only inflamed her more; nothing could change her final decision.

The High Priest left with a deep sorrow in his heart, which was a bad omen. After purifying himself he went back inside the temple and spent the rest of the day and night kneeling before the statue and watering it with his tears.

Lamekis the Elder and Semiramis enter the catacombs

The Sun had barely lit the azure vaults of the temple with its golden rays when music struck the ears of Lamekis. He had dozed off, weary and troubled, and awoke with a start. He knew only too well that they were announcing the arrival of the Queen. She entered the temple alone and after bowing she went to the gate of the sanctuary. Lamekis repeated his sage advice and explained that there was still time to turn back, but her decision was made. She was wearing the crown and her beauty and majesty joined together made her commands so absolute that it was impossible to resist them. The sanctuary was opened and he respectfully presented her with a headband that the Kings used in the coronation ceremony to cover their eyes so they would not know the secret entrance to the catacombs. Semiramis let herself be veiled.

"I am in your hands," she told him, "but I was smart enough to take all necessary precautions for the dangers you warned me about. I know your honesty and the respect you have for the blood of your Kings. I can see them in the details you gave me, the language of your priesthood, and the idea you must have of my power. But watch out, Lamekis, if you abuse my kindness. I have given orders that will be faithfully carried out. If I am not back in front of my guards and my people in three hours, the temple will be leveled and they will avenge the attack on the ruler of these lands by destroying everyone within."

The Queen's determination surprised the High Priest. He had hoped that the fears he tried to instill in her would sway her desire, which was so contrary to the Laws. There was no precedent that the laws had ever been violated; and the death penalty for those who transgressed them should not include the Sovereign, of course. On the other hand, this very penalty would be inflicted on the High Priest because he alone is the secret master of the entrance and the mysteries could not be profaned without his involvement.

Lamekis was so surprised at the Queen's final words that he stood there without moving. Finally he threw himself on his knees and said to her, "Oh Queen, since you want to be faithfully obeyed, you have to know how to act in order to avoid a certain death. The spirit within these men who are going to be honored by your presence down there differs in every way from normal sentiments. Born in the heart of the earth and in ignorance, they know nothing but Serapis and his laws. I will be the first victim of their fury if I give them any reason to suspect that I have sinned against their eternal rules. Like people living in the woods they are brutal and it would be useless for me to vaunt your superiority and the power of the crown, respect and dependency. Even the power you have over their lives means nothing; nothing will calm them. Their prejudice and the law will make them angry and both of us will become victims of their anger.

"I tell you this, Princess, to protect your precious life. You have to wear the mantle in exactly the same way as our Kings during their initiation when they go down into the mystic catacombs where they stay for a day. Like that, the ministers of our revered god, who don't know very much about what happens above them, will take you for their master and pay no attention."

His arguments were too logical to go unheeded. The Queen agreed to be transformed and she changed her orders about when she would come back. When all was done, the High Priest opened the secret trapdoor and led the way holding a torch.

She had to rest several times. The number of steps, already around 2,000, began to frighten her. She thought she was going down into the realm of the dead. But she kept her thoughts to herself. The harder it got, the more curious she became. At the last step a corridor led into a large gallery lit at regular distances by lamps that never went out. The wall was covered with marble inscribed with hieroglyphs showing the mysteries of Serapis. The vast hall was more than 100 measures long and ended in a portico through which could be seen four wide paths lit by an infinite number of lanterns. It was teeming with people who seemed to be doing business like in any big city.

As soon as the High Priest was recognized, a general cry was raised that shook the vaults and the sound of a mournful instrument announced his arrival. When the people heard it, a deep silence followed, the streets were deserted and a thousand new lights appeared, which could have rivaled the brightness of the sunniest day. 12 priests dressed in long cassocks of the finest leather came up and kneeled at their feet. 12 others followed bearing a stretcher with two seats on which the Queen and Lamekis were placed. They walked with a great crowd of people all around them. Semiramis was surprised at this and at that moment she formed a plan that when she got back to her palace she would round up this nursery, which was a feeding ground of rebellion, as she saw it, to make them ordinary subjects.

After walking for about a mile like this, they came to a large square where there was a temple supported by 40 marble columns. An image of Serapis was set on the marble altar and the steps they went up were sculptured with the latest, most delicate and the most exquisite workmanship. The roof of the temple seemed to come straight out of the vaulting, which here was as high as the eye could see. There were 40 triumphal arches through which they entered the building, each with a door carved with the mysterious history of the divinity.

The stretcher stopped before the temple. The High Priest got the Queen down and they clothed her in a bull-skin coat[11] whose tail was held by Lamekis. The 24 ministers followed them up the stairs and to the altar. After Semiramis knelt down at the feet of the divine bull, they passed it three times between her legs, an honor reserved only for the master of Egypt.[12]

After this blessing was made, they put her back up on the throne carried by the 12 priests. Lamekis walked in front with his head now decorated: with a great deal of ceremony he was dressed in a very tall cap with four horns driven in lower down and four others with their points out above. A cow's tail came out of the middle tied with golden ribbons, the god's favorite color. Each subordinate minister had on the same hat, but with only one row of horns and the tail was shorter and without ribbons.

The procession went down a broad street that ended in a gate guarded by 25 priests in short coats. They had wide belts

[11] When a bull died they embalmed his entrails and his whole skin was carefully preserved to be used only by the ministers of the divinity.

[12] The author is mistaken. The High Priest had the same honor when he was sanctified.

from which hung a bull's leg[13] and in their hands they held a kind of pizzle whip. They were all dressed alike: rough black leather with big horn buttons, finely crafted. Their caps had only one horn, but with a crest made from cow ears, very well carved and easy on the eyes. When the procession appeared the ministers were armed and to honor the Queen they held the bull's foot in their hands. The captain of the troop, noticeable by the huge beef tongue he wore as a collar, the sign of his rank, approached Semiramis respectfully, put a finger to his lips and a seal over his heart. With a nod from the High Priest the Queen kissed his head, which was the customary vow not to reveal the mysteries.

The Princess got down from the stretcher and four men brought forth a huge, brass instrument[14] with four pipes, which they put to their mouths. The instrument made a raucous, frightening sound that was used to warn the people to go back home and if any were found in the streets by the guards they would be food for the great leopard.

After the ministers sounded their instrument four times, the gate was opened. The High Priest went past the guards first, followed by Semiramis. When they got to the end of the hallway, Lamekis knocked three times on the door and it opened. An old man wearing a hat, which was a lantern with a hanging light, cracked open a window and the High Priest stuck his head through the opening. Four old men came up, recognized him and whispered in his ear.[15] The Queen had to stick her head through too and they changed her sacred headband for a leather one. After this they let her into a hallway that ended in four galleries, each closed by a door with a window.

---

[13] In the 35th article of the Bosoë law, it is said that the priests of Serapis who guard the underground will carry a bull's foot instead of weapons.

[14] Called Bursoan. The Egyptians used it when they went into battle.

[15] In spite of much research, what they said has never been discovered.

The High Priest knocked on one and an old man appeared wearing a bull's head that he respectfully took off at the sight of Semiramis. The High Priest was recognized and the door opened. The old man with the bull's head threw himself at the feet of the Queen and after this homage he led the way, prancing and jumping every ten steps.

This gallery was called Koroïka[16] and ended in the catacomb Lesmikis where the book of law was kept. No hieroglyphs decorated it. The walls and the vault were all covered with black marble. When the old man got to the end of the gallery he stamped his foot. Three other ministers of the same age knelt at the entrance holding a finger to their lips.

The Queen was frightened by their looks. They had long beards that hung down to their feet and at the end of every strand was tied a bull's tooth; they clicked and rattled at the slightest movement. But what made their sight hideous was that the weight of all the teeth pried the old men's mouths open into the most grisly scowl you could imagine. They were bald and half nude and their withered skin was slashed in so many places and so close together that the scars stuck out like the spines of a hedgehog.

In the middle of the mystic catacomb was the great book[17] whose pages were made of bronze. The High Priest opened it and the sound of the pages falling upon each other was worse than the slamming doors of the most dreadful prison. The three old men helped Lamekis turn the pages and when they found the passage with the King's vow, they all knelt down and swore-in Semiramis.

---

[16] According to a famous author this gallery was covered in hieroglyphs that told the story of Serapis. They say that after an earthquake in Egypt in 1504, out of this buried chamber, as we will see, came a surprising number of bas-reliefs, many of which were carried away to different courts in Europe. Among these was a statue of a high priest with a finger touching his lips and a book in his hand with a cover inscribed with Coroïca or the law.

[17] They still have this book in Tauris, [Tabriz], and they claim that Thamas Koulikan, [Nader Shah], owns it.

After this ceremony, they left the catacomb and went back through Koroïka. Lamekis knocked on the door of Buraïkos,[18] which led to the sacred fire. At this door appeared a man around 40 years old who looked wild: he rolled his eyes in rage and scowled so frightfully at the High Priest that Semiramis recoiled. Lamekis reassured her. There was no reason to ask the name of this gallery—its heat gave it away as that of the fire kept in the catacombs. They saw it at a distance raised on a massive, iron tripod behind a gate of the same metal. The whole hallway was full of the bones of the dead, carefully piled on top of each other, which made them look very graceful. Two young men walked over them barefoot carrying a watering can that they used to sprinkle human skin oil over the mass grave. The Queen urged Lamekis to leave the place because the smell was really appalling. In consideration he cut the ceremony short: they brought her into the catacomb (where she could barely stand the heat), took off her headband, sprinkled it with the sacred oil and put it in the sacred fire. A small flame burned it slightly. Lamekis put it back, scalding hot, on the Queen's delicate forehead. The pain she felt was so bad that she let out an awful scream. And the vault echoed so that it could be heard everywhere around. Angry howls answered and the noise grew so loud that it seemed like the ceiling was going to collapse.

"Ah, Princess, what have you done?" the High Priest cried out. "I warned you that your voice would betray you. If they find out you're a woman, we're lost. This noise I hear coming from all quarters makes me fear for your life. What help do we have to save us from rebellion? You yourself saw how carefully they guard this place. How are we going to escape the rage they think is justified?"

---

[18] Buraïkos or the burning. This place was so holy that for the priests to be allowed to guard the fire they had to be chosen by the god himself. The fire was kept burning with nothing but human bones, which they made combustible by sprinkling them with human skin oil.

He did not have time to say anything else. The gallery doors opened and the underground ministers showed up all together, followed by the people. The High Priest in this emergency resorted to a ploy—make the divinity speak. He went toward them in the grandeur he always assumed and broke the silence for the first time.[19] He asked them arrogantly the reason for their turbulent arrival and their lack of respect.

"Don't you know," he pretended to be inspired from on high, "that Serapis is ready to crush you? I see the foundations of his temple shaken. Oh people, what have you done? They are going to crumble, to punish you for your recklessness. Oh Heavens, stop! Your ministers repent and kneel at your feet for mercy."

He spoke foaming at the mouth with his hands over his head as if to hold up the ceiling about to fall. The ministers, who first appeared ready for rebellion, trembled at his words. They threw themselves on the ground and humbly asked forgiveness.

"If you leave," Lamekis raised his voice, "I will intercede with the god and calm his anger, which I see is at its peak."

He had barely finished speaking before they left and silence fell. The High Priest wanted to take advantage of the fear that the Queen must have felt at what just happened in order to get her out of the catacombs and away from the secret mysteries. But the Princess had a heart that was stronger than most of her sex and her policies of love were in tune with her policies of the state. She wanted to probe the mysteries and go down into the underground Vestasia[20] where they kept the three virgins. The High Priest obeyed reluctantly; he could not disobey her sovereign orders. He led the Queen to the trapdoor Luroë[21] [...][22]

---

[19] The first law was Kroustia or Sitao, i.e. perpetual silence or death.

[20] The most remote underground chamber.

[21] Luroë or the last secret, according to the rites of Semiramis, opened a very narrow marble staircase at the bottom of which was the chamber of Vestasia. There was a mysterious room inside where, after

Semiramis was furious at the High Priest's denial, but covered it up and asked to go back up. She went back the same way she had come and after a hard and tiring walk, they were in the upper temple again. It was full of the Queen's guards; the officers in charge had surrounded the sanctuary. She ordered Lamekis to bring the officers in and spoke to the chief.

"Open the doors," she shouted. "Put them all under arrest and tell the people to listen to me."

Lamekis was distraught by the Queen's orders and threw himself at her feet.

"What are you planning to do?" he pleaded respectfully.

"To utterly destroy a rebellious swarm," she replied, "and tell my subjects about the abyss they're digging for them."

"Ah! Princess," the High Priest cried. "Stop! Shudder at the thought of this idea. You're going to put all of Egypt to fire and sword and the Earth will vomit out entire armies to punish you for your attack."

"Understand, Lamekis," the Queen spoke softly in his ear, "you are dear to me and I will take care of you. But I do not want the power of my hidden enemies to grow any stronger. I have found out their plans: under the veil of religion and on the pretext of putting Serapis on my throne, they will place themselves there and sooner or later the dark caves will vomit

---

going so far just to enter, it was necessary to give real proof of the difference of sexes. The High Priest was apparently prohibited from entering with Semiramis, which, as simple as it seemed, according to the same rites, was the cause of the ruin of the famous temple of Serapis, which will be talked about until the end of days. I am not knowledgeable enough to describe this temple or the variety of mysteries. I leave it to the scholars to enrich us of these treasures.

[22] Here is a lacuna of several pages in the manuscript. I could describe the place, but I have too much respect for antiquity. As well described as the room might be, it would always be an obvious addition. I would rather be faithful than prolific.

out a tyrant and usurp the lawful power. The time has come to destroy their criminal designs."

She got up on the platform with Lamekis and revealed to the people the secrets of the catacombs and told them how dangerous it was to let the enemies keep growing in number and lying in wait to attack. She pointed out how many of them there were and finished her rant citing the kingdoms that were destroyed by such scheming sites. The end of her speech had the effect she expected. The Princess was loved and her words swayed them heavily because of her gracious character. Shouts rang out demanding the destruction of the underground. And only the respect they had for the Queen saved Lamekis from their fury. She arrested him only when they insisted that she had to get to the bottom of the matter. The people demanded that he be held under guard until the next day, when the powerful underground would be destroyed. She gave the High Priest to the guards to lead him to the palace so that he might be close at hand to help in the destruction, or so the Queen said, when really she just wanted to talk to him about her love that was as crucial to her as the action she set in motion.

"Lamekis," she said when she was alone with him in her room, "I have had eyes for you for a long time. In spite of what happened, you are priceless and my feelings for you keep you close to my heart. I don't have to say any more. You can guess the rest. You will share the supreme power with me and in spite of my people's fury I will save you and change their hatred into respect. Answer me. Don't let my rank worry you. You know me and you should know that when a Queen confesses a weakness, she anticipates everything that can happen.

Semiramis waited a long time for Lamekis' response. He was troubled by her words and was battling in the inner depths of his soul. His natural generosity made him feel like a caring father for the people about to be destroyed, which stirred up infinite pity in him and made his soul tremble in fear. But whatever choice he made, he could not avoid the loss of what was most precious to him: Lamekis was a husband and father, but the Queen did not know that. Once the secret was revealed it would give rise to such jealousy in Semiramis, learning why he could not give his love to her, that she would not hesitate to kill all his loved ones. However, knowing that indecision on his part could not stop all these evils, he would rather die in virtue than live in crime and defile his ministry. He spoke to her with this mind. Semiramis tried her charms and tears to seduce him. Like a rock beaten by the waves, Lamekis' virtue upheld him in this dangerous confrontation. He kept to his decision and did not surrender to any hope. Hatred followed upon love and the result of the battle was a command to deliver the High Priest to the people's fury, which was urgently demanding his head.

He was barely out of Semiramis' sight when she repented and sent a counter-order, but it was too late. The people had got hold of him and all the Queen's power could not take him out of their hands. The most furious wanted to chop him to pieces then and there. So, with a saintly tranquility he waited in irons for the end of his life—his virtue gave him a serenity that put him above even the cruelest events.

A Council was held and it decided that he would be burned alive. The stake was set up, they attached him to the post and the ready torches were set on fire. But the righteous Heavens, protector of innocence, burst forth. Thunder roared and the people were astonished. The sky was lit up everywhere by lightning flashes. It looked like the Universe was about to collapse and return to eternal night. Everyone cried out that Serapis was avenging the outrage to his minister. They ran to the stake, untied Lamekis and led him in triumph to the temple. They sacrificed to the divinity, and the Heavens eased up. Calm followed the fury.

But the Queen herself had trembled in fear and then buried herself in terrible grief when the High Priest was swept away from her anger. And her desire for revenge revived. She sent some guards to seize Lamekis, but he was too clever to be exposed to such a danger a second time. He went down into the catacombs, sowing chaos and confusion. Holding nothing back, he aroused in them the desire to defend themselves and to carry out the plans that the ministers had been working on for so long; they said that they wanted to destroy the monarchy, make Serapis the everlasting King and rule under his name and auspices. The undertaking was bold and would have succeeded, but the Queen's policies and determination foiled their criminal project.

The officer in charge of arresting Lamekis reported that he could not be found and had probably gone back to the underground. She led them to the temple and searched it so carefully that the trapdoor to the catacombs was found. Troops were brought in to go down, but were surprised to find it walled up. Workers were ordered to break it down. For eight days in a row they worked at it without being able to get through. As much as they demolished one side, they rebuilt the other. It was an endless labor and they were forced to stop and find another means of access.

The more difficulties they faced, the more determined Semiramis became. The resistance troubled her and she tried every way imaginable to get underground. She brought in countless workers to dig an entrance, but no matter how hard they worked or how deep they dug, they found no trace of what they were looking for. The people began to whisper that it was a fruitless task and believed they should abandon it. But finally after six months they hit a vault. They informed the Queen who wanted to be present when they broke through. They people armed themselves, the vault was broken and a detachment was ordered to go down into the underground. They found a whole city, as big as the capital, but deserted. Semiramis trembled at the news and sent twice as many guards to make a thorough search.

That's what the hidden enemy wanted. They had set up an ambush in the confusing maze that hacked the Queen's troops to pieces. Only one soldier, who was in charge of watching the device they used to descend, escaped. He gave the signal, was brought back up and reported the fatal news, telling them that the number of conspirators was so great and their hideout was so well defended that it was hopeless to take them by force. They held a council after this news and found a very easy method of destroying the rebellious swarm. It was decided that they would write to the High Priest on behalf of the Queen and warn him that if his ministers and the enemy population did not put down their arms and surrender to the mercy of the Queen, they would destroy them without a single person escaping the dreadful fate awaiting them.

Lamekis believed it was an empty threat just to intimidate them. He answered that he and his people were ready to die rather than give up their arms; they were determined to defend themselves; it was kill or be killed. The Queen was informed of their stubborn response and had a ditch dug from the Nile to the buried vault. When they got four measures deep, she had a second letter written to the rebels in which they warned them of the means they had to destroy every last one of them. To prove her threat she wanted them to send four representatives to verify it and she would send four of her people as hostages. The offer was accepted. The envoys saw the arm of the Nile dangerously close to their dwelling and admitted that there was no way to escape being drowned. They asked for six hours to give an answer and then reported the sad news to the underground city. At the end of the period, one of them showed up at the bottom of the device and handed a letter to the guard, who immediately sent it to the Queen. And she read the following dispatch:

To Semiramis from Lamekis, High Priest:

The kindness you honored me with, Madame, deserves my sincere gratitude and now I am ready to bid you an eternal farewell. The least I owe you is a picture of the real situation and of my true feelings.

The cult of Serapis is destroyed. The god's predictions are accomplished, but his temple is eternal and will survive as long as the Earth turns on its axis. The waters of the Nile can destroy his ministers' refuge, but they will never put out the sacred fires that burn in their hearts. His supreme bounty, while suffering the destruction of the temple, long ago pre-

pared a place to shelter us from all powers. Before this letter is read, the people persecuted by your hatred will be in a safe place, a secret underground passage will lead them to the shores of an unknown sea where ships are always ready to take them to the land where Serapis reigns. I thought I should tell you this so that your calm life will not be disturbed and you will have nothing to fear from these men who never offended you for the simple reason that they never knew you.

On reading the letter the Queen was rattled and made them go down into the underground. They searched everywhere, but this time reported that it was deserted and it even seemed that they had taken supplies to survive for awhile, but the maze was so full of twists and turns that it was impossible to know which way the people had fled. The Queen sent down her cleverest officers and they said the same thing. But the Princess was defiant and suspected new stratagems, so she sent down even more guards than before and ordered them to leave no stone unturned to find out how the rebels got away.

The officer she put in charge of this project was the avowed enemy of the ministers of Serapis and did his duty with zeal. The orders were so strict and he himself examined the place so carefully that he finally discovered the escape route. Lamekis thought he could fool them by building a wall behind them as they slipped away, not imagining that they would search the remote corner, but he had not figured on such a clever man as the one the Queen had dispatched. The Commandant recognized that the wall was new and had it knocked down. Two hours later he found that it led to the coast. He sent word to the Queen and he himself was so dutiful that by the middle of the night he had stopped the ship on which Lamekis was about to be saved, since he was the last to leave, putting, like any good citizen, his country's safety before his own. He was caught completely off guard when he was arrested along with two women and three children.

Imagine the joy that Semiramis felt when she heard the news. She celebrated by destroying the catacombs—she drowned them in the waters of the Nile. To top off her vengeance she knocked down the temple razing it to the ground.

When the Queen found out that one of the women arrested on the boat was Lamekis' wife, she was furious. She had recovered from the High Priest's denial of her desires by believing that since he was born in the worship of the gods his heart was love-proof, but if she kept at him, he would eventually succumb to her charms. So this news magnified her anger and revived her passion. She summoned him and her eyes and love tried over and over again to latch onto him. But Lamekis' fidelity withstood her efforts while using all his wisdom to put out Semiramis' fires. His virtuous speeches were of no use; his resistance frustrated her. Her hatred regained the upper hand and she was ready twenty times over to revenge her outraged passion by sacrificing the High Priest and his wife to her fury. But her canny rage, not satisfied with a death that would free them from her tyranny, came up with new and untried ways to drag out the punishment. She had a raft built on which she fastened Lamekis and those with him and she cast them onto the sea without food, water, masts or sails.

Lamekis on the high seas

Here, Oh Sinouis, is where I will start talking about myself. I was one of Lamekis' poor children. I was 10 years old and even at that age I felt all the hardship of our fate. My father was very strong and steadfast. With his wise words and his piety he urged us to resign ourselves to our misfortune. Milkhea, my mother, cried bitter tears. Seeing me and my little sister in swaddling clothes (who would perish before our eyes) broke her heart. The cries of Haronza, the wife of the chief minister of the ruined catacombs, whose daughter hung from her breast, added to our sorry state—the worst, most dire situation possible—so that we hoped for death to bring a swift end to our fatigue.

We spent three days and nights in that dire situation. The death of my little sister started the catastrophe. "Oh Heavens!"

Milkhea cried, snatching her out of the arms of Lamekis who wanted to throw her into the sea to remove the heartbreaking thing. "Give me the comfort of dying with this dear child. Savage Queen, what have I done to deserve such cruel punishment? And you, my son," she looked at me with tear-drowned eyes, "will the Heavens not take pity on your youth? Oh Serapis! Oh hideous fate! Must everything living die?"

Haronza died of weakness on the fourth day. We had no more tears to shed; desperation had dried them all up. An awful silence fell upon us. Only Lamekis seemed to be waiting calmly for an end to this terrible tragedy. My little sister's nanny was driven by devouring hunger to throw herself on dying Haronza's daughter, wanting to eat her in a fit. Lamekis screamed out at the sight and tried in vain to stop her ghastly desire. The horror that I felt made me jump on the woman and wrench away her prey. I bore the marks of her rage—her murderous teeth bit out a chunk of my hand. She devoured my flesh like a fury in front of us while I howled in pain.

This new tragedy, however, saved the life of Haronza's daughter. My mother put her to her breast and took my hand. She tried to stop my bleeding with a bandage and when a few drops of blood by chance fell into the crying infant's mouth, the baby calmed down instantly and started smiling. My mother noticed this and seeing me suck my wound because it helped me feel better, she suggested I give some to the poor little girl. She grabbed it as eagerly and intensely as my mother's breast and soon opened her eyes completely. The gruesome new food brought her back to life. Then Milkhea was sorry that she had not given her blood to save the life of her own daughter. I found some relief and felt a secret consolation whose motives I could not understand. Oh Serapis, how wonderful your decrees are! Who could ever have foreseen what would come of this event!

It was impossible, however, for us to pull through this harsh situation. We were more ravaged by thirst than by hunger. The seawater we tasted, far from refreshing us, burned our hearts. We were ready to be devastated by all this when the wind suddenly changed; heavy rain and hail fell. The raft was filled up and we saw it like manna sent from the Heavens to prolong our sorry lives. We jumped on it eagerly and it tasted so delicious that our energy was, so to speak, reanimated. But as comforting as this was, it did nothing to assuage our devouring hunger. One desire is satisfied and another, more insistent, arises. All our energy was gone and lethargy soon followed anger. Lamekis was the first to give in. In spite of his strength in adversity he fell backward and Milkhea soon did the same. The infant was crying, but my blood still sustained her, even as I felt the pain of my wound come back. My poor life was not going to last long, but the gods did not want to put a quick end to my misery.

The raft suddenly beached on a bank of sand. It stretched out in both directions and was covered with shellfish. The natural desire we have to save our lives made me taste one. It was so delicious that I cried out in joy. "Ah, my father! Ah, my mother!" I cried. "The Heavens have taken pity on us. See the gifts before us. They will bring us back to life."

They both opened their eyes, but they barely had the strength to react. "Oh my son!" Lamekis said. "Let the Heavens preserve us. The kindness of your heart has earned us these miracles."

They ate some and I put some in the mouth of the little girl. It had such a wonderful effect on all of us that we soon felt drowsy. The cruel woman who had bit me in fury was dead and it was very hard for us to unload her from the raft.

Motacoa saves Lamekis

I was buried deeply in sleep, which I had not had for a very long time, but I woke up with a start when I felt myself being carried away by someone. I opened my eyes and what a surprise! I was in the arms of a man with an extraordinary face. I called out for my father Lamekis and my mother. Because of the night I could not make out my surroundings; I could only tell that I was on land. I cried and the man carrying me patted me and tried to calm me down. At the end of an hour-long walk he descended into a grotto where he put me down on a small mat bed. The grief of being taken away from my loved ones almost made me pass out and I was so crushed that I went more than two days without opening my eyes or eating anything.

But on the third day I looked around. A pretty woman, whom I had not seen before, was sitting near me. She seemed worried about my desperate condition. She was talking to me in an unknown language trying to get me to eat what she was holding. I finally tasted some and found it so good that I gobbled it up. It was a kind of rice cooked with meat and the woman looked happy that I gobbled it up greedily.

A moment later the man who had brought me came in. The woman ran up to him and talked excitedly while watching me. He raised his eyes to the Heavens to express his infinite gratitude. I heard the word "Lamekis" in their conversation and I started crying and whimpering, "Lamekis, Milkhea." They looked at each other and repeated the words. The man left, came right back and, holding out his hand, said, "Lamekis, Papo."[23] I understood nothing and kept crying bitter tears.

The Sun was fully risen and I could easily make out the dwelling. The grotto was cut out of a rock and the very high ceiling let in the sunlight through a crevasse in the mountain. Thousands of different seashells decorated it nicely. Water pure as crystal came out of one corner, murmuring pleasantly and dropping into a basin that it had hollowed out and then disappearing into a crack in the rock. In the back of the grotto, across from the fountain, was another ceiling, lower than the first, which seemed to have been purposely made into an alcove. There was a big mat bed with foam that never settled. In the opposite corner was a kind of armoire in the rock with an earthenware dish that was black as a crow and shining like marble. But what really caught my attention was a big animal, almost as tall as a donkey, with black-spotted, sky-blue fur. Its

---

[23] He is no longer.

body was somewhat like a deer, its head like a mastiff and its eyes were gentle and very beautiful; it looked around with an odd expression. In spite of my pain I could not help petting it. It seemed to enjoy that and started licking my wounded hand. Its tongue was soft and so comforting that I let it continue. During this time I looked at my hosts whom I had not yet examined too closely. The man's face was blue and gentle and pleasant and seemed to be in the prime of life. The woman's was pale pink, suiting her, with beautiful, very delicate features. And the way she was dressed totally complimented her.

My host, who had not forgotten, took me by the hand. The woman was busy plucking a kind of chicken with a cat's head and before we left the man went up to her, put his hand on her head and whispered something. She stopped her work and with a gracious smile pulled a hair out of his head and tied it around her ankle where there were several others. I watched these things wide-eyed, but I was even more surprised to see him grab a vase and take out a kind of sponge and scrub my face and hands, which right away turned the same color as his.

We left the grotto on a path hollowed out of the thick rock. The dog went ahead and guided us by his voice through about 400 feet of darkness. When we were out of the underground, we went up a natural slope that led us onto a platform where we could see the sea. On the right were some woods with trees reaching up to the clouds and on the left the view was cut off by a chain of small mountains whose tops were sparkling white. The ground we walked on was soft and so white that I bent down to touch it thinking it was covered with snow; it was very fine foam. My host smiled at my wonderment and said, "Piga, piga."[24] I repeated the words, which surprised him. Then he put his hand on the blue animal and said, "Falbao."[25] The word was barely out of my mouth when the dog jumped on me and almost knocked me down.

---

[24] Snow, snow.
[25] The name of the dog, which means mighty in strength.

The man was surprised at how easily I learned the words of his language and spoke a few others that I articulated with no problem. He put his hand on his head and hit his stomach, saying "Motacoa," meaning that was his name. I repeated it and he smiled and squeezed my knee.[26]

When we got to the end of the platform, facing the sea, we went down by a slope and ended up on the shore. We climbed into a small, round boat with a wheel attached to each side with blades that were used as oars; a double handle turned them both at the same time. He barely touched them and we were moving off so fast it scared me. Everything that had happened came rushing back to me and I started weeping. Motacoa[27] left the oars, came over to me kindly, squeezed my knee again and said many things that I did not understand. Meanwhile Falbao jumped into the sea and started monkeying around so much that I laughed as hard as I had cried.

My host was delighted, but the dog suddenly disappeared. Afraid that he had drowned, I screamed. Motacoa did not think so and started laughing. He touched his mouth and said, "Falbao, Falbao, tou-kat-zi."[28] The words were barely out of his mouth when the dog's head popped up and quickly dove back down into the sea. A minute later he came back up and jumped into the boat holding a big fish in his mouth (or his muzzle, if the critics prefer). He dropped it at the feet of his master. The fish was huge and looked like nothing I had seen before. Motacoa petted the dog's knees and he reciprocated in his way. Then Motacoa stuck his finger in the fish's gills, took something out and threw it at Falbao, who gobbled it up with delight. When the meal, which I thought rather meager for its size, was finished, he jumped back into the sea and did not resurface for a long time, which worried me a lot since I had found an unusual attraction for the animal.

---

[26] Polite gesture in this land, like shaking hands here.

[27] The native's name, meaning son of sorrow.

[28] Come here!

Soon he came back with an even bigger fish than before. He kept this up for a few hours and when there was enough in the boat, Motacoa got under way and in no time at all we were almost back at the rocks I mentioned before. As we moved on, I noticed that the land was cultivated and must have been someone's dwelling. We entered a little bay that brought us to a big area full of people the same color as Motacoa. But what was really surprising and remarkable to me was that the women were the same color, whereas my host's wife looked nothing like them.

We had just landed when a few people came up and touched Motacoa's knee. When they saw my clothes, which were different from theirs, they stood arm in arm and spoke out. Then everyone came running up and pointed at me with their elbows,[29] yelling "clao, clao."[30] One of them (whom I thought was the chief because when he appeared everyone stepped back) came up, touched my knee and plucked out one of my hairs.[31] During the ceremony Motacoa fell on his back and spread his hands on his chest. Then he got up, grabbed the chief's hair on the front of his head and shook it vigorously.[32] The native was pleased with the courtesy and got in the boat where he picked out the biggest fish and then left.

I was too young to pay much attention to everything. I only remember it later after I learned their language.

The people were free to board the boat[33] and they took the different foodstuffs that they needed. When the market ended and Motacoa had traded his fish, we got back in the

---

[29] In this country they only used the finger to point at the divinity and the king; they used the elbow for ordinary things.

[30] Look, look.

[31] No greater mark of respect could be given to someone than to pluck out a hair. And when they kept it, it meant that the person whose hair was plucked was dear.

[32] Only the king was rendered this honor, but over time his ministers pulled out all his hair in front.

[33] No one in the market could barter or trade before the kiaouf or leader had taken what he wanted.

boat and went back to our dwelling. His wife greeted us in all kinds of ways. When night fell they lit a kind of torch which gave off a bright light and whose odor was very sweet. Sitting on the edge of the fountain we had soup made of rice and the chicken I mentioned before. We drank the water from the rock, which was biting and spicy—I only had to drink three mouthfuls to feel a kind of drowsy drunkenness, which plunged me into a deep sleep.

There's no point, dear Sinouis, in telling you the details of the life I led for 10 years in that dwelling. I learned Motacoa's language so quickly that at the end of two years I could speak as well as him. My host and his wife treated me so warmly that I forgot, in a way, my natural parents. I was raised in the religion and ways of the country and when I was initiated in their customs Motacoa put his complete and thorough trust in me.

One day he said to me, "Lamekis, I want to prove my affection for you by telling you my story and your own glorious part in the most important event of my life. What concerns you is the most heart-rending: the death of your father."

"Oh Heavens!" I cried, "What are you saying? Lamekis is dead and you've been hiding it from me all this time! What horrible brutality…"

"You have every right to yell at me," the native interjected, "and to criticize what I've done, but I didn't know you well enough to reveal the awful secret. This is not the time for revenge. It is coming and soon I will give you the means to punish the wicked murderers. Hear me out. My story will teach you about your father's tragic end.

The birth of Motacoa and the jealousy of the Houcaïs

I am the son of the Houcaïs[34] or King of the Abdalles.[35] His kingdom was founded by the great Vilkonhis,[36] whom you

---

[34] This means caliph in the native language.
[35] Abdalles, the people near the zenith.

42

know as the Universal Being. The extent of his realm is vast: my father ruled all the people who lived between the rock that I showed you and the mountain Collira.[37] His power had no limits. My mother, who was white, had been brought from far-off lands and he fell so madly in love with her that he married her.

With this marriage love was coupled with intelligence. Their happiness was perfect. If they ever argued, it was only in their love for each other, fighting over who loved the other more. One day the Queen wanted to get the better of the King and said to him, "Well, the fruit that I bear will decide the matter. If the token of our mutual love is blue, it is undeniable proof that I love you more; and if the child is my color, I will consent that your love is greater than mine. The Houcaïs accepted the test and they waited impatiently for the moment that would decide the crucial issue.

I was born white.

"How can that be?" I interrupted. "You are the same color as the people here."

You will see in time. I use a trick to be blue and it's only to protect your life that we have dyed you that color.

My mother was carried away with joy when she saw me. She was delighted to lose the challenge because of her excessive love for my father. But the King took it very differently. He became glum and gloomy. His jealousy invented all kinds of suspicions about my birth. For some time he considered how to get revenge. From the fateful day that I came into the world, he stopped seeing the Queen, who dissolved in tears because she could not imagine how she had lost his love. Im-

---

[36] The Abdalles recognized only the Universal Being, whom they called Vilkonhis or Father of Light. We will see what they thought about religion in the second part.

[37] Of ice.

agine her surprise when the head kirzif[38] came to her one day with the dreadful kirmec[39] in his hand.

"What's this I see?" the poor Princess screamed. "Is the grandeur of my love to be the height of my disgrace? Am I condemned to death?"

"Ah, Madame," the Kirzif cried, "I am so unhappy to be in this position! If only I could take your place in the dreadful pit of Houzaïl![40] The Houcaïs sentences you and your son, the Prince, to this dreadful punishment. He thinks you committed adultery and has sworn to Vilkonhis that he will henceforth kill all whites who fall into his hands, supposing that of all the people who die, one of them must be the suspected perpetrator of his shame and the father of the Prince."

"Oh Heavens!" Hildaë cried out (that's the name of my mother), "Oh height of despair! How much innocence and virtue must be sacrificed to so much ingratitude?"

Her pleas were useless. The Houcaïs had gained so much power and it was so absolute that he answered only to himself. There was no point in the people moaning and groaning about such an unfair arrest, it was done. They lowered the Queen and me down into the deadly pit in a basket. As was the custom they gave us food for eight days and instead of 1,000 lengths of rope, which was usually used to lower the basket into the abyss, on behalf of the criminal's status they gave us

---

[38] Vizier.

[39] Sealed letter. They only gave it to proclaim death. It was a leaf from a tree that was guarded at the house of the minister or kirzif and was the image of his power. It was kept in a huge pot behind a strong, iron gate whose key the king wore around his neck. When he wanted to get rid of someone he went to the chief minister, opened the gate, tore off a leaf and pressed it against his face—it kept the imprint forever.

[40] The famous pit of Houzaïl is so deep that they never found the bottom. It seems that the author wanted to play with the gullibility of the people living around the pit who claim they descend from Motacoa and reel off the following tales.

3,000, which had never been done before and which eventually saved our lives.

It took three days and nights to go down into the center
of the Earth.[41] On the fourth day the basket came to a stop on
the top of a mountain. The Queen, who was thinking we
would die at any moment, felt us land, took me in her arms,
quickly got out of the basket and ran, afraid that the rope,
which they usually dropped at the end, would kill us. It
seemed that the Heavens wanted to preserve us by a miracle. It
was a worthwhile precaution—an hour later the rope rained
down with an awful racket.

When Hildaë got over her first fear, she examined her
surroundings. They were frightening. The ground was scattered with bones and skulls and the mountain looked like it
was built of nothing but these poor bodies that had been
thrown down there. It was a chilling sight for a woman in my
mother's situation. She hurried down the mountain and saw
new, funny objects as she went. The variegated ground was
oily and soft and the light that broke through created a play of
shadows that would have charmed a less intimidated mind.
But Hildaë was scared of the fate pursuing her and was so
worried that she did not take 30 steps before she went back to
where she started.

"Oh gods!" she cried. "What is to become of me? Won't
the grand Vilkonhis be swayed by my innocence and by some
strange miracle save us from this fatal fall?" This plea lifted
her spirits and she looked more confidently at the wondrous
things around her.

She was surprised to see an incredibly high vault overhead that was cut with sideways openings spaced unequally
apart. Waterfalls came out of some, reflecting the light in a
multitude of colors. Others meandered down fissures that they

---

[41] The reader should pay attention here that the author says it took
three days for the basket to reach the bottom of Houzaïl and later that
it only took one day for Motacoa and Lodaï to come back. It is an
important slip that cannot be understood.

seemed unable to escape. In a farther place a torrent of what looked like heavy silver[42] flowed out of the vault. The liquid was so shiny that she could barely look at it. Hildaë enjoyed (if we can call it that) looking at these wonders for a little while, but many other things amazed her. Turning to the left she saw a sea of fire[43] with many waves; everything around it was covered by dark, purple smoke and the restless flames moved the ground. Closer to us she saw columns of transparent and less restless water,[44] some flowing down and others flowing up. All these miracles of nature were too strange for her to analyze in such a short time and her situation was too critical to ponder over them for long.

Besides, I was weak because I had not eaten in such a long time. My mother saw this and noticed too late that in her desire to save us from the deadly falling rope she had forgotten to take the few provisions that they usually put in the basket. She became desperate and screamed frantically. She tried in vain to remedy the situation by scrambling back up to where it had fallen, but her search was fruitless and her weakness prevented her from continuing. She left the awful place wailing and was surprised to hear a distant voice in answer, "Patience, I'll be with you right away."

She turned and saw a man on the other side of the stream coming quickly toward us. She jumped with joy. "Oh Vilkonhis!" she cried. "You are coming to save me." She went to meet him and as she got closer she could see that he looked like the people who had just banished her. Ah, she told herself, it's some poor creature like me who miraculously escaped the harsh fate to which he was, maybe, unjustly condemned. In the middle of this thought she found herself face to face with the stranger, who stepped back and said, "Oh Heavens, what's this? The Queen! I don't believe it! What awful deed has thrown you down here?"

---

[42] Quicksilver or mercury.
[43] The central fire.
[44] The vegetal soul or spirits.

"Ah!" my mother replied, not remembering the stranger. "Who are you? And how is that I hear my name spoken in this disgraceful place that does not render me honor but rather that covers me in shame by recognizing me?"

"Princess," the stranger replied, "whatever the reason you are here, it can only be to your glory. The grand Vilkonhis does not protect criminals and does not perform miracles in vain. I was sentenced to the infamy of a sure death like you, but I escaped punishment. The Heavens saved me from the deadly fall and aided me in my helplessness. My virtue triumphed. My enemies believed they had destroyed me, but instead they gave me a life unbelievably more peaceful than the one they thought they were depriving me of. Come, Princess, put that precious package in my arms—why, it can only be the legitimate Prince, who is the unlucky partner of our misery." He took me in his arms and bade my mother follow him, telling her how he survived in the unknown land.

For five years since injustice had cast him down there, he had discovered all the monstrous ins and outs of the inner world. His adventures alone would fill volumes. His name was Lodaï and he was a minister of the Houcaïs. Being favored and fair had earned him enemies. His honesty and openness never made his master's subordinates love him; being firm in his interests attracted them to him. He was too smart not to notice that they were trying to destroy him, but he asked only for the uprightness and kindness of the King to prevail over their calumnies. The King stood up to them for a long time, but in the end he fell victim to the suspicions they sowed in his mind. No people were ever more jealous of his authority than the Houcaïs. They made him believe that Lodaï was scheming to usurp his throne by leading a conspiracy. The minister of this complicated plot suggested the likelihood of treason and it worked as they expected. There was a trial and in spite of his innocence the wicked, corrupt judges convinced the King of the crime of high treason and he was sentenced to the pit of Houzaïl. His luck, or better said, the Heavens made it so that when they let go of the rope, it got caught on a branch growing out of a crack in the rock, which stopped the basket's fall four feet above ground. It was easy to get out and jump onto the mountain. And by this unheard of miracle he was the first one up until then to live in the center of the Earth. He was the one who told us about the wonders that are so fascinating today and that I will tell about later.

After Lodaï told my mother all these things, he led her to the banks of the stream whose rose-colored water flowed onto pure golden sand. This part of the Inner Earth was lit perpendicularly and the ceiling was so high that we could barely see it. A mountain of minerals, mainly sulfur and bitumen, rose up next to the stream. Lodaï had built a nice, comfortable dwelling inside it and since he knew so much about the environment he was able to get everything needed to live. He led Hildaë into the refuge and when he had put her on a bed made of the very finest moss, he gave me some water that I swallowed, which stopped my crying, and then he spoke to my mother.

Lodaï's story

Here is the refuge, Oh great Princess, which I made with patience and skill and where I live infinitely happier than in the ranks I was in before. Here I am King. And from my studies since I was young I have knowledge of nature. When I saw that I was banished but safe, the desire to save my life, which the Heavens seemed to be protecting, compelled me to look for food. The few provisions they give to those they throw down here were barely enough to give me time to find something else. But can you die when the Heavens protect you?

The third day I was wandering in this place I stopped on the banks of this stream. I saw a kind of chicken come out of the water, followed by a few others. I was transfixed by how strange it looked and by the novelty of the thing. I kept watching it and it beat its wings and the air was filled with the sweet smell of the water. All of them romped about for a little while on the golden sand of this little river. Their feathers and heads were crimson and black; they had two beaks with the lower one curving down; they walked pretty much like a duck and soon wandered far away from me. I followed them to find out what they would do. They jumped into a hollowed out path lined with pebbles that looked like mother-of-pearl and after a quarter karie[45] they went into the trunk of a tree that six men holding hands would barely wrap around. The opening they entered was so small that they had to duck to get in. When I saw the chickens holed up in the tree I decided to try to catch one. I went up to the opening and looked inside. It was huge and completely hollow. By the light that entered in different places I could make out a large number of these animals each with their young and cooing like pigeons. After examining them for a while I closed the opening with some moss that covered the tree bark and thought about how I could catch one of them.

Looking up I was surprised how beautiful and how high the tree was. Its branches were four times longer than an alder and twice as thick. I had to use my knife to cut one of them off because there was no way I could snap it. Just look (Lodaï continued) at the clothes and furniture I made and you can see for yourself what can be done with it. The discovery pleased me greatly, but not as much as the fruit that hung from it. I had quite a bit of trouble getting some down because they were so high. I had to throw rocks to knock them down and I spent a long time trying to gather them up. They fell and bounced like handballs except that they bounced so high and so crazily that whenever I got my hand under one, it slipped away. When I finally got hold of one of these fruits, I scrutinized it carefully. It was light and as fat as an Indian melon. When I split it open, a clear liquid came out. I was so thirsty that I couldn't find enough of them to quench my thirst. I drank so much that I got kind of drunk and felt groggy. I stretched out at the foot of the tree and fell into a deep sleep.

---

[45] A league of 5,000 feet.

I hadn't been long in my peaceful state when I woke up with a start at the sound of horrifying screams overhead. I opened my eyes and saw the tree covered with those chickens I was talking about. They were all hot and bothered, jumping from one branch to another. I watched their little game for a while and figured that when they found the hole plugged up they got out somewhere higher up in the tree. I opened it up to see if that would change anything, but they just went higher up. One of the little ones was lying in front of the opening, apparently killed in a fall. I picked it up and after examining it I was no longer surprised by the hubbub—it came from the fact that they could not fly. Their wings were really fins folded back on each other and could only be used to swim. Only their back was covered with feathers; their stomach was scaly like a fish. Judging by their claws and their soft skin I figured they would taste great and the experiment I made proved me right.

After this test I went back to the fruit. I was hungry and its liquid had piqued my appetite. I wanted to see if the fruit tasted as good as its color and juice suggested. I ate with delight and found it tasted like the sweetbread we make in our country. Imagine my joy, Queen, for what could be better than being able to save your life? Taking a half dozen of these fruits I was going to leave the wonderful tree to come back to this dwelling here that I had already picked out, but then I saw the chickens leaving the hole I had left open. I snuck up on them, but they did not seem scared. I picked one up easily and petted it; it was very soft. So, I went to the rock loaded with my rich booty and all kinds of encouraging thoughts about my findings.

What can I tell you, Princess? With time and labor I gradually got used to this subterranean home. I dried out the fruit and ground flour for bread. For the dark nights I discovered fire from the bitumen on the other side of the rock. It burned continually and gave me the means to build an oven to bake my bread and cook the excellent meat. It was also veined with a kind of pitch that was bright when lit up and had a nice smell that was good for the health.

I haven't been bored for a minute since I got here. My books now are the wonders and contents of this Inner Earth. When I have lived through the four ages of man, I will still find new things every day. Every time I go out I come back with more new marvels than I know what to do with, so I put them up in a deep closet that I carved out of the rock where I can relax and enjoy myself. I hope, Princess, that in your exile you will be as charmed and amused as I have been.

Forget about your rank, which in reality is only a pure illusion and gives only false pleasures, which you will clearly understand if you think about it. True happiness depends on the things around us. My experience proves it and I hope that you will agree before too long.

Motacoa is raised underground

Hildaë was comforted by Lodaï's wise words. What calmed her completely was how easily I got used to the new food he gave me. Not only did I like it, but it was also so good for me that I grew before their very eyes. 12 years passed in total calm, untroubled by the sicknesses or worries that constantly bother us in the world. I was raised by the wise Lodaï, who taught me what he knew and when I was old enough he told me about my birth. They were surprised at how strongly I reacted to the King's injustice against my mother. I was so angry that I sometimes disturbed our tranquility and whenever our conversations turned to the subject, they always ended with me swearing that if ever I saw the light of day again, I would spend my life putting my mother back on the throne where she deserved to be. Lodaï lectured me in vain that I should not dream of such things because it was impossible to return to Earth. I shook my head at his protests and kept saying that I had a hunch that it would happen. Events proved me right, that a secret intelligence was giving me a glimpse of the future.

As I got older, my thoughts about everything that Lodaï had taught me expanded and focused on everything I could

51

see. He taught me philosophy, but natural philosophy, not with prickly words but with things that are clear and obvious and I was so preoccupied with the miracles that I saw everyday that I often forgot to take care of myself. The research I was doing sometimes took me 10 or 12 karies from our home and I got lost twice. My mother and Lodaï, who loved me tenderly and worried about me a lot, begged me badly to stop alarming them, so for a while I did not go far and I made sure I got home to sleep.

One day when I went into a crevasse in a rock on a wide, clear path I found a flowing vein of such beautiful, perfect liquid[46] that I wanted to find the source. It was thick and the color of gold, but what was really amazing was that instead of following the natural downward slope, it flowed steadily upward. I followed it for more than three karies and the farther I went into the heart of the mountain, with light slanting in, the wider and rougher the path became. I had to sit down to rest and I looked around. Through a crack in the rock I saw something so bright that I jumped up and ran to it. As soon as I got up close to it, I heard an awful hiss and I shrank away. I had discovered a dreadful animal, crawling on its belly, folding and unfolding on itself like it was rolling. I started running at full speed up the mountain because the monstrous worm was behind me and seemed to be chasing me. I was sorry, then, that I had not followed Lodaï's sage advice and I made a resolution that if I escaped this hideous threat, I would never expose myself to danger again—the oath of young people in danger that they forget when it's all over.

I was out of breath and the enemy in pursuit was slowly gaining on me. I could hear the noise it made dragging itself along and the hissing got louder. I was at death's door when I saw four feet above me another strange looking, but very different animal. I screamed at the sight of it. Not knowing what else to do, I hid in a hole on my left. I was so scared that when I grazed myself with my own hands I thought the animal had

---

[46] The author seems to be talking about gold.

seized me and I shivered. But my enemy had other things to worry about. It was attacked by a formidable athlete that stood up on its hind legs and found the right time to strike. I saw the snake or worm coil up and spring out at its adversary hard and fast. Its mouth was open and a tongue armed with three hooks shot out of the gaping chasm. The slightest touch could have felled its enemy. Falbao, the same dog as you see here, Lamekis, (for it was him) dodged his attacks like an agile fighter by jumping to the side whenever the worm uncoiled and by this tactic wore him down. The fight lasted for a while like this until Falbao suddenly jumped on his enemy and cut it in two with his lethal fangs. The two parts tried to come back together again, but in vain: the skillful victor took one and threw it 30 feet away. After this precaution, which was no doubt done instinctively, he came back to the battlefield and looked around. Finally seeing me he dropped the head of the terrible enemy at my feet. He lay down looking at it and looking at me with eyes that cheered his victory.

My mind was so confused that I did not know what to do. My nerves were numb from fear. Falbao and I sat there looking at each other for about an hour until the animal finally let up the tension; he got up, took three steps forward and came back. It looked like he was inviting me to follow him and his gentle eyes gave me confidence, but because of my fright I stayed back afraid of being eaten. I cannot say if sympathy was the reason he took care to reassure me, but whatever his reasons it worked wonders—he came up, wagged his tail and nuzzled against me. I ventured to stretch out my hand to touch him. He lowered his head and gave me all the signs of gentleness that he could, so I plucked up all my courage to leave. He walked ahead and I followed. After one karie I was so tired that I had to take a rest next to the vein of gold. Falbao did the same and lapped up the liquid. I saw him try to lick a wound on his back, but his neck was not flexible enough to reach it. Then his eyes seemed to beg me for help. I cupped some of the liquid gold in my hands and rubbed it into the wound. He stretched out and let me do it. There was also a wound on his back paw and I was surprised that as soon as I applied the liquid the wounds healed. I, too, had grazed myself, so I put some of this divine balm on it and was relieved right away.

After resting a little while in this place, Falbao got up and I followed him. After a few more karies, imagine my surprise, Lamekis, when I found myself on top of a mountain in mid-air, which convinced me that I was in the regions that my mother and Lodaï had talked so much about. I felt a secret joy, enchanted by the splendid sight of nature. I stood there without moving, dazed, in awe of the beauty of the bright day while my eyes wandered over the immensity of the sky. I spent two hours like that, unable to get over my astonishment and if a new adventure had not pulled me out of my lethargy, I might still be there.

I was sunk in this ecstasy when I felt someone touch me. It was a man the same color as Lodaï. At first I thought it was him and I reached out my arms, but they hung back down when I did not recognize his face.

"Ah, young man, what are you doing here?" the stranger asked. "Are you running away? Where are you going? To your sure ruin. Where do you come from? Don't you know that you are in the empire of the Houcaïs and he has ordered all whites to be arrested and brought to the capital to be sacrificed?"

Imagine the impression those words had on me, Lamekis, finding out that I was in the empire of my father whom I hated more than anything else in the world with a hatred born in childhood for the sake of my unjustly banished mother who was dearer to me than the fate that had torn me from her arms. The dangers I had just faced had lulled my thoughts, but the stranger's speech woke them up and I fully felt my loss.

"Oh Heavens," I cried, "where is this barbarous King you're talking about who covered my mother in shame and sacrificed her to his anger? Where can I find him? Ah! As young as I am, my hatred will give me enough strength to take his life...but what am I saying, good gods! He's my father. The Houcaïs gave me life..."

"What's this I hear?" the stranger cried out. "What are you saying? You, the son of the King of Abdalles! Obviously fear has made you crazy and wild! But I can see a resemblance in your face. And your color almost...I recognize...but no, it can't be. Hildaë died a miserable death in the depths of Houzaïl and her son shared her fate. But, listen mortal, whoever you are, flee! Go back to the cave you came out of! Someone less compassionate than me will arrest you. The order is for everyone, everywhere. Since the day our Queen Hildaë brought a white into the world, it's happened to many men of this color. All the King's subjects are spies and the punishment is so strict against anyone who disobeys that no one would dare break his inhuman laws; not only would it cost him his life, but also the loss of his goods and family."

I stood there without moving as he spoke. Many different thoughts passed through my worried mind. In spite of my prejudice an inner voice rose up for my father, but fear, which was inseparable from my looming fate, got the upper hand and I cried out, "Whoever you are, protect the son of the great Queen whom Heavens' kindness saved from a more tragic fate. Vilkonhis saved her from death, but oh, how much bitterness does she suffer now? I was her consolation and she has lost me. She has shed so many tears already! Oh my mother! Will I ever see you again and calm your soul? O Lodaï!..."

"What are you saying?" the stranger interrupted. "What names are these? Hildaë is alive and you're her son? What proof can you give of these extraordinary things?"

"My story," I replied, "and Lodaï's, who is alive."

"Lodaï!" he interrupted again. "Surely you've lost your mind..."

"No," I continued impatiently, "it's easy to prove the truth. I can lead you through this cave to the center of the earth where the pit of Houzaïl is only one way in. There you will see the Queen and Lodaï."

The stranger cried out again at these last words. He cast everything into doubt when he happened to look at Falbao whose weird face made him shudder. The animal seemed to be listening to us and the stranger could not move an inch without the animal looking like he wanted to eat him. His foaming mouth was hanging open and his eyes were furious. I was so preoccupied with the stranger that I had not paid attention to him. I trembled, too, and got so scared that I fell backward. The animal ran to my feet and looked so gentle and humble that I trusted him again. The stranger's eyes were all agog and he wavered between fear and admiration. I reassured him and told him how the animal and I had become so close. The adventure impressed him.

"I'm starting to believe," he said, "that there's something extraordinary in your story. I'll even admit that I'm getting interested, though I can't imagine why. I'm curious to know more, but still it's too dangerous for you to stay here any longer. Follow me. My cabin is in the middle of the desert nearby where you will be safe from any fanatics. There we can get to the bottom of this and see if you can convince me that you are the son of the Houcaïs. If so, I won't disappoint you. Even though I'm by myself here, I can get things moving. I don't live alone by chance. I have my reasons that you will appreciate when you know why, but I would be a criminal if you really are who you say you are."

Saying this the stranger led me into the dark woods. After many twists and turns we came into a little valley watered by a river where his house was. Along the way he told me that his name was Boldeon, the first Prince of the Houcaïs' blood. After the disgrace of my mother the King married again, but had no children. He was so in love that he had this Princess' brother, Ruraos, recognized as his heir provided that he and his successors exterminate all the whites found in his and the neighboring realms. A few months later he retired into the royal cave[47] and Ruraos mounted the throne where he ruled as a tyrant who was so detestable that all the nobles of Abdalles preferred to flee into faraway provinces rather than obey the usurper.

---

[47] The royal cave where once the King enters, he never leaves.

When we got to Boldeon's house and washed up, he was eager to hear my story. I told it so naturally and sincerely that he could not help but believe me and he humbled himself as if I were his legitimate Prince. I kissed him and he recognized me as the Prince and swore to me that he would spill his blood to put me back on the usurped throne. Then he let me in on the plans he had made to get rid of the tyrant since the Houcaïs was cut off from everything, just like his contact with the nobles of Abdalles who would form such a formidable opposition that Ruraos would surely fall. Boldeon had pretended to travel to far-off lands to accomplish his plot without suspicion, so no one knew about his house, which was near the capital and also in range of the conspirators whom he could contact when the time came. He told me that he would not let them know about my arrival, but would keep it for the final blow to incite the people in case the tyrant's power got the upper hand, but that it was absolutely necessary that I go back down into the depths of Houzaïl to get my mother and Lodaï to prove my bloodline. Not only did I agree with his plan, but I was elated by it and we resolved to carry it out. The next day I found where I had come out of the abyss and I hoped that I could find where I had grown up. But, I could count on faithful Falbao who was constantly showing me new signs of loyalty. I already knew his bravery and now with him and the weapons we could take, there was no danger we could not face. But, Sinouis, we did not figure that the depths of the earth were inhabited. We would soon find that out, too.[48]

---

[48] This is obviously an error in the French original. "Sinouis" should be changed to "Lamekis." Whilst the overarching narrative is one being related by Lamekis to Sinouis established right at the beginning, the "we" being referred to here is Motacoa referring to himself, Lodai, Hildae and Boldeon. Earlier, on page 54, Motacoa acknowledges Lamekis as the recipient of his tale: "Imagine the impression those words had on me, Lamekis, finding out that I was..." And then, "my unjustly banished mother who was dearer to me than the fate that had torn me from her arms." The latter phrase: "the fate that had torn me from her arms" is obviously a reference to the death of his

The worm men

The evening star had just appeared on the horizon when we left Boldeon's cabin loaded with the supplies needed for a journey that might take very long if we got lost. When we got to where we had first met, it was not hard to find the cavern entrance and the mysterious vein was only a few feet inside. I pointed it out to Boldeon and told him about the miraculous effect it had on Falbao's wounds after the battle with the snake.

"Aha! Motacoa," he said. "It can't be! Wonder of wonders! How long have I been searching for this divine vein? Don't regret your bad luck because it has brought you this treasure. This alone is enough to make us the happiest of mortals. It's one of the greatest benefits we could hope for. This vein contains the universal remedy and whoever has it is guaranteed to live without sickness and be forever healthy unto the grave."

Saying this he cupped some in his hands and drank three times, inviting me to do the same. After doing this we sat on a big rock and ate a light meal while Falbao lay down nearby. The liquid worked its wonders and soon put us to pleasant sleep.

I had barely closed my eyes when a mysterious dream churned my senses. I thought I was somewhere in the Inner Earth where I used to go before I left. There was a rock of talc, shiny and strange, that was very precious to me. Inside it was a kind of natural crucible in which the wondrous water was constantly boiling. When the fiery heat poured it out, it con-

---

mother, given that he and his mother spent many years underground with Lodaï. So if we assume, incorrectly, that Mouhy is simply, and without a line break or parentheses, switching over to the main narrative of Lamekis and Sinouis, the "we" of the sentences on page 57 contradict the fact that Motacoa's mother (Hildae/Nasildae) has died by the time Lamekis comes into the care of Motacoa and Nasilae. (Ed.)

gealed and took on the strangest forms that I examined for a long time.

Then I dreamed that I was in a cave where the back was laid up by an earthquake and revealed a bright corridor. The ceiling was dotted with different colored gems that sparkled so brightly that my eyes could barely stand the fire. I went in. It ended in a big room that was decorated with so much beautiful art that it looked like our most skillful workers had been there. In the middle of the room was a table made of a single opal with an exquisite mother-of-pearl armchair in front of it. On the table was an open book with gold letters. I went up to it and, being alone, I could not hold back my curiosity: I read a sentence that stood out. It said, "You, mortal, cannot ascend a throne that belongs to you unless the marriage with Ascalis[49] puts you there."

These words seemed so fitting to me that I cried out, "Oh Vilkonhis, let your will be done!" Hardly had I said this when two winged men appeared, like the ones we picture as Spilghis.[50] They held a finger to their mouths and motioned me to follow them. I obeyed. They led me into another room, paneled with gold and in the middle was a bed on which a radiantly beautiful woman was sleeping. Her skin was the color of rose and her features beyond compare. I knelt on the ground and contemplated the young beauty whom I had not noticed was stirring. She sighed in her troubled sleep. Without knowing why, I shared her troubles. One of the Spilghis tapped her with a crystal rod and she woke up screaming, which made the two celestial men vanish. The stranger's reaction affected me. I opened my mouth to say something reassuring, but I felt myself rising up despite myself. She jumped out of bed and grabbed my arm to help me, but a zenghuis[51] struck the divine

---

[49] The color of rose.

[50] Angels.

[51] Mouhy at times waits for the second mention of something before he footnotes it. He also, at times, will repeat a footnote (such as defining a unit of measurement). This, for example, is the first mention

woman's hand and she collapsed on the ground. I wanted to avenge this treachery, so I turned around to see what barbarian had the gall to attack and I found myself staring into the ghastly face of a monster, holding me in its arms, and I got so scared that I woke up with a start.

Boldeon was waiting impatiently for me to wake up because he was upset by my restlessness. He urged me to tell him what was wrong. I was so disturbed that I did not answer for a long time, but I finally got hold of myself and told him about my dream.

"It's not for nothing," he said, "that Vilkonhis speaks and this new evidence is sure proof of your birth. It is said in one of the prophecies that a woman the color of Ascalis will give birth to a hero who will make the Abdalles happy and their most valuable goods will be due to him. Oh Motacoa, if the oracle speaks through you, I hope you will be happy and become beloved and honored! Let's move on under the auspices of this divine omen; the master of the sun guides us. Can we get lost when we are led by such a powerful hand?"

Talking together like that we went into the depths of the mountain. Soon we came upon the snake that Falbao had conquered. It was still alive and its dying eyes were dreadful. The dog looked away and seemed to want me to do the same. I followed my instinct, which was a good thing because the awful snake struck out when it saw us and its forked tongue broke off a piece of rock. We sped up and after three karies or so we got out of the cave.

I was going to take a path that I thought I recognized and that I believed would lead me to Lodaï's grotto, but when I turned around I could not see Falbao. A grave anxiety took hold of me. I had got used to the animal and I loved it. I yelled at the top of my lungs and cried while Boldeon ran around looking for him. I did the same and as night was falling we got lost. No matter how loudly I yelled, nothing answered.

---

of a zenghuis, but the explanation footnote is on page 63. We have obviously left these anomalies intact. (Ed.)

"Oh Heavens, here I am fallen into bad luck again. Falbao! Falbao, whom the gods gave me for comfort. Oh, I will never see you again! And you, Boldeon, whom I led into this awful desert, what is going to become of you! Wandering around and worn out by remorse as much as by walking, I'm going to lay down under the weight of sorrow and close my frightened, troubled eyes."

Weariness and weeping was starting to make me drowsy when I heard a dull, terrible sound. I opened my eyes. "Oh Heavens! What is this I see in the light of the subterranean fires! What horrifying sight is this?"

A man (can I call it that?) was coming toward me. His head, arms and chest was like a man, but the rest of his body was like a worm, except that he was as big as the thing that Falbao had battled. He was huge and moved using his coils. Sometimes he dragged himself along with his hands and sometimes he stood up straight. His nose was very fat and flat and bent down into a point that almost covered his upper lip. His eyes were small and round and completely surrounded by thick eyebrows. His horrid face was marbled red and his beard and all the hair that covered his body grew together.

Barely looking at him I yelled and ran away as fast as I could, turning around now and again, knowing that sooner or later I was going to fall prey to the monster. Leaning on his hands he bounded forward so far that he almost caught me, but then against all hope I saw Falbao running to my rescue. What a relief! When the worm man saw him he turned tail and rushed away. Falbao followed him. I got worried and called out to him as loudly as I could because I needed him around and could not stand the idea of losing him a second time. When he came back I petted him and the lovable animal answered in his way. He went ahead and I followed him confidently.

We had barely gone 30 feet and I heard horrible screams. I was ready to run away again, but I stopped when I heard my name called and recognized Boldeon's voice. He was begging for my help and in spite of the fright I had just experienced I had to run toward the cries. My dog, as if reading my mind, went first and was on the trail in no time. Imagine how I felt after rounding a corner and seeing Boldeon in front of me in the arms of one of those monsters running away with his prey at full speed. Falbao followed them, but the worm man thrust forward with so much energy that whenever the dog got near him he jumped forward in a single bound and was 30 feet farther on. During this awful chase I could do nothing but follow at a distance, but seeing my dog scare everything he saw gave me confidence. We ran for around an hour and I was starting to peter out when a cave suddenly appeared in front of the monster and he flung himself inside. Falbao chased him and since I was desperate and afraid of being alone again in such a scary place knowing what kind of creatures lived there, I followed them.

I entered a large opening lit up so brightly by bitumen that it was easy to make out the minutest details. I went trembling into this dreadful place and had not gone 60 feet when the road split into four parts. I was in a terrible quandary because they all seemed to go in different directions. Which one had Falbao taken? Three of them were lit by bitumen snaking through the rock, but the fourth was deadly dark and horrifying. I was not sure what to do, but then I saw a bunch of those monsters coming down the middle path straight in front of me, apparently trying to tell me something. I was so gripped by fear that my legs shook and had no strength to move. In vain I tried to get hold of myself; my nerves refused to obey. Meanwhile, all the hideous faces surrounded me, twanging awful flute-like sounds.

After huddling together, one of them grabbed me with his strong, sturdy hand and shrieked, shaking me with all his might. What could I do against the iron fists of a giant? The monster put me under his arm and hurried down the dark passage. He held me so tightly that I was about to faint and he noticed it. Afraid that I might die, he grabbed me by the feet and carried me like that. Around 20 constantly buzzing creatures followed us. After walking for an hour like that, which seemed like a century in my uncomfortable position, we came out of the rock. I was so shaken up by the bouncing monster that I passed out, but snapped out of it right away because of the new, painful way of carrying me—by the hair. I screamed in pain and they twanged fluty again. The result was to carry me by the neck. As uncomfortable as this was, it was gentle compared with the others.

After walking half a karie like this an odd building came into view. It seemed to touch the sky, which I could see here. Its foundation looked like four shapeless columns made of a strange material supporting the building that had a round door, a square façade and a statue of a worm man whose two tails and coils formed the entablature. The building extended on both sides and the back looked like it was attached to the mass of shiny rock. A great number of worm men were coming and going, or better said were bouncing around on the platform, and others were crawling either up or down the ramp that led to the door of the building, which was guarded by several of these monsters who stood out from the others by a kind of short cape made of those crimson feathers I mentioned before. They wore a cap that looked pretty much like a dried pumpkin decorated with gems and in their belts they carried zenghuis[52] made of shiny metal. But the most terrifying of all were their ghastly faces.

When we got to the building the monster carrying me made a stupendous jump to the door, which was more than ten measures up. The guards surrounded him when they saw him loaded with me and one after another they brushed their hand over my face. After this ridiculous, annoying ceremony, we went through the door into a huge room where 100 guards were lined up, looking surprised to see me. Then, the one carrying me, who could obviously go no farther, gave me to the first guard and he gave me to the second who gave me to the third and on and on I went faster and faster from hand to hand across the grand hall and through others that I did not have

---

[52] Sword.

time to examine. Finally I arrived at a large door decorated with the most precious things that were found in the center of the earth and they put me down. Everyone in this big room came up and stared at me as hard as they could. A minute later the door opened and a daffodil-colored face that looked like a woman popped up with a finger over its mouth. At this sign the usual buzzing stopped and the people stood still. Then the door closed again very softly. But what really struck me was that I distinctly heard yapping that sounded like Falbao. I listened more carefully and had no doubt that it was my faithful dog.

I was concentrating on this when the door flung open. I had never seen such a strange and beautiful sight: there were four rows of worm women marvelously dressed and covered in gems. They carried a six-branched candlestick with pieces of wood burning like candles that lit up the room furnished with the most wonderful things you could imagine. It was a square room that went back as far as the eye could see and ended in a colonnade of transparent stones with very high arches. The middle of it was covered with a dome encrusted with many shiny, precious minerals. Behind this arch, which you could call "de triomphe," was an elevated armchair. Sitting there was a woman whose beauty captured all my attention and kept me from looking at anything else. Because of the distance I could not see her face clearly, but I was moved and could tell that she was shaped like me. Little ribbons of those feathers I talked about girded her body, arms and legs, showing off her perfection. Her hair was the most beautiful black in the world, partly floating over her breasts and shoulders and partly fastened with a stick covered with diamonds that were no less beautiful for being uncut. I sighed seeing myself so far away from this charming beauty, but a piercing cry rang out from the foot of the throne and I quickly turned my head. How happy I was to see Falbao. He had seen me and whimpered loudly to come join me, but he struggled in vain against the collar around his neck and his sad cries testified to it.

Lamekis is swept into the sky

I had gotten this far in Motacoa's story and Sinouis was paying close attention when I saw that the sea was boiling and a column of water rose up carrying the ship with it. We shouted out in the face of this new danger and the crew woke up. When they realized what was happening they started wailing in sorrow. The column and the ship, however, kept rising higher and higher until we were carried into the clouds. The sight was awful and we thought that the column would collapse at any minute and we would plunge and sink into the sea. There was nothing to do but resign ourselves to fate. We kept rising with a frightful noise and little by little got closer to a bright region that we were justifiably afraid was fire since we were already feeling a heat that became more and more unbearable the closer we got. And we could already make out the circles of the universe. We could feel the painful, burning torrid zone near where we were headed. Everyone hid in the hold to delay the end of their lives at least for a few extra moments. I alone, embittered by my bad luck and convinced that human wisdom could do nothing against eternal decrees, abandoned myself to whatever was in store. Already the fire was devouring me. I felt about to burn up when a whirlwind spun the ship around and lifted it from the column that was holding it up. In the blink of an eye it rushed through the vast space of the universe on top of a cloud and finally came to a stop in a huge tree. The cloud slowly dissipated into the air above and left us perched on the branches. From there I saw a strange land and several big cities.

The tree we were in was unbelievably tall. "Oh Heavens," I cried out, "will I always escape a danger only to fall into another? What will become of us? The slightest wind can fling us down! When, Oh Serapis, will you stop chasing me?"

The crew was unaware of what happened, but when they noticed that the ship had stopped moving, they ventured out. What a surprise they all had at seeing the extraordinary situation we were stuck in. We discussed what we should do and the unanimous decision was to try to get out of the ship as carefully as possible to see if it was solidly supported. I was chosen for the exploration and after checking things out I found that the weight of the ship had nuzzled into the branches so securely that there was nothing to worry about on this account.

I told the good news to the ship. They decided that we should go down and get on solid land if it was possible. We started uncoiling rope and tying the ends together to make them long enough when a sudden wind, followed by an awful storm, shook the tree so hard that we thought the ship would plunge down at any minute. Three of the crew, who were trying to lower the sails that the wind was sweeping away, were thrown overboard and surely died a horrible death. The example made the rest of us more cautious and as the storm increased in violence we ran scared to hide in the depths of the ship.

Part 2

The Island of the Sylphs

We were in this state of confusion and talking to each other about the danger and the new, extraordinary situation we were in when an even more fantastic event happened. An unexpected noise broke out overhead. We listened carefully. It sounded like people were working on the ship with axes and hammers. A minute later we saw the boards of the powder magazine (where we had taken refuge) removed one by one. We all screamed together when we saw the ship being taken apart and then the crowd of winged monsters working together to destroy it. Some were taking down the masts while others were cutting the ropes; others still were loading up supplies. Every one of them looked excited to be contributing to the destruction. It did not take long for the monsters to strip off the top of the ship, but it was enough for us to observe the startling creatures: their heads were very fat and topped a body that looked like a bird; they used their two huge wings to slice through the air and under them were two strong hands.

The only thing left of the ship was the floor on which we were sitting, so we just waited to be thrown out of the tree, but instead each of us was lifted into the air by the monsters who flew off in different directions with their prey.

The monster who picked me up flew out in front with one of its partners carrying someone else. The way it was holding me did not hurt, quite the opposite, but what scared me was that I felt like I was flying by myself, feeling neither the arms above me nor the body that must have been pressing against mine. But in spite of this marvel, my philosophy calmed me down by convincing me that nothing could change destiny. I abandoned myself to my fate and was bothered by nothing but the curiosity to know more about the extraordinary

67

Being whose power I was under. So, I chanced to reach up to its body and was flabbergasted when my hand went through it like a sword, feeling no resistance to my touch. I closed my fist but only grabbed empty air.

"Oh Heavens," I screamed, "where am I and what Demon is taking me away?"

Until then I had heard no sound. The monsters flew in utter silence. But as soon as I screamed, a voice like a hoarse flute spoke to me in my own language. "What! Can Lamekis be scared and astonished? What's the point of penetrating into the center of the earth and dipping into the heart of wisdom if, in spite of all the ordeals, he belittles himself?"

I was amazed and could not figure out by what strange fate the monster knew my name and language. "Spirit or Ghost," I replied more calmly, "how do you know me?"

"Some day the mystery will be revealed to you," responded the Intelligence (for it was one), "I am not allowed to tell you anything else for now, except that I have always been watching out for you."

"But where am I?" I asked. "Where are you taking me?"

It continued, "We are going to the Island of the Sylphs[53] where Scealgalis[54] reigns. It's a miraculous island that is touched by nothing impure or material, except for Dehahal[55] and the mysterious tree in which your ship fell, which is why we dismantled it and flew you away, so that you crude beings not sully the ground you walk on. You are going to be at Scealgalis' palace soon. The rustling of the air should tell you

---

[53] It is in the middle region, next to the moon. Some claim that it is the cloud that follows it.

[54] Scealgalis was an Egyptian. In his time he got such a great reputation as a judicial astrologer that he was regarded as divine. The cabal made him a god.

[55] The name of an admirable man who, through his abstract and profound study, was able to remain like a man of the world. He will be spoken of below.

the latitude. After you have examined his divine palace, we will strip you of your humanness in the Ceolbhaume."[56]

The Spirit stopped talking after this, but encouraged by its kindness I ventured to ask one more question. "Holy Intelligence, what has become of my dear wife? Is she still alive? Can I hope to see her again some day?"

"Hope," the Sylph snapped back, "but don't ask any more questions."

That made me sigh and I looked over at another Spirit flying a little farther off. I was glad to see that it was carrying my dear Sinouis. I called out to him and saw that my friend, devastated by his disgrace, had recognized me too, but had not said anything. Reassured by my voice he answered, "Where are we? Lamekis, what's going to happen to us? Are we still alive or is this just a dream?"

I was about to respond when the Spirit glared at me and put a finger to its mouth to tell me to keep quiet. Sinouis apparently got the same advice because he did not say a word, just looked at me and sighed.

However, I felt like we were slowing down. We were so high over the land that I could see many other globes[57] that seemed no bigger than the sun seen from the Earth. But the ones we passed closer to were so big that I could barely see the whole of them. These globes seemed to sail through the sky like ships on the sea, but their movements were as precise as the most skillfully constructed clock and every time one moved away from us we were blasted as by a strong wind.

After flying through the sky for a little while, encountering new wonders at every step, the Sylph suddenly folded back its wings and plummeted. I looked down and the objects, which were so small before, grew bigger and bigger. We passed by a great, luminous globe[58] that looked three times

---

[56] Mountain of fire or rather cloud composed of fumes from the ground that the slightest rustling fuels and sets on fire.
[57] Lamekis seems to claim that the stars are all different worlds.
[58] The sun.

69

bigger than the Moon. Then I felt a fierce heat that I would not have been able to bear if the Sylph had not noticed my reaction and started flying at an angle, which thus alleviated most of the heat. I tried to avoid the rest by putting my head in the shade of the huge wing, but this soon became useless because the rays of the sun passed through the feathers like through ice. The wing itself looked like it was made of fumes, like the iris, reflecting a thousand different colors whose brilliance I could not stand.

Then the two Sylphs, Sinouis' and mine, reached the magnificent, extraordinary palace. It looked like it was built on a still cloud. Its walls were made of ice from which the reflected rays of 20 stars flashed 100 different colors. They were transparent and if it was not for that blinding brightness you could have seen all the way inside. The palace was octagonal and the roof looked like one of our domes. A Sylph was posted at every corner, each one blowing a new fangled trumpet that looked like crystal. A ninth Sylph was flying around the castle and was armed with what looked like a scythe like we picture Time.

The sound of the trumpets was sweet and harmonious, composing a perfect, touching unison that moved the soul with such vivid impressions and such divine ecstasy that it was almost irresistible. As astonished as I was at so many extraordinary things, I was more surprised at what the Sylph told me.

"The time is coming when matter and spirit will battle. This palace you see belongs to divine Scealgalis. His decrees are continually announced. He sees you, reads your heart and weighs your good and bad deeds on the scales of his justice: if you are not saddled with iniquity, you will be initiated in his mysteries. Oh Scealgalis," the Intelligence cried out putting its two hands together, "take pity on the weakness of mortals, protect the one you have entrusted to me and in the trials that he will undergo don't let the Black Spirits outweigh the virtuous tendencies that I have inspired in him."

The Sylph had barely finished his prayer when a ray of light shot out toward us from the palace dome as fast as lightning driven by a falling cloud. I moved and screamed, afraid that the Spirit would drop me. The Sylph started sneezing so loudly that I thought I would go deaf. I later learned that on this island they sneezed instead of laughing.

But I soon had other things to wonder at. Up to this point I had not felt anything touching me, but after circling the building three times I found out that the Sylph had a material body and that its arm was hugging me tightly. Then a jolt in the air brought on by a violent whirlwind made me look up in search of the cause and I saw a very high mountain that looked like crystal a karie[59] away. From its summit rose up a bluish, sparkling flame, like saltpeter. The Intelligence that was carrying poor, trembling Sinouis cleaved the air on this side behind us. It took long enough to get there for me to look at the Sylph that was flying in front of us. It looked like it was six feet tall with a head attached directly to its shoulders; instead of arms it had two wings with white feathers. Its body, as I said, was like a bird's except it had no feathers and its backside ended in a point like a lizard. Under its wings it had strong, hairy arms. Its body and face were milky white with no other color to be seen. Its features were perfect, incomparably beautiful, but what was really amazing was its hair, which was so long that any Sylph could have covered its entire body with it.

All the Sylphs of this great species (because there were two types, as we shall see below) looked the same as this one.

We were close to the crystal mountain when the Sylph looked at me and said, "I am going to leave you here, Lamekis, and you will need all your courage. You skirted the torrid zone without hiding like your shipmates, but you only scraped the fringe. Now you are really going to enter the Ceolbhaume, the mountain you see there, and the 40 days of quarantine[60] will go by like a second."

---

[59] A league.
[60] Place where things brought from distant lands are purified of bad air.

71

"Heavens!" I screamed, "What are you telling me. How can I pass through that all-consuming fire without being burned?"

"Well," the Sylph replied sneezing, "only the spirit, not the body, suffers in this trial. I will tell you something that I probably shouldn't: if your soul is great enough to speed you through it, the fire will respect you. But if you wait for me to help you escape and you feel the slightest fear, the fire will punish you for your weakness." While he was speaking we reached the mouth of the burning mountain. I had no time to look at it because I got scared seeing poor Sinouis hurled down by his Sylph. He screamed horribly as he fell into the volcano. Flames shot up and howled, shaking the air. Right then and there I forgot all the advice. I was frozen in fear by what I had just seen and turned to question the Sylph, but it lifted its arms and reminded me of what it had said. I closed my eyes and jumped.

The Ceolbhaume

I cannot remember exactly how I felt just then or what I experienced when I entered the volcano, but what I can remember is that far from being burned by the fire, I felt cool and peaceful. So, I opened my eyes. I was sitting on ground that was white and as soft as down. Sinouis was lying four feet away in a deep sleep.

I looked at my surroundings. The ground was moving and rolling like ocean waves. Many Sylphs of the same species were coming and going and walking on their hands. Hundreds of them passed by others who stopped to looked at us without any of them coming close. I was so preoccupied with watching their movements that I did not even bother to look up.

If I was struck by the things around me, I was even more struck by what was in the air. A great many Spirits of a very different species were flying above my head. In size they looked no bigger than a parrot and they seemed very serious about what they were doing. Many of them were flapping their wings at each other and I saw some plunge down next to me. But wonder of wonders! As soon as they touched the ground they vanished completely, invisible.

I sat watching all these new marvels for a long time after opening my eyes, but I soon felt a gnawing hunger. I got up, went over to Sinouis and had a hard time waking him up. "Oh god!" he cried. "Where am I? Lamekis, is that you? You did say that I was going to share your misfortunes, but I can't do it. The fire I passed through consumed me. In the name of what is dearest to you, don't touch me—I'll crumble to ashes. By what miracle did you escape the burning furnace? I don't exist anymore."

"What are you saying?" I was astonished at his mental breakdown. "To say you don't exist is to exist. You're still the same, Sinouis! I'm as surprised as you are by everything we've been through and I've told myself a hundred times that I'm sleeping and dreaming. But whatever it may be, whether we're asleep or awake, let's call upon Vilkonhis. His wisdom is always great, his plans are just and his providence is inscrutable. Let's submit to his will, for the Supreme Being will never abandon us before the day when all our troubles will end."

After saying this I tried to take Sinouis' hand and lift him up, but he was still obsessed by the idea that as if he had been branded by irons he would be reduced to ashes if he moved. He begged me not to touch him. I tried the best I could to convince him that the vapors of a dream caused delusions like this and in the end he believed that after such an experience I was probably right.

We were not sure which way we should go, but having glimpsed a building in the distance we decided to try to get there. When we began walking, we were surprised to be going constantly downhill, even though the ground looked very level to us. For me, experienced as I was in the extraordinary and having made it a principle to surrender myself entirely to destiny, I was not surprised by this new wonder. My physical needs preoccupied me completely and we hurried up to get to the building that gradually took form. The houses around looked like black, upside down cones.

It was a clear, bright day, but all of a sudden it became dark and black, which scared Sinouis. "Oh Heavens," he cried, "what does this change mean? What hideous country are we in?" He stopped himself and started screaming. I urged him to tell me what was going on and he stammered, "Lamekis, Lamekis, a beast, a monster, a something is on my shoulder. I can't get it off. It feels like its mouth is stuck to my ear."

"Well," I tried not to laugh, "another scare like you turning to ashes."

"No, no," he blurted out, "it's absolutely true. In the name of Vilkonhis, don't leave me. I'm scared that we'll get separated in the darkness and you're all I have to keep me calm. Try to get this pesky thing off me." He took my hand and put it on his shoulder.

"Fear has addled your brain. I don't feel anything."

"So, I'm becoming mad," he howled. "Is all this just to make me hopeless?"

At that very moment the sunlight suddenly appeared and naturally we looked up into the sky where we saw three, equally bright suns forming a perfect triangle; in the middle was a star more brilliant than the most perfect diamond. This extraordinary phenomenon was so amazing that I forgot all about my raging hunger. The rest of the sky was poppy red and the horizon looked square instead of round.

My awe was interrupted by another scream from Sinouis. "Ah, Lamekis," he said stepping back, "look at me and tell me if I'm wrong."

"Now what's the matter?"

"Oh, Heavens," he went on impatiently, "don't you see the monster I'm talking about? Now it's on your shoulder."

"I don't see or feel anything," I answered.

"Then your eyes are bewitched."

"No," I responded. "And the proof is that the animal that you say is on me is absolutely on your shoulder, but don't let this scare you since it isn't doing any harm. Why do you torture yourself? We're in a world of wonders and we have to let things take their course."

After walking and talking like this for about two more karies on ground that wrinkled under our feet, we reached the cone house. We went up to the gate guarded by two Sylphs whose faces looked like mirrors in which I was not surprised to see an animal on my shoulder as well as on Sinouis'. But in spite of my courage I flinched when I felt a cold mouth against my ear that told me in my own language, "Lamekis, don't go through this gate. Here is the dwelling of baleful Intelligences. Go left and you will see the palace of divine Scealgalis in the distance. Hurry up and get there and don't heed your needs or desires."

While the Spirit was talking, I stared at Sinouis, who seemed to be concentrating on the whispering of a small black monster whose color I now saw. I wasn't wrong; it was talking to him, but saying something very different.

"Lamekis," Sinouis pressed me, "let's go into this house. When we have gone past the gate all these wonders will stop. We can find there everything we need. The Spirit assures me that we will be kindly welcomed there and we can rest and finally enjoy a charming, peaceful future."

"Vilkonhis help us, Sinouis," I interjected, "we have to ignore it. That future is all bad. It's better to endure a little longer rather than risk the happy fate awaiting us for some frivolous hope. Sinouis tried to battle against my decision. His gnawing hunger (and mine, too) made him so persuasive and decisive that I almost gave in to the burning temptation, which would have spelled our ruin.

But the Spirit spoke to me a second time. "Stop, Lamekis. If you fall into the trap, you'll be lost. You can only gain happiness by controlling your desires."

While it was speaking, I saw a huge number of these winged animals flying to the left and right of us. Those that came out of the house to the right were black and those that were on the left were white. Both groups started flying over our heads and came so close that we could easily have reached out and touched them. What was really odd was that the white ones did not mingle with the black ones even though they seemed to be all mixed up together above us.

Sinouis was really begging me to enter the house, but I held firm to my decision to go to the left because of the second advice. A soft murmur started growing louder as we argued, but I only made out the voices of the white Spirits, which were like reeds swaying in the wind while the black Spirits sounded harsh and confused.

In spite of Sinouis' insistence, I won the day and convinced him that it took a noble and generous soul to sacrifice our needs for the glory of appearing before the divine Scealgalis and that one cannot be great without earning it. The precious partner of my latest adventures finally agreed and followed me to the left. We had barely made up our minds when the black Spirit that was perched on his shoulder flew off and was replaced by one of the opposite color.

The band of whites sliced through the air in total rapture and as we left the house we saw the blacks sink into the roof from where thick black smoke rose up every time one of them went in.

The path became firmer and changed color the farther away we got from the fatal place. The sky seemed endless and the three suns appeared to be following us. A magnificent view rose up in front of us: the same clear palace that we saw before appeared right in the middle of the road we were taking. On our left was a field of blue grass dotted with flowers that were bigger than I had ever seen and that shook as if a raging wind were blowing, even though there was only a gentle breeze that felt nice and fresh. The view on this side got lost in a sea that sunk into the horizon.

The ground we walked on was white as snow. I reached down to touch it, but my fingers went through it so easily that I felt nothing. We could not imagine what it was except maybe a standing cloud and we were amazed that it could support our weight.

On our right was totally black where the night cut through the day as if a fog had been ripped away in a straight line.

However, our pressing hunger no longer devoured us. We were in a state where the tranquil soul played with itself, so to speak, and happy to do so it aroused no cares or desires. The bad luck feeling that had stayed with me, gradually faded away and if the shadow of the past still tinged in my imagination, it was only as an inducement to the future.

Sinouis interrupted the sweet reverie I was sunk in. "Oh Lamekis, the state I'm in is so different from the one before! The new wonders I'm constantly seeing fascinate me instead of scaring me. The needs that usually bother us so much have left not the slightest trace of what we went through. I remember things cheerfully and even catch glimpses of the future, but I care so little that it's as if I were thinking of nothing, not even myself. Lamekis, are you, too, feeling such divine harmony."

"Yes," I replied. "Your situation describes mine exactly, but be careful of getting the causes mixed up: the inner peace that we feel, that makes us so happy, is less the effect of this marvelous environment than the fruit of the good choice we made. If we had surrendered to the wicked advice of the black Spirits, our souls would now, perhaps, be drowned in bitterness and tears—a picture of what happens to us every day when we face two different wills that each pull us in separate directions, one to good and the other to bad. Only the soul decides, determines and designates one or the other that will make it rejoice or regret."

I was about to move on to other thoughts when the road we were on was suddenly cut off by a cliff. We were astonished to see that we were in a region higher than the ground, giving us a good view of where we were. The Moon was not far from us and looked like it was on the same level. Its dull shine reflected strange rays. The night that cut off the right side looked like it was attached to the ground and it was only broken off on our side by the rays of the shining beacon of the world. What we had thought were three suns were actually three stars, mistaken because of how close together they were. The shiny, transparent palace seemed to float in the air without any kind of support and it was not far from the Moon, which we clearly saw turning like a great wheel on its axis.

We looked toward the right and saw countless white and black Spirits rising and falling toward the ground, forming a cloud that blocked out the light. We were forced to double back. The cloud that was carrying us was disappearing, slowly melting away in front of us.

Oh Vilkonhis, I said to myself, let us share in your heavenly knowledge. Should we wait here for higher orders or go back to where we came from?

Then the Spirit told me not to be afraid and to wait patiently for what would happen. Sinouis and I sat on the road with no fear of anything, contemplating the different things around us in profound silence.

We analyzed everything with that secret satisfaction you feel when your soul expands in the marvelous. All of a sudden a wild wind rose up and scattered the cloud of aerial Spirits that was cawing above our heads, which gave us good reason to start worrying.

Soon we saw two bodies slice through the air. They were too far away to be recognized, but they seemed to be heading for us. A moment later we could tell that they were the same ones that had taken us away from the ship. Their eyes were shining like stars and they left behind long trails in the sky that took a long time to disappear. Their path was silvery and seemed to be directed toward the transparent palace. When the Sylphs were at closer range they did not look like they were flying anymore but rather walking on level ground, which hooked up to ours. When they reached us we stood up.

The one who had spoken to me several times before said, "Lamekis, the time of wonders is coming. Happiness should be a reward for your virtue, but it is a little thing among men! This is the palace of the divine Scealgalis. Your soul, which stammers now, will soon speak, stripped of the carnal flesh that obscures the celestial ray. You will enjoy never dreamed of pleasures, but only acquired on a final condition that is horrifying to mortals—just to hear it can freeze the most hardened will in terror and up until now no one has dared to meet it. That's final proof of the weakness of men, who prefer cowardly love to the immensity of this reward.

"At the palace gate," the Sylph continued, "is a material place reserved for the great proof. When you enter it everything that disgusts you now will vanish. Your human functions, which have stopped in our regions, will start up again. You will be able to eat and taste sumptuous delicacies. You will be served like on Earth and exposed to all the fantasies of men. If your will endures and you can resist all the desires that will grip you, you will be considered worthy of initiation in the mysteries of the divine Island of the Sylphs. 30 days of battle against yourself will be enough to put you in this state and prepare you for the removal of materiality. The great operation is done in this way: four half-Sylphs, like my partner and I, will be chosen to skin you alive and at that moment you will feel all the pain that nature can give. Your skin will be completely taken off your body and carried to the storeroom made for this purpose by the admirable, headstrong Dehahal,[61] the tenacious philosopher who was so desirous to be one of the

---

[61] A Phoenician philosopher who was convinced that the middle region was inhabited by aerial spirits. He tried so hard to get there that he finally succeeded by filling a bunch of bladders with dew, which lifted him to the solar meridian on the day of the equinox. He was the first to enter this region after being found worthy by Scealgalis who at first wanted to cast him down to Earth. He himself asked to be stripped of humanity, which was granted him along with a place at the edge of the island. A tree had been carried by the winds onto the Island of the Sylphs and it was agreed that he would keep it to put ships in, when columns of water carried them up into the clouds. He placed it in such a way that the sea had never since then been sucked up from the region without the uplifted ships crashing into the extraordinary tree. A Frenchman who recently came back from the Island of the Sylphs guaranteed that the tree had been removed.

inhabitants of this island that by his determination he earned not only admittance here, but even the right to keep his opacity in the empire, which has never been granted to anyone but him. The tree in which your ship is resting is less a monument of his vanity than a witness of his love and kindness for his fellow creatures. One day you will know all the marvelous things that this great man did, but you need pure ears to hear them. I am not allowed to tell you any more at this time, but not to leave you in doubt about your role, I can say that if by cowardly disgust and foolish self-love you refuse the goods that have been prepared for you, you will be cast back down to Earth and you will crawl like a reptile, with the body of a reptile but with your same mind, which will be a never-ending punishment and will make you regret, too late, having chosen cowardly sensuality over manly suffering at the price of happiness and immortality."

Having said this the Sylph beat its wings and went back the way it had come with its partner. The speech made me think and made Sinouis scared. We both spent a long time buried in our own thoughts.

The Palace of Scealgalis

"Lamekis," Sinouis cried out, "sad partner in misfortune, are these then the goods that have been promised to us? What is to become of us? What are we going to do? What decision are we going to make?"

"Nothing is more certain," I replied, "than to surrender to our fate, to suffer the eternal decrees and go through the trials that have been set out for us. What is life compared to the immensity? Shouldn't we sacrifice everything in the hope of being eternally happy? What does it matter if we lose the Earth? Doesn't it cost more than it's worth? And if it's true, as the Spirit said, that eternal rewards would crown our pains, should we hesitate to suffer for a little while in order to be worthy? Oh Clemelis,"[62] I burst out, "I will face the dangers, evils and the cruelest punishments in the hope of seeing you again. The happiness I'm told about is obviously you and I will run to it."

With this I set off with joy and Sinouis followed me on the new way that the Spirit had prepared for us. Soon we saw a house that looked like it was made of huge blocks of marble. A large avenue of beautiful trees laden with fruit that looked and smelled delicious led up to the entrance of the palace. Hardly had we started on this pleasant path when we felt the desire to eat the beautiful fruit. The Sylph's warning held us back. We got a grip on ourselves in spite of the hunger that was back, controlled our desires and reached the palace court with the secret satisfaction of having won the first round.

A transparent, precious metal gate surrounded the court. A number of people dressed and acting like us were walking around. We even thought we recognized some of our travel companions and felt a secret joy, convinced that the same fortune had reunited us in this place. We tried to go up to them to be sure, but it was no good walking—we never got any closer. As soon as we noticed this, we stopped.

"Obviously," Sinouis said, "there's a spell on our steps and I'm starting to think that we're in the palace of illusions."

I was getting ready to answer him when a young man with a kind face came up and invited us to enter the palace. He walked ahead and we gladly followed. He had a nice face and his voice was persuasive and pervasive.

"Sir," I said, "can you tell us if you are one of us? Your appearance, which is so different from the inhabitants of this environment, would make me think so."

"My name is Dehahal," the young man replied. "I come from Phoenicia, my philosophy is immortal, I live in the universe and my way of thinking and acting has made me worthy of the happiness I enjoy."

---

[62] The Egyptian wife of Lamekis.

81

"Sir," I continued when Dehahal had finished, "we are very pleased to meet you! We have already been told about you. We respect and trust you completely. Please instruct us and guide us."

Dehahal answered, "I can only hope for your sake that you will persevere. I will leave you at the entrance in front of us; my rights stop there. My only power is to bring you here and to take away those whose behavior makes them unworthy of staying here."

He spoke and pointed to the entrance that opened onto four big rooms. He waved us in but when we turned around to thank him he was gone.

Sinouis and I looked around surprised at what had just happened, wondering if we should take the path shown to us because we were afraid that it might be a trap and that the young man was sent to put us on the wrong track. But his face was so impressive and his voice was so trustworthy that we went in. The place was exquisitely furnished. On one side it opened onto the courtyard I mentioned and on the other onto a splendid garden as far as the eye could see. A stone and metal bas-relief showed a group of stories that must have been very interesting. It was all the furniture in the room.

We crossed the room and entered a splendid hall, lit from the garden, whose vaulting was unbelievably high. The metal ceiling sparkled like thin ice and the large windows encircling the walls were embedded with gems so skillfully wrought that the light passing through them was the most wonderful and strangest I had ever seen. Everything that was not transparent (between the windows, the doors, etc.) was gilded with different colors. We counted 50 doors across from as many windows around the room and the huge space was so quiet that we felt both respect and fear.

In the middle of the hall was an altar supported on four twisted columns like we had never seen before and made of an unknown (perhaps) precious metal. There was a statue made of something like diamond that represented a figure like the

Sylphs who had taken us from our ship and it was so perfectly sculpted that the closer we got the more real it looked.

We were still hoping to find someone to put an end to our doubts and wanderings, so we crossed the hall and went into another room. The same solitude prevailed there. We left right away and entered another. Again the same silence and uncertainty.

We wandered around like this from room to room for quite a while. Seeing no end to the solitude we decided to go back to the main hall, if we could, and rejoin the people we first saw walking around the courtyard. With this in mind we doubled back the way we had come and paced through the labyrinth, but it was impossible to find the hall again. No sooner did we leave one room than we found ourselves in another and if night had not fallen upon us we would probably have kept walking around uselessly.

But a gnawing hunger was consuming us. What were we to do in that dire state? Tired out from having walked so far we were crushed and the dark night was daunting. We groped around feeling for a place to rest while waiting for the day. Fortunately we stumbled upon a sofa, or something like it, which was very lucky under the circumstances, and we took a break from our labor.

Sinouis and I sat there for a while without talking. My dear friend was lost in sorrow if I could judge by the deep sighs he fetched from the bottom of his heart. As overwhelmed as I was by our situation, still I tried to comfort him and told him everything that came into my mind. Whether he was less resilient than me or less accustomed to the rigors of fate, my words did not have the effect I was hoping and found no hold on his troubled soul. On the contrary, his harried heart wept bitter tears again and I sympathized with his desperation. I had no idea how to calm him down, so I decided to distract him by telling him more of my adventures in the hope that he would see how wrong he was to compare his sufferings with mine. I asked him if he was willing to listen while we were waiting for morning and he urged me to try to remember where I had left off.

"Oh Vilkonhis, do I need to try to remember? Such things never leave our memory when love has burned them into our hearts."

Continuation of Lamekis' Story

Oh Sinouis, the rest of my adventures will show you how many trials a mortal must suffer. You saw how I was born in the catacombs and then cast on the sea by the inhumanity and fury of a jealous Queen in love and how I was taken from my parents when I was just old enough to know about my tragedy but too young to do anything about it. Then you saw how I went to the home of a foreigner whose religion and customs were so different from mine. However extraordinary the beginning of my story might seem, the rest is even more amazing. You will see this easily enough when I get back to talking about myself, but for now I will continue with the adventures of Motacoa, which I remember is where I left off.

You remember, of course, that he was the blue man who raised me and loved me so much that he told me his story so that...

"Don't worry about it," Sinouis interrupted. "In spite of all the strange things that have happened to us, I haven't forgotten a word of your story. You were at the part where Motacoa recognized Falbao, that marvelous animal, attached to the foot of the throne on which a radiant, beautiful Princess was sitting. How could anybody forget such strange events?"

Sinouis' memory proved to me how closely he had listened and I hoped that what I had left to say would distract him from the black thoughts of his present state. Thus I took up the thread of the story.

Continuation of Motacoa's story

Motacoa continued: If the sight of Falbao surprised me, I was even more surprised when I heard my name called from the throne. I approached with admiring respect. Imagine my surprise when I saw the Princess up close and recognized her as the young woman who appeared in the dream I had after drinking from the divine spring, the dream in which a monster had stolen her away when I wanted to avenge the wicked blow that cut off her hand. The vision was so striking that I could not go up to her at first like she asked and find out what miracle had brought me into the Trifolday[63] world. Recovering at last from my surprise I bowed low and in this position went up to the foot of the throne to obey the charming Princess. But as soon as I looked up at her my astonishment caused me to faint.

A dull noise followed this unexpected event. The rows of worm women started milling about and humming frightfully. Four of these monsters from the four sides of the throne came at me armed with a zenghuis.[64] Scared by this I jumped toward Falbao and guided by his instinctive sensitivity he struggled so hard to help me that he broke his chains. The monsters got scared and ran away from his fury as he jumped onto the throne. Then the women guards fled out the doors, taking the Princess with them and leaving me alone in the hall with Falbao.

Imagine how surprised I was at what just happened. The first thing I did was to congratulate my wonderful dog. And he accepted my show of affection, or rather of gratitude, with all the joy he could show in his way. As embarrassed as I was, his presence gave me confidence against anything that might happen, as proven by the fear that he inspired in these people. At times I felt like I was losing my mind in search of the cause of these wonders: my imagination wore itself out, but could find no valid reason. So, what I felt when I first saw the Princess,

---

[63] The Inner Earth.
[64] Sword.

which had vanished in my fear, took hold of me again. Now that I was safe from immediate danger I scolded myself for letting her be taken away and I resolved to find her again no matter what it took. With this in mind I left the hall through a round door and soon found myself wandering in a maze of dark alleys. The paths were so hard that without Falbao at my side to lean on I would have fallen down any number of times.

I wandered around like that for a long time without finding any exit until I finally noticed a glimmer of light. There was a ceiling skillfully paneled with everything precious from the Earth, but what was remarkable was that the different products of the inner world were placed in such a way as to make a kind of bas-relief that pictured men and women to form the body of a story. As I went farther on, the light from some burning torches, spaced apart, lit the area more and more and revived my courage. After a few hundred feet the vaulted hall led to the bank of a very big canal whose water was mercury and as rough as a storm-tossed sea. I was also amazed by a stream of burning sulfur on my right because I figured that this nearby fire had to be the source of the boiling canal. I stepped back because I could not stand the crippling smell. Falbao was ahead of me, heading left toward a door I had not seen, which opened onto a bright room lit by the same kind of torches, which very quickly revived my dulled senses. In the middle of the big room was a mausoleum of different colored stones that pictured a normal man. Four inhabitants of the Inner Earth supported the monument in different positions befitting their effort and the mournfulness of the place.

I was marveling at this tomb, which made me think that this world had two kinds of men, when I heard a voice speaking my language, coming from the next room. The sound of the voice struck me to the core and I rushed toward the half-open door. I stopped to listen and heard it speaking.

"No, barbarian, I will never be yours. Your persecutions are useless. I'll bury myself in a dark grave before lying down with a monster like you. Keep your empire to yourself. I don't want to reign over it. Give me back to mine and my dear country. Isn't it enough that your jealousy killed my father who refused to let me be taken by his murderer? Your accusations of me are useless: I'm not responsible for these strangers coming to Trifolday—I've never seen them before. Your jealousy blinds you to the point that you don't even see that they're a different species from me. You say that I swooned at the sight of one of these strangers, that he was my lover. You say that my excitement at seeing him proves it and this extraordinary creature, the basilisk that is so dreadful to your nation; you say it came here into your kingdom at my behest and by the information I gave to this rival conspiring against you. You say you know how to take revenge, that they are ready to die and if I don't succumb to your desires, I too will be punished with death for my treachery and stubbornness. Go ahead. Do what you want, barbarian. My innocence will vouch for me for my happiness. But fear the vengeful gods—they leave nothing unpunished. Sooner or later the Heavens will take revenge on you for all your cruelties."

The voice stopped there and the woman speaking started weeping bitterly. I was sure it was the Princess whom I was looking for and her lament was all about me. The only difficulty for me lay in the authority and skill of the barbarian who was obviously the leader of the place.

I was lost in thought, not knowing what to do, when a terrible shriek came from behind the door and I boldly pushed it open. What a sight struck me! My Princess was lying on a strangely built bed of foam, on the verge of death at the hands of a worm man who was holding a zenghuis over her breast, dangling it in mid-air to take cruel pleasure in watching the beautiful woman suffer all the horrors of death. At the unexpected sight of me he started to strike.

"Stop, wretched monster," I screamed and threw myself at him heedless of his hugeness. "I'll die before you finish your savage deed." The force with which I threw myself at him, which he was not expecting, or maybe being flustered by the crime he was about to commit, caused him to drop his zenghuis. With his powerful hand he grabbed me and was going to crush me in his arms. I was already losing my breath when Falbao, who had stayed back until then, jumped on the monster. This unseen aide was so frightening to him that he dropped me and tried to jump away, but it was too late. The agile Falbao had already got hold of his neck and in one fell swoop he brought down the huge mass that fell lifeless at our feet.

The Princess was so taken aback at this sudden turn of events and so unspeakably scared of my wonderful dog that she screamed, "Heavens! I'm lost. Save me, noble stranger, from this frightful monster. I'm not an accomplice of Za-ra-ouf..."

"Don't worry, Princess," I put my hand on Falbao's head as he stared at me like he was awaiting my orders, "this faithful animal only attacks persecutors. Are there any more? Show me and they will all be wiped out. What just happened is not the first time I've witnessed the bravery of my faithful dog and his effect on these strange people of the inner world."

The Princess, still scared of Falbao, listened to me and slowly recovered. "Sir, what do I owe you? Without you I would be dead. What can I do to show my gratitude?"

"Let me devote my life to you, which is as dear to me as yours and allow me, Princess, to be your eternal servant."

The lovely woman opened her mouth to answer, but in the doorway across from where I had entered two worm men appeared. At the sight of us, or rather of Falbao, they left in a hurry, buzzing furiously. The Princess, who paled when she saw the monsters, afraid that they would take vengeance on her for the death of their king, started worrying again in spite of the confidence she should have had in me.

"Oh Vilkonhis..." she cried out.

"What's this?" I cut in, staring at her. "What venerable name am I hearing? Ah, it makes me think that you come from somewhere close to where I'm from. What miracle has brought you to this place that should be unknown to all the earth?"

"Alas," the Princess said, "a nasty trick and hard fate led me here. It would not take long for me to tell you my story, but I have to admit that I'm not calm enough right now to satisfy your curiosity. The death of the King by your animal will very soon have very dangerous results. 10,000 of his subjects are maybe right now preparing to avenge the regicide. How are we going to save ourselves from their attack? I can't imagine how we can be safe. The most obvious solution is to flee, but where? At least you must know the labyrinth better than I and can find some secret exit."

The Princess got more worried when I told her I did not know anything about it, but I made a quick decision and urged her to try it with me anyway, putting our faith in the great Vilkonhis whom she had prayed to—surely moved by our trust in him, he would guide us and protect us wherever we went. The Princess, filled with religion, looked up to the Heavens and followed me, leaning on my shoulder. We left through the same door I had come in and entered the mausoleum room.

The Princess started crying bitterly when she saw the tomb. "There, Sir, is the height of inhumanity and the cause of my sorrow. The death of that barbarian Za-ra-ouf can hardly atone for the crime of having cut short such a precious life. Oh, my father," she let loose a torrent of tears, "however innocent I am of this crime, I am still the fatal cause." She turned to me. "This magnanimous hero is the great Lindiagar, my father, King of the Amphicleocles, whose tender love for me brought him here with the bold plan to take me away from the tyranny of wicked Za-ra-ouf. I can still hardly believe it."

I took the liberty of interrupting the Princess to tell her that at the moment time was of the essence. After kissing the monument reverently she kept crying, but followed me. We sped up and were about to leave the dreary place when the passage was blocked by a crowd of people holding zenghuis and bustling toward us. I could not help feeling scared and wondering whether Falbao could save us this time from a seemingly inescapable danger. The Princess and I became even more desperate for our safety when Falbao, who had walked ahead of us at the sight of the monsters, stopped short and stood still. With his head raised he looked like he was frozen there by the size of the crowd and the danger, but I thought differently when I saw a man of my species coming toward us, armed. Keeping his eyes on him, Falbao slowly went to meet him and far from looking furious, he showed respect in his own way for this stranger and came galloping back to me as if I should congratulate him for his discovery.

The Princess and I, in our state of utter confusion, frozen in fear, could not fathom the cause or the effect. Falbao stared at me, waiting for me to do something. Soon all these mysteries were cleared up when I recognized the man coming toward us. "Ah, Boldeon!" I cried, leaving the Princess and running up to him. "Is it really you I see here at the head of my enemies?"

"No, Sir," the kind minister replied. "Violence alone has forced me to take up arms. These monsters are frightened by the death of their King and scared of your faithful dog who they think is a horrible basilisk. They are convinced that he has no power over men of our species and their Council has decided that they will use me to chain the animal up and thus save them from his fury. They said that if I didn't do as they asked, they would kill me, so I accepted, but, Motacoa, I don't think that the arms they gave me are supposed to be used against you. How sweet it would be to prove to you right now the respect I have for my rightful ruler by risking a hundred of my lives, if I had them."

He said this and turned around quickly, brandished his zenghuis and ran toward the monsters who looked like they were waiting for their plans to be carried out. The Princess tried in vain to hold me back. I followed my friend without the slightest fear of danger to stop me. But did I need to worry? Wasn't Falbao there? The faithful animal got a whiff of my plans and passed me up running toward the monsters and barking so hellishly that the crowd turned tail and rushed away. Falbao wanted to go after them, but afraid of losing him I called him back and he came running. Sure of our escape now, I went back to get the Princess who was frozen in fear and could hardly stand up on her trembling knees. We passed through the room whose bas-reliefs I recognized from before, where several monsters lay trampled by their wild flight. It took us more than four hours to find our way out of the labyrinth. Boldeon, who was following Falbao, was the first to announce that we were out of the palace of darkness. After around two more karies without meeting any obstacles, we ended up in a place that was familiar to me.

I shouted out seeing the expanse of plain that I had visited a hundred times. "Thanks be to Vilkonhis," and I congratulated the Princess. "Now we're safe from the monsters that we were so afraid of. Soon, Boldeon, you will be in a familiar country. Yes, Princess, you are finally going to have a rest from your labors. Oh mother," I cried with joy, "you're going to be in bliss and you, father, Lodaï ..."

"Just Heavens," Boldeon could barely contain his joy, "are we finally going to be happy?"

"Yes, Boldeon," I said, "nothing is more certain. I know this place perfectly. See that crystal rock over there with thick smoke coming out of it and purple fire—I often used to sit in wonder at how feeble mental theories are in the face of such wonders like the natural crucible inside that opening where the purest metals constantly boil, which the perpetual fire sometimes makes liquid, sometimes material and often permanent. I find the slanting light that passes through the crust of the earth here beautiful as it filters through the bitumen on the right, winding its way for a long time before dropping down next to the house that Lodaï built. We still have around three karies until we get there if the Princess, whom I fear is exhausted, allows me to carry her. The extra weight will be precious to me and make the thorny road shorter, especially if we will tell each other the strange events that have brought us together."

The lovely Princess was calmer after I guaranteed that we were safe and seemed flattered by the attention I showed her. She hoped that she could follow us without any trouble, so Boldeon, to start the program I came up with to pass the time, told in his own way about the dangers he faced since the fatal moment when the worm man took him away.

Boldeon's adventure in Inner Earth

You can imagine my distress when the monster grabbed me. The enormous leaps he made to avoid your faithful Falbao shook me up so badly that I thought I would die at any moment from the pain. But in spite of his agility and cleverness in avoiding his pursuing enemy, he would have been caught sooner or later if the far-sighted orders of the King, who warned his people that the basilisk (that's what they called Falbao there) had shown up in their land, had he not had them dig trenches all over the place as traps to keep the people safe from the murderous effects that the dog naturally had over this species.

Falbao could not avoid being caught in one of these traps. The monster that had grabbed me stopped and went back to see. He was delighted to see that the spring in the trap had chained the dog by the neck. The poor animal was struggling as hard as he could to free himself from the restraint while the worm man looked on with pleasure, watching the animal watch me sadly. He twanged some words at me in a language that I recognized but that I did not hear. Thinking by my silence that I did not understand, he tried a different language that I did not understand at all and the clever monster ended up speaking so many languages that I finally heard my own and said so. He looked glad and asked if I knew the animal that had chased him and that was now chained up, believing that I was so calm because I was used to seeing his kind and if my country produced them (he added), as was rumored, we should be congratulated for not being in the same situation as his people who became mortally passive at the sight of one of them and died right away if they were unlucky enough to be touched by its drool. I answered the worm man's questions by lamenting my fate and that of a friend who maybe had the same bad luck as me. The monster scowled hideously at this.

"Tumpingand," he said, "bad luck depends on prejudices, what you're born with. They make the little instinct that nature gives you wander off. Vile excrement of humanity, you are too happy with what happens to you by chance. Give thanks for this to the great Ver-fund-ver-ne[65] and that your misshapen species, cursed by us, has a Princess that our emperor loves. On behalf of this beautiful Tumpingand[66] our sovereign has granted life to the monsters of your country, when chance brings them down here. Otherwise at the time of your enslavement you would be led to the temple of Ver-fund-verne where we would skin you alive and burn you on the altar. Give thanks also, I tell you, for the accident that brought our ruler into the kingdom of the Amphicleocles. That is why the elders of Kin-zan-da-or,[67] for the sake of the Princess Cleannes' abduction, were exempt from the severe law I just mentioned. Instead it was decided that henceforth every Tumpingand who happened to be found in the kingdom would be mutilated in the body parts that are different from ours and these thighs and legs would be thrown away like the disgusting protrusions of humanity that they are, which is far better for them since these useless, shapeless limbs are the only reason they are rejected by the great Ver-fund-ver-ne.

"As for you, barely sufferable Monster, your capture came at just the right time because of the honor of being mutilated with the Princess whom we haven't been able to convince to stay here peaceably and who, maybe to get out of it, with her awful stubbornness got the monarch to agree that the operation would only take place when two Tumpingands could serve as an example. She was clever because it's been more than a century since a human came into our lands and it didn't seem likely that it would happen any time soon. But Zara-ouf, being the King that he is, very easily got the elders of

---

[65] The divinity worshipped in the center of the Earth in the form of a grotesquely huge worm.

[66] The name given to all nations that differ from the people inside the Earth, which means foreigner or stranger in their language.

[67] The plain where the High Council gathers.

Kin-zan-da-or, the Council that counterbalanced his authority, to admit that they could not, in spite of their great respect for him, override the law that gave the Tumpingands a month to meet the terms of the mystical operation and that everything they could possibly do to beautiful Cleannes was ordained by the Fingaïd,[68] the decree they resorted to only in the most urgent matters of state.

"Za-ra-ouf, who loved the Princess but according to the laws of his kingdom could only marry her after the mutilation, was not angry at the stubbornness of the elders of Kin-zan-da-or. The Fingaïd gave him hope because there were so many of his subjects taking part in the hunt that someone was bound to catch some Tumpingands for him to fulfill the promises that Cleannes made.

"So, what can I say? The Fingaïd is over today and a human monster has been captured for the King. Thanks be to Ver-fund-ver-ne. I've got you and for that I foresee that the Prince's joy will be complete since I assume that your partner is the prey (or will be soon) of one of us. But an extra benefit that is a hundred times better than the prize, as valuable as it may be, is the great fortune to have the basilisk in our power so that it will no longer leave its mark of death on our lands. The elders of Kin-zan-da-or, who until now have kept a faithful tradition of everything that has happened since we owed our existence to divine Ver-fund-ver-ne, say that the last time this cruel enemy of our species appeared in our lands more than 20,000 of our inhabitants died and it took three hirzidos[69] to catch it in a trap like the one you see here. Imagine, Tumpingand, everyone's joy when they hear the news of the basilisk's capture. Take comfort," he looked at me with kindness, "because you are not unlucky to have fallen into my hands. I am respected by Za-ra-ouf—I am his Grand Bagdhaf.[70] You

[68] Public tracking or hunt.
[69] Years. They are counted by the people of the Inner Earth by the number of assemblies of the elders of Kin-zan-da-or, which are called every 225 days.
[70] Great Hunter.

seem to possess a purer instinct than an animal of your kind usually has. After the mutilation I mentioned, I will give you the esteemed privilege of going to the cages of the King's menagerie, which is a wonderful benefit only given to the most admirable productions of nature."

After saying all this to me, the monster resumed his normal step[71] and we soon met a lot of his kind. Seeing me they gave signs of great joy, which became more and more excessive when the worm man talked to them. He was probably telling them (unfortunately I did not understand a word of their language) about the capture of the terrible basilisk. They got all excited and jumped higher and higher and made all kinds of strange gestures, too many and too confusing for me to describe. After celebrating in their way the common good luck, each of the monsters came and wiped their hand over my face and then went their separate ways to spread the news. Two of them stayed with us, one walking ahead and the other behind.

You can imagine, Motacoa, (Boldeon continued) how many thoughts were going through my head and the justifiable fear that should have alarmed me. But considering that it did me no good to torture myself and struggle against evils that could not be helped, I forced myself to resign to the will of Vilkonhis. Nothing calms the mind in adversity like religious sentiments. I found myself completely changed after this inner submission and was able to think about what was happening to me and about the conversation I had had with the monster whose slave I had become. I was not surprised at the names he called humans; everything that is different from us and our kind and our preconceived ideas usually acquire the title of monster or barbarian without seeing that these names are legitimately used only for those who act against reason and against their own principles. But what really did surprise me was to hear my language spoken in these places that were so different from where I was born. And I was even more asto-

---

[71] To leap and bound.

nished since the monster said that it had been more than a century since anyone of my species had been in their extraordinary world.

I certainly should have been worrying about more important things, but I could not resist the desire to learn more about this quandary. And the worm man answered, "How's this? After I talked to you, you thought about what I said and used your mind! I never imagined that a Tumpingand could reason. Well, with this in mind I will try to answer some of your questions. The trip is still long from here to the capital so I will have time to give you a rough outline of our history. And I think I owe you this considering how we met and since you are curious I have no doubt that you will be pleased to hear it."

Za-ra-ouf and the worm people

We owe our origin to Ver-fund-ver-ne, who illuminated a philosopher among us called Za-ra-ouf, who dictated our laws whose strict and religious observation promised the reward of passing from the inner world to the higher world where they revel in true light and really see the divine torches that are its principles.

The punishment for those who violate these precepts consists in the eternal deprivation of this promised light.

The wisdom that shines in these laws gave Za-ra-ouf such well-deserved respect among the people of Trifolday that they elected him King and submitted entirely to his power. He proved himself so worthy of this high rank that he wanted to counter-balance his authority, so one day he gathered his people on the plain of Kin-zan-da-or and there set up the elders, who still today keep their name from this plain, as preservers of the laws that had been made public and accepted, with such sovereign power that they can depose the King himself if it were agreed.

Za-ra-ouf was as great a philosopher as he was a wise lawmaker and foresaw that his species was not the only one that inhabited the inner world. To guarantee its preservation he said that if it happened that other peoples invaded the kingdom his people would unite to destroy them and never form any alliance with them.

To the privileges of the elders of Kin-zan-da-or he added that they would elect their rulers, excluding his own posterity in the hope that virtue and valor would win the kingdom's vote.

When Za-ra-ouf died, his successors kept his name. But when the elders of Kin-zan-da-or were not satisfied with the third King whom they had elected, they published a decree whereby it was ordained that in the future everyone aspiring to the crown could not be admitted among the candidates unless they traveled three dikhados and brought back some positive proof of some unknown wonder that might be useful and beneficial to the country.

This new law not only gave us great Kings, but also through the discovery of one of these Kings we know today about the hideous immortal beast, the basilisk, who can single-handedly destroy all of this lower world. And by the experiments this King did on some subjects condemned to death we learned the ways not only to protect ourselves from it, but also to use it, after capturing it, to destroy others of its kind[72] who might come after it.

The King who came after this one was elected over all the others because as proof of his labor he brought back two Tumpingands, an extraordinary wonder. Before that they were unknown. The story of his voyage was that these monsters had come into our country through an opening in the crust of the earth. They were let down by a rope in a basket that they clung onto. He chanced to be there when one of them fell and was surprised to see loads of these monsters lying dead on the ground with coils of rope piled around, proving that these barbarians were planning to invade their states, but had not yet managed to find out how to succeed.

---

[72] This only took place in the first century.

After this report the elders of Kin-zan-da-or held an important Council in which it was decided that the commissioners be elected to be brought to the place specified by the aspirant and after making an examination they would put many guards there so that every time Tumpingands showed up they would seize them and send them to the capital where they would be sacrificed to Ver-fund-ver-ne.

For the living monsters in their custody the Council decided that they would keep them and have two elders of Kinzan-da-or study the monstrous species to try to understand what kind of instinct they had. The two chosen to study the Tumpingands up close found out that their crude instinct could reason, so they strove to learn their language, which they managed to do after a few dikhados. This knowledge led to more and more and the report they finally made to the Council was very worrisome to the wise men because according to the Tumpingands the place where they came from seemed to be the promised land of the Trifoldaysters since it was lit by the principles of light.

The elders of Kin-zan-da-or were divided on the matter and the findings of the report would surely have divided the kingdom and created a new sect had the High Council not been wise enough to foresee such consequences and order the Tumpingands to be put to death and that in the future no living specimens would be kept. However, they figured that it was of the utmost importance to learn to speak their language, but only for a few elders and the King. This was a political decision so that if the unheralded revolution of the monsters ever took place, they would be prepared to face it and crush it.

Our history says that for centuries there was a guard in the very place where the first Tumpingands were found and they caught many more. But one day they caught three hideous basilisks, the sight of which killed two thirds of them and the rest were so scared they ran back to the capital to tell the tragic news. The King who was reigning at the time wanted to take charge himself and led even more guards than before to meet this enemy of our species. The King himself and most of the guards behind him lost their lives.

The next King proved himself no less determined and made it his duty to find a way to protect his people from these new enemies. To accomplish this he had a bunch of traps dug, but his efforts were useless. The elders of Kin-zan-da-or were afraid that if they kept guarding the place all the Trifoldaysters would be destroyed, so they ordered that in the future there would be no more guards in the places where the basilisks chose to live.

This wise precaution was a grand success. Two centuries passed without any Tumpingand showing up and without any new incident, which caused us to almost totally forget about the past events until today.

Za-ra-ouf, the prince reigning today, whose intelligence and activity earned him the throne, was coming back very late from the hunt one night and came across a Trifoldayster on the road who said to him, "Stop, Za-ra-ouf, here's what's bothering me: the torch of happiness enlightens strange people whose kingdom is inaccessible. Up there is a Princess the color of Ascalis who is the object of desire of all the Kings. I hope Za-ra-ouf will not let himself fall under her charms. The terrible enemy is keeping watch over his spouse. Fear the fate that has been prepared for you, a just punishment for ravishing the wife of your chief minister! Oh cowardly elders of Kin-zan-da-or, your disgraceful tolerance will get the punishment it deserves. Za-ra-ouf, the only way to appease the anger of Ver-fund-ver-ne is to lay your scepter at his feet, go back into the nothingness that you were tricked out of and under the sacred vaults of the temple atone for the crimes you are stained with."

Za-ra-ouf was taken aback by the boldness of the Trifoldayster. He paid back the oracle with a swipe of his zenghuis that laid him at his feet. But whatever he did, he could not get the words out of his mind. His soul was sunk in melancholy. Alone and lost in thought he fled to those who had once been so dear to him and shut himself up in the heart of the palace.

He often spent many months there without a public appearance.

One day, being more absorbed than ever in his dark thoughts, he was absently looking at the tradition of his people[73] to distract himself and he stopped at the place where the Tumpingands appeared for the first time. The story interested him so much that he looked at it several times.

The next day he gathered the elders of Kin-zan-da-or and informed them of a voyage he planned to make, he said, so as to dignify his reign by discovering in person the spot where the Tumpingands tried to invade the kingdom and he would find a way to put guards back there after such a long absence.

The Council tried in vain to stop the project by telling him that it had been so long since a monster or basilisk appeared that he should leave things alone. But nothing could shake him. He left with only one of his ministers and after being away for three dikhados, he reappeared carrying the beautiful Princess I talked about. He told the elders of Kin-zan-da-or all about his voyage and after winning over the great Moulhoubouk[74] he convinced him that Ver-fund-ver-ne had forever destined the abducted Tumpingand to be Queen of the Trifoldaysters and that she would give birth to a magnanimous Prince who would open the gates of happiness for them and exterminate the whole race of enemy basilisks.

The elders of Kin-zan-da-or were fooled by this trick and not only changed the law that forbade the King to marry, but also, in consideration of the benefits promised by the Princess' tubes, abolished the law requiring every Tumpingand caught in the kingdom to be put to death. And to indulge the people's prejudice, which could have resurfaced against the future Queen, they decided that instead of death, as the old rules demanded, they would mutilate the species, as I said.

---

[73] The tradition is recorded in bas-reliefs, as writing was not in use then, and this method was so ingenious and so cleverly accomplished that the most minor parts of a story were displayed.

[74] High Priest of Ver-fund-ver-ne.

Now, Tumpingand, (the worm man finished up) you can get over your surprise at hearing me speak your language. I am an elder of Kin-zan-da-or and it's one of my privileges and it's lucky for you that you fell into my hands. If you take my advice and your instinct is strong enough to ask for your monstrous limbs to be cut off, I promise to make your life easy here and you will never stop thanking Ver-fund-ver-ne for the good fortune of having met me.

Boldeon in Trifolday

To make me trust him more the monster spit in his hand and smeared it on my face. That's how these people make an oath, a practice I would have willingly forgone, along with everything else. After this ridiculous ceremony whose heady smell made me sneeze, it was his turn to ask me hundreds of questions that I answered the best I could.

After three days of walking we came to the capital where the palace, as you no doubt know, is the entire city. There they led me into Za-ra-ouf's chamber. He seemed buried in deep sadness and at first would not even look at me. The monster who brought me had a long talk with him; then we left and I was put inside a prison cave.

"I'm as surprised as you are," the worm man said, "at the treatment they're giving you, which I wasn't expecting. I can't understand why the King is so upset. He must suspect you of evil designs because he gave me a stiff warning to keep a close eye on you. The Princess herself is coming here for something. But whatever's happening, don't worry—I didn't give you my word for nothing. I'll go to the court and when I find out what's going on with all this, I'll come back and fill you in. What I suspect, however, is that Za-ra-ouf is maybe remembering the prophecy of the Trifoldayster whom he killed on the hunt. There's a bad feeling in the air. Ver-fund-ver-ne preserve us lest the state be destroyed forever."

Saying this the monster left and I was drowned in a thousand thoughts, each one more troubling than the last. The intelligence and courage that I should have had at my age were useless to me. But what else did I have? Should I have ignored the fact that the older we get the weaker we get? The dangers and perils that I faced trying to get back your father's throne, Motacoa, were nothing compared to what I was facing then. I looked sadly around my underground prison where the weak light filtering through the cracks was only good for highlighting all the horror.

I was kept in suspense for three days awaiting my fate. Sad, woebegone and listless, I could not even bring myself to eat. The food was so different than what I was used to that I could barely look at it. But my body, devastated by an overlong fast, could no longer fight my devouring hunger and I pounced on the roasted slug that lay among the food they gave me. I was eating this awful meal against my will when I heard the rock rolling back from the opening. I shuddered at the sound, but rushed over to learn my fate. I saw the monster I knew and listened to what he had to say to me.

"Tumpingand, I have lots of news to tell you. You were right to think that the same thing was happening to one of your comrades. He was captured the same day as you and the sadness you saw the King sunk in was from the interest the Princess showed when she saw him. He suspected that the monster was from her country and he became jealous like he'd already shown. He imagined that this Tumpingand was maybe the Princess' lover and had come to steal her away from him, as was tried once before by one of your species who was put to death and later discovered to be her father.

"Duly warned, the King gave secret orders that the Tumpingand be brought to him. But what bad luck! And what is everyone's worst nightmare…the hideous basilisk that you saw caught in a trap has escaped. Everyone is scared. Why was its life saved by the leniency the King showed for the Princess? When we brought the animal to him the Princess assured him that the species was common in her country and that they only had to give it to her—she knew how to tame it and far from being a threat she would make it useful by slowly getting it used to the people of the kingdom. She convinced him that the harm coming from its eyes only happened when it was really angry. The King was seduced by all kinds of things like that and allowed the monster to be handed over to the Princess—fatal trust! She might be the cause of all our ruin.

"So, duly warned, as I said, that the Princess' interest in the Tumpingand held a mystery, Za-ra-ouf secretly hid under the Princess' throne so that when he was brought in, he could catch them as accomplices or lovers. But oh, the disastrous consequences! When the monster of your species was first brought in the Princess fainted. What more can I say? The basilisk broke its chains and protected the Tumpingand with its deadly looks and murderous foaming mouth. But their days are numbered. Everyone ran away scared and is relying on the traps to catch the terrible animal again. The elders of Kin-zan-da-or have assembled and I told them about you, bragging about your reasonable instinct, which might be useful to us on this sad day, but they argued with me and want me to bring you before the Council. So, follow me and if you can be of any use right now, you will have our fullest gratitude."

The monster had barely finished talking when a crowd of his kind showed up in the cave opening. Their buzzing was horrible and scared me. "Don't be afraid," the worm man said to me, "it's me they want. They've come to tell me about some awful new turn of events."

One of the monsters was very animated speaking with him. He finally turned back to me, slapped his face and cried out, "Great Ver-fund-ver-ne, what have I just been told? Za-ra-ouf is dead and the Princess stolen away. The basilisk is responsible for this tragic turn of events; everyone is running away from it. The people are desolated and the elders of Kin-zan-da-or want to see you right away."

Then the monster grabbed me and leapt out of the cave. I was brought to the Council followed by a huge crowd of people buzzing bitter laments. Right as I entered a deep silence fell over everyone. The elders whispered together and then the one who brought me put me in their midst. "Tumpingand," he said, "the elders of Kin-zan-da-or have discussed our sad situation and the assurance I gave them that your species lives above ours and was born in the land of happiness where the principles of light are. Now they want me to tell you that the throne has been vacated by the death of Za-ra-ouf and they will promise to make you King if you deliver us from this horrible monster who persecutes us. Take this zenghuis as a faithful pledge of our word. Go and if under your auspices we are victors and the basilisk falls, you will be carried straightway into the divine temple where the great Moulhoubouk will place the sacred crown on your head."

I was so surprised at this extraordinary proposition that I took the zenghuis without saying a word. It was barely in my hands when all the elders of Kin-zan-da-or surrounded me and made the customary oath by spitting in their hands and wiping my face. If I were in my right mind I would have used the weapon they gave me to avenge this ridiculous ceremony, but at the time I could do no better than suffer it. Figuring that I would meet up with you, I guaranteed the elders that I was ready to do anything they wanted. The spitting intensified and they led me into the palace where I met you.

Motacoa's reunion

The Princess confirmed what Boldeon had just said and was about to add a few other details when I looked to the right and interrupted her with a cry of joy. "Oh Heavens, my mother and Lodaï are at the edge of that spring where a greenish elixir flows. Vilkonhis, I am in debt to you forever!"

I spoke so loudly that they heard me at the spring. My mother, sitting there sunk in deep reverie, heard the sound of my dear voice, jumped up and recognized me from afar. "Oh son," she cried rushing toward me, "you've come back. I won't cry anymore." She had no time to say more; I was already in her arms. My dear mother's joy was so overwhelming that I feared she might die of it. Lodaï, who was running up, stopped to gather some useful herbs when he saw my mother's soul ready to fly away. As dear as I was to him and as curious as he was to know why I had been gone for so long and who the strangers were, he continued to help my mother and only paid attention to me when she was completely over the shock. Then he showed me all the joy he had at my return.

We spent more than an hour sharing the pleasure of seeing each other again, fumbling through what had happened to us. Lodaï told me he thought as much because he suspected that the center of the earth was inhabited. He even told me that he had once caught a glimpse of one of the monsters I described, but was so scared of being caught that he was very careful to never again wander off farther than two karies from his home, which was why he repeatedly warned me to stay nearby. He often repented not telling me the whole story, but knowing how precocious I was he kept quiet, afraid that my curiosity would do what chance ended up accomplishing. Then he told me about how desperate my mother was while I was gone and that it was a miracle she never gave up.

After the first bursts of emotion at our reunion, Lodaï recognized Boldeon. The two longtime, close friends looked at each other with inexpressible joy. My mother could feel something about the Princess and about what I felt for her and she hugged her with as much tenderness and affection as if she were her own daughter. Then we started off for Lodaï's house and when we got there Boldeon told his faithful friend and my mother everything he had told me about my usurped throne. The two great men of state agreed on what should be done to win it back for me without running any risk. In their plans the beautiful Nasilaë had to get married. I was ecstatic when I saw that everything was heading for my happiness, but even more so when I learned all about what the Princess had sacrificed for me.

After a few days of well-deserved rest we begged beautiful Nasilaë to tell us how she came to be carried away by the monster Za-ra-ouf. She was more than happy and when she introduced herself as the Princess of Amphicleocles, Boldeon and Lodaï spoke up. Lodaï said, "We shouldn't be too surprised at this extraordinary news. What strange chance, great Princess, pulled you out of such a mysterious state? Allow me," he turned to me, "to tell the Prince why we are surprised. It will be a good introduction to your story."

The story of the three sons of the Sun

The kingdom of Amphicleocles borders that of the Abdalles. Tradition says that the people never had any relations with their neighbors from your state, Motacoa, so, it's not surprising that you don't know about these things. But, that you might understand the Princess' story a little better, it would be good to tell you a few things about this extraordinary kingdom.

Our history teaches us that the people originate from Hor-his-hon-hal, the third son of the Sun. They say that one day the Father of Light was about to go back to his aerial palace when he spied a girl bathing in a river in a dark forest. Her name was Phiocles. The tradition is interrupted at this point to show that it was the first creature to appear in the world and that before this mortal was created, the Earth was inhabited only by animals and it owes its being to the intervention of the Sun and the Moon by a ray that fell straight down onto a female serpent, which died giving birth to the world. The same tradition says that Phiocles was nursed by a she-wolf, which took care of her until she did not need her help anymore.

Hor-his-hon-hal, the meanest of the Sun's sons, conspired with his brothers to rid themselves of their father who punished him often for his evil inclinations. Their father learned about the parricidal plot and threw them down to the Earth, saving them from harm by forming a cloud that vanished when they reached Earth.

Phiocles was returning to a grotto where she would spend the night when she met Abdalles, the older brother of Hor-his-hon-hal. Instead of running away she gladly went up, enraptured to see another like herself. Abdalles was charmed

106

by the beautiful mortal and soon got over his exile after Phi-ocles took him into her grotto. The nation of the Abdalles owes its origin to the night of this first encounter.

One year later, while Phiocles was returning from the forest, she met Thumipgand, the other brother of Abdalles. The sight of this child of the Sun, the handsomest of the broth-ers, enchanted fickle Phiocles. She responded to the desires of the new lover, but afraid that Abdalles would catch her and punish her for her crime, she hid away in another grotto where she spent three years with him. After this period of living in darkness flighty Phiocles abandoned Thumipgand while he was sleeping. Tradition does not say whether Phiocles' fickle-ness produced any children, but as I'm speaking and thinking about what happened to you in the center of the earth, I sup-pose that the Tumpingands, who are spoken about so much, must owe their origin to Thumipgand—they are the same name even though they are pronounced differently.

Phiocles was racked by remorse and decided to flee as far as possible in fear of meeting some other of her lovers' brothers. One day as she was going down a hill she saw a man coming up to her. She started to run away as fast as she could, thinking that it was Abdalles or Thumipgand, since she did not know they had a third brother, Hor-his-hon-hal, who was the person in question. When he saw the beautiful creature his desire was awakened. He chased her but only caught up to her in the night as she fled into a grotto.

Since she knew she could not escape from Hor-his-hon-hal and was sure that it was Abdalles or Thumipgand who had caught her, she threw herself at the feet of the third son of the Sun and spilled her secrets, praying for forgiveness. Hor-his-hon-hal heard her story and suspected that she was talking about his brothers. He was delighted that the charming lover had fallen into his hands, but did not want her to commit a third betrayal, so he locked her up in the grotto every time he had to go out to get food. As time passed he became head of a numerous race and passed a law that put to death anyone who had any communication with the neighboring states, which was daily growing bigger through his brothers' posterity. To prevent his people from disobeying the law he had an insurmountable wall built around his kingdom, which took 100 years to complete. The wall was so high and so closely guarded that our history claims that only one man ever left the state of Amphicleocles—a man named Zo-ra-hod. He was a philosopher, curious to know the truth of all things through personal experience, and his intelligence told him that beyond the great wall he would find other men and other lands. He imagined he could fly by imitating the birds, so he fashioned wings and one day when he was on guard duty on the wall he unfolded them and soared away on the winds. He drifted into our country and it was through him that we know the history of the Amphicleocles. The Princess can tell us if what I just said is confirmed by the tradition of her country.

The Princess is interrupted by the toad monsters

The Princess, who had listened to Boldeon with pleasure, was surprised to hear him so well informed about the history of her nation. She assured us that the summary he made differed in very few points from what she knew. "As for the great wall, it was only built because Phiocles had been caught trying to escape from Hor-his-hon-hal. In his initial fit of anger the Prince wanted her to be put to death, but during the preparations for her execution he was moved by her begging and pardoned her on the condition that she herself lay the first stone of the great wall (which still stands today) and that she stay in prison until the wall was high enough that she would never think of escaping again. He was painstakingly careful about the work, so it took ten years before it was in a state to fear no escape attempts by Phiocles. But he did not know how tricky a woman could be when she has made up her mind to do something.

"Phiocles was bent on leaving Hor-his-hon-hal and one day she finally disappeared. No matter how hard the Prince searched, he could not discover how she managed it. Out of his mind and furious that in spite of his vigilance he had been duped by Phiocles, he kept building the great wall and so that his people not have to worry about the future he passed a law that decreed all the girls in his kingdom be kept in a perpetual prison and only be allowed to see the man whom their family destined them to marry.

"As I tell my story," the Princess went on, "some of our customs might seem very strange to you..."

Up to this point not one of us had dared to ask the beautiful Nasilaë the extraordinary reason behind her Ascalis color. My mother, who was less used to it and more curious (being a woman) could not help saying something about it. "We were wondering..." she said with an eager and bewildered smile.

"Concerning ourselves, the tradition says that Hor-his-hon-hal, from whom we originated, was the color of a red poppy and Phiocles was white. The Amphicleocles men have kept the color of their first father, but the women are still white like Phiocles and their skin, as you see in me, has got only a faint hint of color from the head of the clan."

The Princess of the Amphicleocles was about to start her story, sitting next to us, who were silent and all ears, when we heard a sound like a stampede of horses and yelling and screaming and we all jumped up, afraid to find out what it was. I was the first to leave the house and stumbled back in dread at the sight of a horde of monsters a hundred times more frightening than the ones we had just escaped from. They were as tall as a man and from afar looked like toads, except for the face, which was vaguely human; they were naked and their skin was yellow with black spots. They were riding huge worms like horses with short, stubby legs. The troop marched in order and one of the monsters in front carried an owl with its wings spread out on a staff. Lodaï, Boldeon and I ran scared into the house. My mother and the Princess were frantic seeing the fear on our faces and begged to know the reason. In this new plight we could think of nothing to do but barricade the door. Falbao, who had been sleeping, suddenly jumped up on hearing the stampede and tried to encourage us with his fierce looks. His first move, when I made for the door, was to follow me, but Boldeon held him back and the loyal animal, as docile with us as he was vicious with our enemies, went and sat at the feet of the Princess and my mother.

We were trying to figure out what to do in this perilous situation when we saw the dreadful face of a monster appear in the slot that served as a window. We screamed at the sight and Falbao jumped at the opening, trying in vain to squeeze through. He knew by instinct that he could not do it and went to scratch at the door, looking at us, begging us to open it. We were too scared to do it, so Falbao finally gave up and started digging up the ground. It was sad to watch him failing at this new plan, but all of a sudden we saw the ground start trembling and Falbao fell headfirst into a hole that opened up under his feet.

Part 3

The toad men

We were dazed, amazed and cruelly dismayed by this new wonder. Lodaï, whose courage was shaken by nothing, was brave enough to approach the hole that the rest of us backed away from. An example is always a great influence when it is set by respected people. I was ashamed by my show of fright and by the impression it had made on the Princess of the Amphicleocles, so I hurried to follow the minister.

The opening Falbao fell into looked pretty large to me and the underground, lit by a strange light, looked pretty easy to enter. I did not think twice about what to do. The fear of losing my faithful Falbao and of giving a bad impression of my courage compelled me to go in. Even with the impact that the charming Nasilaë had on my heart, it was useless for her to call me back; her appeals had no more power. My recklessness had already pushed me forward. The path I wandered was swampy and scattered with rocks, but I heard Falbao from time to time and his voice guided me. I soon found the exit from the dark cave.

Just as I was starting up a kind of natural, uneven slope that led to the exit I heard awful cries (among which I could make out Falbao's barking) and I stopped to try to pinpoint where they came from. But I could not see a thing around me, so I hurried out, took a few steps forward and, Heavens! What did I see? A mismatched, furious battle was unfolding a few feet away. A legion of monsters surrounded Falbao and his famous strength was fighting with raging valor in vain. And in vain did the death of a hundred monsters, heaped up around him, work as a defense for the stalwart animal—and the pile was growing. The advantage that I saw him have over the worm men was of no account here. He was preparing to die. He was already staggering, covered with blood and wounds and was slowly waning under the attacks of the cruel enemies.

You can't imagine how I felt at the sight of this tragic scene and even more extraordinary was that his defeat was not due to a lack of strength or bravery but to a strange spell. The weapon they used against poor Falbao, what was laying him low, was none other than the deadly Owl flag I mentioned before. The foul face seemed to stagger him and stun him with its gaze. He chanced to look at me and a ray of hope flashed through his misery—but bent on his downfall his enemies soon blotted it out. His eyes were shrouded in tears; his strength failed; and then he howled loudly and fell backward.

As soon as he hit the ground all the monsters jumped on him at the same time. And just then, overcome by the lovable animal's fate, racked by his ruin and by all that I owed him, not thinking about my weakness or inability to help, I stormed onto the battlefield, armed only with a pointed stick as hard as steel. I hit the dreadful monsters hard and Wonder of Wonders, they fell back. At the sight of me they all ran away wailing and screaming. Before long the cowardly mob had abandoned the place and I was alone with my dear Falbao.

I was carried away by the joy of having saved him from impending doom, but still did not stop thinking about what had just happened. If I could have taken advantage of the fact that the sight of me was so frightening to these new inhabitants of the Inner Earth, I would have, but I was more affected by the sad state of my faithful dog than by the glory of my victory. I could only think about taking care of him and bringing him back from the brink of destruction. My tears were enough to show my grief. I talked to him, comforted him and used all the pet names I had given him in friendship to express my love and regret. I tore off a piece of my clothing to stop his bleeding wounds, but my care was of no use. His eyes only opened, it seemed, to say a final farewell to me. Closing his eyes again he licked my hand. He took a deep breath that I knew was his last and it was so devastating that I fell on top of him crying bitter tears.

When I got over my grieving, I was lying face down on the ground. But knowing for sure that my lovable dog was no more, I was still lost in sorrow. A sudden attack wrenched me from my moaning to think about my own safety. The enemies, who had run a certain distance away, saw me covering my face and got some of their courage back, which my face had robbed them of. They were so careful coming up that, buried in grief as I was, I was soon surrounded before I knew they were there. Then I was grabbed from behind. I yelled loudly and jumping up quickly to defend myself. The fury in my eyes, or better said the secret spell in them, was so suddenly and so tremendously scary to this crowd bent on my destruction that it went howling away again.

The event was too weird and shocking to give me time to wonder about the cause: it was not normal for an army to flee before a single man, but that is exactly what happened. On more careful reflection, I could not help thinking that my eyes sealed my victory and their gaze hit the enemy hard, causing it to flee. Armed with this confidence I looked around at my environment and as I turned my head I saw a monster covering its face with its hand to avoid my dangerous eye and threatening me with the Owl flag. I was more disgusted than scared by this useless tactic and pushed it back, filled with anger at what these monsters had done to Falbao. With my other hand I hit the bearer of the foul flag. Just as I came up to him, he dropped dead at my feet. The hideous Owl shared his fate, smashing its head and shrieking as it died. An awful howling echoed in the land after the final death throes of the bird, whose loss was obviously very important and precious to them.

As logical as it was to be astonished by these things, I only paid them a little attention: I was completely preoccupied by Falbao's fall. A ray of hope lit up in me. Maybe, I thought, the loss of blood just made him pass out. I turned around to check and what a surprise I had to see Falbao up and running toward me. I cried out in joy as he came up. The lovable animal expressed his joy by jumping up and scampering around. I petted him with all my heart and looked into his jubilant eyes while I tried to figure out what the secret principle was of this miraculous transformation. After backing up a little Falbao stopped short, twitched and started howling with deep sadness in his eyes. His blood, which I thought had stopped flowing, started gushing out of his wounds again. The animal fell at my feet and looked like he was begging for my help. What could I do? What was going on? I had absolutely no idea of the fatal cause that lay at the heart of these stupendous changes.

Hearing a noise a few feet away I looked up and finally uncovered the mystery. A foolhardy monster, obviously devoted to the safety or glory of his fellows, had separated from the crowd of enemies carrying a new flag on which another Owl was perched, staunch and looming. The monstrous hero covered his own eyes with a kind of shield and mounted on his worm horse was galloping toward us.

Falbao's howling got louder as the monster got closer and when he collapsed seeing the Owl held up at the end of that foolhardy arm, I knew for sure that the gaze of that hideous bird affected him like his affected the Tumpingands and I had reason to believe that mine had the same murderous influence on our present enemies.

As soon as Falbao was spread on the ground the monster spurred his worm steed and came at me brandishing his flag, obviously thinking that the sight of the animal would have the same effect on me as it did on Falbao. I grabbed onto the contemptible flag in my enemy's hands trying to make him look at me and find his undoing, but knowing now from experience that the Owl had no influence on me he kept his eyes closed and forgetting the brave plans that had separated him from the army he gave up the glorious flag, kicked at his monstrous steed and rejoined his compatriots much faster than he had left them. I watched him go and saw the welcome he got on his arrival. His partners were obviously furious at seeing him come back without the glorious standard they had entrusted to him and bludgeoned him with clubs. After this righteous lesson all the monsters went into hiding.

Astonished by all this, but then figuring that I knew the reasons, I left Falbao to crush the Owl's head against a rock and throw it into the bushes. The shriek it let out with its final breath ended like the first time with an even more frightful howling from the hidden monsters.

My experiment was not in vain. Falbao stood up before me to prove that the death of the Owl gave him back his life. Without everyday examples of the effect of antipathies, wouldn't we call these things fictions? But, philosophers, you are still far from the knowledge you brag about. And why do you continue to search in the Heavens for mysteries that are beyond your mediocre intelligence when you can't even explain the least of things here on the earth you crawl on?

Although I was worn out by all these events, I decided to get far away from the dangerous place. Seeing me turn back to where I came in, Falbao walked ahead of me and let me know how happy he was to be leaving there. Soon he was at the entrance to the cave waiting for me to follow him in. All of a sudden I saw him take a leap and I started running, scared that there was some monster in ambush, but the sight of Boldeon calmed me down. He had been worried, came searching for me and looked delighted to see me again.

On the road I told him everything that happened. "Vilkonhis be praised!" he shouted. "Let's get to Lodaï's house fast. You have to give some comfort to the worried Princesses. They are all terribly depressed and just seeing you will pull them out of it, Motacoa. The Queen has proven her motherly love for you in her tragic fright, but the Princess of the Amphicleocles has shown that you are no less dear to her. She loves you, I am sure of it, and if my assurance doesn't fill you with joy like it should, it does me: I see your destiny fulfilled and I believe that everything will happen according to our desires."

His words filled me with a quiet rapture. I loved beautiful Nasilaë so strongly that my young heart never believed it could feel such things. I was burning with desire to see her again and quickened my pace to get there. When I showed up, the sadness and tears were replaced by joy and cheer; and I had to repeat what happened to me. Nasilaë interrupted me at the part about the Owl's powerful effects. "During your adventure," she said, "you learned some interesting details about these people. My extraordinary stay among the Tumpingands gave me the opportunity to hear many things about them. At least what you are saying and the way you describe them makes me think that they are the same. If that's the case, we have nothing to fear—they came here for Falbao. There are mysteries that I will explain later. In the meantime, we shouldn't worry about them. They are not brave enough to take another stab at it."

The Princess' speech managed to reassure my mother, who at first could not get over her fright, while the latest events gave us plenty to talk about. Lodaï told us that one day when he was far from his house he came across such a monster, but it ran away so fast that he barely had time to catch a glimpse. We figured that Lodaï's gaze was the reason for the monster's hasty retreat and the Princess confirmed as much when he had finished his story.

So, night fell and we stopped talking. After taking care of our bodily needs and preparing a bed in my mother's room as comfortably as the space allowed for Nasilaë, we said good night and went to bed. Before going to bed Boldeon and Lodaï had a long discussion about what we should do to get out of the dark room we were living in. Before the adventure with the monsters it was agreed that the Princesses and I would live in the center of the earth until Boldeon's final preparations were ready to put me on throne because they were afraid of us falling into the hands of the usurper. But what had just happened changed the plan, because now we knew that the Inner Earth was inhabited by different peoples and we would be running new and dangerous risks everyday. After careful consideration it was decided that we would go to Boldeon's secret hideaway on the road that I met Falbao on and once there we would wait for the results of the minister's plans.

It took three whole days for the Princesses to get over their fright and fatigue, during which time it was decided that Lodaï, being the most experienced of us all with his years of living in the Inner Earth, would scout out the places we could leave from so we would not be in danger. When everything was ready the next day we went to my mother's grotto. The Princesses had had a rather bad night, but they were better than the day before. It seemed to me by my mother's talk and by the flattering kindness the Princess showed me that they had been up talking about me and had decided that they would take the first opportunity to marry me to the beautiful Princess of the Amphicleocles.

Part of the morning was spent discussing the current situation. In what the Princess said, she showed us how intelligent and insightful she was and that she deserved all the wonderful praise she got. My heart, which barely had time to recognize this during the constant flight we were in since I had first laid eyes on her, was filled with the sweetest satisfaction and without any notion of why or how, love entered my soul. I felt a secret joy that affected my organs and made all my senses tingle. I could not look at Nasilaë without feeling something strange inside me, which my ignorance did not understand, but whatever it was my heart adored it and made it the most precious treasure.

After a meal of those chickens that Lodaï found, which were exquisitely tasty, we turned to the Princess, who was ready to tell her story.

("It's amazing, Sinouis, that even though so many extraordinary things happened to me, as you hear, I haven't forgotten a single thing." I took my friend's hand and continued, "It's useless for me to repeat that this is still Motacoa who is telling the story and that up to this point he has still only indirectly mentioned me once.")

The Princess saw us silent and knew we were ready to listen. She nodded graciously to my mother and began her story.

The story of Nasilaë

Lindiagar, called the Great, Ruler of the Amphicleocles, the 77th King of this name, is the one who brought me into this world. According to custom he made the counting[75] of all the male children born at the same time as me and they were brought to the palace of Kaiocles[76] to be raised until I was old enough to be married.

I spent my childhood in the temple according to custom[77] and when I was 13 years old the High Priestess purified me of all the impurities of my birth in the rays of the sun, duly dismissed her minister,[78] and delivered me to the assembly with

---

[75] The day, hour and minute of the birth of the Princess of the Amphicleocles were announced in the kingdom with the decree that all the seraskiers, or judges, make a verbal inquiry to verify the births of all male infants born at the same time as the princess. The Council of Astronomers authorized the certificates, which were then sent to the court and deposited in the archives. The verification was made among the fathers and mothers of the children and when it conformed to the law the newborns were marked and at the expense of the city were taken away to the palace of Kaiocles.

[76] The palace was the second temple. It was here that they brought the children born at the same time as the heir or heiress of the crown. Of course, if it was a prince, they brought only the girls.

[77] At birth the prince or princess successor to the crown was brought to the temple of the Immortal, called Fulghane, where they were raised until they were of marrying age. The High Priestess was in charge of their education.

[78] When the heir of the Kingdom of the Amphicleocles was 14 years old, the general assembly of states was convened in one of the temple rooms. The High Priestess led the prince there and declared him of age. After this ceremony she left and the prince was paraded into a secret room of the palace that was held only for him. Then an audience with the sovereign was requested where they told the reasons

certain signs[79] that I was of age to convene the assembly of the palace of Kaiocles and choose a spouse.

Even though I had been raised in the secrets of the temple and should have accepted the dictates of our religion and our laws when I was old enough, I began to feel a frightening aversion to the practice of two laws that were totally against my way of thinking: that of never being able to see my father seemed opposed to all natural sentiments—it was a policy that obviously came from accustoming the King, from an early age, to consider only his subjects as children. This seemed to me to be too cruel and going too far. The longer I was forbidden the honor of embracing a father whom I loved a lot, the more I desired to do so. The last years I spent in the temple brought me to the point that I was dying to get out so I could accomplish my secret goals: I was planning to find a way to fulfill my desire to see my father.

The other law that my mind rebelled against did not offend me until I was told that I had to go to the temple of Kaiocles on the third day to choose a spouse. My young heart trembled at a custom that was so contrary to my lofty thoughts. What! (I told myself in secret) I'm going to make a blind choice of some despicable, loathsome blood to give an heir to such a noble father, my master and King! These thoughts grew so strong in my heart and bothered me so much that I got sick

---

for their convocation and presented him with the Mourche-by, the act of cession of the High Priestess, whereby she stated that she handed the prince over to the assembly and swore by Fulghane that he had been purified and she had made him pure and without stain, which duty she asked to be relieved of according to custom. Then the king sent her away, since he was bound by law to trust the statements of the priestess and the assembly and he was forbidden by law to ever see or have any relation with his children.

[79] In turning the Princess over to the assembly, the High Priestess swore by Fulghane that she was a virgin and old enough to give heirs to the state. On this day the King's daughter was dressed in a white tunic of fine linen and on her breast wore a golden sun with rays the color of fire.

over and over again. The Karveder[80] came twice a day on behalf of the King to find out how I was feeling. He had been told by the Lea-Minska[81] about the awful melancholy I was sunk in since leaving the temple and the serious change in my health, so the Karveder respectfully asked me why I had changed and become so glum.

As insistent as the minister was, I hesitated for a long time to confess the secrets of my heart. He was as clever as he was dedicated to my father and turned me every which way so that, of course, I finally confessed my desire to see my noble father face to face and my horror at being separated from him forever by marrying. It was only the first confession that mattered. Naturally I opened up to him and said that as long as I could remember I was tormented by this desire and that just the hope of satisfying this natural yearning had kept me alive until then, but on the eve of entering the fatal temple of Kaiocles my trembling soul was ready to vanish away. Getting carried away I stooped to the most pitiful prayers and ended up assuring the Karveder that if he did not get the King's beloved permission to see him, I would fall into a ghastly grave long before him.

The minister was surprised at my fit and at what he heard and did everything he could to calm me down, but to no avail. All my tears and my cruel situation touched him. He promised that he would tell the King everything and that he would do everything in his power to bend the King to my desire. His

---

[80] King's chancellor. He had the privilege of the King's ear and of carrying out his orders, but his most important role was as messenger between the King and his children.

[81] A simple priestess chosen by the general assembly as the princess' governess until she got married, who then changed her title to first lady-in-waiting after the marriage. Gregory of Tours, in his observations on this, wisely said that this kind of assistant, coming from this organization, was a political maneuver of the religious ministers to know all about what happened in the heart of the state and to protect the holy power in case the sovereign authority saw things too clearly and encroached upon its privileges.

assurances comforted me and I awaited his return restless and excited.

The Karveder did not come back before the end of the day and I did not know why he was so late. I was afraid that telling the King my secret had caused his disgrace and this doubt troubled me more than anything. A thousand dire thoughts ran through my mind. I was alone in my room with nothing else to think about and I fell headlong into sorrow and tears.

I was so preoccupied with the thoughts rolling around in my mind that I did not notice how strange it was that I was left alone since the Karveder's meeting. The Lea-Minska, who left when he arrived, according to custom, had not come back to my room. That was something that violated her duty because according to the law she was not supposed to leave me except under the circumstances just mentioned. But she soon showed up and the reasons she gave for her absence calmed me down.

The shadows of the night were chasing away the daylight and the Lea-Minska and I had just finished the sacred duty that obliged us to pray at sunset when the Karveder showed up. I was anxiously waiting in my room.

"Princess, wake up" he said on entering, "get yourself ready to welcome the King, your father. He has agreed to fulfill your desires. His Highness will be here in the middle of the night."

"What?" I cried out. "Can I be so lucky as to have such a dear visit?"

"Let's talk more quietly," the minister cut in. "We have to keep it very secret. You are obviously unaware, Princess, that this hoped-for favor will be the ruin of you and the end of the King's reign if the High Priestess and the people get the slightest wind of it. The laws are strict and the grave threats against the King in case of an offense are so well engrained in the hearts of his subjects that any argument would be pointless if they really felt abused by him. That's why the King hasn't satisfied your wild impatience for so long. But forewarned like yourself, he badly wants to see his dear Princess who is so beloved by him. He has overcome all difficulties and found a sure way to meet with you without risking the crisis that might result. The Lindiagar and I have agreed that to avoid anything leaking out I have to go to the Priestess and if she becomes suspicious, to be sure that she can't find out about or barge in on your meeting. I thought I should fill you in on all these things, Princess, to lift your spirits, which I naturally suspected were troubled."

After saying this the Karveder left to join the Priestess. About an hour later he came back and told me to prepare for the King's visit, that nothing would interrupt the priceless happiness of being together and that he was going to inform him of what had been done so he would have no worries about what he wanted as badly as I did.

I admit that it was almost too much for me to be on the verge of a blessing that I had desired for such a long time. Never had a Princess of the Amphicleocles been singled out for such an honor; and to this sweet thought was added the hope of being freed of the cruel law of choosing a spouse among the vile pretenders, a hope that my hatred of this custom made almost as dear as that of seeing the face of my noble father. Just the idea of these things relieved me so much that I barely felt the sickness caused by melancholy and grief. A troubled mind can devastate the body, but when it gets better it straightens out as easily as it was bent.

The third hour of the night was sounded by the Bouch-chouk-chou,[82] my room was purified and scented with fragrant

---

[82] Public criers whose express duty was to announce the hour because clocks were not in use in this kingdom. The Amphicleocles divided the night into 24 parts between sunset and sunrise using a fountain whose basin was large enough that it took exactly one half hour to fill it. When the water reached the edge, they watched for the first drop to fall and then turned a key that emptied it in one minute flat. The Bouch-chouk-chou on duty at the fountain sounded the hour at this instant with a kind of horn that was heard by the others placed at suitable distances so that at the same moment the entire city was told what time it was.

disks and at the sound of the Great Prayer[83] all the elementary spirits went back to their vortex and left room for the divine Intelligences to stay pure and holy. Dressed in a simple, golden yellow tunic I was ready to welcome my father and King. I was counting the minutes, the seconds and I was already getting worried when I heard a dull knock that made me quiver in the hope that it was the promised sight so long desired. But what did I see? The Karveder was standing there without the royal scarf, which was the sure sign of the King's arrival.

"Heavens," I cried, shaking with fear, "what's happened to the King? Where is he? Has he changed his mind? Could it be that he's gone back on his word?"

"No, Princess," the minister replied, "you will see him. But what will happen to us because of his blind indulgence? Our secrets have been betrayed. The Lea-Minska either heard us or figured it out. The High Priestess knows about the King's plan and through her channels the people have been stirred up; they're screaming for your sacrifice according to the laws so as to appease Fulghane,[84] who they say is angry. The people are afraid of the evils foretold and have surrounded the temple demanding the sacrifice. The great Lindiagar is trying in vain to calm them down, but nothing can break the old superstition. With this grave danger threatening your lives, the King sent me to tell you to follow me to safety to a secret room away from the rumblings of the mob."

---

[83] These people were convinced that the atoms that we breathe were so many pure or impure spirits depending on whether they did good or evil. There was even a belief among them that when the impure spirits were chased away by the good spirits, they suddenly died and were transformed into hideous, always inauspicious reptiles. Their theology taught them to protect themselves against this awful misfortune by pronouncing three mysterious words that they typically called the Great Prayer.

[84] A statue or representation of a monstrous man from whom they claimed emanated the principle of all things and whom they worshipped under the name Fulghane.

"I will see him, then?" I was filled with joy. "I'll be lucky enough to embrace my noble father?"

"Yes, Madame, but we don't have any time to lose. Get a hold of yourself because in our present situation we can't be too careful."

The risk I was running put me at the mercy of the Karveder's sage advice. He led me through strange underground passages carrying a torch in one hand and helping me along with the other. After walking like this from one area of the palace to another, we climbed a secret staircase that he told me led to the King's chamber. When we got there he went to the door of a closet and blew into the lock.[85] The door opened right away. Then the Karveder motioned to me to enter. I was struck deep down at the sight of the great Lindiagar, who came up to greet me warmly. I barely had the strength to embrace his knees.

"Cleannes,"[86] he said, lifting me up and putting his hand on my head,[87] "don't worry. It won't do any good for the High Priestess to try to ruin you. I am not the slave of my people's shouting or their blindness. I worship the great Fulghane, but reason has taught me to tell the difference between the laws that come from divine wisdom and those that were born of the ministers' politics. Up to now I have done the best I could to walk in the ways of virtue and I don't think I deserve this horrible punishment of ordering the death of my own daughter. This is not the first time I've glimpsed the secret plans of the High Priestess. I never condescended much to her ideas and

---

[85] It was forbidden for any of the King's subjects, no matter what their rank, to scratch or knock on the doors of rooms where the king was present. There was a hole lower down to blow through to ask for entry. Behind the door stood a deaf, mute dwarf who acted as doorkeeper and whose job was to keep his ear glued to the opening waiting for the breath of air.

[86] The name of all the princesses of the Amphicleocles, which means, in their language, heiress of the empire. Nasilaë, the name of this one, was given to her according to custom when she entered the temple.

[87] The laying on of the Kings' hands was the greatest of their favors.

always firmly opposed her schemes and now she's trying to make me sorry for this. Her plot and intrigues look like they have the upper hand, but I have clever, infallible ways to stop her. For the moment, Cleannes, we have to let the mob rumble and shield you from the initial frenzy of rebellion. However far the rebels might go, they will not be so reckless as to profane the sanctuary of my palace. Nevertheless, Karveder, do as I say. As soon as the Bouch-chouk-chou has announced the general assembly and the temple is open, run and tell me."

The minister left then and none too soon. The privilege of breathing before the King, which was one of his favors, did not apply while the King addressed him, which made the sovereigns very concise in giving orders.

When I was alone with the King, my good father abandoned his tiring image of grandeur. He took a torch and brought it close to my face to examine my features. He looked pleased at what he saw and kissed me. I reacted gently and affectionately, like any loving daughter who knows how valuable such a thing is. The King sat me next to him and spoke intimately about how hard it had been for him not to see me. I took the opportunity to confess my worry that the present troubles would make him regret his decision. He reassured me, but at the same time could not help complaining bitterly about the aggravations of the crown, especially when a Monarch was thoughtful enough to make it his duty to fulfill his functions scrupulously. His bad mood even made him envy the condition of an ordinary subject.

"At least," he said, "an individual can enjoy himself and is not a slave to appearances and abuse. When he is guided by reason he can act accordingly and being respectful he can enjoy truth. Isn't it dreadful," the Lindiagar continued, "that a King has to suffer the wicked customs and caprices whereby they marry off his children? How many kinds of warped ideas have come from these unequal unions? What! Because our ancestors handed down to us bad laws that are far from common sense, we have to be ridiculous enough to respect and preserve them? How can we still reasonably reconcile the fact that he who is bound to be master of this empire will have a father who is a subject born to obey[88] and who owes his elevation and eminence only to his pretty, bewitching eyes. Could antiquity persuade me, then, that the Sovereign's saliva has the power and virtue to ennoble a subject and purify him of his baseness?[89] Is this kind of King any different than the least of

---

[88] The Law of Kaiocles said that the ruler's last child was the heir apparent. The state acknowledged only the first three as the King's children when the Queen, their mother, had been chosen in the temple of Kaiocles. So, with the third birth she was shut up by one of the priestesses of Fulghane and no longer lived with the King. If the Queen was the daughter of said King, she had the privilege of renouncing her husband after the birth of a prince or princess, but when this happened she could not marry again. If the Queen happened to die after rejecting the King, the High Priestess played the important role of regent after the death of the Queen until the general assembly in the Council of Seven (spoken of below) chose who would govern and succeed to the eminent dignity of ruler of the Amphicleocles.

[89] The King's saliva was highly venerated among these people who claimed that when they had the honor of being moistened on the forehead not only were they ennobled, but also impure spirits dared not approached them. When the heir or heiress of the crown went to the temple of Kaiocles, it was their saliva that designated their spouse, but this valuable grace was given only after a general examination of the suitors, which ceremony was described by the learned Scaliger in his treatise on these antiquities. When the princess Cleannes entered the temple of Kaiocles, the doors were barricaded. They blindfolded her and led her into the royal hall. When she was sitting on the throne that was prepared for her, a priestess removed the blindfold. The steps forming a semi-circle around the throne were full of all the predestined males dressed only in their natural graces. If Cleannes made a decision on first sight, the assembly was broken up and the spouse was announced at that very instant to the people. But if the Princess happened to appear uncertain, she had as many days to chose her husband as there were suitors. The wise Heinsius, who commented on this, added that the heir or heiress of the Amphicleocles had to pass one day with those wishing to marry in order to examine the character and countenance of each. The same scholar informs us that the children shut up in the temple of Kaiocles were

his subjects? Hasn't experience proven the opposite, that a prince's bodily and mental impairments are the same as any other man? Time and time again I've revolted against these shameful fanatics. Time and time again, hoping to open the eyes of these blind people, I've tried to understand the sacred, esteemed opinions of those who carry the vote, but, Princess, these people whose higher education should enlighten them, are so pigheaded that they are ruled by their preconceptions and the crowd's weakness consecrates these eccentric customs. Do what it may, reason cannot penetrate the shadows of ignorance. It's like they enjoy the darkness and are ashamed to clear away the clouds of pride, sloth and feebleness."

I won't tell you everything that my father's wisdom and learning had to say on the subject, but his final thoughts were to encourage me to share mine with him. Naturally I trusted him and confessed. He was surprised to learn that at my age I had already shaken off the veils of prejudice. He was especially happy when I told him of my opposition to the marriage custom that I was bound to be sacrificed to. How I spoke about this matter surprised and touched him.

---

called Kails and each of them were kept in a cell under lock and key, since it was forbidden by law for them to have any communication with one another. It was in one of these cells that the prince or princess made the examination. Strabo, moreover, observes that there was a secret peephole in each of these cells through which a priestess watched what happened with the two people. If a Kail happened to be chosen, the prince or princess had to stick to the choice that love favored. Abbé Aubignac in his research on the ancients claimed that this happened three times over three centuries and that the people of the kingdom noticed there was never a happier reign. The famous De Thou, who expanded on this more than any other scholar, tells the story of a prince named Heliobol who spent 22 days in the temple of Kaiocles for his examination. The following year 17 successors were born, which started a very fierce war 15 years later on the death of the King, their father, over which of these children should get the throne. The High Priestess pronounced an oracle on these divisions whereby all the rivals were excluded and she became regent until the general assembly could convene and elect a new king.

"Oh my daughter," he kissed me again, "the gods be praised! I see my blood in your enlightened soul and also the Heavens' gift promised so long ago. May these same Heavens make the signs you give me conform to the great prophecy.[90] Everything seems to point to you alone, Oh great Vilkonhis,[91] whom I worship and who, by a miracle, showed yourself to me and made me see how ridiculous these false gods are. Accomplish your work and enlighten a heart that seems to be worthy to be consecrated by you. If it can be done, let this Princess be the chosen one whom you promised so long ago. If it cost the life of her father to fulfill the divine decrees, I resign myself completely. Let my death bring happiness to my

---

[90] Tradition had it that one day the people were gathered in the temple of Fulghane to pray for his mercy because of a widespread sterility brought on by a famine. The god's statue turned its back on the people, trembled and cried out. The people were dismayed at this frightful omen, threw themselves on the ground and shouted even more loudly. Their fear increased when lightning struck the roof and brought it down, exposing the inflamed sky. A voice boomed forth, "You will not always be powerful, Fulghane. Your altars will be destroyed when a princess looks upon her father and gets from him my name and my laws." After these words a divine music sang, "Praise be the airs, a princess will triumph over Fulghane, overthrow his altars and ministers, be taken away from his blasphemous subjects and in the center of the earth she will find a faithful man who will restore the true worship and bury the bones of his father and his king and return to the kingdom to build a temple for Vilkonhis.

[91] In the few fragments of the history of Lindiagar that have been preserved by the ancients, we read that coming back from the hunt one day, a venerable old man appeared to him and made a sign for him to follow. When the king obeyed, the specter covered his eyes with his hand and asked him if he saw clearly. The prince answered no and the old man said, "Well, Lindiagar, the same cloud that covers you now obscures the eyes of your mind. There is only one being who should be worshipped. Kneel down at his feet and recognize the great Vilkonhis. Come back here tomorrow at the same time and you will receive his laws and learn that a princess of his blood will build a temple for the being of the airs. The Historian of the time said nothing more. Apparently the Lindiagar followed the old man's orders.

daughter and my people—I am worth nothing on such important occasions."

I loved the King, my father, too much not to be troubled deep down in my heart by his last words. I urged him to tell me what he meant and if I had to be so unlucky as to bring these happy days to an end.

"Don't be alarmed, my daughter," he replied, "a divine hand has counted them and nothing can slow them down or extend them. Even though it's true that you play a part in the end I talked about, just thinking about the positive things that will come of it is enough to fill me with joy. Cleannes, stop crying. It's not right. We're not made to fight against the Heavens and we have to accept both its presents and its plagues. Isn't it a great honor that it wants to use us as an instrument of its glory? No, we shouldn't wonder that such happiness is earned through trials and tribulations. The heavenly spirit inspires me, but the reward that waits for both of us is magnificent, it is above anything the human mind can imagine." The King saw me wrapped in this enigma and continued, "Princess, let's leave it at that. Truth just spoke through my mouth, but I cannot yet explain it to you."

In spite of his advice, which I took as an order, I was still, maybe, about to ask more when I heard an awful noise. The Lindiagar did not look worried. He put his finger to his lips and motioned me to follow him. After leading me into a secret room and before leaving me there alone, he told me not to worry or be frightened because his presence alone would clear away the clouds of rebellion. But as much as I trusted him, his words could not reassure me.

I threw myself around my father's knees and begged him to let me come so that we could at least face the danger together. He frowned, looked hard at me and told me sternly that his kindness should not make me forget that he was my father and my King and as such he wanted me to obey. Those were his final words; he closed the door and left. For the rest of the day I was anxious and afraid. I heard muffled sounds telling me the rebellion was still going on and I prayed to the Heavens for my father's safety—he had become even dearer to me since I met him. His kindness and gentleness came back to my troubled mind and made me scared that at any minute they would announce his death and then I would fall prey to the rebels. Not knowing is cruel, especially when there is no way to delude yourself.

I spent the night in this awful state even though I heard no more noises and the change should have convinced me that the troubles were over. I was starting to despair when the Karveder suddenly showed up.

"Princess," he told me, "dry your tears. The King, your father, has triumphed. With his profound wisdom he has broken through the dark clouds covering up the schemes of the High Priestess. At this very moment she is being punished for her detestable designs. In front of the altars and the people Sovereign tore off the lying mask she used to seduce them. The event is too important and too indicative of the Monarch's wisdom to be left untold. As a faithful witness, I will give you an accurate account."

After saying this, the minister brought me into the King's chamber where he sat me down and sat himself at my feet and related to me the following:

The King and the High Priestess

During the time that the King was with you, Princess, the Council of Seven[92] gathered in the temple of Fulghane. The High Priestess, who alone had the right to convene them, had

---

[92] History does not tell us the origin of this council, which proves how old it must be. What is certain is that it had immense power. It alone had the right to call the general assembly of states, to set the agenda and resolve the most important matters. It had the right to declare war or peace and to reign under the high priestess during an interregnum. Its members were the elders of the kingdom. When a seat was vacant, the council had no authority until it was filled. To be admitted, a person had to have lived four generations, be sullied by no passion and to have rendered four important services to the state.

done so. She appeared before them at the foot of the statue, dressed in dark and gloomy clothes, which she wore during public catastrophes. Beating her chest she exposed the evils that the state was about to suffer because of the transgression of the laws and she painted a frightening picture straight away into the holy transports of the furious oracles. Her face changed, convulsed, her rabid eyes popped out of her head and seemed to weep blood and tears. She foamed at the mouth as Fulghane himself spoke through her, "Councilors, you are the venerable columns of this empire and its strongest support. Hear me! The foundations of this state are shaking and ready to crumble. The huge mass of the universe is breaking apart and only the touch of my mercy sustains it. I have commanded in vain; I am not obeyed. My altars are not stained with the blood of the guilty Princess. You scorn my laws. Her father has stolen her away from Fulghane. And why is Fulghane waiting to reduce you criminals to ashes? The sanctity of his ministers is all that holds him back. But if the sacred fire is not fed with the blood of the guilty before the end of the day, all the Amphicleocles will perish!"

After this the High Priestess lowered her head and went back into the sanctuary. The Council of Seven, scared of the oracle, left the temple and announced to the people, who were stunned at its convocation,[93] the anger, threats and commands of the god they revered.

Like a subtle, vile poison rebellion infected the hearts of the people. The crowd rushed to the palace and tried to storm in, shouting out for the Princess. The Council of Seven would not let them enter, reminding them to respect the sanctuary of their Kings. One of the Seven said that the Council would ask the Monarch for the grace that his subjects longed for. This guarantee calmed the people down and they waited more patiently for what would happen next.

---

[93] The Council never gathered except in the direst emergencies of the state.

While this was going on, I waited here for my Sovereign's orders. After he left you, seeing him overwhelmed by the extraordinary measures he took to grant you something expressly forbidden by law, I was afraid of the consequences if they got wind of this secret deal between you and the King. I was thinking about the risks we were all running when the Council of Seven came to the door. I got flustered at the sight of them. You know I'm the only one allowed to enter the chamber; anyone else will pay with their life if they try. In spite of my anxiety I ran up to them, presented the sacred Kiargouh[94] and asked the wise men how they became so reckless as to disobey the customs that their own vows had consecrated. At the sight of the formidable sign, they humbly closed their eyes and said that they knew that death was the price of disobedience, but their role was to sacrifice their lives when it concerned the glory of the Sovereign and the safety of his people and if they were doing their duty, they were ready to die. With that they started moaning and crying out so loudly that the King soon heard it in his room.

I was doing my best to convince the Council of Seven to go away when the Lindiagar showed up. We all closed our eyes at his sudden appearance. The Seven held their breath, put a finger in their mouths[95] and turned their backs. The King took two steps back.

"What's this?" he yelled. "Has Fulghane come down from his eternal throne? Is he here in these regions? Has he

---

[94] An effigy of the King that the Karveder wore around his neck. It was used as the seal of the King's orders to his subjects and they had such high respect for this sign that when it was presented before them they closed their eyes as if they were unworthy to look upon the sacred effigy.

[95] A finger in the mouth was still a sign of respect. A learned English commentator has given a good reason for this: he claims that the fear of suffocating by holding your breath for so long produced this respectful stratagem because you can breathe like this without being noticed.

broken the great bronze book?[96] Are the laws destroyed and am I deposed?"

The Council of Seven got worried and did not know what to say.

"Speak," the King continued, "and confess yourselves before I let you breathe."[97]

The youngest of the Seven[98] fell on his back and started shouting the troubling news about the capital being shaken up by Fulghane's oracle. When the sage had finished, the Lindiagar ripped off his left babouche[99] and gave it to the oldest of

---

[96] This book was 18 feet long and 12 feet wide and was filled only with periods and commas, but it was the way these characters were arranged that gave them meaning. All the laws were written in this great tome, which was only opened in the direst emergencies of the state.

[97] When the ruler of the Amphicleocles allowed one of his subjects to breathe, it was to command him to die. The people were raised in such submission that when the word "Ookhilgrhouk" was repeated three times, the one it was addressed to went home, covered his head with his shirt (a sign of banishment), gave the mark of superiority (the thumb of the left hand, which he cut off himself) to the head of the family and then went to the temple of Fulghane with the closest of his family who considered it an honor to die with the outcast. When the victim of this superstition had shown his mutilated hand to the priestesses, they sang a hymn in honor of the god, bound the guilty one's head with a fire-red bandage and then hanged him by his arms in front of the statue. The lucky ones had the sweet consolation of dying before the idol that they imagined was possessed by the god. This death was not considered dishonorable by the Amphicleocles, but quite the opposite, as Strabo confirms, it was sought for as a reward for services rendered. However, Abbé Aubignac contradicts this, saying that there was a minister named Koïl in the reign of Taphaik who asked the King for the favor of dying in the temple of Fulghane, but that he died of old age and not of hunger there because the priestesses took special care of him.

[98] In this kingdom the youngest were the oldest and enjoyed all the rights of being such.

[99] The King's slipper. When he took it off his left foot, it was a sign that they had to carry him to the temple.

the Seven,[100] who lifted it up at the end of his sankdakhar.[101] The six other Council members, who were listening to what was happening, lifted the King[102] and on his order carried him to the temple of Fulghane, preceded by the one holding up the royal babouche according to custom.

The people surrounding the palace were not expecting to see their King carried by the venerable Council of Seven.[103] They turned their backs in resentful respect and followed them backwards to the temple of Fulghane where they expected to

---

[100] The Greek here must not have been understood because the oldest were bestowed with the most menial tasks and Cyrano says that the honor of carrying the standard was conferred only on the youngest priestesses, i.e. the oldest according to the customs of the realm.

[101] A rod covered with a snake's skin, topped off with a toad, a sign of the Council's dignity.

[102] The way in which the King of the Amphicleocles was carried was very particular: only the priestesses had this magnificent right. They did it five at a time and took turns every hour if the trip was long. The King lay face down on the ground and the first priestess lifted him by his hair. The four others carried him by his arms and legs. Aristotle mentions that they carried the sovereign in this way with his face to the ground so that careless eyes not meet his by chance.

[103] This was an important event in the history of the Amphicleocles. Only the priestesses of Fulghane had the honor of carrying the King before this. Afterwards the Council of Seven held this right, as well as that of carrying the royal babouche.

When the sovereign was on the move, the Bouch-chouk-chou announced it with a particular sound. Then, all the people had to get to the road and when the babouche came into view, they had to turn their backs in respect and spit in the air to cool it down. Heinsius, who said everything that could be said about ancient customs, pointed out that pneumonia came from this ceremony because the good people's affection was so deep that, especially in hot weather, they spit so much and so hard when the king passed by that they usually ended up worn down by the procession. The same scholar definitely proved that we descend from these people, just like fathers who hand down their bad qualities to their children—these are facts that we cannot deny.

see a strange uproar. The Bouch-chouk-chou's cries[104] had warned the priestesses of the King's coming and they came before him dumbfounded both by his coming and by the way he was being transported. The sight of the royal babouche held them in respect and as was right, they went back into the temple where I followed in order to inform the High Priestess of the King's arrival.

When I told her, she turned pale and staggered, but trying to hide it, she asked me very nicely why the King made such an outrageous breach of their rights[105] and what important affair could make him appear before the divinity, notwithstanding the law that forbid him to be in the temple except on the designated days.[106] The Lindiagar, showing up just then, spared me the embarrassment of answering the High Priestess and as soon as she saw him, she went back into the sanctuary and placed herself first at the foot of the statue. Nobody spoke while the King ascended his throne. Here was where that conniving woman waited to assault the King. Without his diplomacy and profound understanding, he would have been lost. The High Priestess had power over the throne in that she represented the god of the Amphicleocles, but on the High Throne[107] the Lindiagar was her equal and only the people could upset the balance on one side or another, as they chose.

---

[104] When the King left his palace, the public criers, as I said before, announced it throughout the city. Afterwards none of his subjects were allowed to work and these outings became holidays for the Amphicleocles. Year after year they were announced and celebrated throughout the kingdom.

[105] The right that the priestesses had to carry the venerable body of the sovereign.

[106] The King could not enter the temple without the High Priestess's permission, which she only gave four times a year.

[107] The highest throne in the temple where only the King could sit, which only happened in the most important matters of the state. But when the sovereign had his own reasons for asserting his authority and could persuade the high priestess and the assembly to let him ascend this throne, then his power was absolute. He could change the laws of the state or make new ones as he wished and his decrees were

The High Priestess trembled when the guards at the pulleys were ordered to take down the Glis-koar.[108] She tried in vain to shout out against what she called an obvious attack on the laws of the kingdom. Since the Lindiagar was treated so magnanimously on this important occasion, the Priestess's protests sounded frivolous. The Sovereign was already on the High Throne—that's all that mattered.

The Bouch-chouk-chou had barely finished their extraordinary announcements[109] when the people there turned around, filled with emotion, and lifted their eyes to the Monarch. Only the old men had the honor of seeing him on the High Throne and as all the young people were denied this wonderful privilege, there was a great cheer by everyone. The King's majesty uprooted the rebellion in an instant and engraved respect and love on their hearts.

In his great wisdom the Lindiagar did not want to let the positive momentum die down; he thought it best to take advantage of it to reach his goals. As soon as he made the sign, all the leaders of the state gathered around the royal cap[110] and silence fell over all. The High Priestess was at their head and bent her nose to the ground.[111]

---

accepted with as much veneration as if Fulghane himself had given them.

[108] The device that they used to bring the King up to the high throne.

[109] Since no one of the subjects was allowed to look at the sovereign in the face, he dropped a brass ball when he had to give orders. Those who were to take charge of them, listened and passed them on to the respective officers.

[110] The custom in this country to ask for silence was to throw your cap at the nose of those you wanted to be quiet.

[111] The High Priestess only had to show this mark of respect to the divinity, but when the King presided she was forced to show him the same submission.

When all these things were arranged, the King turned his back to the statue[112] and spoke to it, explaining everything after dropping the big Tak-lak-lak ball:[113]

"O Fulghane, it is to you I speak. You see before you a King whose authority comes from your immutable decree that cannot, according to the rules of your divine justice, be taken away from him undeservedly. I call upon you, Divinity, forever revered by my people, to judge me according to the dignity that I deserve and that has brought me to the eminent position I occupy. I also appear before you as a submissive slave. As such my eyes are closed and respect your luminous rays. Allow me, Sovereign, to justify myself. Exonerate or fulminate, but speak through your mouth."

After saying this with determination but respect, the King was quiet and looked like he was meditating. Then he put on the royal cap[114] and spoke to the High Priestess.

---

[112] The King performed the same rites before the statue as his subjects did before him.

[113] A brass ball on which was engraved the privilege accorded to the people by the king to breathe and look at him in the face, precious rights that they enjoyed only once during each reign, unless, as is said, some important reason made the sovereign bring it out. This right was so dear to them and they desired it so fervently that when the year began they greeted it with these words: "God protect our King for us and may he ascend the High Throne." The benefits the people might enjoy were: the general amnesty of all their crimes, both spiritual and civil; the release of prisoners; the dismissal of debts of every kind; the right to renounce a wife and to contravene the normal rule of birthright on behalf of a favorite child; a woman's permission to chose a successor to her bed among her husband's family. But the most wonderful was that granted to the old men, at least 100 years old, to die in the small temples instead of in the sanctuary of Fulghane. Only the King, the High Priestess or the general states could honor a subject with this favor. It was a peculiarity of the kingdom.

[114] A hat made of sweetbread and golden spider silk that was ten feet high topped by a figure of the sun turning on a pivot. The sovereign

"Oh Magna Fakhaldak, raise your head, breathe and heed my words. Who are you? High Priestess of Fulghane, the divinity we revere, were you put in your eminent position for the growth or the destruction of the kingdom? You fire up rebellion, set my people against me, accuse me of breaking the laws, the oracles speak and thunder through your mouth, they judge me and condemn me in my innermost heart. Are your accusations well founded? Am I guilty? Is it you or Fulghane that condemns me? Now we have to accuse each other in front of this divinity and in the presence of the people gathered together. High Priestess of Fulghane, it is up to you to make him speak. Me, the Ruler of the Amphicleocles according to the Heavens, I know where to find my judge and chief. Woe upon the proud and insolent! Woe upon the rebellion and the guilty."

When the King finished speaking, a frightful yell rose up to the sacred vaults. The Priestesses got scared and started screaming, obviously following the feeble voice of their leader shouting out that they were disrespecting the statue and wrath would fall upon this attack in no time. The people got worried by the threat and it seemed like the rebellion was about to break out again, but the King on his High Throne put a stop to the revolt by shaking his head three times and pronouncing the terrible Fazakmalodzi.[115]

The power of this sacred word brought on silence right away. The Lindiagar shouted at the High Priestess again. "Magna Fakhaldak, since Fulghane is silent, the holy bronze

---

only wore the cap on this most important occasion of ascending the High Throne.

[115] This word meant the King's head when it was pronounced by the ruler and thus it was not obeyed. There was no hope of pardon for the guilty; death ensued and they were deleted from the register of immortality. The people had a big book in which every individual was registered. The king was its trustee and they superstitiously believed that the prince was born with the right to destroy them by erasing their name from the book.

book will speak and decide which of us has broken the good laws that are written there."

After this the King threw out the ball[116] on which was inscribed the order to open the sacred case.[117] As soon as I reached the venerable cabinet, the astonished people turned their backs, closed their eyes and struck their pose of submission.[118] The four Foukhouourkou[119] each opened their side of the cabinet and before bringing it down they blindfolded me.[120] Then I started singing the canticle of Tulkoë[121] and the priestesses finished it. The Kriskrougandil[122] took out his Loushaikis[123] and using a gold stylus[124] read aloud the founding laws of the kingdom, which were brought from the Heavens by the Kirkirkantal.[125]

---

[116] Before the King sat on the throne, he took the orders that he had to give written on bronze balls that were kept in the archives and recorded every 100 years to serve as rules for his successor.

[117] The place where the great bronze book was kept.

[118] When they opened the book of laws, the privilege of sight stopped and the people had to turn their backs like with the statue.

[119] State leaders who were in charge of guarding the book of laws. They could not accede to this honor unless they could prove that four of their ancestors had been in the great Council of Seven.

[120] Only the Foukhouourkou, the King and the High Priestess could see the great bronze book. Everyone else present at its opening had to be blindfolded.

[121] Hymn sung only during public celebrations. It began with the words "Thanks be to you, Fulghane," etc.

[122] The grand reader, under the High Priestess, was the most important person in the kingdom.

[123] Crystal glasses with square, hollow lens in which there was a greenish liquid that magnified objects.

[124] A needle whose point guided the eyes over the characters.

[125] Spilghis or the first angel of light. Tradition claimed that the bronze book was brought from the heavens by this sacred intelligence and the laws within were written by his hand. The veneration they had for this book was so great that their most serious oaths were sworn on its covers. If someone was found to transgress these formidable oaths, they were handed over to the priestesses who put him

When the Reading Minister got to the article about the High Priestess, the King clapped his hands[126] and ordered me to have him look for the passage concerning her. I informed the Kriskrougandil that after he found it he should read aloud the article, which ran something like this:

"If somehow by the maliciousness of human nature our Magna Fakhaldak is ever in opposition to the Ruler of our dear people and a fundamental disagreement follows or because of concealed hatred or personal interests the kingdom is put in danger of ruin, we order them both to step down from their thrones and after invoking us to bow down before our divine image and holy laws. Then they will stand up at the same time, put their foreheads together and after stepping away from each other the distance of one body[127] they will both hit each other. Then our justice will be shown and the guilty will be punished."

At the end of this passage the Reading Minister clapped his hands and informed me that there was a reference at the end of the article. I told the King and he ordered that it be found and read. It was explained in the following terms:

"In order that all equality be observed in this formidable decree and that the people always have reason to praise our wisdom let the High Priestess accuse the King in person of breaking our laws and voice her complaints about him. We

---

to death by tickling—this was the greatest punishment among these people, which humanity later discarded.

[126] This signal for the Karveder to know that the king wanted to speak with him.

[127] All scholars have disagreed over this passage. All the authors who mentioned it have explained it differently. The most serious say that the distance is measured by the length of an arm; others say that it was six feet, the average height of the Amphicleocles. As the subject remains undecided today, I prefer not to have the final word. What I can say to explain this is that the way people fought was to knock their heads together and hit each other until one of the fighters was conquered. Scaliger claimed that this way of fighting only took place among the nobles.

grant her the right to speak first unless the sovereign is not on our High Throne, then he is allowed the first word. After the accusation the guilty party will speak in defense and for judgment will use our laws that mention the crime concerned. If the article of law cannot settle the matter, then we grant the people assembled together to make a definitive judgment and the Council of Seven will register it as a duly authorized law."

The Kriskrougandil stopped there, lowered his head and closed his eyes. Taking advantage of the right granted him by the law, the Lindiagar spoke out and accused the High Priestess of using her sovereign power to destroy the crown's heiress and of leading the people to rebellion. Worse than that he backed everything up by saying that the solemn Priestess caused all this through a lack of respect for the sanctuary of his palace when she entered without observing the formal law that forbids it under penalty of death and that is so firmly and expressly worded that the Karveder himself can enter only by backing in.

To these terrible accusations the King added that of having induced the Council of Seven to profane his palace, an even more serious crime because she knew very well that this infraction would be the cause of the venerable Council's destruction,[128] which might take a long time to restore.

The King finished his speech earnestly praying by the sacred heel[129] of Fulghane that the High Priestess, before heaven and earth, confess the secret motives that led her to these odious crimes. The Magna Fakhaldak, before answering, wanted to accuse him in turn, but the order coming from the High Throne was without appeal. She would have to break her

---

[128] When a minister of the Council of Seven got the death penalty, all members suffered the same punishment.

[129] For the Amphicleocles this prayer was so powerful that they believed the slightest concealment of truth was revealed by a clap of thunder. These people were so blind that all mysterious or sudden deaths were blamed on it.

word and face the people's fury. So, she yelled loudly[130] and explained herself as follows.

"May Fulghane be forever blessed. May his High Priestess die because her virtue is suspect and you, Monarch, may the highest justice pay you according to your deeds. Oh Chief of the Amphicleocles, dear people whose divinity I serve, breathe[131] now and heed the motives that forced me to mix up spiritual and civil matters. Let Great Being strike me down even if the truth comes out of my mouth. Why, Fulghane, do you abandon me?"

When the High Priestess had finished she came down from the Throne, threw herself at the foot of the statue and soaked it in tears. After a few minutes she tore off the sacred headband[132] hiding her white hair which otherwise would have aroused pity and respect. It was lucky that the law forbidding the people to look upon her was in effect because her venerable appearance could have affected them and made them revolt again, which would have been even more dangerous since religion would have been at the heart of it. The King himself was touched by the sight. In fact I saw[133] that he was so touched that he covered his face and turned his head away. We are not safe from first impressions.

The Magna Fakhaldak dried her tears and spoke. "Now I am ready, Lindiagar, to respond to your accusations. Why have you beseeched me? What forces you to make me reveal secrets before the people that they should be ignorant of and that ought to be buried in deep silence? Wouldn't it be better that the death of your daughter bury them with her in the grave? Oh, you are going to be tremble. The Princess who has been handed over as heiress of this empire is not the one who

---

[130] The High Priestess preceded her speech by yelling in order that the people fall silent and be twice as attentive and respectful.

[131] The High Priestess, like the King, had the right to give this permission.

[132] A kind of collar of four rows made of the teeth of those who were granted the right to die in the temple.

[133] Only the Karveder had the right to open his eyes in the temple.

should reign. By confessing this I am condemning myself. The priestesses who were responsible for raising the infant, the one lawfully called to the throne, when making her pass through the flames of purification according to custom,[134] unfortunately let her slip out of their hands. They tried hard to save her life, but oh harsh fate, all their efforts could do nothing to prevent her face from being totally disfigured. And the poor priestesses were afraid of being punished, so they concealed the tragedy; they substituted the oldest for the youngest[135] and thus, in time, I delivered that child to the general assembly as the heiress of the throne.

"That's my crime, people, which I would never have known about if one of the priestesses hadn't been angry and resentful enough to take revenge for a well-deserved punishment and tell the Princess about the real heiress and the secret of her birth[136] and about the changeling, obviously making her think about the laws of the throne, which legitimately belonged to the other, and the harsh fate that was in store for the consequences of this baneful substitution. The Princess was astonished to find herself the innocent victim of a secret ploy

---

[134] Before being presented to Fulghane, the newborn prince or princess was passed three times through the flames of a furnace, which was called the purification.

[135] The High Priestess, like the King, was not allowed to the see the crown heirs. They were raised in a separate set of rooms.

[136] It was expressly forbidden by law to tell the crown heirs about their parents, although a writer of the ancient celebrations has proven through an historian of the Amphicleocles that a queen of the realm, jealous of being made to observe the laws, argued in the general assembly that the law in question had been forgotten for a long time and for proof of her accusation of the priestesses disclosures she declared that when the children under their watch were 10 years old they were told the secret of their birth and whether they had a brother or sister shut up in the temple. And she added that when she learned through the same channel about the cruel law that made them kill a crown heir at birth, she was so horrified and so scared of having lost a brother or sister that she resorted to supernatural means in order to have no children.

and deeply affected by everything she would lose. Having no stomach for the never-ending duress she was about to suffer and scared of the death destined for the prince or princess who owed their life to their sister, the proud Princess announced herself the reason for her presence in the temple—she revealed the cruel secrets. She found willing minds, touched by these offenses, and arranged such dangerous stunts that in fear of the deadly results she might cause I thought I should convene the High Council of Virgins[137] to clean up the emergency. I was terribly worried and got wind that the impending decision leaned toward sentencing the Princess to be killed in the temple and announcing it as such to the people. I was afraid of the possibly tragic results of this double election of Princesses,[138]

---

[137] This council was made up of all the priestesses whom various changes had separated from one another. Those of the temple of Kaiocles, although inferior to those of Fulghane, presided and had two votes each.

[138] This is one of the most remarkable incidents in the history of the Amphicleocles. To really understand it we must remember that they only gave the name of crown successor to a prince or princess when the Queen had no more children. If the king happened to die before the legally stipulated number was filled, his widow was taken to the temple of Kaiocles the day after the funeral to choose a second husband among the Kails, who were kept in the temple until their death for this very purpose. It is also necessary to mention that the council of seven, at the birth of the King's second or third child, stamped the seal of their number, e.g., the third was marked on the head with three stamps. In his description of the overthrow of the empire of the Amphicleocles, Scaliger failed or forgot to mention these important points. If he were aware of them, he would not have suggested in his description of the civil war between the princesses Cleannes and Nasilaë that the latter, in spite of her incontestable right proven by the mysterious mark, was forced to yield the throne to her sister, who was excluded by law. Heinsius, better informed of the matter, has shed light on the incident in saying that when the armies were ready to fight, Princess Nasilaë, who was not very bloodthirsty, urged King Motacoa, her husband, to convene the Council of Seven, part of which was in the army, and in the presence of both party leaders to check both sisters' heads and respect the decision of the reunited

not to mention my other fear of scandalizing the kingdom by showing that in the midst of peace a war was brewing. Struck, I say, by all these righteous considerations, I broke up the Council as was my incontestable right[139] and made the priestesses follow me to the sanctuary.

"When we got there I had recourse to the divinity, but I prayed in vain; it was deaf to my voice. Three times I tried to utter an oracle and three times the divine spirit withdrew and cast me into lethargy. Fulghane was angry and gone from the sanctuary. Moaning because of his constant refusal, I ordered the Sacred Vigil.[140] Every organ in my grieving body fell into a deep sleep. A cold sweat, chilled by some mysterious dream,

---

council, which worked, as we will see in the course of this important story. I have to admit, in passing, that I owe this solemn author, whom I just cited, for some of the information I have provided to elucidate the difficult passages in the adventures of the Princess of the Amphicleocles.

[139] The High Priestess's authority was so broad that she called and dismissed the council as she wished. She held the power of life and death not only in the temple, but also throughout the kingdom. The King alone could grant a pardon, which her rights did not allow, but he could also not condemn one of his subjects to death without her approval while the High Priestess needed only that of the Council of Seven, which was never refused.

[140] Madame Dacier explains the ceremony as follows: When the High Priestess deemed it necessary to call the sacred vigil, every virgin prepared herself by cutting her hair and performing the ablution in the officially sanctioned fountain where they all jumped in together. After the bath they went back to their cells where they had to drink a certain amount of wine (about four pints—the older ones could drink six). After this holy preparation they went to the temple with the same amount of "spirits of wine," or grain alcohol, and all the medicinal herbs they could stand. Then they surrounded the statue and sang a simple hymn. After the hymn the virgins danced around the idol and to prove their submission and respect they sprinkled the feet with the rest of mysterious liquor that they got drunk on. The same scholar says that whichever drunk virgin fell down first was recorded among those aspiring to be High Priestess. It was an incontestable right to become so when there was no other candidate thus honored.

seeped out of my pores, announcing the presence of the god I served. I saw him. He came to me.

"You try in vain to appease me," he said in wrath. "You are breaking my laws. Discord reigns. The crime has been committed. Tremble, Priestess, for my temple is about to collapse on your head. The foundations of the kingdom are going to fall and everything will perish."

"My fears multiplied at these words and I think I fell at the feet of Fulghane while the guardian spirit[141] begged him to have mercy on the Amphicleocles.

"Go," the god continued, "and pour the blood of Princess Nasilaë[142] on my altars;[143] only that can appease my anger."

"Overwhelmed by the grace that Fulghane had deigned to grant, I woke with a start and told the frightened priestesses both the dream and the oracle. The doors of the temple were opened on my orders and the judgment of the divinity proclaimed before the assembled people.[144]

---

[141] Tradition said that Kirkirkantal was the first King of the Amphicleocles and they owed their peaceful government to him.

[142] The oldest according to these people's way of speaking, and so the youngest.

[143] Human sacrifice was in use among the Amphicleocles and the people believed that it was so pleasing to the gods that when it was demanded of them or when they were afflicted with a plague, they sacrificed the best of their people on the altars of the gods. On this pretext the King and the High Priestess, when they got along together, got rid of enemies who threatened them. This superstition lasted until the reign of Motacoa who became so powerful that he abolished not only these horrible practices, but also all the laws opposed to common sense and reason.

[144] The people did not have the right to enter the temple except when the King was on the High Throne. Outside of this ceremony, the doors stayed shut. The people remained in a big forecourt with their bellies on the ground until the doors were opened. Then they got up and turned their backs until the temple criers told them to leave. (The criers were eunuchs and appointed to guard the sanctuary). When the priestess gave an oracle, it was engraved on a brass ball that was thrown in the air and whoever was the most agile and caught it had

"Those are my crimes, King, and here are yours. You transgressed the divine and human laws at the same time: you entered the holy temple without being purified. And how? Being carried,[145] oh profanity, by men who, in spite of the purity of their rank,[146] are excluded from our mysteries. You

---

the glorious honor of announcing what it said. Another honor attached to the first to catch the ball was that he was given the first vacant public office. But on the contrary, if a subject dropped the ball, he was straightaway punished with death. These two motives produced much skill at catching and many years often passed without the unfortunate event of dropping the ball happening. The ball was thrown only three times in the air. The fourth time it was sent to the temple where it was deposited in a big chest, which was used as the archives of Fulghane's ceremonies.

[145] The king was such a holy personage that only the priestesses were allowed to touch him and everything that he used was handmade by these virgins. Ménage, in his work on ancient banquets, observed that the King of the Amphicleocles always ate alone and his food was prepared in the temple.

[146] They took a census of the kingdom's subjects in the capital every year. The record contained the dates of birth, names and positions. When a man passed the normal age, they put his name in a special record and he was maintained at the expense of the state. All the elderly lived in the temple and made up a kind of council to resolve any problems concerning tradition, though the real reason for them being there was as a breeding ground, so to speak, for the Council of Seven. When a member of this venerable body died, they took all of those who had lived for four generations and locked them in a special room surrounded by guards to prevent any ploys or tricks in the official election. Before entering the election room, they were purified by fire and then had to swallow an awful drink that cleansed their bodies of the previous night's food. After this wise precaution they were locked up and left for six days and nights without any food. Before sunrise of the seventh day all the ministers of the state came to the election room, opened it very carefully, with much ado, and whoever had survived the famine would fill the vacant seat. If more than one old man happened to be alive, they locked them up again until only one survived. We have to mention the way the ministers greeted the old men on the seventh day. The chief minister at the head of the others entered the room on the left and when he found an old man stretched

invited them in without the supreme will and glorified yourself for no reason, with no order, against the law. You sat on the High Throne and from this holy seat you accused me and in the heart of this sanctuary you usurped a power that emanates only from the Heavens and belongs only to me. You distort your oaths and open the sacred book without mystical counsel. These are your crimes against the divinity.

"As for the civil, you broke the law that forbids you having any contact with your children, profane King. I call Fulghane as witness to this and the Lea-Minska and the Karveder, that cowardly, conceited minister. Didn't you see your daughter? And don't you know that for this awful crime the people and their descendants have to be forever outlawed.

"Were the priestesses of Kaiocles informed according to custom? Isn't it the rule that after Princess Cleannes left the temple your first order should have been to inform them so they could prepare the Kails for the sacred ceremony?[147] Am I

---

out, he grabbed the beard, lifted his head off the ground and said, "Molbok," i.e. sleep. He repeated it three times, letting the head fall back each time. When it was thus proven that the old man was dead, all the ministers cried out, "Molboken," which meant he sleeps. This went on until they found a survivor who had to line up the bodies and then put himself in the back row of the dead. To mark his election they adorned him with a strap from which hung all the heads of those who aspired to this eminent position. Then they led him to the temple with all the people cheering and there the high priestess got the choice approved by Fulghane by cutting off one of his ears, which she wore around her neck when they sang the hymn Tulkoë.

After this sacrifice, they led the old chosen one to the palace of the King, who knew about it and appeared on a balcony to ratify the election by spitting on the forehead of the old man, who was thus cleansed of any impurities that might have remained.

When these duties were done, the cavalcade started from the palace. The new councilor got up on a chariot to which were attached all the corpses whose heads he wore and that served as proof of his worthiness; and the chariot was pulled by the group of old men he had left.

[147] When the priestesses of Kaiocles were told that the princess had to be taken to their temple, they gathered all the males who would be

being stupid? King, I call you to witness that you're trying to destroy the custom of holy marriage. Blind Prince, until now you have proven worthy of the throne, your birthright that you upheld so virtuously. Why do you want to give it up through impiety? Oh King of the Amphicleocles, pull yourself together and don't leave the temple until you have gratified Fulghane. Sacrifice a vain affection to him. Bring out Nasilaë so that she can atone for her crimes on the altar; so that Cleannes, the only heiress, can go from the temple to the palace; so that the second order of the priestesses be carried out and to satisfy both, since the statue is angry, we will cross our thumbs[148] and cut them with the sacred knife and let the fire consume them[149] and along with them the crime and anger. Oh Fulghane, power of life, absolve and punish."

The violence and fury of her voice swept the people back believing that the god himself was being explained. The Priestess' venerable appearance, which many people glimpsed, brought out a dreadful murmur. The King, who knew that the last resort was called for under such drastic circumstances,

---

used in the marriage competition and to test who was old enough to get married and who could face the trials they brought them into a long hall and there each of the men got a bow and lined up. They drew the string at the first signal and shot an arrow with their name carved in it. The target was a double-bottom drum stretched so that if an arrow just touched it, it would stick. After the signal and after the competitors let their arrows fly, they were taken back to their cells and the drum was examined. They recorded the names of the arrows that were found and from this the priestesses told them their fates.

[148] A way of making honorable amends among the Amphicleocles. Far from being subject to shame and insult, it was glorious among these people because they claimed that one of the great deeds of man was to admit one's errors and gratify those who were offended.

[149] Fire among the Amphicleocles purified all imperfections. It was so venerated that it was used as the seal of all public acts. The way of stamping a paper was to burn it in the corner.

threw his crown into the crowd of people.[150] This unexpected action recalled them to respect and silence.

"Oh Magna Fakhaldak," the Lindiagar raised his voice in anger, "what good are your tricks and how can you escape the punishment I have prepared for you? Doesn't the statue's silence in this drastic time condemn you? Fulghane reacts when you are alone and stays quiet when you need his voice.[151] But it's up to him to judge your abuse of his ministry. However, let's prove this very important point that provoked the present troubles. Let's pass over the horrible crime of changing the order of the succession of the state. As great an evil as it is, we can try to fix it. Is it so hard to put things back in the order they should be in? I grant the switch; it is fair. But I want the right of primogeniture to be established. The Princesses, my daughters, are both dear to me and on this basis I have to treat them the same. So, Magna Fakhaldak, what do you have to say to that? Are you worried that the mask is falling? The truth will win out and the mystery be revealed. Only one word is needed to expose you.

"Priestess, it's your turn to learn a secret that should be kept quiet forever, but that your tricks have forced me to reveal now. At the birth of my children the Council of Seven enjoyed the secret privilege of being at the side of the Queen and they marked the newborn's skull with a mysterious seal kept under lock and key in the nuptial room.[152] What I'm tell-

---

[150] The last resort to recall the people to their duty when they had strayed and the way of abdicating the kingdom—it was a tacit approval when the people picked up the crown, but when they turned their back on it, it was a sign that the abdication was not acceptable and then the sovereign had to take it back and continue his reign.

[151] The King, as has been said, was of a different religion than his people and this statement was ironic to make the high priestess understand that he knew all about the ploys she used to assert herself and seduce the people.

[152] The room where the queens of the Amphicleocles gave birth guarded by two priestesses who were relieved every day by other virgins from the temple of Kleocles. This is still one of the customs

---

ing you is a truth that cannot be cast in doubt: if the Princess whom you told us about is taking her rightful place as heir, her head will be marked with the mysterious sign and the Council of Seven here can verify it. But if it is a fraud, if the Cleannes coming out of the temple is not the real Cleannes, there will be punishment. Let's get the fire-mutilated Princess out of criminal negligence..." The King noticed that the Priestess was opposing his orders. "Obey! If I am committing a crime, violating the laws of the sanctuary, Kod-si-kad-zaïd."[153]

How the authority of sovereigns has great power over his people, especially when these rulers are respected by their virtues! The Lindiagar's order was carried out with no problems. Someone went off,[154] according to custom and law. The Magna Fakhaldak was so crushed knowing that her ploys were finally going to be discovered and they would soon know all about her dark designs that she descended the throne and started to go off to get the Princess.

The King, your father (the Karveder said), fearing that the Priestess was escaping or taking advantage of the break to stir up new troubles, ordered the sanctuary to be kept under guard and no one could leave until everything was cleared up.

The trial of the 12 tables

I was up to this point in the wonderful story of Motacoa, and Sinouis was so attentive that he was barely breathing so he would not miss a word when all of a sudden the darkness around us turned bright as day with piercing, glaring rays. We

---

that the politics of religious ministers use to have emissaries in the heart of the palace so that nothing can happen without their knowing about it.

[153] Let the punishment fall on my head and may the heavens be praised.

[154] The King was not allowed to give orders to the priestesses and even less so punish them when they deserved. Justice was done in the temple on the order of the high priestess, whose power was totally despotic.

stood up, dumbfounded, and looked around. My partner in misfortune cried out in joy when he recognized them. "Vil-konhis be praised!" He stepped forward and motioned me to follow. "Oh Lamekis, what a sight! The spell is finally broken and here we are in this wonderful room. What a pleasure! The tables are set and piled high and all these wonderful guests around us are drinking and eating. They're inviting us to join in. Isn't it time to take a break from all the wear and tear? Don't you see, Lamekis," Sinouis went on, "we've finally made it to that longed for bliss. Obviously the good cheer is shining in all the things around us. The beauty of the women who we can see here in the feast and the number of different tables that are set up in the room are all proof enough of the happiness of those who are allowed in and the grandeur of the master of this place—it can be none other than the great Scealgalis whom we've heard so much about. The Sylph didn't lie to us. Let's go, Lamekis," weak Sinouis wound up, "let's follow their good examples. We'll offend the great King if we go hungry here where everyone seems to be invited to enjoy themselves and be merry."

After saying this my travel companion left me and went up to one of the tables where several people of both sexes were indulging in the charms of voluptuousness. I tried in vain to call back my easy-going friend, but he was already sitting down and a young woman, as pretty as Venus, was serving him delicacies with eyes only for him, eyes full of fire and tenderness that invited him not so much to make cheer as to make love. I turned away my own eyes and sighed. It was all too seductive. My excited heart was flying after the goods that my reason fled from. I looked around the huge room where all kinds of amusement was going on and I could barely tell how big it was. The ceiling was incredibly high and looked like the sky with all the stars shining on an azure night. The light was so cleverly set up that it seemed to shine out of the painted planets.

I spent quite a while enjoying the sight of so much beau-ty and trying to figure out how the light was physically produced, which was enough to light up the whole room even though it was obviously a trick. Then I noticed the paneling on the walls and I was not so surprised to see that it was made of fine, polished crystal, cut and beveled so that the facets reflected off one another, multiplying the hidden source of light.

After checking out all the different objects decorating the room, I went to Sinouis' table with the idea of getting him away from such a dangerous place, which was becoming even more so as the thorns of hunger were starting to torment me. The sage advice of the philosopher Dehahal could barely hold me back and my own wariness kept me at a distance while trying to urge him to follow me. But what a wonder! If my weak friend heard me, he did not recognize me. All I could get out of him was a look in his eyes infused with wine and love. The guests around him saw me standing back and tried to seduce me into joining them, but as sorry as I was for it, I felt I had to flee. It pained me to have to abandon a friend, but I could not get lost with him. My hunger was acute and the sights and smells would not have taken long to overcome my reason. Running away from so many attractive objects was the only way to halt my burgeoning desires. So, I fled.

And then a soft, silvery voice, penetrating me deep down, said, "Lamekis, is this how you abandon me?" I knew the voice and turned around and ran toward it. Good god! What did I see? Was it a ghost or Clemelis herself? I fell into her arms and, cruel fortune, the illusion vanished, the wonderful ghost disappeared; I was hugging only the wind. I stood still and bursts of laughter broke out. I turned around again toward the one whom I took for the dear object of my affection and I saw her; I recognized her again. But what a surprise! A light mist was slowly evaporating. The features that were so dear to me were fading away and other, more material ones were taking their place. I waited, trembling, for the extraordinary transformation to finish. And who was there? Instead of Clemelis I recognized the Sylph whose advice had warned me about what would happen here. It looked stern but sympathetic. I wanted to go up to it and beg it to get me out of that tantalizing place. I approached with my arms held out, but it was no good. The Sylph was no longer there. It had disappeared.

I felt all the harshness of fate pursuing me. Then I made a firm decision to resist all the attacks that might come against me and to get out of that deadly place at any cost. But the tender friendship I had for Sinouis made me try once more to wrench him from the destiny that threatened him. I went back to the table where I had left him, but he was gone. I sighed in sorrow.

"Poor friend," I cried, "why did you let yourself get dragged into the seductive charms of voluptuousness, which surely appeared under this mask of lies only to drag you down into the awful pit of vice?"

I started walking away and thinking, trying to avoid looking at the tables I had to pass by, but at every step I found new temptations. All my senses were attacked by the most formidable enemies: on one side a graceful, enchanting voice sweet-talked me; elsewhere the scents of sumptuous dishes tickled my taste buds; a third, more dangerous attack, because it was felt stronger, made me quiver—a hand, softer than satin, took mine and tried to sit me at a table and my eyes snuck a peek at the perfect beauty who was inviting me to fulfill my culminating sense. The Heavens graced me with resistance. I closed my eyes, held my breath, covered my ears and started running as fast as I could.

I ran for half an hour without stopping, stumbling and staggering the entire way until I finally took a painful fall. For a few minutes I was dazed, but I heard nothing that led me to believe that I was still in the room. I dared to open my eyes and found myself in a room lit only by a dome. The walls looked blank and all the furniture was very modest. In the back of the room I found a marble balustrade that blocked off the entrance to an area where I saw a young man dressed in blue. The only food he had was bread and a bottle full of a liquid that was clearer than crystal. I thought he looked familiar in some way. He was reading a big book and once in a while looked up at me. Sometimes he even picked at the simple meal in front of him, but he seemed less interested in this food than in the spiritual sustenance he was devouring with his eyes.

Part 4

I watched the young man with a secret satisfaction that filled my heart with quiet joy in spite of the hunger gnawing at me more and more. All of a sudden I heard my name called. I quickly turned around because I recognized Sinouis' voice, no doubt about it, and I looked for him eagerly, but he was nowhere to be seen. I thought that my imagination had got the better of me and fooled my hearing. The brain is often so preoccupied that it muddles its fibers and the results agitate the soul such that it takes as real the sounds and visions that the deranged machine offers up to it. Then it wanders off and gets lost in a mess of ideas that it can make no real sense of.

I was beginning to think this was the case with me when a deep sigh and tear-choked words told me that it was no illusion; the weeping really did come from my partner in misfortune. I searched again in vain. I still heard his voice, not far off, but I could not find the source. Anxious now, I turned back to the young man shut up behind the balustrade. The way his eyes stared at me made me look at him differently. He watched me kindly and it looked like one of his fingers was trying to point something out to me. I followed the direction and looking down at the ground I saw a pitiful owl that was staggering around on its wings as much as on its feet. It looked dark and gloomy, wearing its depression. For some unknown reason, I was touched by the sight of it and started crying, which blurred and obscured my view. Then I knew where the voice and sighs were coming from.

"Oh Heavens!" I cried. "What does this awful metaphor mean? Great gods! What is it trying to tell me?"

"A happiness to come," the young man exclaimed in a tone that calmed my troubled soul. "Dry your tears, Lamekis, and come sit at my table. Through your perseverance and your resistance to pleasure you have been found worthy of the real goods with which the divine Scealgalis rewards truly virtuous men."

Almost before he finished speaking my heart fluttered, my sight became clear again, my legs regained their strength and I went up to the balustrade with a kind of confidence that I had lacked until then. I recognized the young man as the same one whom we had met when we entered the palace. It was Dehahal, the great philosopher, whom we had heard about. Two Sylphs, whom I had overlooked or maybe were hidden from me when I entered the mysterious room and whom I recognized as the same ones who had carried me and Sinouis away, were guarding the entrance of the balustrade. One looked like jolliness was painted on its face and the other stared sadly down at the poor owl I mentioned.

When I got to the gate the happy Sylph opened it and motioned me to enter. It looked like he was congratulating me and was glad to see me go in. When I greeted him with respect, Dehahal pressed his hand to his forehead, which I took as a sign of thanks.

"Eat and drink," the young philosopher said, "you will find this sober meal sweeter than you would have found the myriad of sumptuous dishes that were offered to you."

I obeyed since my dire need outweighed my shyness and surprise. I ate only bread and drank only water, but I had never had a more exquisite meal in my life. Virtue made the stew and a peaceful heart the pleasure: there are no delights that can equal these two boons. Dehahal watched me kindly, smiling from time to time. "Lamekis," he said when he saw I had had my fill, "is there anything else you want?"

At these words I became worried and my present calm was broken. The image of Clemelis surged up in my mind, as well as the recent loss of Sinouis and his transformation, which I had no reason to doubt. All this made me feel how many different kinds of misery were crushing me. "Sir," I cried, kneeling at his feet, "don't you know how I feel? Haven't you seen into the depths of my heart? Can you think that I can be happy in this situation?"

"Lamekis, Lamekis," the young man clapped his hands, "you are still a long way from perfection!" The way he spoke and the piercing look he gave made me very ashamed. With my eyes cast down shyly, I could not bring myself to look at the philosopher. I waited in fear for what would come out of his venerable mouth. I wanted to hear it and yet I was afraid.

Finally he said, "Get up, Lamekis, and listen very carefully. You have reached the blessed moment when the soul is freed from its weaknesses and vain desires and revels in the priceless luxury of no longer being obsessed.[155] Until now I have not been able to tell you how to behave or give you any helpful advice, but now things have changed.[156] The perilous trial of the 12 tables,[157] which you passed gloriously, gave me

---

[155] The Sylphs had no doubt that the soul was immortal, but they did not think that when it left the body it flew directly to the blessed or cursed places that its deeds had earned. They were convinced that the substance (that's how they referred to the soul) went into mortal bodies on blessed or cursed planets and that they stayed there until the end of the world. Then the Universal Being, whom they call Noc-kha-dor, gathers them up into the great heaven where they are suited up with bodies made by his hand, one for each substance, whose beauty or ugliness will make them happy or miserable. When they taught their children the basic principles of their sect and asked them what Noc-kha-dor did, they answered, "He grinds down our fathers' bodies and makes new ones for them to wear according to whether they followed his laws or not."

[156] Dehahal had the right to favorably direct those who are thrown by chance onto the Island of the Sylphs, but he could not keep them from the constant traps that the black spirits maliciously laid out to harm them and get hold of their substance. But when a mortal chose freely to resist all the temptations of vice, then the philosopher could show up and lead him into the port of happiness.

[157] Scealgalis allowed the black Sylphs to appear to men in the most attractive forms to tempt them to evil. The trial of the 12 tables was one of the most dangerous to experience. If you were lucky enough to

responsibility and confidence in you, as well as friendship. The first proof of this is to give you a basic idea of the venerable Island of the Sylphs. Before joining it, it is terribly important that you know its laws and customs. After learning what the price of admittance is, you will search the depths of your heart and make the most important decision of your life whether to stay here or go back to where you came from. Don't fool yourself, Lamekis, the journeys and troubles you have suffered so far are nothing compared to the moment of initiation.[158] And I'll tell you, it would be better for you to go back into the void you were dragged out of and crawl like a reptile on the earth than to dare to show up at this second trial[159] if you are not absolutely sure of a glorious success. There's no middle ground here. Either you soar into bliss or plunge into the horrors of eternal misery.

"Let's begin, lucky mortal. But before going into detail, which can bring you the power to move mountains and make

---

get through without falling into the traps, you earned the right to call yourself initiated.

[158] By this is meant the great skinning ceremony, which is when you are skinned alive. See Part 2 (above), *The Ceolbhaume*.

[159] Of being skinned alive: when they entered the place where this barbarous deed was done, they announced that the skinning, as cruel as it was, signified the abandonment of all things that one was most attached to. When the proselyte was ready to sacrifice everything to the glory of Scealgalis, (formal litany), the executioner Sylphs left him to prepare for the ceremony. This interval was given to the black spirits to try one last time to make him succumb to temptation. They appeared in their most attractive forms, as the most beloved of the proselyte, to arouse his desires. If he was unfortunate enough to give in to the seduction, the executioner Sylphs came back and skinned him alive. But instead of this punishment being the last step to happiness, it led to ruin. After the skinning a Sylph brought him back to earth where, to punish him for not following the good, he lived for one year in torment and despair of having lost the greatest good that could ever be hoped for and was promised to him.

rivers flow upstream,[160] every profane spirit must be re-moved,[161] every vice cleared out and for the first punishment of these weaknesses he will go down, until called out, into the dark manors[162] where the black spirits rot."

After saying this, Dehahal clapped his hands seven times.[163] An awful, mournful cry followed and the melancholy Sylph at the railing took off after the poor owl, who started fluttering around trying to escape. The black spirit grabbed him by a wing and they both disappeared.

I cried seeing what just happened and looked pleadingly at the philosopher, ready to ask him to pardon the poor bird, but his firm look held me back. And yet it was not hard for me to see that Dehahal was affected by his command. The sadness in his face and the sighs he let out left no room for doubt that even if his state of perfection had stripped him of all human concern, he still held a modicum of compassion and sensitivity. But the cloud of emotion did not last long; it was quickly eclipsed by a calm and tranquil face; and then he addressed me.

---

[160] The Sylphs claimed that there was so much strength and energy in the way their history was written that there was not a single passage that could not move mountains, dry up the seas, etc. I felt it necessary to edit out all the advantages they attributed to this claim, which were set out in detail in my original manuscript. Today we are so strict that we can never be too restrained: the bombastic gibberish of hypocrisy is fashionable everywhere and we must conform.

[161] Dehahal was badgering the black spirit and the owl. The passage will be explained forthwith.

[162] The Sylphs believed that there was no happiness beyond their island and life on Earth and the planets was the real hell where law-breakers were cast.

[163] If a Sylph was on his island or in any other place, he had the right to be obeyed by clapping his hands seven times.

The story of Dehahal

I am the first philosopher[164] who dared to think of the bold plan of discovering the Island of the Sylphs, where we are at the moment—this Island that is so praised by scholars and the object of their deepest and most abstract study and yet remains a mystery and fiction for their various imaginations.[165] At an age when most people are worried more about having fun, I had already surpassed all ordinary, natural knowledge and with my keen, clever father as guide I soon traversed the thorny paths that his experience and knowledge laid out for me. The strangest phenomena and the most difficult to explain were nothing more to me than thin veils that I easily exposed. The visible stars, as well as those that are barely seen

---

[164] The vanity of Dehahal is insupportable and his speech pretty much proves that whatever state of perfection the man had reached, he still had some traces of his former weaknesses since it would be easy for me to show in the heart of this story that Dehahal was not the first to be transported to the mysterious island, as he claims. It was written in their tradition that a certain Csekaliel, a Phoenician, had been transported by a female Sylph who had fallen in love with him and had children who made up the third species of inhabitants, which will be discussed elsewhere.

[165] I agree with the author that the Island of the Sylphs has always been regarded as the dwelling of Intelligences where all metaphysical knowledge comes from. I agree, too, that it is 70 leagues or stadia of night phase away. I know that it is said that the cloud that follows the Moon is the base of this mysterious island and this should not be doubted. Everyone knows that Fagelle, the former Calvinist minister, recently deceased, made the voyage in an extraordinary adventure that will be described elsewhere. So, I agree with all these things, but I am not of the opinion that the island is inhabited and governed with the order that is claimed. If I can reach it myself to clear the matter up, I will add a supplement to this work on my return from the island and, to leave the scholars nothing to be desired, I will provide undeniable evidence to establish the momentous proofs.

because of their fantastic distances,[166] were followed step by step by my enlightened eye and I knew their orbits before they were completed. My knowledge increased and expanded to such a degree that my mind began living in the Heavens more than in my body.

But can man ever finish contemplating the unlimited? The farther I went on this divine path, the more I loathed crawling on earth. One day I was sitting and daydreaming on the seaside, sadly moaning about my mortal coil whose materiality opposed the lightness and expansion of my ideas, when I first saw the floating island[167] that was moving around like a whirlwind, spiraling around in wide circles. For more than four hours I watched its troubled course, carried over the surface of the sea sometimes to the west and sometimes to the north. Finally I ran up on a nearby hill to get a better look at its deviations. The sun was high in the sky, there was no wind and the calm waves could not have been pushing around the floating island. I could not find the reason why; no physical law could provide me with a satisfying cause. I was lost in thought, naturally caused by such a phenomenon, when the island was violently shaken up, started spinning like a top and then a piece of land covered with shells and Roc eggs[168] broke off and rose gradually into the air. I stared fixedly at the mass of land as it went up slowly, ponderously. The sun beamed down on the surface and looked like it was stopped by a kind

---

[166] It is presumed that Dehahal is talking here about the planets. Gassendi has made a very exact count of them, which the reader can use to figure out this passage.

[167] Tavernier reported that in the Atlantic Ocean he came across an island that was sailing a few miles away from his ship and he said that it was inhabited by black men who were built differently from other men.

[168] The Roc is a huge bird that is found around the South Pole. It carries cows off in the countryside, but in this country the animals are as big as elephants. Judging by this we can imagine how big their eggs must be.

of gum in the half-open shells.[169] I even thought that the burning rays shot through the oily, swampy pores in a few places and sucked up, so to speak, the roots and juices concentrated there. I was measuring (if I can use this word) the range and force of the rays, which seemed like so many lines attached to the land, when a new phenomenon awed me. Three of the Roc eggs, half-buried by their weight with the sun beaming straight down on them, suddenly shot up into the sky as quick as an arrow.

I was watching all these things very closely when I noticed that the land started tilting and slowly heading down to the sea again. But I got over my astonishment at this change of movement when I saw a thin cloud[170] come between the sun

---

[169] It is true that sunlight makes this impression. If a reader has any doubts, he can easily check it by taking a coach to the nearest port at sunrise to see how the spectacle is produced. The first beams will barely hit the water when the oysters, which cracked open during the cool night, will close in fear of being dried up by the heat. But like all inhabitants of shells, (like with men), there will be a few lazy ones and the sunlight will take advantage of their negligence, slip in between their shells when they are not completely closed, and quickly pry them open. That's why you always find so many empty oysters on the seashore. Common people who are not apprised of natural mysteries and take everything literally, have always believed that the sun loves oysters and before starting its day it has oyster stew for breakfast. With no disrespect to philosophical secrets I thought I should explain this passage so that we not fall victim to ignorance.

[170] This phenomenon happened in the year of the world 2,400 of the Egyptian Era. Here's how Aristotle described it in a supplement he wrote for his Dioptric, which he forgot in his pocket on the fatal day when he fell into the Euripus Strait. His contemporaries say that the piece was finished, but we have this fragment that I publish here after a copy that the doctor of the Great Mughal sent to me a few years ago: "The Sun had not appeared over our hemisphere for three whole days, but on the fourth of the month Oklouk at the second hour of the day, it was seen in all its brightness. The people were not used to losing it for so long and breathed a sigh of relief on its return. They ran around the country to enjoy the holiday of its welcome presence. But everyone stopped in surprise when they saw a bright body rise up

and the piece of land. It took the force of attraction away from the rays, but was not thick enough to prevent them seeping through, which obviously kept the body afloat and prevented it from plummeting.

But the cloud causing the drop dissipated and the land gradually rose again. When it reached a certain height it moved faster and looked like it was losing mass, becoming visibly smaller and smaller. I kept it in sight until it disappeared completely.

The event cast me into deep meditation. From this body's attraction I concluded many, very important things about physical facts that I had struggled with until then. I realized that the great bodies of the universe, like the Moon, Earth, planets, etc., got their movements from the sun's motive

---

into the sky and gather up all the rays of the Father of Light! The ministers of the temple of Jupiter were stunned by the phenomenon and bid the people turn to the god's mercy, saying that the comet in the skies was a powerful enemy rising up to overthrow his bright throne. The frightened people kneeled at the foot of the altars, screamed and wailed and waited for the universe to crumble at any moment. But the strange body was moving back and forth, sometimes totally eclipsing the sun and obscuring the Earth and then letting it reappear again like normal. The battle lasted for three hours, during which time the people were afraid that the sun would be overcome by how swiftly the phenomenon arose. However, when they were least expecting it, the comet suddenly faded away and disappeared completely. The priests of Apollo took advantage of this natural event to glorify themselves among the people by telling them that it was only through their prayers that Jupiter came to help Phoebus. Everyone believed it and ran to the temple to give thanks. For myself, not easily giving in to the errors of the common crowd and having examined things deeply, I figured that the phenomenon was a foreign body that the Sun's heat had attracted and then dissolved when it got too close." There's Aristotle's report on the matter. I thought I should cite it in this important place to prove without a doubt the passage in question. Moreover, it tells us something about Lamekis's chronology, which is a significant benefit that should never be overlooked and that I always strive for in my works—it costs me dearly, but can we ever do too much for the public?

164

force and that their movements were greater or lesser according to their distance from it and the strength of its rays, whether moving or not. This problem led me to another that proved to me even more strongly that the vapors sucked up from the Earth by the sun had to be carried up and coagulated, so to speak, by the degrees of heat and when they became bodies and were no longer supported by the oily juices forming it they lost their floating balance and dropped onto whatever was under them, which causes terrible catastrophes that are so startling because we don't know why. I also found that the rays were not caught in the coagulated mass of pores where they could be spread out to one another, but they slipped through and gave a false light to these pores.

The fruit of my observations and the subsequent flowering of thought in me spawned a desire, more fervent than ever, of supporting theory by practice. It had been a long time since I craved to have commerce with the higher Intelligences that inhabited the Ether. Although the learned writings of our ancient philosophers did not confirm that they really existed, I had never doubted that since there was life in the universe,[171] one of its largest parts, the sky, had to produce creatures that shared in its lightness and density. I reasoned very clearly that since material bodies and fluids housed animals, the air and

_____

[171] The Sylphan philosopher says that all the atoms that make up the universe are animals of different shapes and sizes that live and breed according to the instinct of visible creatures. He offers this maxim to explain the duration of nature's movement, demonstrating their regeneration as an indisputable point that compensates for the mortality of the species, which changes into other volatile substances to feed its kind who by their lives preserve the necessary movement that keep all the parts of the universe going. From these physics the Sylphs draw their knowledge of the creator and say that nothing offers stronger proof of its power than the variety found, according to their system, in all living atoms. Comparing it, then, with the uniformity in the human species, they show that of all animals man is the only one predestined for glory and his soul is immortal by this distinguished preference. These are the two pivotal points of the philosophy of the Island of the Sylphs.

matter had to generate and contain volatile substances higher than all known animals. My father had been given the precious manuscript of an immortal philosopher that proved to me that many sages were set above all others by their privilege of having real commerce with these Intelligences, which was such an incomparable advantage that they were led to the highest degree of metaphysical knowledge.

Although I had no sure indications, I was convinced of what until then I had only suspected because of the constant contradictions in men's thoughts and their fickle will, sometimes for and sometimes against, born and nurtured by an unknown inspiration, which the common crowd calls contemplation or reflection—when there is a choice between two things, at one time they lean toward one and at another time toward the other and sometimes they are so indecisive that it seems that there are two, totally separate wills in them that yield only to a higher being, which makes the final decision and moves the body or mind battling with itself. The names common people give to these changes in the soul seemed vague to me and did not at all reflect what I thought about the subject. I found it much easier and more natural to believe that the spirits created within the sphere of the universe were the causes of the contradictions that we so often fall prey to and that it was their good or bad nature that made us more or less unfortunate. I figured too that the soul, as ruling judge and absolute master, gave itself up to the good or bad Intelligences and then, being completely obsessed, followed its guide blindly.

I spent years contemplating these things and rarely did a day pass that I did not try to prove to myself these solid theories. I often went back to the place that first inspired me with the positive notions of the elevation of bodies into the sky. There I worked hard to figure out how to reward myself with traveling in the air. I would have worked for nothing because the mind is too obsessed by the body for these operations to be clear and distinct, but chance ended up accomplishing what so much study could not.

One night as I was climbing up one of the highest mountains in Phoenicia, my brain was so overheated grinding away at this project that I got a burning thirst that I could not ignore. In spite of my great contempt for the body, I started searching for a source of water to quench my thirst and wandered over the mountains for two or three hours. The harder I searched the worse I felt. On the brink of exhaustion I had to resort to drinking the dew that came from the night's humidity on the blades of grass where I lay down. I cupped as much as possible with my hands, but my burning head would not cool down so I laid out a handkerchief on the fresh grass. As soon as it was soaked with dew, I tied it around my head and felt so much better that in no time at all I fell into a sweet, peaceful sleep.

A strange, pleasant dream hovered over my tired senses: I felt like I was lifted off the ground and was carried into an atmosphere that was brighter than the sun. A wonderful palace made of clear stones rose up before me. A strange race of people like I had never seen before milled around, walking on the clouds, while other winged people flew through the skies. I walked slowly but confidently toward the massive men. When I got close enough I tried to talk to them, but as soon as I raised my voice they ran away screaming.

Dreams can be so odd that they change your way of thinking. A coward, while asleep, can overcome a danger that would scare him stiff just remembering it when he wakes up. And those who are afraid of nothing, when they close their eyes, their knees shake at something they would laugh at when awake. Well, that's where I was, I who had dreamed for so long to be blessed with knowledge of the Intelligences: I was afraid of the mere vision of them. I was barely close enough to see them, but my cowardice got a good look and at the sight I tried to run away in fear. One of the monsters (as I considered them) grabbed hold of me and threw me from on high to the Earth. My fall was so painful and seemed so real that I woke up screaming.

The Sun was beaming straight down on the mountain and everything was lost in its blinding light. Barely half-awake I did not understand right away the strange thing happening in the sky, which I had caused unknowingly. My troubled dream was obviously the reason why the dew-soaked handkerchief had come undone, fallen to the ground and was all of a sudden flying around in the air. I thought that it was being carried on the wind and I quickly got up to catch it, but it was already out of reach and rising higher and higher. But what really surprised me was that there was not even a breath of wind. Therefore, I concluded that the sunbeams were attracting it. It flew out of sight so fast that I knew I was right.

Convinced by this second proof that heat had this power of attraction and the air, its principle, could also attract earthly bodies, I wanted to try a more conclusive experiment right away. When I got back, I filled up a bunch of bladders with enough dew to carry out my project. Nine days before attempting my novel, reckless enterprise I started eating less and less, drank a lot and only answered the call of nature when it was absolutely necessary, convinced (as I was) that the dew water permeating all the porous parts of my body would lead to success. And to overlook nothing, I had a robe made of light cotton that I soaked in the wonderful dew during my entire fast. I was sure that the success of my project relied principally on this liquid.

Finally, one day when the sun was at its hottest, I went with all my preparations to the high mountain where I had had the mysterious dream and where my plan had been drawn up. I wore a harness with 200 bladders tied in a circle around it and two wings skillfully made, attached to my back like a shield, which I could move with my arms and I thought might help keep me afloat in case a cloud came between me and the sun. In a word, my precautions were so thorough and clever that it was impossible for my project to fail.

I waited very impatiently to be lifted from the Earth. My accurate compass, made with my own hands, showed that the Sun was entering its equinox and the thick steam from the humidity of my bladders warned me that I was about to see my plan go in action. Four of my bladders suddenly left the ground and little by little the others followed. My body was rattled by the movement, but was still too heavy to give in to the force of attraction. In my excitement and desire to leave the Earth I stood on my tiptoes and like a veteran high jumper trying to get off the ground, I jerked and pumped myself up and down. At last my efforts succeeded and my feet left the ground, but my body stayed still, unmoved. I was sorry then not to have got more bladders since it seemed that a few were still lacking to carry my weight. But I was wrong. The Sun was still not strong enough to suck me up. I was sure of it. Second after second the pull became so strong that six of my bladders broke their cords and shot up into the sky like arrows. My clothes, which had soaked in the dew for a long time, were fuming and created a thick cloud around me, obscuring my view and keeping me from seeing that I was rising up incredibly fast. My body seemed to open up and all of its pores felt pricked by sunbeams like by sharp, hot irons. The force of pressure was so great that I had to close my eyes and mouth— I felt like every part of my body wanted to escape through these openings. In short, the whole thing was so violent and so upsetting to all my organs that I got sick, intoxicated and I passed out.

I must have floated through the sky for the entire day because when I came to I did not see the sun anymore. It's true that I could see a countless multitude of stars just like it wherever I turned my head, but some were a little less bright and others looked brighter and the rays coming from these stars had a much weaker force than the one I saw as chief, which was also bigger than the others. I was not surprised at staying in the air without the initial force of attraction when I saw that the number of rays emanating from all the planets moving around me looked like so many swords whose blades crossed each other to form a kind of vault, which, despite their individual weakness, was able all together to support a heavy body. I also noticed the astounding fact that the bladders that had carried me into the air were all dried up from the heat of the sun and instead of lifting and supporting me as before, they were dragging me down by their extra weight. There was no doubt about it when I examined things more closely: without the crisscrossed rays supporting me, I would have plummeted from the sky into the unknown abyss.

After I had enough time to figure that there was really no danger in this and my body weight was of minor importance at this elevation (like a small boat floating on an endless sea), I needed to experiment to see if I could force it to move forward. To do this I thought it necessary to let go of the bulky bladders that were dragging me down, so I used the knife I had brought and started cutting the cords that tied them to me. As soon as I severed one it shot off like an arrow and was pushed by little, invisible globes farther and farther away, spinning around like a top, until it was out of sight. It was really pretty fun for me to watch the different ways the bladders took off into the air and the different paths they took when they were released, but I paid dearly for my fun, as you will see.

I was barely done with two thirds of the job when I felt myself spinning and unable to stop. I was going up toward a big, square body that emitted a pale light. I clearly saw then that the weight of the bladders and cords had served as a kind of counterweight against the force of these little bodies that were creating a whirlwind. I had been like a ship whose anchor held it back from being carried away by the current. Convinced of my reasoning, I stopped my task, but could not resist the whirlwind that kept spinning me around and pushing me toward the square body. Then I thought that I could use my wings to counteract it if they were not too awkward. As soon as I stretched out my arms the spinning stopped, but all the little globes ran against the flat figure at the same time and I felt myself hurled up toward the square body. The closer I got the bigger it got and I knew that there was nothing I could do to stop, but it looked like ground to me and I was hoping to be able to land there until I started veering off to the right and gradually moving away from it. I'll say in passing that the body was not lit everywhere, it was huge and only the highest parts of it, jutting up, caught the light, which made me think that it was the Moon and that the deep, dark areas were the spots we see from the Earth.

I was wrapped up in this observation when I was suddenly pushed into a liquid cloud that soaked me like I was passing through a river. Luckily the crossing was short, otherwise I might not have made it. It was like fresh snow, except for the color, which was purple, and the taste of sulfur, which proved that it was not from Earth.

After getting through this pesky snag, I found myself in a calm, clear sky. A cloud, whiter than snow, seemed to separate the other climes. I breathed freer and felt happier there. A delicious, healthy odor revived my dulled, tired spirits and I had an inner feeling that I had finally reached the goal I had sought for so long.

The shaking of the little globes, which had carried me up to this point in the sky, stopped all of a sudden and I saw a wonderfully built palace in the distance, which I felt eager to reach. But no matter how hard I beat my wings, I could not move a step forward. It was like a powerful hand was holding me back against all my efforts. In this unexpected difficulty, I remembered the weight I was carrying and I cut the rest of the cords and bladders that I thought were hindering me, but I got no farther out of my rut. I thought that the weight of my wings was also a detriment to my forward progress, so I unhooked my belt and let them go. This, too, was useless. I only had my clothes left and I ripped them off in anger and frustration. After all my vain efforts I was still not moving and now I was naked and hanging in the sky like a planet pinned down and only good as an ornament.

I started to get worried (what more could I do) in this extraordinary situation. I kept waving my arms and legs in the vain hope of being able to get out of the sluggish state, but I was unsuccessful. I racked my brain trying to figure out the obstruction, but it was all a mystery to me. Finally I resigned myself to the will of the Heavens and since I was not in pain, it was not hard for me to surrender to fate.

So, hanging in the sky like that and able to do nothing with my body, I figured I should make the best of the situation by examining everything I could see. I first looked at the cloudy body beneath me, which appeared oval and the strange rays striking it helped me make out some movements on the surface of the mass, which looked terrestrial to me. For the most part this new world looked very much like our Earth: I could spot mountains, seas, rivers and streams and using the spyglass I had brought with me (and was the only thing I had kept) I saw cities and towns and even some men, no bigger than flies from that distance, moving so slowly that I could barely see them.

To the right of this new world I saw a star that was brighter than the others and seemed to be lighting the land—I took it for the sun. From my vantage point I looked over the universe. Everywhere I looked I saw similar worlds, each one surrounded by a myriad of stars that made for its particular sky. Thus I supposed that every planet was a world like the one I had left, with its own sun, moon and orbits and despite the immensity of the universe, everything was built in perfect and exact uniformity.

I was admiring these things when the sky was suddenly crowded with a legion of living bodies cawing like crows and flying around all helter skelter over my head. Their number was as astonishing as their form. None of my books had prepared me for how they would look, which made me believe that I was the first one to get close enough to observe them. My pride convinced me that I had been singled out to witness this marvel. Among such spirits I felt so free that I dared to ask the closest Intelligence why I was nailed down, so to speak, in the sky. I asked the question in Chaldean, which I thought would be the most suitable language to converse with the spirits.

"Tremble, curious and profaning mortal," it answered in a hard, hoarse voice, "and fear the attack you are making. Are you not aware that the divine Scealgalis is the Sovereign here and he allows nothing impure? May the great King live forever and may they all die who aspire to know without being purified in the Ceolbhaume and by the dreadful skinning of materiality."

The Sylph had barely spoken these words when a chorus of similar spirits repeated them melodiously. The harmony was so powerful that I felt like the matter around me started moving. It was also so touching that I myself was shaken out of the inaction that had been troubling me. A dark night quickly followed, during which a male voice, whose beauty was inexpressible, sang a hymn to the glory of Scealgalis. I won't tell you about it, Lamekis, because you're not allowed to learn it until after the universal skinning.

(I took the liberty of interrupting the young philosopher here. "Is it allowed to ask you if the wisdom of the island's ruler had predestined you? I mean, your carnal ears heard the marvelous hymn without being purified, which privilege I cannot enjoy until after the final trial."

"That's a very good question," Dehahal responded, "but I can only tell you that the gods are the masters and they can favor someone for no reason but their own supreme will."

His observation was too sound to say anything more. I kept silent and Dehahal continued.)

When the hymn finished four Sylphs grabbed me and sliced through the air very fast. I don't know what divine, hidden force got hold of me, but I was not scared at all. On the contrary, I very coolly asked the Spirits what they planned to do with me.

"Cast you into the eternal fire," said the one who had already spoken. "Don't you deserve this punishment for your arrogant attempt to get to the Island of the Sylphs?"

"The Island of the Sylphs?" I broke in, carried away by joy and unaffected by the threats of punishment. "What? I have arrived at my longed-for destination? Ah! The cost would never be too high for the incredible pleasure of being here."

The Sylph stared at me. "Aren't you scared of dying?"

"No," I said, "because first I will have the happiness I've desired for so long."

"Kaliskiki,"[172] the second Sylph shouted. "Be careful what you are doing. This man is different than common mortals. The law orders us to cast everyone who is met on the Laeteecaklak[173] way into the Ceolbhaume,[174] but whoever is found on the Zi-al-bis[175] way does not fear death and thus he is special and in this case the law says that every foreigner shall live if does not fear death."

My Sylph guards gave in to the sage advice of the one who seemed to be protecting me. They went a little ways off and held a kind of council. It was decided that they would purify me in the Lakindakis[176] and during my ablution they

---

[172] The most serious oath a Sylph could take. The word meant "on the head of Scealgalis" and when it was pronounced you were obliged to follow the advice of the speaker.

[173] The way from the Island of the Sylphs to the Moon. These Sylphs were declared enemies of the lunar inhabitants. Not only was it forbidden by law to have any communion with them, but it was mandated to kill any they happened to meet. That was why everyone found on this way was seized and mercilessly thrown into the Ceolbhaume.

[174] See note on the Ceolbhaume at the beginning of Part 2. This is the same place with the slight difference that those who were thrown in without the mark of purification burned for all eternity.

[175] The cloud that apparently joined the Island of the Sylphs with the Earth. It was a special way and the Sylph guards were forbidden to deal with anyone found there without first informing Scealgalis.

[176] In Sylphan language it means "universal force." According to the astronomers, this place in the sky is located below Saturn. The Intelligences claim that it is where all matter dissolves into fluid and its impetus is given by the action of the fiery motive force. The sky is called glacial and changes according to the position of the Sun—when it is farthest away the sky is changed into ice, but when it gets closer the ice becomes hail, the hail turns to snow and when the sun is closest the snow becomes rain. The Sylphs look upon Lakindakis with great veneration. On coming back from a mission they purify themselves there like in a sacred bath that washes them of all the

would tell the Sovereign all about me. Then, one of the Sylphs left and the others carried me higher into the sky. When I had climbed hundreds of leagues into the sky, the extraordinary brightness of the stars was so strong that I could not stand the fire and I had to close my eyes in spite of my overwhelming desire to see the marvelous beauties that filled the Heavens.

Oh Lamekis, I cannot describe this brightness except by saying that it was stronger than anything you can imagine and despite veiling my eyes I saw through my eyelids the greatest spectacle the mind could ever dream of. What words could describe this magnificent sight? Only a divine mouth could express it and if it did, what mortal could understand?

Try to imagine, if you can, the combination of everything the human mind can conceive along with everything that fiction can imagine. The sky was violet purple, transparent and bold, and shining like with a million suns, each brighter than the next. Great starry circles of different colors seemed to support the vast immensity of the Heavens. In every direction there was no end to be seen because there was no end. Extension was followed by space and space by extension.

I looked straight up over my head and saw an extraordinary, opaque mass in the shape of a bee with outstretched wings. It was as big as the biggest whale and its back was covered with scales, moving as it breathed. It had countless feet in perpetual motion and when they rubbed against each other it sounded like the clatter of swords. As for its head, it is hard to say. It was like no other species of animal. Its face was long and square, shaped like a trapezoid, wider on top. In each of the angles near the collar were swellings in which were housed octagonal eyes whose visual point was a kind of sharp arrow that darted in and out like the swinging pendulum of a clock. At the other end of the head was a wide beak like an ostrich. The animal breathed so heavily that the beak opened and closed to pump the air in and out. The feet of this enorm-

---

stains that they might contract in the profane atmospheres where their duties led them.

ous bee had three claws that each had a human head hanging from it and each of their faces was twisted into a different expression of despair. Instead of hair on the animal's belly it was covered with crystal plates layered like roof tiles, but shining brightly and each with an image of a star on which you could see land, cities and people but all of it quite strange and far different from ours.

I was so astonished by all this and especially by the hideous hanging heads, whose desperate expressions were constantly changing, that it took a long time for me to realize my situation. Feeling all wet and starting to lose courage, I opened my eyes. You can't imagine how horrified I was. I was swimming in a river of blood and being raised up steadily by a column of the same liquid. I looked up in the sky and what did I see? The beak of the hideous bee was opening. I thought it was just breathing, but it was actually trying with all its might to suck me in and swallow me. I lost my head then and started wriggling around and waving my arms in fear, like a drowning man. I struggled to escape the looming danger, but my efforts were useless. The column rose higher and I was soon in range of the deadly beak. Then the monster shook its huge head, moved forward, opened its mouth wide, sniffed and swallowed me whole.

I closed my eyes in horror. I felt myself being ground up, like wheat grain in a mill, by a rack of teeth that were as sharp as razors. My soul was soon separated from my body, but by an unheard of marvel every part of my hacked up body felt its own pain. Only my eyes remained whole and slipped through its teeth. They watched the gruesome dismemberment of the body that they had once belonged to and recognized the soul that looked like a coiled spring, struggling to escape the bee's crop engulfing it like a pocket closed tight, but in vain.

Besides their normal abilities my eyes seemed to have taken on those of my other senses, which had so often affected them. Worried about what was happening to their body they looked around in the huge belly of the fly. Since there was light filtering through everywhere it was easy for them to see what was happening inside the animal's stomach. The limbs were not yet ground up enough to be unrecognizable, but the animal's muscles, like a thousand hammers, were beating them so hard that they were gradually losing their distinctiveness and were being mixed up with the boiling blood that was thickening and changing color.

My eyes could find no trace of my head in the munching belly of the awful bee, but found it near the heart. It was full of holes spitting out a red, fiery spirit that slowly seared the skull. The brain looked as black as ink and throbbed as wildly as the flank of a steed after a long run.

I was astonished at how my eyes could think without a soul, but I soon got over this surprise when I saw that there was a fiber at the end of my pupils that was connected to other lineaments coming from my soul, which stiffened as it struggled to escape.

I was still in wonder at all this when my eyes were attacked by a horde of insects that were obviously born out of the putrefaction. They were so small that if there were not so many to make a thick cloud of them, it would have been hard to see a single one of them. They were round with a stinger that kept pricking my eyes, which were missing their eyelids that could have warded off the repeated assaults, but instead the liquid in my eyes poured out into the animal's beak. Despite its being emptied, the liquid could still feel in horror the animal's tongue licking it and sucking it down into the stomach where it finally lost all feeling, or better said where it became lethargic.

Meanwhile my soul, which was still trying to escape and reunite with its body, suddenly felt itself drawn up and enclosed again in the brain it had left. Then my eyes opened and I saw they were attached to the head and the head to the body, which seemed to wake up as if from a deep sleep. On closer examination, I found that I was back to myself and instead being inside that awful place, I was sitting on the back of the bee whose carnivorous beak was doing all it could to swallow me back down. Scared of this I kept moving around to escape

177

from it, but the bee's neck was so flexible that my efforts to avoid becoming prey were in vain. The moment finally came when I was about to be gulped back down and suddenly a Sylph appeared, thundering out, "That's enough! Scealgalis is satisfied." With that the animal disappeared and losing my support, I tumbled in the air.

But there was nothing to fear! I was in the arms of the Sylph. He became invisible in an instant, but reappeared when he sneezed and smiled at me. "I got the mercy of the Island's Sovereign and after the customary preparations I will introduce you to him."

His words made me happy deep down inside. Lamekis, I cannot express how delightful the spiritual goods are. When I got to the foot of Scealgalis' throne, I could not stand the divine sight. My soul felt like it was soaring off in pleasure, all my senses were lost and I became lethargic.

I was drawn out of the peaceful state by the melody of a chorus of divine voices. Why couldn't I stay like that for a minute longer? But I opened my eyes and then closed them right away in horror. I was being skinned alive and my blood was pouring out of all my pores. Four Sylphs were there, wringing out my stripped skin like a wet sheet. Even though it no longer belonged to my flesh, I felt everything they did to the skin with convulsive pains.

I screamed so loudly that I quivered. A fifth Sylph came up, armed with a steel stylus whose point was as red as if it had just come out of a burning forge. "Dehahal," it said, looking at me proudly. "There's still time. You are suffering impatiently, but you can still stop your torments. The hide of your wretched body has not yet received the sacred marks. It's up to you whether you want them or would rather go back to crawl on the Earth that your virtue pulled you off of. Think about it. But realize that you are the only one who has been given this royal gift from our divine Monarch without passing through the trial of 12 tables. This favor is worth more than a thousand lives. And realize, too, that if you go back to your old self, which he wants to strip you of completely, you will forever lose the goods that you aspired to for so long."

"No, no," I cried out in sorrow. "I'll go back into nothingness before I think or act so cowardly. Do it! Skin me a thousand times, as long as I can rejoice in the supreme happiness of sharing in the sacred goods."

I had barely finished speaking when the four Sylphs beat their wings and the air rang out with cheers. Silence followed and the four Sylphs stretched out my skin, each one pulling their side tight. The Intelligence with the stylus went up and with the burning, sharp point imprinted the following privilege, which was painfully engraved on my heart at the same time:

Privilege of Initiation:

"Scealgalis, by the grace of the Great Being, Ruler of all created Intelligences and all that will be, Dispenser of the divine rays that give life and take it away, hidden Creator of all the insects and reptiles, Driver of the great circles of the Universe, Primary Instigator of the internal and spiritual movements of earthly animals, Protector of sentiments, Alembic of all the natural and metaphysical sciences, Sole Possessor of the Great Work and of the liquefaction of all the fluid planets, Creator of all elixirs. For all the Sylphs, both white and black, emanating from the Great Being. Greetings. Our dear and well-beloved Kaagilgon, having humbly shown us that in the earthly formation of the Phoenician animal Dehahal, he would have been summoned, called and chosen to be his guide and spiritual leader and therefore he would have carried it out with so much care and diligence that the breath of the black spirit never would have tarnished the napping of Dehahal's heart unless Kaagilgon had been fortunate enough to get hold of it so that he could inspire it with the desire to see us up close without any outside help, as was fitting. For this he prayed that we look upon his applicant's grand character and more than human courage, trying to get us to grant our letters of grace to be received bodily on our divine Island under the conditions that conform to our laws, ways and customs and that he will never return to Earth, according to our just policy, for fear that our secrets will be revealed and profaned.

"For these reasons, wanting to treat Kaagilgon well and to recognize the vigilance, talent and zeal in his spirit, as well as to give him the signs of my wholly royal kindness, through the sealed gifts of my breath I grant him the right to bring the said Phoenician Ladinkakis, his student, and in addition, by special favor, I let him be eaten by the great bee, my honored insect that I hereby command to digest him but only on the condition that after the kneading is done it give up the applicant in one piece to Kaagilgon to skin him alive and afterwards to teach him my laws, ways and customs so that he can enjoy all the privileges that my unmatched gentleness grants to my subjects, except for invisibility and immateriality, which will only be granted to him three days after his death on the condition that this privilege be inscribed all along the applicant's skin and this skin be handed over and hung in the treasury of my archives to be used accordingly. I command, entreat and order all the officers who are living on this Island and who are envoys to the earthly world to recognize Dehahal as one of my third class subjects and to take him by the hand so that he will enjoy all the favors that I have granted to him. I order my Loug-hou-kou[177] to have all this published by my Laniska[178] so that no one can pretend to be ignorant, despite the desperate shouting of the black spirits to oppose it. Given in my fantastic palace on the Island of the Sylphs with no date or year."[179]

SCEALGALIS,
By the King without counsel, LOUG-HOU-KOU."

---

[177] Guardian of the royal pen who acted as the secretary of state.

[178] The great bee. It had the privilege of proclaiming Scealgalis's orders. For this, every citizen living on the island had to give it a certain number of corpses, which the Sylphs got from the inhabited planets.

[179] It was forbidden on the Island of the Sylphs to date anything or have any time-measuring instruments, thinking that true happiness had no limits and was subject to no change.

When the privilege was engraved on my skin, the Sylph Kaagilgon was carried away with joy. He gave me the spiritual accolade and split his tongue, the greatest of all favors.[180]

But, Lamekis, I hope that what follows will show you how sweet it is to purchase bliss.

Hardly had my old human skin been deposited in the treasury of the archives[181] when my wasted muscles were suddenly covered with a new one. And as soon as I was decked in this bodysuit my mind understood things in a completely different way than they had before. My once spellbound eyes saw clearly now and knew the truth.[182]

Only one essential formality was missing for my initiation: the sacred reading of the customs, laws and manners.[183] Since it was the basis on which an aspirant had to rely and I had the right to share these treasures (when one is made worthy by the steadfastness shown in the trial of the 12 tables), and since I have the right to tell my story so that it might serve as an example and introduction,[184] I will tell it accurately so

---

[180] Peculiar favor and one of the greatest that a Sylph could give to a mortal. It consisted in breaking a tooth. For even greater distinction Kaagilgon broke four of his for Dehahal. History says that such grace was never given to any other man, which makes gives all scholars great respect for this philosopher.

[181] Tower in which they kept the skins of those who rendered great service to the island. The skins were used as dowries for the daughters whom the state married—it was the greatest good that they could bring to their husband, a sure proof of their special nobility. In the grand ceremonies the women wore them like long coats and were thereby set apart from the ordinary nobles.

[182] The Sylphs claimed that before being skinned the mind was weighed down by matter and saw things through a cloud making it impossible to tell the difference between the true and false.

[183] It seems that the author wanted to slip this in: that one cannot truly be an upright man without being thoroughly instructed in the laws of one's country.

[184] Dehahal gives an important lesson in this passage to those whom the ministry has put in charge of leading other men by teaching them that a good example is the best way to put and keep them on the right

that you can meditate well on it and make the right decision about what you still have to suffer before reaching your goal. For, as happy as you will be to get there, as much and more will you have reason to groan if you have qualms about such a divine state in your time of temptation. Then unhappiness will fall upon you and rage and desperation and an eternity of evils and suffering.[185]

After the extraordinary renewal of my skin, I was led in pomp to the Opaque Palace[186] (where we are now) by Loughou-kou, flying at the head of countless Sylphs singing a divine hymn. After the first group came the semi-Sylphs on foot on the cloud Kikizigambis.[187] In their mouths they had a kind

---

path. You can glory in your good just like you must recognize your faults. The first produces admiration, the other punishes pride.

[185] The philosopher insinuates here that it is not enough to strive for the good, you must persevere in it. He also seems to be saying that the loss of happiness because of our own fault drags in its wake such cruel regrets that it is the worst imaginable punishment. See Hensius, *On Suffering*, p. 42, vol. 5, Holland Edition.

[186] Built of tiles of thunder just like the tower of archives and all material places. The author is mistaken in saying that no body suffered on this island, unless he tacitly omitted the earthly exhalations petrified by the sun where everything was created in the air, as unique to their substance.

[187] To really understand this passage you have to have an idea of what the opacity of the island was like. The best comparison is to the way Venice was built. Put the sky in place of the sea or, if you'd like, imagine that there were solid clouds that could carry the third-class inhabitants of this region. For, no offense to the original but the Island of the Sylphs is of a mixed nature. It is so well known today that I would be abusing the reader's pleasure by trying to prove such a basic truth. Enough Frenchmen have returned to back up what can only be mentioned in passing here, but since life is full of unbelievers, who spend their time doubting everything, let's pray they are honest enough to make the journey themselves to the Island of the Sylphs. The story of the philosopher Dehahal shows the way to get there. With such clear details it cannot be hard to reach and we can hope that after coming back they will want to do justice to the truth.

of Triton horn instrument[188] that made a sweet, melodic sound. Kaagilgon was at their head carrying a flag with a picture of the great bee vomiting out a mortal. The painting was transparent and drawn with sublime skill.

I followed the second-class inhabitants[189] of the Island, dragged along by four semi-Sylphs by my hair with my belly to the ground. The march lasted 15 painful hours during which time I could not help silently cursing all philosophy and philosophers.[190] However good we are deep down, the human always shows itself somewhere.

From where the procession began up to the avenue of the Opaque Palace, the third-class inhabitants[191] of the Island lined up on the side of the road. In their hand they held a dish,[192] like a chafing dish, that gave off a pleasant, fragrant smoke forming a big, thick cloud around them. The sound of the horns came from far enough away that it was no bother. Behind the row of citizens were the Sylph women[193] covered

---

[188] We see here that the philosopher was also an orator and could not help making such a rich comparison. The text translated word for word says that the instruments called Triton horns were human bladders with three holes that they continually blew with their lips. The wind coming out of the holes made a very sweet, very odd sound.

[189] Semi-Sylphs changing species every 12 hours. What the common people call sprites or pixies.

[190] Which shows that patience and perseverance are the necessary virtues to reach the greatest happiness. Yet it seems that the author gives philosophy a slap in the face here because he is tired and fed up.

[191] Composed of normal men who were favored or recruited by the Sylphs.

[192] The first condition that a man had to fulfill when he became an inhabitant was to always carry his dish. It looked like the bottom of a lamp hanging from an iron handle and in it he had to keep a very pungent gum burning in order to keep away the black spirits. In the course of time they became so used to it that they could never live without it, even if it were outlawed.

[193] Women appeared only in public celebrations. There are two kinds on the island. The first kind, born of the Sylphan race looks like

with their Cankragard.[194] Even though their form was different than our women, I could not help finding them attractive. The third line was formed by the mortal Peu-plau-keki[195] of our species. I watched these beauties wantonly and if it were not for the painfully awful way I was being dragged, which was torturing me, I would have been very sorry to give up this eyeful. But it is terribly difficult for a soul to have sensual thoughts when the body is steeped in suffering.

After the Peu-plau-keki the march was closed off by the big Sylphan horses. The species astounded me: the animal's head was like a stag but instead of ears it had two transparent wings; no neck, a perfectly round belly and instead of a tail it had a fan of feathers that opened and closed like wings. The horses were ridden by a different kind of semi-Sylph. I could

---

them. Despite their extraordinary figures they are so beautiful that mortals can fall passionately in love with them. The second kind of woman is normal like ours. Whatever the Sylphs might say about how crude we are, they are naturally inclined to love our women. When they find one on Earth who pleases them, they find a way to kidnap them and reasons to get them accepted on the island. Later on we will see some special features that will explain this passage better, which is pretty difficult in the original.

[194] Ashes of burned fingernails that the women had to cover their foreheads with to show that they were nothing but dust compared to their husbands. Fortunately there is a passage in Gregory of Tours' *Ceremonies* where he deals with the subordination of women toward their husbands. He says that on the Island of the Sylphs the women are so respectful and so subordinate that they were not allowed to walk on both legs. The greatest favor a husband could give his wife was to let her change feet, but it was only given on special occasions. The learned minister from Charenton goes even further and assures us that if by chance a woman stumbled or was caught on both her feet, they cut one off right then and there and she was forced to wear it around her neck for the rest of her life. The author gives the credible example of the wife of a chief minister, which would be too long to reproduce here.

[195] Women married by the state who had the right to attend the grand ceremonies.

not see their head, but they had an eye in each of their shoulders and their mouth was placed above their belly button. When they stretched out their arms I could see their ears covered by a bell-shaped layer of skin. Their hands were normal except that the fingers were attached with pliant flesh that let them move every which way. The strange bodies ended in large, fat thighs with rounded points at the end that made them jump instead of walk.

In the middle of their chest was a large nose whose nostrils were on the back, which they used as a trumpet—the different ways of touching it made different sounds.

I learned later that this strange species came from a people who lived on one of the nearby planets. One of their chief ministers had revolted against the fundamental laws, wanting to believe in a higher power than theirs, and was thrown off the planet and received by a Sylph who accepted him and his followers on this Island.

When we got to the gates of the grand avenue of the Opaque Palace, the parade stopped for an essential ceremony whose strict observation I thought would destroy the fulfillment of my happiness because I got so impatient.

The people were not allowed to go any farther. I had to separate from then at this moment and accept their compliments, though some decided to rant and rave at me. The Loughou-kou, a strict observer of custom, was very pleased to do me the honor of showing me to the assembly. He grabbed me by my ear[196] and lifted me in the air while giving a heartfelt, elegant speech as a defense of my behavior during the trials and the reasons why I deserved the glorious benefit of initiation.

It was terribly hard for me to listen to my own panegyric. The orator would not stop and to make matters worse his

---

[196] Sign of particular distinction when a Sylph meets another inhabitant of the island and wants to show his respect; he pulls his ears and drags him around like that, which means "I respect you, you're a good man, you can count on me."

bombastic speech was punctuated with such wild gestures that my poor ears were livid and flayed.

When the speech was over, the people applauded.[197] It's true, however, that I caught a glimpse of the cabal of critics and a few of them were protesting some of the bold compliments and daring rhetoric used by the orator. But they got over it and everyone approved the novelties.

I was put back down on the ground to accept the farewells from the audience. Each of the classes sent their deputies to congratulate me on becoming one of their members. The ceremony that went along with their compliments was not one of the least painful experiences I endured up to then. It was, however, a distinction that had to flatter my vanity since it was a sure sign of consideration that tickled me as delicately as you could when you want to make someone laugh, but which hurt me no less than the former pains.

When the people had left Kaagilgon allowed me to walk normally.[198] I was in dire need of this favor and without it I do not know if I could have put up with being dragged on my belly for much longer because it was really very painful.

It was with great pity that I went down the grand avenue. Looking up into the bordering trees I saw the most spectacular sight: to understand it, you have to know that the people are

---

[197] The applause was made by picking up stones and throwing them at the head of the speaker. The more contusions he got the more people liked him. After the speech there were men with the specific duty of picking up the stones that had been thrown. Then they put them in a balance and invited the critics to get onto the other side. They were accepted, however many of them there were, and when there were no more they hung the scales. If the stones were heavier they recorded the approval of the speech and it was used as a model for young orators. As for the critics who had stood firm against it, they threw them in a well that was heaped with the same stones that proved their envy and treachery.

[198] Surprising acquiescence that would put this passage in doubt if so many other authors mentioning it did not incline us to believe it, since no mortal was allowed to walk on the ground of the sacred island until he had been initiated as an inhabitant.

forbidden on the grand avenue unless they accept the scaffold on the major holidays as is stipulated in their privileges. The scaffold in this case consists of being hanged by the nostrils on poles that are highly praised on these solemn days. There were so many of these curiosity seekers that for four hours on the road not a space was vacant of these voluntarily hanged men. If I were not worrying about the pain that I wrongly imagined they must have felt, I would have found it a pleasant sight, even more so since they were doing exercises with their arms and legs[199] that I cannot describe but were weird and yet nice to watch.

When we got to the first courtyard of the Palace the triple signal was given and everyone who had shown up until then disappeared quickly. They put me back on my belly, crossed the courtyard and scaled the stairs, dragging me by hair the whole way. I protested and yelled as loudly as I could. I felt like I was bleeding and that there was not one part of my guts that was not on the verge of spilling out. In fact, I was so convinced of this that when I finally had the chance, I touched everywhere I hurt, sure that I would be chafed and bloody. But everything was fine and the only discomfort I felt was a dampness[200] that had the lovely smell of rotten venison.[201] Our imagination invents half our evils. After this brief examination, I felt only a superficial pain and figured that I owed the

---

[199] The citizens of the island were great jugglers and hustlers. What is mentioned here is practicing all the agility and artifice to do the most extraordinary things. It was from this island that swindling came to Earth and when a man excelled in this craft you can be sure that a black spirit was in him and could be found under every cup.

[200] We can assume that Dehahal's suffering, with exaggerated details, was only in his mind and the dampness he talks about comes from his overworked imagination.

[201] This would seem to be ironic and surprising if we did not know that the more unpleasant a smell was, the more welcome it was on this island. On this basis, a modern author cracked a joke that when we passed foul wind, it was a Sylph caught in our body trying to escape.

fortunate situation to the solidity of my new skin and it would serve me well in the future.

As soon as we entered the magnificent room where the triple roll[202] was kept two Sylphs grabbed me by my feet and hung me in the air to listen to the reading of the sacred history. They opened an altar with a statue of Scealgalis on it, but before taking out the roll, they pulled out two of my teeth[203] from each side and burned them before the idol using the reflected rays of the sun. A Sylph sat on the ground with a special instrument that he filled with the smoke from my burning teeth. When it was filled up he squirted it into my mouth so hard that it blew out of my eyes and ears. The operation was so violent that I started bleeding out of everywhere blood could possibly issue.

I thought I was going to give up the ghost considering my condition, but no sooner was the triple roll taken out of the sanctuary than the bleeding stopped. And then a Sylph forced a crystal stone[204] into my mouth that as soon as it touched me it calmed me down. My soul quivered in joy and my balanced mind listened eagerly.

The author's story

Part 4 finishes here and no trace of Dehahal's story is found in Part 5, which makes me think that there is a considerable lacuna or a number of missing pages in the manuscript. I

---

[202] The triple roll was made of a human skin that was so strong you could shave off three layers without weakening it.

[203] The Sylphs claimed that they were harmful to conception as they were earthly bodies that the volatile spirits could not pass through. No inhabitant of the island was allowed to keep them. The first thing they did to a newborn baby was to pull out its gums in order to destroy the very roots of these vile accessories.

[204] The author did not interpret this passage well. The stone in question was a piece of ice and the cold stopped the bleeding. One can never be too careful when translating: the slightest ambiguity casts a dark shadow, which happened more than once in this work.

thought I could compensate for it by looking among the most learned writers for some passages that might help me finish this interesting story and ended up spending two years in the best libraries leafing through all the scholars who wrote anything on the subject and especially those who commented on the adventures of Lamekis. I started to get discouraged by so much wasted effort when an extraordinary adventure happened to put an end to this work, which deserves to be mentioned here.

One day when I was coming back from the Bibliothèque du Roi, very depressed after spending a whole day leafing through 20 volumes without finding anything at all concerning the lacuna, I noticed as I turned off Rue de la Richelieu that I was being followed by a big, black dog that would not stop staring at me. My affection for these domestic animals prompted me to pet it and it seemed happy that I did so. I went on my way without thinking that it would continue to follow me and I got home paying no attention to it.

During the night I had disturbing but extraordinary dreams and the strangest thing of all was that they were all about the big dog. Nevertheless, when I woke up I forgot all about the dreams as I usually did, except that when I put my head out the window they came rushing back: the black dog was there at my door looking at me. Its determination to follow me and stare at me when it saw me made me shiver—I was so shook up that I had to have some chocolate to brace my stunned senses. I felt better and went back to the window—the dog was still there. I figured that he must be hungry and his staring eyes were nothing but pleas for my sympathy, so I brought him something to eat, but instead of jumping at the piece of bread I offered, it started howling with such an astonishing voice that all the yapping little dogs in the neighborhood left their yards to come to see what it was, and a bunch of basset hounds started barking in the distance at the big dog whose deep voice was so aggressive that it scared them. The neighbors were upset by this canine stir and encouraged their dogs to chase off the awful howler. A guard dog being goaded by its master tried to come up, but was thrown down and pounced upon so furiously that the rabble cooled down.

But my neighbor obviously took personal pride in his dog's strength and felt insulted by what had just happened, so he picked up a piece of sandstone and threw it hard at the victor. Imagine his and everyone's surprise when the stone was swallowed whole and the dog kept howling. The good people imagined it was a sorcerer; the smartest got furious and accused each other of causing it. Finally they all went back home, not wanting to be exposed to the anger of the mad animal.

However, a new challenger, who had not shared his plan with anyone, came out with a rifle, gave warning, took aim and fired. But his gun misfired. He used all his wiles to light the powder. He shouldered it again and a second failure. Maybe the powder was wet; he had to replace it and did the same with the flint. A third time cocked and our hair was standing on end. A frivolous hope! The cock was sprung, the priming pan opened and the powder just sat there.

The entire neighborhood was stunned by the marvel. They started moaning and groaning that the dog was definitely a sorcerer. For myself, who saw things differently, I imagined that there was something extraordinary involved, but the dog only wanted me personally. With this in mind, I got dressed and went out. When the black dog saw me it stopped howling and started wagging its tail. The brave man who had tried so hard to shoot it came up to me and told me very empathically everything that happened. I told him I had seen the whole thing and I whispered to him to give up his plan because all his efforts would be in vain seeing that the dog in question was a werewolf. I advised him to be on his guard since after all the harm he had tried to do he should be scared that the dangerous animal would get its revenge by eating him up the first chance he got. When I finished I turned the corner and left the brave man turning whiter than the whites of his eyes.

I could not take another step the entire day without the black dog following me. Not knowing what else to do under

190

such extraordinary circumstances, I went far out of the way so that if there was some unknown mystery, I could give the dog a chance to let me know what it was. It seemed to work. Going toward the suburb Saint-Antoine, it went down into the ditches and turned around as if inviting me to follow. It was getting late and as much as I wanted to satisfy my curiosity (which you must think only right), I did not think that at that time of night I should expose myself to a situation that might prove dangerous without taking the necessary precautions. With that in mind I turned back and found a coach to take me back home.

The next night I was startled awake by very pleasant music coming from the road. My passion for this art got me out of bed thinking of the beauties milling around my neighborhood of La Butte Saint Roch. I was curious to hear and find out who was being serenaded, so I stuck my head out the window. And I was amazed to see in the light of four ominous torches carried by four shaggy dogs a dozen white great danes holding paws and dancing around the big, black dog that was barking a tune and keeping the beat and melody. I rubbed my eyes, thinking that I was still asleep and the mists of some extraordinary dream were causing this strange sight. It took a long time for me to realize that I was totally awake and that the big dog had a reason for being so set on following me.

Part 5

I stared hard at the extraordinary sight before me and was trying with all my might to imagine how dogs could talk and act like people when a new and even more amazing scene interrupted my thoughts and grabbed my attention.

Oh Intelligence, you who inspired me so many times, you who controlled all the actions of my life, you whom I can feel acting inside me and who never abandoned me, guide my pen, direct my words and tell, with the fire that is so natural to you, the marvels that I witnessed. Without you what mortal would dare to describe such wondrous deeds? Don't they have in them the divine character of truth? Yes, no doubt. They offer the mind convincing and consoling ideas. And you, sublime philosophers, great Dehahal and famous Lamekis, who are still alive today after so many centuries, light me up with your immortal rays. It's done. I have it. The spark has flashed and I feel it inside me—let's begin.

The four shaggy dogs who were lighting the dance of the danes with torches and had not moved until then suddenly got up, jumped all together at the big black dog and set its fur on fire. A black, smelly smoke rose up and became so thick that soon I could see nothing, but I could hear a howling that was so awful it made me shiver, in spite of my resolve. A cold sweat ran down my forehead. The principles that I always armed myself with against all events in life were useless—it tried to make me blush for being so weak. The human succumbed. I withdrew, closed the window and my eyes and buried myself in bed where things happened to me that I cannot think about without shuddering.

I was so afraid that I did everything I could not to think about it. I tried to hide deeper in my bed. I felt something cold and hairy lying next to me. My hair stood on end. I wanted to jump out of bed, but a horrible nightmare kept me nailed in place. I could barely breath and could hear nothing but a loud noise in my room like people coming and going and discussing some important affair.

An instant later I felt my eyes opening against my will. I brought my hands up afraid that they were betraying me, that they wanted me to see frightening things. But it was useless! Two powerful arms were one step ahead of me, holding down my hands and forcing me to make use of my cruel sense of sight. I yelled in terror when I saw my tyrant: it was a worm man, exactly like I had described in *Lamekis*. The worm part was what I felt cold and slimy in my bed; the rest of the body was behind me holding me down like I said. I naturally tried to get out of its grip, but an awful, nasally noise threatened my life if I continued to squirm. Finally, I sighed in sorrow and gave in to whatever was going to happen to me.

They were not as unpleasant as my fear had imagined. I'll say, on the contrary, that they looked very much like my former conception of them, which proved to me the truth of an idea I had about our eternal memory. But I really had to be surprised at seeing that what until then I had thought was only a figment of my imagination now bore a real, genuine relation to past events, which had really taken place and in which, obviously, I was involved somehow, since I had described them in such detail, so precisely and accurately in the adventures of Lamekis, which I had published more than two years ago. What was about to happen would prove all this.

I was, as I said, in the position of a man forced to watch what was in front of him. I was quietly and resentfully moaning under this control when a mysterious-looking woman suddenly appeared, pale and racked with guilt. "You know me, traitor," she said to me. "Aren't you afraid? What did I do to be painted with such black, nefarious colors? Don't you recognize Semiramis, the offended Queen whose shadow, as powerless as you thought I was, can still make you sorry for having revealed my weaknesses unless you do as I say. There is only one way to make up for your vicious attacks on my reputation. Change the people's minds. The adventures of Lamekis are not finished. Do it. And give me back the honor that was taken away by your vile work. In the next parts, take back all the bad things you said about me. Then I will forgive you and contribute all the credit that my crimes earned for me in hell to fill you with a fire that will be appreciated in the results of your work. Take revenge for me on the wisdom of the High Priest Lamekis by making up some secret Memoir that shows him to be a villain. Boldly say that he himself wanted to take me down and I knew how to resist him. Above all, hide from posterity my awful desperation after being exposed by Lamekis and his family on the sea, with no masts, no sails and no provisions. In no way admit how I died. Paint my guilty end with the colors of virtue. The worst punishment, when we no longer exist, is to hear our reputation torn apart. Since that fatal hour when your book appeared, my torments have multiplied. Readers add to them every day and thus to the horror they feel against me. Do what I say and you will relieve my sorrow. Cruel author, can you refuse me?"

With that the Princess disappeared and it seemed like an army of snakes followed her as she screamed out that they were tearing her apart. Just punishment for her hideous crimes!

I did not have much time to consider it. A large number of all kinds of characters passed before my timid eyes. A man with a blue face like I wrote about in *Lamekis*, dragged on a leash by the Furies, spoke to me out of foaming mouth: "Tell the world about my tragic fate and make my story serve as an example to jealous, distrustful spouses. My anger made me deny everything virtuous among women for doubting my wife's loyalty. It's a horrible crime to condemn someone without listening to them, to punish them without proof! Poor Houcaïs! What good was my sweet love for wise Nasildaë[205] if it only burned to throw her in the abyss and cover me with

---

[205] [Motacoa's mother, also called Hildaë—not the princess Nasilaë—tr. note]

194

blood and horror? How many victims did I sacrifice to take my revenge for an imaginary attack? What was the point of so much bloodshed? To prove to me through my repentance and remorse that I alone was guilty, that I was the abomination of Kings? It's a deadly power when it is used only to commit crimes! Listen, you who were chosen to write all these wonders, and learn how I found out about my injustice and crime. I owe you this explanation. A higher authority, the protector of the innocent, is forcing me. What you don't yet know about will serve to restore the honor of a spouse whom I was unworthy of and for whom I suffer for eternity."

The story of the Houcaïs

Nasildaë had just been thrown into the pit of Houzaïl. I was furious at having to lose such a dear wife and decided to kill the wretched architect of the alleged seduction. To do this I ordered the Balkagous[206] to arrest all the white men found in their states and to send them to the capital for me to sacrifice for my revenge. Not content with the arrests, I appointed men to find out on the sly if anyone was hiding them out of sympathy and if any of my subjects were affected by some unlawful compassion, they themselves suffered the death sentence that was meant for the miserable white men they were protecting.

All my time and energy since the loss of Nasildaë was spent in questioning and putting to death the white men. I held on to the hope that in the end my thoroughness would earn me the sweet satisfaction of seeing the lethal instrument of my dishonor fall into my hands, but alas, after a few years of blood and crimes I decided to find comfort for my sorrow in the arms of another woman. I shut myself up with her in the royal den, but to no avail! The idea of revenge and my suspicions buried me in the most dreadful melancholy. In a fit I stabbed the new queen when I caught her dishonoring me. This proof of women's wickedness made me think of them

---

[206] Governors of the provinces.

195

with horror. And still, I had a dream that brought back my desire to prove Nasildaë's infidelity and to kill myself if it turned out that she was innocent. I was inspired by my mysterious dream: I witnessed the birth of a white boy by a white woman although her husband was my color. It seemed that this vision proved Nasildaë's innocence—what happened was a natural phenomenon and in no way dishonored me. To be absolutely sure of such a delicate matter I decided to find positive proofs that would leave no room for doubt.

For this I ordered the Balkagous throughout my kingdom to find white women at any cost and send them to me. They had quite a hard time obeying me because of how cruelly I treated this species. Even though I had not had any women of this kind killed, they were convinced that my hatred had grown and I wanted to spread it to anyone related to them. I had foreseen this problem and given sure guarantees to the contrary and I put the fear of death in the officers in charge of this mission if they did not carry out my orders within a fixed period of time. So, I had reason to be satisfied. After a few months 40 of them came to me from different parts of the country and right away I did with them what I had planned.

I shut each of them up with a man of my species to see if it was true that a white child could come out of such a coupling. To make no mistakes in this experiment that was so important to me, I kept its purpose to myself alone. What more can I say? At the end of a year 20 of the women gave birth and 5 of the children were born white, both girls and boys. I did not want to know any more. I judged myself guilty and the most miserable of men.

As soon as I was convinced of the truth I became desperate. I wanted to die, but, oh, how hope always shines in our soul. Before accomplishing my final act I wanted to try everything that could possibly be done. So, I had all the cords that were used to cast the poor men and women into Houzaïl tied end to end and after reaching a length of more than 10,000 fathoms I planned to go down there myself.

Maybe, I thought to myself, I would find a clue of what happened to my poor wife. In any case I would die of the same punishment—that was the least I owed to her offended *manes*. The project was no sooner planned than carried out, in spite of the opposition of my chief minister in whom I had confided and whom I had chosen to drop me down into the earth's opening.

The night was set for the grand project. Before going down into the pit of Houzaïl I gave a letter with the Royal Seal to my chief minister in which I named him regent of my kingdom. He would govern it until I came to take the scepter back. Properly speaking, in any case, I named him as my successor. I knew him as an honest man and he had so often proved his skill and loyalty by opposing all the crimes I was inclined to commit that I had no doubt that my people would be grateful for such an equitable choice, which might make up, in some way, for all the harm I did to them.

After that I got in the device built for the purpose along with a criminal whom I had chosen to accompany me for his punishment. It took us three days and nights to descend. On the fourth day the slave and I stopped moving. I had agreed with my chief minister that if by some unforeseen miracle I reached the bottom of the abyss, I would pull on a string to follow out the orders I had given. Around an hour after the signal was given, the device lifted up again in order to let down the provisions and slaves that I might need in my plan…[207]

The author's extraordinary adventure

The Houcaïs was at this point in his story when a winged man who yelled out, "That's enough," suddenly took him up.

---

[207] The author's Intelligence convinced him that he would be told the rest of the Houcaïs' story. When the favor is granted, we will be sure to let the public know.

Instead of my ceiling I saw the sky where he went farther and farther away. I watched them go for a long time.

After losing sight of them I looked down to examine the objects around me, but darkness had followed the brightness of the beautiful day and it was completely silent. I made a quick movement and found out that I was free again and the hideous monster haunting me was gone. I took a deep breath and thought about all the wonders. My sound judgment led me to believe that everything I had seen was a pure illusion born, perhaps, out of my feverish work. I ended up convincing myself so completely that the fanciful visions were the result of overwork that I resolved to give up *Lamekis*. I would become crazy, I rationalized, and I was getting close. I had to try to keep what little sanity I had left.

I spent the rest of the night between contemplating and nodding off peacefully. Just after sunrise I awoke with a start. As usual I got up to work half-asleep without thinking of the strange events I had been victim of the night before, but moving around chased away my drowsiness. My mind cleared up and I remembered everything that had happened. I realized that the danger had passed, so my fears vanished as well. The morning light was a comfort and I resolved again to treat the night's adventure as an illusion.

"Ah, obviously I'm right," I said aloud, "I have to stop this abstract work. My brain is overheating and will end up becoming deranged." This said I quickly searched for Part 5 of *Lamekis*, which I had already begun. "Send it back to nothingness," I said. "Tear it to pieces. I will banish it forever."

What a fright I had saying this! I heard a howling that seemed to come from the street and it sounded like the dog that had caused all the trouble. And now I had no idea where I was. I rushed to a window and what did I see? A dog with blue fur that I knew by its mastiff snout to be the same animal that had followed me. Didn't I have reason to be amazed at the transformation and to think that what had happened was not as fantastic as my reason led me to believe? I could barely keep my eyes on the dog—its eyes were so fierce and piercing that I could barely look at them. It stared at me, wagging its tail like it was glad to see me.

I did not know what to think or do. I could feel my heart beating fast and I was about to faint when I felt a slap on my shoulder. In the state I was in I thought I was going to be the victim of another prodigy. Wasn't the strange blow an omen? I shuddered and showed all the signs of utter fear. And then a burst of laughter that I recognized reassured me. It was a lady friend who sometimes had coffee with me and I felt ashamed of myself. Too jealous of what the reaction might mean, I asked her to look into the street to see what was happening.

"But, there's nothing there," she said with a look of surprise.

"You don't see anything?" It was my turn to look surprised. "An animal? A strange dog whose fur is not like a normal dog's? It's right across from us, wagging its tail and staring at me..."

"Come on, you're crazy," the lady said. "You're just having fun, I guess, or you're working too hard and getting dizzy. Your imagination is making you see things. I'm telling you, I don't see anything," she repeated when I shrugged my shoulders, "unless you're so amazed by that black dog sitting in the alley."

"What?" I almost screamed. "You think that dog is black?"

"Of course," she replied wide-eyed, "or you're dreaming or, as I said before, you're having fun at my expense. I don't see the point of the joke. Let me in on it whenever you feel like it."

I was furious at her stubbornness not to agree with what I saw so clearly. It was the middle of the day and I could not believe that I was dreaming. I was wide-awake and felt fine. The lady could not deny it, but she swore to me in all seriousness that I was having trouble with my eyes and when the coffee was brought she asked my servant to be a witness—he corroborated her so naturally that I had no more doubts that I was losing my mind.

Yes, of course, I said to myself, it's slipping away. My work is addling me. Well, I'll give it up entirely. Hopefully it's not too late!

That's what I was thinking, but it did not last long.

I was talking and acting so strangely that the lady left advising me in friendship never to have someone over when I was working. "It makes you weird or else you're acting like this just to get rid of whoever is interrupting you. Either way you're an insupportable bore."

She concluded her short speech by leaving. In spite of my affection for her, I was glad to see her go. I was out of sorts and when the mind is worked up it doesn't like to be distracted. The soul needs solitude to recover—the more you try to stifle or stall it, the more it suffers. That's what I felt.

When I was alone I sounded myself out. After testing my mind a little I figured that it was healthy and sound and my body felt fine, so that could not be the problem. With that done, I decided that the vision of the animal that was disturbing me, that was the spitting image of Falbao in *Lamekis*, the brave and wonderful dog, was real and meant something specific to me. It made me think of a time in my life that I never spoke about because of its peculiarity. Here is the perfect opportunity for me to unburden myself of it. The public, which has shown an interest in my life up to now, will not be upset if I entertain it like this. I won't try to convince you to put any faith in it because it is too extraordinary to hope that anyone will take me at my word.

I was crossing the Tuileries at 11 a.m., carefree and without a worry in the world, when all of a sudden I heard someone talking in my ear. I spun around, but no one was there. I stopped short, a little taken aback, but was even more so when I realized that without opening my mouth or uttering a word I was clearly answering the strange voice and holding a conversation with it. The dialogue lasted a while and I was so afraid of interrupting it that I closed my eyes and listened like a good audience.

I stayed in this extraordinary state long enough to recite a "Miserere" and it would have lasted longer if it were not for the misplaced generosity of a good woman who saw me standing in the middle of the path with my eyes closed, not moving. She took me for a lost, blind man and kindly offered to lead me where I wanted to go, being sorry, she said, that such misfortune befell someone of my age. As angry as I was to have my mental activity interrupted, enjoying it so divinely as I was, I could not help laughing at the old girl's imagination. She looked astonished when I opened my eyes and as she went on her way she mumbled, "Excuse me, Monsieur, for waking you up. I would never have imagined that you were asleep standing up."

The reader is no doubt anxious to know what the secret voice told me and what it was all about—there will come a time when I will satisfy all curiosity, but for now I cannot linger on the matter. Let's go back to where we were.

Remembering this experience, I had no doubt that the adventure with the dog was fantastic but real and I resigned myself to whatever might come. I got dressed and left in order to follow the animal if it wanted to lead me somewhere as it had done before. A steadfast man is only surprised the first time; when it happens again he will try everything—as will be proven in a moment.

I was barely on the street when the dog, which I can call Falbao since it looked just like how I depicted him in *Lamekis*, came up to me and acted as happy as ever to see me. I responded in kind and as I was anxious to know what he wanted I motioned with my finger to walk and I was ready to follow. He understood me, barked in joy (or so it seemed to me), turned the corner and left me to follow.

He led me straight into the ditches separating Paris from the suburb of Saint Antoine. This time I forced myself to venture in. He stopped at a timeworn opening in an old wall and went through. I had to bend over to follow and had all kinds of trouble dragging myself along the hard 100 feet. There were rocks and roots blocking the passage that I had to break to move forward. Then, for almost a quarter of a league, I was walking between two walls that looked like they were built as dams. Falbao kept turning around to reassure me, it seemed. My good feelings for him gave me courage and I trudged on.

After a lot of road and fatigue, Falbao turned to his left, but he was barely out of sight when 30 bats and as many owls flew out making a dreadful noise. I was pretty frightened, but I rose to the occasion and abandoned myself to fate; Falbao, who had come back, managed to put me back on track. The new road he led me on was wide, smooth and very bright. It was paved with marble and cleaner than it should have been. The surface was wet, probably from water leaking through the walls, I thought, and was rather proud of my discovery: history had taught me that there were once underground temples dedicated to the pagan divinities of the dark house of the dead. I figured that I was on one of these pathways and the thought of this made me a little calmer than I naturally should have been—as I said before, the mind, like the body, can get used to anything, it is only the first steps on a hard road that count. The mind is resilient and easily joins in.

If I made a detailed description of the adventure I am about to tell, I would have to say some ghastly things. I came across many graves and all kinds of evidence of the barbarism and inhumanity of the ancient pagan priests. The sights were too offensive to retell. I can say that the catacombs seemed to have been built only as a theater for tyranny and with that I close the curtain and come to things less terrible and more comfortable for me.

At last we arrived at an iron gate through which I made out another passage whose marble walls were engraved with hieroglyphs. At the end of this passage was a marble door with a Corinthian arch, which opened onto a large vestibule lit by five globes giving off a dim, pale light. I had no doubt that this was where Falbao wanted to lead me. He scratched at the foot of the gate and it opened. We got to the vestibule, but instead of going up the marble stairs he turned to his right and went down by other stairs. It was lit by two globes like in the vestibule and although the light was dim it was enough to see things clearly.

More than 500 steps to go down before we finally reached another vestibule, but it was full of golden bas-reliefs. I was more than a little astonished at what they represented. I saw all the adventures of Lamekis described in the first four parts of the work, executed with such skill that there was no mistaking them. Every cartouche followed the sequence of events in the story. Falbao looked like he was inviting me to look over them. Since I was ready to do anything he asked I examined them closely.

The first[208] showed a sacrifice to Serapis performed on a ship in gratitude for the end of the storm that had put Lamekis' ship on the verge of destruction several times. I saw Lamekis and Sinouis on the deck, the only ones not sleeping, deep in conversation. In the same relief I saw Semiramis go down into the underground temple and I could see in the skillfully etched expression how afraid she was. Then the procession of priests where every person and especially the Queen were perfectly distinguishable. Beneath this I saw the destruction of the underground by the Nile at the orders of the Queen; Lamekis on the open sea with his family; the death of Milkhea, his wife; the death of his daughter and of Haronza and the wild behavior of her daughter.

In the next bas-relief I saw the deep sleep in which Lamekis and his family were plunged; the awakening of the High Priest's son and his abduction by the strangers; his surprise; the humane way he was accepted and raised by Motacoa, son of the Houcaïs and Nasildaë.

In the 4th cartouche was shown Nasildaë's descent into the pit of Houzaïl; her meeting Lodaï who had been banished like her; the adventure of the monstrous worm that almost ate Motacoa, her son; the unexpected aide of the admirable Falbao. On the left I saw the moment when Motacoa, followed by Falbao, got out of the Inner Earth and met Boldeon who prom-

---

[208] The following descriptions are of Part 1.

ised to put him on his father's throne. On the right of the bas-relief was the awful encounter between Motacoa and the worm men followed by his and Boldeon's abduction by the monsters; the horrible way they dragged him by his hair; the extraordinary building where they brought him; the strange sight of the naked worm women in the room which the beautiful Ascalis presided; Falbao reappearing to Motacoa who thought he had been lost forever.

In the 5th I clearly saw the ship carrying Lamekis on a column of water up into the Heavens and resting on top of a tree. I saw the astonishment on all the faces. The fall of the three sailors carried away by the winged creatures was not left out, nor the flight of the crew into the ship right after.

The 6th bas-relief[209] showed the amazing way Lamekis' ship was marooned by the Sylphs carrying everything off. I saw Lamekis and Sinouis snatched away by the winged monsters. The bottom of the picture recalled their dropping into the volcano and I could see Sinouis fearing for his life and the sky crowded with Sylphs.

Lamekis' astonishment at the white Sylph perched on his shoulder was perfectly recognizable in the 7th when its mouth was up against his ear whispering sage advice. It was in stark contrast with Sinouis and his black spirit. The two figures were exquisitely depicted. In the distance I could see a dwelling. Sinouis looked like he was urging Lamekis to enter. The latter resisted the temptation and taking his hand tore him away from the imminent danger. The picture hid nothing, not even the facial expressions. Everything was artfully told.

The 8th picture showed how Motacoa was saved from the four monsters around the Ascalis Princess' throne. On the bottom was the battle between Motacoa and Za-ra-ouf and the victory over the latter by the brave and faithful Falbao. On the left I could see the total defeat of the monsters by Falbao's rising and Boldeon's bravery in his attack.

---

[209] Part 2.

The story of the three children of the Sun was the subject of the 9th. In the background the Princess telling the story was scared by the unexpected arrival of the toad monsters. I saw Falbao digging furiously at the ground and the alarm on all the faces.

The 10th bas-relief[210] reminded me of the deadly battle between Falbao and the toad monsters and his defeat caused by the awful owl. The other side showed the fury with which Motacoa attacked the monsters to free his faithful dog from their overpowering blows. I saw the monsters' fright and flight and the care Motacoa showed Falbao to bring him out of his stupor. In the distance appeared the second battle; the conqueror scoffed at the new assault, threw out the owl staff and put the enemies to flight again.

The adventures of the Ascalis Princess took up the 11th picture. I saw her guided by the chief minister with torch in hand to satisfy her pressing desire to see the Lindiagar, her father, which was forbidden by law. Never was inner satisfaction pictured better than was expressed on the face of the Princess of the Amphicleocles at this crucial moment. And I read on the King's face the joy he felt at seeing his daughter. That's all there was in this part of the sculpture. On the left was depicted the moment when Lindiagar suddenly showed up in the middle of the Council of Seven, his majesty in his critical speech and the dismay of the Council. On the right I saw the procession of the King to the temple of Fulghane; his entrance into the sanctuary and the respect caused by the royal babouche. In the distance could be seen the sanctuary, the High Throne where the Lindiagar was in his glory and the dismay of the High Priestess in humiliation at the foot of the statue. I read the scorn on her face. Everything was so well expressed that the whole story came rushing up in my memory.

The surprise of Sinouis when the light followed the darkness; the vision of the tables and guests; the betrayed joy of Lamekis believing that he had found his wife Clemelis

---

[210] Part 3.

again; his flight after recognizing the threat to his virtue; these were the subjects of the 12th and last bas-relief.

After examining this final bas-relief, Falbao lowered his head and went to the back of the room. I followed him and he pushed open a door directly across from the one we entered. Never in my life had I seen anything so strange. It was a big gallery with mirrored walls, as clean as they were extraordinary. Instead of reflecting what I looked like, they reflected what I was thinking and everything I had seen in my life. The number of images scared me and I stepped back, but a bright flash struck me all of a sudden and melted my astonishment because I looked toward the back of the room: a throne as bright as the sun stood there. Because of the flashes of light I could not tell what it was made of, but what really surprised me was that it was surrounded by all kinds of animals that all seemed buried in a deep sleep.

I was getting unsettled by all these wonders when Falbao suddenly started barking. His howls echoed in the chamber and the light vanished into darkness with such a horrific noise that I was completely frozen in fear. I fell backward and passed out.

I will never forget the extraordinary dream that troubled me. I felt my soul disconnecting from my body and flying into the immensity of the Heavens. It reveled there in its avid thirst for knowledge, which it had sought so often before its freedom—a wonderful and charming state! Why did you vanish away? Oh, happy lethargy, why didn't you last forever? I saw…a whirlwind…but, hidden power that stirs around in me, your orders are supreme, forgive me—I will be quiet.[211] Either I would say too much or not enough.

---

[211] At the exact moment when the author wrote this passage and was about to describe his mysterious dream, his hand suddenly went numb and could not move the pen. With the idea that the paralysis was caused by bad circulation, he took the pen with his left hand and tried to continue writing. By some unheard-of prodigy, it, too, refused to work. With no doubt that the difficulty was caused by a hidden power, he figured he had to submit to the internal orders. Indeed, his

Struck by all these mysterious experiences, my soul expanded with so much energy that it generated the heat that my senses had destroyed: I regained consciousness with this life-giving strength. My eyes were barely open and the first thing I did was to look at the throne. Imagine my surprise to see Falbao there talking earnestly with all the animals as if they were making some important decision. I did not recognize their language, but I guessed that their attitudes and gestures embodied their spoken ideas.

I was marveling at these things when a human cry made me jump to attention. "Come close and see," the voice yelled. I thought I recognized it. I approached and would you believe it? Falbao, the extraordinary dog, suddenly changed shape: his shaggy head slowly lost its animal form and became human. The rest transformed almost imperceptibly, but I soon recognized the Armenian whom I had traveled with and who is mentioned in the Preface to Part 1. At the same time all the animals took on human form and by their clothes I could tell that they were from different countries.

Completely flabbergasted by this fabulous event, I stood there gaping, like I was about to scream, when the Armenian imposed silence by putting his finger to his lips. "Listen to me," he said. "Don't interrupt or it will be your ruin. Right now you can become like all the wise men whose happiness you must imagine by everything you just saw; it's up to you to get there like they did. Listen carefully to me now."

Dehahal appears to the author

I am the philosopher Dehahal whom you talked about in your story of Lamekis. You were sure that you made it all up while writing, but you did nothing except remember things that really existed and still exist. The great Scealgalis allowed me to appear to you during the trip, you remember, to clear up

---

submission was accepted right away. As soon as he decided not to speak about it, he was given back the use of his hands.

your clouded understanding so that you can teach men how good their sovereign is. It was I who has inspired you so far and whom you secretly called the Intelligence. Take advantage of my teachings, the time has come when my spirit will leave you. Only a furrow left behind by my departure can remain in your soul. May it please the Highest Power that it be enough to lead you to the good I desire for you and that, in the end, you deserve, unless you rely on your poor senses more.

De Mouhy, it was I who was driven by sacred desire to be transported to the divine Island of the Sylphs; I who came up with the idea to fill up the bladders with dew[212] so that the heat of the Sun would lift them from the Earth. By my inspiration you described how I was horribly eaten by the great bee and by what miracle, after being digested, I came back to life and regained my natural shape. You did not forget that I owed my preservation to the Sylph protector who snatched me away when the great bee was about to gobble me up again and that I was able to pass courageously through the awful torment of initiation by letting myself be skinned alive and engraved with the sacred characters of Scealgalis. I would criticize you for not having told the rest of my story as I inspired it in you if I did not know about the obstacles preventing you.[213] I could have supplied (I even wanted to) the missing parts by writing them myself, but I was advised by those around me that the subject was too lofty and abstract and a little too indelicate to honor earthly men with it. I wanted to appear to you to explain my intentions in person because the care you have taken until now to inspire mortals with virtue and knowledge of the greatest good made me want the best for you. Now it is in your

---

[212] Part 4.

[213] The story of Dehahal had been written in full and I dare say that it is as interesting as you might imagine, but the strict censor was convinced, since he heard no more from the author, that it could be replaced by more than 30 pages of scholarly explanations. Unfortunately for the public, there was no rough draft of the manuscript and the original was not kept after being approved. That's why the rest of the story was not told.

hands. Choose—you can end up being initiated among the fortunate. You know how I came to the greatest good. A burning desire will lift you up. Speak. They are ready to skin you alive, to engrave the sacred marks of initiation on your heart with the burning stylus. The great bee will obey and you will be eaten. These are the favors that I can offer, you only have to consent and it will be done.

The book writes itself

Dehahal waited quietly for my answer. Everyone around the throne was looking at me, ready to congratulate me, figuring that I was going to jump at such a kind offer. But I was so far from feeling this! Just the thought of it made me shudder in fear. How could I endure it? I answered with courage and respect that I was not fortunate enough to enjoy the goods purchased in such cruel places.

I had barely finished speaking when Dehahal, his court, his throne and the room disappeared and I found myself back in bed, shaking and covered in cold sweat with a roll of paper in my hand. It took me a while to get a hold of myself, but there was nothing else wrong with me but shock. I slowly came back to my senses and thanked heaven for the present it gave me in its extraordinary way. I had no doubt that the roll of paper contained the rest of the adventures of Lamekis. I opened it and was stunned: it was written in a strange, unknown language. Yet, judging by some of the marks and the arrangement of sentences I guessed it was Chaldean. I felt better knowing that I could find a translator.

I went to find a specialist in oriental languages and I showed him the manuscript. He examined it and said to me, "I don't recognize these characters. They don't look like anything men have ever used." I went home sad, thinking that I would never succeed in my project.

More than six months went by without thinking any more about it when one morning while I was working on a book of piety[214] I heard a sound in my office like a mouse gnawing away at something (or someone trying to dig his way out of prison). I opened my drawers with gloves on ready to catch it if I could. It was useless. The noise continued but I could not find what was causing it.

I stopped looking and listened carefully. It sounded like my papers were moving around. I opened all my drawers again but everything was completely undisturbed. I was dumbfounded. Finally, when I got to the bottom drawer, just as I was opening it, I jumped back: one of the manuscripts there was leafing back and forth like a fan in the hands of an annoying flirt—perpetual motion. What was I to think about such a wonder? I sat there for two hours like a rock, not being able and not daring, I admit, to change the situation.

I tried to pluck up the courage and determination to pick up the shuffling manuscript, but my hands refused the noble deed. All I could do was stare at the miracle—it changed soon. The book suddenly jumped out of the drawer, onto the left side of my desk and lay still. The change made me feel better. I was bending over to see which of my works was acting so strangely when another wonder made my hair stand on end. One of my pens rose up out of my writing case like a needle drawn by a magnet, dipped its nib in the ink and then started writing on the paper that had been prepared to continue my next work. It looked like the pen was tracing French letters; I even made out some words. It also looked exactly like my handwriting—there was no mistaking it.

I was so amazed by all this that I could barely breath. But the pen stopped writing all of a sudden and went to the open manuscript. It made some corrections on the open page and when it was done the page turned, ready for the next. "Well," I let out, "either the devil's mixed up in this or I'm dreaming." (I didn't have control over this exclamation). "Neither one," answered a voice that seemed to come out of my desk. "Don't be scared, sit down, watch and write."

---

[214] *The Motives of Conversion for Use by the People of the World.*

If everything that had just happened filled me with fear and panic, imagine how I felt when I heard that voice coming from I know not where. I was scared to look at my desk. The pen was still writing and continued to do so for more than three hours. By this time I had slowly gotten used to everything and felt calmer. I was patiently waiting for the end of this extraordinary adventure.

Nevertheless, I was starting to grow tired of my attitude when that voice spoke again, "That's enough. See you tomorrow." The pen stopped immediately, solemnly dried itself on the sponge and lay back down in the writing case. The manuscript slid off my desk and went back into the drawer. After this the drawer closed by itself and sounded like it was being locked.

Only the book on which the marvelous pen had written stayed there, apparently undisturbed and unmoving. I dared to look and was amazed to read a title written in capital letters just like I used in *Lamekis* with a slight change: Part 5. I sat down and read. It really was the next volume, written so like my own hand that if I did not see it being written, I would have sworn that I had written it myself. I found 20 pages of writing in my style and except for a few unfamiliar ideas everything followed the previous parts to a T. My imagination was on fire with so many extraordinary things that it compelled me to open the drawer to try to clear up, as much as I could, this incredible phenomenon.

No sooner did I make this brave decision than I carried it out. I opened my desk. The manuscript that was put there looked the same as the one with the unknown idiom given to me in the vision of Dehahal. I tried to take it, but it jumped, got away and rolled up into the back of my desk.

"Stop!" cried the same voice that spoke before. "It's not time yet." I backed away and ran out of the room thinking that if I never returned it would be too soon.

Eight days went by before I could bring myself to go back, but I was forced by absolute necessity to return. At eight in the morning I went to the room and wonder of wonders! A young woman, divinely pretty, was sitting in my armchair, writing. Every other vision was forever far away. I should not have stared at her like I was bewitched, but beauty has this effect—it pulls you in instead of pushing you away. My first reaction was to run away, my second held me back. Should I be afraid of such a beautiful woman, I wondered? If the Intelligence that was always with me looked like this divine person or if this was it, what did I have to fear? Convinced by this I looked at her more boldly.

She was blonde, had a dazzling white complexion, charming features and curly hair that fell over her shoulders. She wore a white silk dress pressed with a pale blue design; a scarf made of extremely fine chiffon hid part of her throat. Her perfectly formed arms were almost bare; the sleeves of her dress came only to her elbows and were bound by heavenly-blue silk that gave a limitless brilliance to her finery. I could not see her eyes because she kept them lowered, intent on her work.

I would really have liked her to look up. I was in serious trouble. Come on, I told myself, could I run away from such stunning charms? Could it be that my fear and lack of courage had blinded me to the point of missing out on such precious moments?

I barely had time to think this because the lovely woman sitting at my desk looked up and gave me a smile that struck me to my soul. What a face, great god! What beauty! My senses sparkled and I ran to her. Nothing could hold me back; I would throw myself at her knees. I opened my mouth to spill out my heart, but the divine beauty lowered her head, put it into one of the drawers and slipped in as easily as a fox in its hole. That was all I could take. I stood there with my arms outstretched, my mouth open and my eyes glued to the desk in utter astonishment. What else could I do?

A fit of righteous anger shook me out of my stupor. "It's too much!" I shouted. "Whoever you are—Intelligence, invisible woman, devil—stop playing with me. What do we have to do to sort this out?"

A burst of laughter came out of my desk, telling me that it wanted to have fun with me more than to hurt me. "Go ahead," I said, holding myself back so that I would not show my fear. "Laugh. If I had the same abilities maybe I would do worse."

"Work, work," the voice cried out. "Time lost is gone forever."

"Let's work, then," I answered, still angry going up to my desk. "I just have to make up my mind whether I feel well enough to obey."

More laughter answered me. I was getting used to it, so it did not bother me.

Finally, to put an end to this unprecedented adventure, I took the pen and got down to writing. As soon as I put pen to paper the book in front of me started shaking. I was about to get up, but the voice said, "Nothing to be afraid of. Read what is written to the end. The Spirit will do the rest."

I did what it wanted, took the manuscript and read. I was just getting to the last line when a sudden inspiration took hold of my imagination; I started writing with amazing speed and did not stop for a month and a day. At the end of this time I was hungry, left off the work and took care of my physical needs. I ate and drank for 31 hours without stopping. After that I slept for three days and nights and on the fourth I woke up. Everything that had happened to me seemed like a dream and I have thought it so ever since.

What is certain is that when I returned to my desk I found *Lamekis* finished. The public can believe what it wants about the wonders. It would be too hard for me to try to convince it. Whatever it was, here is the rest of *Lamekis* that the public seems to want. I'll be happy if the work keeps me in its favor. And if good intentions deserve sympathy, there is no author in Paris who deserves it more than me.

Continuation of the story of Lamekis

The philosopher Dehahal stopped short then, looked up at the sky, presented himself and was raised up, ordering me to do the same. His order was carried out. "Lower your eyes," he told me, "and listen as closely as you can. The truth itself will speak from my mouth. Whatever prejudices you still have will disappear. Your soul has been worried about its destination until now—all its doubts will end and it will be serene. Lamekis, what wonders await you! Will you be able to experience them without dying of pleasure? Worship the Almighty. May He be praised forever.

"O Noc-kha-dor, Being of Beings, Mover of the universe, do not let me profane your sacred story by leaving anything out. And you, divine Scealgalis, inspire me…The Heavens open, the holy rays beam down and heat me. Let me begin…[215]

After Dehahal finished this wonderful story, he resumed his own.

Decide for yourself, Lamekis, if my soul was enthralled by so many wonders and truths. I felt already initiated in the Universal Being that they had just described to me so perfectly. Who could have done that but the Being itself? It was not a God depicted by puny mortals who cover him with all their passions, who fill him full of vengeance and jealousy, who make him cruel and make him revel in the eternal loss of those he created. In the portrayal given to me I recognized a Supreme Being whose eternal happiness needed nothing but itself to make it solid and lasting. The world created by its omnipotence and incomparable bounty had only one goal: grandeur and generosity. To pull living things out of nothingness

---

[215] Here is where the royal censor cut out the text. It concerned a system on the divinity and thoughts on the other life, appropriate for all good people. Even though the author printed this work in Holland and was thereby free to include the passage, he kept it out with the idea that an honest man should obey the laws of his country and never, on any pretext whatsoever, break them.

to make them happy without making them buy their happiness—this seemed to me to be the true attribute of the divinity. Its admirable laws were dictated by the same spirit, striving to pay back their observations by different rewards appropriate to their perfection, and seemed to have been given not to make people wretched but to raise their hearts by recognizing their divine legislator. The loss of these promised rewards by forcing the offenders to assume a new life on Earth to start everything over again is the only punishment announced to those who are not found worthy of the graces offered to their virtue. That is a wisdom and kindness belonging only to Noc-kha-dor. In fact, nothing is greater than this conduct; a mortal pays the tribute to nature when he has not earned the good given to the practice of virtue. Noc-kha-dor created him to make him happy and this weak mortal, by acting against the spirit of his creator, makes himself unworthy. Then he takes on another body and enters on the lists again. The experience engraved on his soul teaches him that it was his own fault he lost the good that belonged to him. He is forewarned that he can still get it if he acts differently than before by worshiping and glorifying the supreme kindness. He agrees that he was unworthy and by this act of humility, born out of the sense of justice in his heart, he gets Noc-kha-dor to pour out enough grace to give him the strength that he previously lacked to reach the blessed state destined for him since the beginning of time.

Oh lucky Lamekis, did you really understand that grand passage that announced to man that he was not created to be eternally lost and that the words "eternal" and "forever" are only a fleeting moment for the great Noc-kha-dor? Do you realize the majesty of this passage and the dreadful blasphemy of those who have limited the omnipotent by giving him the passions of revenge, mercilessness and fury against the creatures fed by his august hand and warmed by his eternal breath? Noc-kha-dor explained himself: that he is great and good, Lamekis, and he said nothing about rewards and punishments. Didn't they explain his grandeur like that to make it worthy of our adoration?

I was deeply affected by what I had just heard (Dehahal continued). Only a while afterward did I notice my wound was bleeding again—the triple roll with the divine history written on it had just been put back in the sanctuary when it started up again. One of the Sylphs holding me up by my feet handed me over to his partner and forced open my mouth, stuck his hand inside, grabbed my tongue and led me around the Island in triumph. All the people were waiting to congratulate me on the glory I had just received. The universal acclamations and praises given to me calmed the bitter pain that I was starting to feel again, which disappeared completely in that special honor I received.

The Loug-hou-kou planted a stake in the earth with his holy hand. At the end of the stake was an iron hook to which he fastened my tongue. This was the final ceremony. All the Sylphs of the Island came up in fours to congratulate me. Each gave me the customary ceremonial honors: the first, the oldest, advanced backward until he was next to me, then he plucked out a hair from my beard and slapped me. He went back crying out, "Ab-kal-hous."[216] The second, armed with an iron rod, hit me on the head saying the same thing. The third slapped me on the ears, put his fingers up my nostrils and pulled at my nose, making me sneeze hard. The fourth, less privileged, only had the honor of spitting in my mouth, but with as much spit as he could muster.

After all the Sylphs and the Loug-hou-kou had paid me their homage, the Loug-hou-kou grabbed the stake and at the same time four Sylphs grabbed me around my body and the Secretary of State yanked out my tongue. I felt no pain during this last honor. A tongue three times bigger, filling up my whole mouth, instantly grew in and took the place of the one that was so ceremoniously extracted and was carried now on the end of a staff. I had to follow it like everyone else and when it was put in the temple, everything stopped and I became like you see me now.

---

[216] May you always be happy.

The punishment of Lamekis

I could not help breathing a sigh of relief when Dehahal finished his story. I wanted desperately not to have to imitate his deeds.

"What's this I see?" the philosopher shouted. "You're pining inside. Could it be that these things that should be leading you to the greatest goods are making you unhappy? You're growing pale. Your weakness is making you see these minor trials as cruel punishments. Speak up! Your response will decide your fate. And don't worry if your calling isn't for the sound repose, I exempt you. I will have you brought back to Earth in consideration for the virtues you have shown up to this point and especially the way you behaved in the trial of the 12 tables. This one grace, such as it is, will be granted you. After that, nothing should prevent you from speaking."

While Dehahal was speaking, I remembered the words of the Sylph who brought me to the Island when he said that I would be condemned to crawl like a reptile on the earth if I did not attempt the trial. I shuddered at this alternative.

"Lord," I cried out in fear, "as much as I want to imitate you, I don't feel as steadfast in physical suffering as I was in the moral virtues. If I am skinned alive, hanged by my feet and tongue, I have to admit that it will only be with bitter regret."

"Well then," Dehahal erupted, "go back to Earth. Follow me. Scealgalis will allow it."

"Oh Heavens," I said obeying him, "how harsh is human destiny if eternal good is only purchased at the price of such horrible suffering! Why did the Almighty not give us the strength to resist it?"

"What's this?" Dehahal shouted furiously, pulling out four of my teeth. "Now you blaspheme!" He clapped his hands seven times and a cloud of black spirits covered the sky. The savage philosopher screamed out, "Let them have you. I give up on you! After suffering the triple Gul-gin-hak[217] to atone for your crime, you will be cast down to Earth where you will crawl until a new order is given."

You cannot imagine my terror at his words. Although I did not know what this punishment was, I had no doubt that it was the worst. With that in mind I wanted to throw myself at his feet and cry for mercy, but the philosopher had already disappeared. "Oh Vilkonhis," I prayed, "take pity on me. You are my only hope."

I barely had time to finish this short prayer; I was already being swept up by the black spirits. Oh Heavens! Who can imagine how they took me away. Each of them grabbed a part of my body with five of them on each hand and foot lifting me by my fingers and toes. The rest of the troop went to my head, combing out my hair and each one grabbing a strand. My whole body was pulled and tugged and finally hauled up brutally into the sky. Then I was sorry that I did not let myself be skinned alive—it certainly could not have been more painful. My cries were useless; nothing would calm their cruelty. They sneezed at my suffering and their monstrous bodies showed an air of satisfaction that proved the blackness of their souls.

Oh Vilkonhis! Could it be that you won't come to help me in my direful need?

After carrying me like that for a long time, they stopped on a thick, black cloud and hung me by the scruff of my neck on a clamp attached to a tall pole. It felt pretty good considering what I had just been through. Every extremity of my body from my toes to my hair, every strand of which stood straight up like a needle, was tensed, making me feel like a hedgehog. Little by little the tugging stopped. I could breathe again and look forward to the end of my troubles.

But I should have remembered those menacing words: "the triple Gul-gin-hak." It meant three different punishments. I could not look forward to a quick end.

---

[217] A punishment on the Island of the Sylphs.

Then I heard yelling and I opened my eyes (which I had kept closed until then). I saw four big Sylphs coming in from four different directions with paddles in their hands. The black spirits were lined up so that they looked like an audience waiting for a play to amuse them. And yes! I was on the mark. One of the Sylphs came up and grabbed me with his strong hands. Another whacked me high in the air with its huge paddle like a handball. I went straight up and fell back down onto another's paddle that whacked me just as hard. It hurt a lot, but was nothing compared to the pain I felt when the clumsy Sylph let me drop, playing around with his paddle and failing to hit me. I hit the ground so hard I lost consciousness. It was the best thing that could have happened to me in the situation.

The next punishment I was condemned to was the cruelest, even though it hurt me the least. When I regained consciousness, imagine how astonished and sorry I was to see the staggering transformation I had undergone. Dare I say it? I was a snake and maybe the most hideous that nature had ever produced. I crawled on the ground, lived in a dark forest and caused everyone to run away from me.

After finding myself in this dreadful state, I coiled up in despair and tried to poison myself with hundreds of deadly bites. "Vain efforts!" shouted a voice from the sky. "You will crawl until a faithful woman turns you back into your former shape. Blessed be Scealgalis whose incomparable kindness has prevented your punishment from being eternal. Without the trial of the 12 tables that you passed, there would be no mercy. Your blasphemy would have brought upon you the final death.[218] Behold and praise the great Noc-kha-dor. He left you the power of speech so that you might use it to get closer to the final moment that will finish you off. Sinouis, to help you out, has the same gift. Being with your dear friend will help you bear your evils. He is in the woods. That, Lame-

---

[218] That of the soul. The Sylphs claimed that the eternal punishment is to return to the void, to nothingness.

kis, is all I could do to help you. I could have done better if you had wanted to."

After this the voice was silent. It did more than enough to calm my fury. Hope is a healthy cure to our sufferings. I could get back my former shape. All I had to do was find a faithful woman—that was not impossible. The power of speech that I still had was a treasure. And Sinouis was alive. Obviously I had to find him, my partner in disgrace, who could help to get through this. That's what I was thinking at the moment.

I spent the rest of the day slithering next to a stream hoping to meet poor Sinouis, but I searched in vain. Around the middle of the night I heard moaning and groaning. I raised my head to listen better and I seemed to recognize the voice. Thinking it was my faithful friend I dragged myself to where it came from. I had barely gone an eighth of a karies when I heard it say, "Did I have to leave all behind to follow a man who ruined everything he touched? Great god, how far has my friendship sunk me? Don't I see the whole world curse me, making me hide because of my bad luck and shame?" Bitter tears choked these words and I was touched to the bottom of my heart.

I hurried to get to the tree where Sinouis was. My keen eyes spied him: he was stamping on a branch and looked just like when I last saw him, that is to say, like an owl. I spoke to him and made him recognize me. At first he was so afraid that he fell off the branch and if it weren't for his wings he would have died.

I tried to console him and he answered sorrowfully, "Is it really you, Lamekis? I guess since you're here again I might be less unhappy." After these seemingly friendly words, he came down, but, in spite of everything I said to reassure him, he would not come close. He admitted that I looked terrible and he could not control his fear. I used this to comfort him: "See," I said, "as hard as your fate is, it's nothing compared to mine because you are horrified by me even after knowing that I am the same Lamekis who used to be your friend and for whom you left everything. How hopeless do you think that makes me feel?"

Sinouis looked ashamed by this. There is no better comfort than to meet someone worse off than you. He found that he was lucky not to end up looking like me and the thought calmed him down enough to tell me everything that happened to him since our separation.

Sinouis is turned into an owl

I had just left you,[219] Lamekis, dragged away by my senses, and I dove back into all the delights that were offered to me. I was so drunk that (should I say it?) I barely remembered you existed. But, great Vilkonhis, who in my situation would not have surrendered to so many temptations? In the past, dear partner in disgrace, I loved an adorable Phoenician girl who was stolen away by a rival barbarian. My entire life since that loss has been spent searching for her, but to no avail. My motivation for the last trip came as much from the hope of finding her as from my friendship with you, Lamekis—it's time I admit it.

I saw her at one of the tables. She was so pretty and adorable. What devoted lover could resist such charms? I threw myself in her arms and made up for all the tears, troubles and tribulations that her absence had caused me. But, oh fatal return, I barely had time to enjoy such a sweet, longed-for good because the beauty that I loved slowly lost her charm and her sweet, desired beauty disappeared and so, too, did the rest of her vanish away and transform into gruesome, monstrous features; and I saw a black Sylph. I wanted to scream out in fear, but I could no longer control my organs. My arms wanted to stretch out, my feet wanted to run away, but I could not move or, better said, they were disappearing. Oh great Vilkonhis, you who allowed this, what a frightening shock I had. I was an owl. And grotesque. My fate made me

---

[219] Towards the end of Part 3.

tremble and I looked daggers at the cause of my misfortune. But instead of all those tantalizing dishes, I saw nothing but vipers and instead of guests there were dreadful monsters. I ran away and hid and you know the rest. A black spirit seized me and threw me in this forest on the Island of the Sylphs where I have languished ever since.

Lamekis and Sinouis in the forest

I was not surprised at Sinouis' story—he had earned his fate. For me, who had resisted the trial of the 12 tables, I could not help grumbling to myself about the cruelty I suffered. I remembered perfectly well that they had allowed me to ask for a favor that should have been granted to me. We never get justice. I forgot that my blasphemy had made me unworthy and that it is not enough just to start doing good, we have to persevere. But does not one grievous wrong destroy all the good deeds of the past? Obviously yes and I should not have been surprised at my harsh fate.

Sinouis and I sat there a while without talking. Finally, I broke the silence and told him what had happened to me since our separation. In spite of all the sensual faults of my dear friend, he criticized me for my lack of determination after being so set on getting to the greatest good. I agreed with him and did not try to make excuses for my weakness. Much of that night was spent with us pitying and comforting each other.

Just as dawn's rosy hue appeared on the horizon Sinouis interrupted me, "Let's get out of here. The cave just over there is my hideout and we can use it as our den and talk without worrying about being interrupted."

"Well, who's going to do that in this deserted place?"

"Oh," Sinouis replied sadly, "if I show myself for a minute longer the inhabitants of the woods will eat me. The ignorant crowd believes that I am the enemy of light and I can't stand its brightness. I thought that myself before, but I've learned better. In truth the owl hides at mealtime, but it doesn't like to. It escapes the light more than hides from it—it's afraid of all the other animals. Lamekis, would you believe that all the other dwellers in the sky, birds of every species, come together to jeer at it? You can already hear their screeching. And that's nothing compared with what will happen if I'm stupid enough to wait out here for them. Imagine that what you are hearing right now is a kind of general warning that I'm here and a universal summons to bring together all the birds in the area. When they are all gathered together and know what's going on they will surround me on every side, knock me out and end up pecking me millions of times with their angry beaks to show how stupid I was to wait around for them. I've thought about letting it happen."

With that, Sinouis flew listlessly back to his refuge. It was just in time. He was barely off the ground when a cloud of birds of every species I could imagine rose up above the trees heading for him. The flock was crowing and cawing deafeningly and kept it up when they alit on a rock. I was so galled that if I could have possibly punished them all I would have done it with immense pleasure. But I could only hiss at them and I did so bitterly while crawling to the cave where I, too, took refuge so that the alarmed birds would go away or at least take a break from their insistent cacophony.

The cave I entered seemed bright and very clean. A stream of water, clearer than crystal, murmured through it. At any other time I would have loved it. Looking toward the back I was surprised to see two owls. They were so alike that it was impossible for me to tell which one was Sinouis. One of them seemed to be avoiding the other, which was trying to nuzzle it.

"What's this all about, Sinouis?" I asked. "There are two of you? Could it be that you've made a friend of the same species?"

"No," my sad friend replied, "this bird you see is really a bird. It obviously thought that I would answer its instinct. It's a female and I look like a male. My coldness obviously made her think I was indifferent to her, so she's courting me, trying to tell me in her language and in her way that I'm suitable for her and she loves me. After repeating this declaration to me the lovely old hen asked me very nicely to build a nest with her and fill up this empty cave with our little ones. Do you think I accepted the proposition? Do you think I can respond to her fervent desires? I'm furious at this new situation. I was almost cruel. I told her that I swore never to love another, but she keeps coming after me. I just said that if she keeps it up I'm going to leave this den and she said that she would follow me wherever I went. What torture! What should I expect from this new punishment?"

"Is it really a punishment to be loved?" I asked and I could not help laughing inside at this state of affairs. "Why don't you give the old hen some hope that you might succumb to her tenderness some day?"

"Ah!" Sinouis got worked up. "I was careful not to let her get out of hand. She's so vivacious and so used to getting her way that last night she tried to surprise me in my sleep. I had to peck her off with my beak. Think about what would have happened if I indulged her!"

The insensitive owl could say no more. The hen, in fact, was all over him. He had to stop talking to defend himself. As miserable as I was, I could not help laughing at this wonderful scene. Their conversation was very lively; their voices sounded like broken jugs. Finally Sinouis had enough and figured it best to leave and take refuge next to me. The passionate hen followed him lovingly, but when I hissed at her she got so scared that she flew away and hid in a dark crevasse.

Sinouis admitted that I had just done him the most important service that anyone had ever done for him in his life. "Really!" he said after thinking about it and in all seriousness. It was too much for me, but can we be so inconsiderate—I was rude enough to be amused by his affliction. But I was soon going to be sorry for this and be punished for my offense. As close as we are to our friends, it is all too true that we do not feel their pains as sharply as we feel our own. To be humane, you have to have suffered the same pains that they do and then you can be truly caring and sympathetic. That is what I was about to learn.

We spent a few hours talking sadly about our misfortunes. "But as cruel as they are," I said with a certain respect for eternal decrees, "shouldn't we thank the creator for leaving us the use of our reason and tongue?"

"What do you mean?" Sinouis flapped his wings impatiently. "Wouldn't it be far better actually to be what we only seem to be? Wasn't our reason left to us so that we can feel how miserable we are?"

"Don't be so contrary to the submission to the Almighty," I replied. "The absolute master of all things does not do anything that is not as just as it is grand. The day will come when you will feel how excellent his decrees were. The gross fog of our humanity prevents us from understanding and is the source of your offensive groaning. Take this from a friend who loves you and who does not want to see you any unhappier. My blasphemy put me in this state and your transformation was because you were too quick to please yourself. Let's be humbled by our experience. True wise men would learn from it, only fools scorn it and fall into despair."

These few words made an impression on poor Sinouis and gave me time to think as well. We prayed fervently to the sovereign Being of Beings and then totally resigned ourselves to its will. This piousness, so appropriate to our humiliating situation, calmed us down.

Sinouis stared at me. "How about finishing off our stories? That would be a good way to distract us from our worries."

"Good idea," I said. "It's a sure way for us to prove that we are alive only to endure the journey. You'll find that out soon. I'm a perfect example." After thinking about it for a minute I resumed the story of the Princess of the Amphicleocles,[220] told by her to the Queen, Lodaï and Boldeon. I reminded Sinouis that it was still Motacoa speaking.

---

[220] From Part 3.

The story of Nasilaë continued

If your noble father showed his keen foresight by this wise order (the Karveder continued) the Magna Fakhaldak showed how wily and clever she was by escaping the righteous wrath of her ruler. She slipped into the pedestal on which she had placed the idol and hid herself from her deserved punishment. The Lindiagar was informed that she could not be found and had the inner temple searched meticulously, but he was not surprised that the Priestess had escaped. Still, he did not want to get down from the High Throne until she was found—enemies of her ilk cannot be dealt with softly. A wise politician, thinking about his own safety as well as the state's under these circumstances, has to fight to the death with such enemies.

During the search for the Magna Fakhaldak, who stayed in hiding, the so-called Princess, who was favored by the Magna Fakhaldak, was brought to the Lindiagar by the priestesses. The incontestable right that gave the authority to the High Throne, which put it above all the laws, allowed the Ruler to satisfy his pressing desire to see the Princess. For this he ordered the veil to be lifted. The priestesses, confiding in their superior, tried to resist. They cried out that the order spelled their condemnation, but it was no good. The Karveder made them obey and the Princess' face was unveiled.

"Good God!" the Lindiagar yelled and struck the Tok-ho-dor[221] three times. "Can it be that such black lies are dared in Fulghane's Sanctuary? Isn't this the Princess that the fire consumed? And she was supposed to take the place of the other? Oh, my Bil-bou-gan-gan,[222] see and judge for yourselves!"

---

[221] A square bell that was rung by the king to let the people see and breath. The privilege was given to the people hardly once a century.

[222] My children. The king only spoke to his people in general using this expression.

The people had heard everything and, being allowed to look, they discovered the lie. They shouted out in anger to sentence and submit the High Priestess to the Fa-ris-bouk.[223] The King approved the judgment, calmed the crowd down and ordered that the girl who caused the condemnation of the High Priestess tell everything she knew about the plot or else suffer the same punishment. The young girl was scared by the threat, threw herself at the feet of Fulghane, turned her back to the King and after these signs of respect confessed that she was the daughter of the Magna Fakhaldak. Her mother's constant hatred of Princess Cleannes, whom she could never bring herself to see as Ruler, cooked up the plan to have her take her place and be protected if her dealings with the males were ever found out, as she might fear because of the hostility against her in the temple and the suspicions she had that her secret would be discovered.

The confession was so appalling to your noble father that he tore out half his beard in despair. The people saw this and out of duty and respect wanted to show the same proofs of their indignation—they wasted no time in imitating him. In less than a minute all the beards were torn off. The old men, because they were too weak, ran to the strong hands of the young and were plucked to the last hair.

That is where things stand at the moment, Princess, (continued the Karveder). The great Lindiagar is convinced that under such circumstances you have to make an appearance so that the sight of you will assure your incontestable right to the throne. The sacred mark that you have on your head will prove who you are and will protect you against any deadly tricks that the present troubles might cause.

---

[223] Distinctive punishment. It consisted of being put on a press and flattened like a sheet of paper. The liquid that came out was burned in front of the statue and the skin that was squeezed out was enshrined in the temple with a bas-relief showing the cause of the punishment.

"Why didn't you tell me this before?" I scolded. "I would be in the temple right now. You've made me lose precious time."

"No, Princess," the Karveder said, "the people are in the inoupisoir.[224] It would have been dangerous to interrupt their fury. When the Sun has gone down you will appear before the stunned people. These are the orders of the great Lindiagar. After that, Abska-kou.[225]"

The terrible word was too strong for me to add anything. I kissed his eyes and waited for the appointed time. The Karveder put my head between his legs and in this respectful position brought me to the gates of the temple. When the Sun was at its awaited point we entered. My noble father saw us, rang the Tok-ho-dor, lectured the people in my favor and made me mount his throne. He covered me with his cap and recognized me as Cleannes, i.e. Queen. My first act of authority was the destruction of the two laws that I had always hated. The natural custom of enjoying the presence of those who gave us life was reestablished in all its splendor and on the same day I ordained that all the males kept in the temple of Kaiocles be sent home, totally free of the princes and princesses of my race to marry whomever they wanted and proved worthy of.

The changes were not well received. The people grumbled. The Lindiagar, who was not expecting me to take things so far, made me see the consequences. I was about to say to my noble father that the supreme authority should be put

---

[224] A kind of delirium ordained by the worship when they want to sway the divinity. Once started it could not stop until sunset.

[225] This word is difficult to translate. The scholars explain it in several ways. Heinsius says that it means "there's no more to say." Scaliger is sure that after this supreme order it was not allowed to answer and it meant, "be quiet." It does appear, however, that in this case the respectful Karveder would not have used it with his master's daughter who was going to become the ruler. The Abbé Ménage feels the same and I thought it best to follow him, even though Madame Dacier fights long and hard against it, as well as de Fontenelle in his *Errata*.

above all considerations, but my attention was distracted by a general cry that broke out, caused by a great wonder. Fulghane was turning like a weathervane on its pole. The awful thing was going to give a divine order. I was dumbfounded. The King himself, in spite of his prejudice against his own religion, seemed shaken up. The statue stopped and let out a deep sigh. Our amazement magnified. In a clear and intelligible voice it spoke, casting dismay and worry on all the watching souls.

"So, it is done. My people must perish, the temple must be destroyed and I must leave this place forever. A proud King has raised a crooked daughter to annihilate my laws and their wicked subjects have accused my High Priestess, refused to obey my divine orders and defied them. If my divine power had not warned me of their awful projects, they would already be trampling my image under their guilty feet. Tremble, Amphicleocles, you are all going to die. There is only an instant given to you to repent. There is only one way to appease my anger and get back in my favor. The Lindiagar must be cast down from the High Throne and his daughter suffer the punishment that Magna Fakhaldak was unjustly condemned to. Let her daughter, and mine (that is a secret I want to reveal), be raised on the High Throne and exercise the sovereign power. Only then will I pardon you. Otherwise I will strike you down. I have spoken."

As soon as the Oracle had spoken, the people rose up in anger and wanted to obey. The Lindiagar, who was never as magnificent as in the most terrible dangers, threw his cap at the people, rang the Tok-ho-dor and ordered his Karveder to take the guards, force open the Sanctuary and smash the altar under the statue.

"I am being wronged and you are being seduced, Bilbou-gan-gan!" he shouted. "Fulghane is not speaking. It's a trick—Magna Fakhaldak is hiding inside. This amazing prodigy is nothing but one of her tricks. If things are not as I say and after going to the statue Fulghane really speaks or shows sure signs of his presence, then I will step down from the High

Throne. I myself will sacrifice my daughter to the divinity in compensation for the crime and I will seal it with my blood. After that, Abska-kou."

These words were spoken so majestically they froze the people who were ready to use lethal force. A humble silence fell and everyone waited for the results of the royal promise. They were not a little surprised at the ruler's insight. The Magna Fakhaldak was found inside the statue. Her old, ashamed face was buried in her hands. They had found the machine that made the statue turn and other tricks that would be too long to go into detail.

The people were outraged at being the dupe of the wicked High Priestess for so long and she and her daughter and all her subordinates fell victim to the people's unbound fury. They begged me (because I was recognized as the Ruler) to get out of the temple, go back to my palace and leave them free to satisfy their vengeance and anger. I thought it best to give in to their just requests.

Two hours later the temple was destroyed to the very last stone and the guilty were punished. Throughout the kingdom the great Vilkonhis was worshipped instead of the impotent Fulghane. Temples were dedicated and you could say that a great revolution had been accomplished without the state being attacked at all. It is always the case that when the truth is heard, it wins the day. By recognizing a supreme being the Amphicleocles found so much justice and humanity in their laws that they willingly and quickly bent under the gentle yoke. The great Lindiagar was made their minister. What glory after reigning as powerful King over their hearts and giving to his people so many proofs of his kindness during his reign. Now he crowned it all by working to make them happy until after death. Oh Heavens, it is you who accomplished this important work! How indebted we are to you for being so blessed? The Amphicleocles will praise you forever.

Part 6

The kingdom of the Amphicleocles enjoyed a profound peace. My father and I shared the throne and were calmly deciding its destiny when an event, as extraordinary as it was ill fated, altered our tranquility.

The Karveder came before me one day very disturbed, which foreshadowed the evils we were soon bound to fall victim to. "Two huge and incredibly powerful monsters have just appeared two leagues away from the capital," the minster told me. "This news coming from a neighboring city's governor caused me the utmost dismay and I ran, Queen, to inform you so you can take the appropriate measures to protect your states against the evils that this dreadful event might cause."

The matter seemed so important to me that I immediately went to my father's room to tell him. On hearing the news he changed color. "Oh, my daughter, the time of the prophecy has come. I praise the divine Being for everything. Fulghane was destroyed by our hands and the consequences are inevitable— I've been waiting for them." After this my illustrious father told me about the oracle[226] that foretold the day of our first blessed meeting. We worshipped the great Vilkonhis together and completely resigned ourselves to his divine will.

The Karveder, who was waiting for the end of our conference and for orders to deal with the awful news that he had brought, was quite surprised at our calmness. He tried in vain to make us destroy the worm monsters or at least to keep them away but our opinion was not to stand in the way of our destiny. He respected this and sighed when he kissed our heads. No doubt he left grumbling about our blindness.

Some time passed without mention of the terrible invaders. They were seen no more. But one day as I was walking in

---

[226] See Part 3.

the palace gardens, Za-ra-ouf, the terrible monster who was defeated by Motacoa's bravery, suddenly showed up, grabbed me and stole me away. My cries and those of my father did nothing but speed up my abduction. Oh harsh Heavens, my abductor ran faster than the winds! Another of his species sped in front of us to forge the path he had to follow. It would never be possible to believe the incredible leaps the two of them made and how fast they got away. At the very beginning I fainted and only came to after we had arrived in that awful den that was destined for me.

Za-ra-ouf, King of these monstrous people, as I said, did not wait to tell me his feelings. "Beautiful Tumpingand," he said as soon as he thought I was ready to listen, "I love you and want to make you the happiest of mortals. My kingdom is limitless and you will see the friendliest Trifoldaysters turn yellow with grief for the great honor that I'm favoring you with. But in order that you enjoy the favors I'll heap upon you and that you not miss your country and your rank that the great Ver-fund-ver-ne called you out of, you must know who I am, my great qualities and how hard it was for me to get to you."

The story of Za-ra-ouf

Of all the Kings reigning in the Inner Earth, I can honestly and humbly say that I am the greatest, the friendliest and the one who has attempted the most extraordinary things. Everything I have done so far has been the result of deep meditation. My predecessors tried in vain to break into the bright domain where the light shines freely, but I alone succeeded. At first my objective was only philosophical curiosity, but your reputation for wisdom and beauty reached even me through channels that you will soon learn about and it hastened my plans, inspired them with a feeling I had never felt before. My magnificent heart was completely obsessed with being in your charming presence. Bow down before me and listen carefully.

One day while I was reexamining one of the places where the light came right up to me, I heard the nearby stamping of stumpy worms.[227] I hid behind a rock planning to catch one of the monsters[228] when they showed up. I had been waiting for this great luck for a long time. The tradition of my kingdom had taught me that these savage people had a secret[229] that could infallibly destroy our cruel enemies[230] and more than one of our Kings had spent his time and energy trying to find their lair to make them give up this so-called secret. But all of their efforts so far had failed. These people were so horrified by us that they fled with as much energy as we spent trying to catch them. We had no idea why. No doubt it had to with some natural disgust, but whatever it was we never knew why[231] and yet it would have been really sweet to add this distinguished honor to my glory.

I do not know if the monsters smelled me or if I was wrong about them riding their fantastic horses, but whatever the case, I only saw a few stumpy worms with no riders come peeking through a crack in the rock where I was hiding. I decided to catch the first one within reach hoping that if I succeeded, it would lead me to its masters. I was just about ready to try it when one of them walked up slowly and sleepily,

---

[227] Fat, thick, monstrous worms with stumpy limbs. See end of Part 2.

[228] These worms were so fast that they were extremely hard to catch. Only the toad monsters had the ability to capture them and tame them. It was big business in the Inner Earth. The worm monsters bought them for the most beautiful Trifoldaysters. The toad monsters worshipped them and considered them the most desirable possession. The ardor to enjoy the women caused bloody wars, but the worm monsters always ended them with their unequalled bravery.

[229] He is talking about the carrying of the owl. See beginning of Part 3.

[230] Za-ra-ouf means the Basilisks; he calls all animals like Falbao by this name.

[231] Père Maimbourg claimed that the toad monsters' hatred for the worm people came from the fear of their teeth, which were hollow and housed a little black beast that killed the toad monsters if they were unlucky enough to get too close.

making it easy for me. I jumped out of my hiding place and onto its back. It was so scared that it started running at full speed and I held on so tightly, in spite of its bucking and galloping, that after two days I arrived in the country bordering our empire. The monster had barely got through the opening of the Inner Earth when he started suffocating. The same thing happened to the one my chief minister was following me on. Both of us stood a long time in awe of the magnificent sight before us. Our eyes could barely stand the sight of the eternal sky.[232] We took the first path we saw and after walking for three days we ended up at the foot of a surprisingly high and majestic wall. I had never seen the likes of it before and I was eager to know the reason for such a wondrous work.

It took us more than a month to walk around the wall. Its enormous size made me think that it marked the boundary of some extraordinary kingdom since the rulers were so careful to forbid entry. The more things I found blocking my burning curiosity, the harder I tried to overcome them. It was not an easy task, my beautiful Tumpingand, but I'm sure you know that, so I'll skip this part.

My minister and I found no way to breach the wall as simple as digging a hole and going under the wall into the wondrous kingdom,[233] but we lacked the tools to get started. After discussing the problem we agreed that we should go to

---

[232] Za-ra-ouf and his minister were so dazzled by the brightness of the light, which their eyes were not made for, that they were blinded for a few days. History says that they hid in a cave where they slowly got their eyes used to it. It is not mentioned here apparently out of pride and arrogance.

[233] The worm monsters were like moles. They could dig so easily that they could travel underground from one place to another just like walking. A scholar made an interesting comment on this passage: when a worm monster wanted to go underground it stood up on its tail and like a drill it turned round and round with amazing speed. It used its hands to throw out the dirt and if it was really in a hurry it ate it and when it resurfaced it could spit it out like it was just useless waste too heavy in its stomach.

the first town to find some and that if they refused to treat us kindly we would force the inhabitants to lend them to us.

But we had another problem with this. A simple town appeared on our left and as soon as we entered all the people ran away in fear. It was a little surprising to us. There was only one old man, whose decrepitude rooted him there, to help us out. In spite of being really scared he wanted to talk with us to help us in our project and give us a rough idea of your kingdom's traditions. What he told us was amazing and instead of giving up, my mind was completely made up.

These people, I told myself, must be very wise to be so determined to break away from the rest of mankind.

The old monster[234] lent us some iron tools that we could use to reach our goal. It took all my resolve to forge on. No underground trip was ever so hard for a Trifoldayster. After a month and a few days we entered your realm. We had learned through experience that the sight of us was frightening, so we were careful to travel only at night. During the day we hid in the woods.

After 15 days or more without meeting anyone or coming across any habitation, we finally saw a grand Kou-i-ouf[235] that was so strange that the minister and I laughed together for more than two hours. But we were wrong. People have their customs and what might seem ridiculous is really only unfamiliar. We decided to get through the wall and to enter the building in the middle of the night to take the residents by surprise and force them to answer all the questions I had to satisfy my curiosity.

It was basically just three things: First, to know if the bright star shining on you was a god that you worshipped or a creature that we might have relations with; second, what miracle allowed you to live with those monstrous growths that

---

[234] Men of another species are monsters in the eyes of those who really are.

[235] Palace. Its façade was magnificent. It had no doors or windows and the entrance was on the roof, accessible by a very tall ladder. The effect was remarkable.

we did not have; and third, if you were intelligent. A Trifol-dayster philosopher seeks knowledge and will risk everything to get it.

The old man I talked about and whom I asked these things seemed so poorly informed that I snubbed him like the monster he was. My opinion was that the people closed up within the walls were the sages who could resolve the thorny problems. Was there anything else needed to drive me forward in my search?

The time of night we were waiting for came. Soon we were in a room where a Tumpingand girl was lying in a box[236] with a male of her species. They were both in a deep sleep. I went up, uncovered them and was not surprised at what I saw. "Oh Ver-fund-ver-ne," I cried out, "can your glory be mani-fested in such mysterious ways?" And I threw the covers back on the monsters. I got tired of waiting for them to wake up, so I pulled the nose of the Tumpingand girl who started scream-ing like a snake. I couldn't help laughing at how quickly she buried herself in the arms of her male and so to have a little fun I pulled them both by their legs telling them that if they kept making my head spin with their screaming I would rip out their teeth and skin them alive like they deserved.

My words made them as gentle as moles.[237] I took ad-vantage of their tameness to satisfy my curiosity on the points I mentioned. I was not too surprised at the mental instinct with which they answered my questions, but when the Tumpingand young man told me your story, beautiful Ascalis Nasilaë, and described your charms, what did I feel? Right away a tumul-tuous heat burned my noble heart. I could not understand how you got on the throne, calmly, how determined you were to destroy that false, baroque divinity and how wise you must be to keep it all going. All this joined to your beauty and gentle-

---

[236] The monster calls a bed a box because the Amphicleocles slept in closed alcoves, a fashion that has been passed down to us.

[237] A comparison that the people in the Inner Earth often use.

ness captivated me. I decided right then and there to steal you away and make you happy.

I won't bore you with all the steps I took to put my plan in action. Just know that I got you to be with me without you knowing a thing. I have to confess that I love your rosy face—it makes me forget about those awful, disgusting limbs. I abducted you and you know the rest. Now, pay even closer attention, I'm going to finish.

I chose you to share my ever-so-sweet favors whether my people groan about it or not. I have unfailing ways to bend them to my will. Rejoice and bury your pride. Your court will consist of the most beautiful Trifoldaysters of my kingdom and soon you will reign over the strongest and bravest subjects of this land. You will be served by the stubborn people who tame the stumpy worms, a mark of distinction that no Queen has ever had before you. Let your tears be tears of joy.[238] I'll leave you now. I have nothing more to say.

Nasilaë finds her father

I cried, it is true, after that depressing conversation and though the monsters were fooled by my appearances of joy, I suffered nonetheless. I prayed to Vilkonhis and to my father for help. My despair brought me 20 times to the point of killing myself, worn out by my laments and my suffering. My beaten body surrendered to sleep and I had a nice dream that in the end calmed my worries. "It is you, Universal Master of all things, who comforted me with this dream to foretell the end of my troubles." The dream's message was too important to pass over in silence. So here it is:

---

[238] The purest proof of happiness for these people was to cry. If this note were here a few centuries ago our scholars would not have fallen into the gross errors they have when describing the funeral rites of ancient people, who, far from considering death a great misfortune, thought it was the greatest blessing. That was why their dead were followed by crying mourners—to make their joy known and to rejoice for them.

I was in a sumptuous room lying on a bed surrounded by aerial spirits who were talking together in an unknown language. One of them hit me with a crystal wand that had a wonderful effect: I could instantly understand their foreign language.

"Princess," the Spilghis said, "the time has come for you to lose everything that is dearest to you. Sacrifice it to the one you worship. The loss will be replaced by someone who will make you happy and the most powerful Queen on Earth. His name is Motacoa. Remember this name well and remember also that Vilkonhis is the Universal Master and he should be worshipped everywhere you rule."

Saying this the spirit disappeared. In his place a frightening monster brandished a zenghuis. I screamed in fright. It looked like that insidious Za-ra-ouf and he was trying to grab me. A handsome young man showed up ready to help me, but he was snatched away by another enemy of my peace. I was so affected by the violence that I jumped up to stop it, but as I stretched out my arm my hand was sliced off. It hurt so much and seemed so real that I woke up with a start, panting bitterly.

(I could not help interrupting Ascalis Nasilaë here (Motacoa said), surprised as I was by the perfect similarity between her dream and mine. The Queen, my mother, and those listening were also fascinated by the peculiarity. After answering a few questions on the matter, the Princess continued her story.)

Although the dream made a strong impression on me, it was nothing compared to the second conversation with Za-ra-ouf. Indeed, how could I have anticipated the new persecutions being prepared for me? What kind of proof of love was that? No one ever did the likes of it! After repeating that I had become the most precious thing in the world to him, the tyrant told me that since it was not the custom in his country to have legs, thighs and all that, he managed, in order to prove his love, to have them cut mine off so that nothing would stand in the way of me being his Queen. It was useless for me to protest that I did not want to be his Queen or to be mutilated.

Looking proud and confident, which angered me, he tried to prove that both were necessary, stupidly dwelling on how much better it was going to be for me afterward.

As firm as Za-ra-ouf was on the matter, his passion for me delayed the barbarous operation. But alas, I paid dearly for his acquiescence. One night while I was brooding over my unlucky destiny, I heard someone walking softly, trying not to make any noise, in the room next to mine. I trembled in fear and screamed out.

"Stop screaming, Ascalis Nasilaë," said a voice that went straight to my heart, "or you will lose your father who is risking his life to see you again."

Oh Heavens, how delighted I was to hear that! I got up, went to meet him and threw myself in his arms. A long time passed in this sweet embrace until a thought broke in: we could be caught. A dozen worm women were on guard in the next room. I told this to the Lindiagar and he said, "I am prepared for everything and I know that it is morally impossible to escape my fate. But my daughter, I will die happy."

"Father, let's go, let's run," I urged. "We don't have to risk our precious lives. We must be able to get out of here if you could get in so stealthily."

"I only hope that the extraordinary means that brought me here can fulfill our mutual desires! I will tell you, but first, hide me somewhere so I can wait for the plot to unfold that alone can accomplish our desires. If we can get two days, Za-ra-ouf will be finished and you will be free. That's what I need and it will work, if the glory of the sovereign mover of all things allows it."

I was pretty stunned by what he said, but without saying a word I thought about where I could possibly hide my noble father from prying eyes. I did not want to take any risks— chance always destroys the best-laid plans. My bed was big and I spent almost all day and night in it crying, so since I had no reason to leave it, that is where I hid the great Lindiagar. He agreed that it was the best place. After getting as comfortable as he could, he told me how he came to be there.

The Lindiagar's adventure

As heart-rending as your abduction was for me, Nasilaë, I did not lose my head. I ordered my Froul-bracs[239] to do their best to follow you and promised that whoever could tell me where you were would be given a province as a reward. A few days later one of them came back. He had kept you in sight and left only when he saw you enter this place. I was so happy with the news that I showered him with riches to add to his governorship and he was so thankful that he offered to risk his life to take you a message and bring one back, but, my daughter, I loved you too much to confer this mission on anyone else. This loyal subject and I prepared to come find you together and steal you back if possible. The plan I drew up was irresponsible, but I was defiant; I paid no attention to hurdles or snags.

No sooner had I formed the plan than I put it in action. The Froul-brac and I left and after a long, tiresome march we came into the center of the earth. I will spare you all the dangers I faced and the close calls I escaped. It would take three days to tell you everything and right now time is too precious to waste. I will only tell you about the adventure we had near the capital, which gave me hope of seeing you freed. The great Vilkonhis did this, I'm sure, for our mutual consolation. I hope that he wants to bring it to a happy end!

While crossing a rocky place, we heard ghastly screams from somewhere nearby. I stopped and looked around, but it was so dark there that I could barely see a thing. I slipped between two huge stones and saw something awful. 20 monsters were surrounding another and torturing it violently: the

---

[239] Runners. They were so fast that they did 10 karies (i.e. 10 leagues) in an hour. This is not surprising when you consider that they ate only feathers, cork and spider webs, light food that was more than a little conducive to making them supple and spry. I owe this important information to Madame Lévêque who took the trouble to elaborate it in one of her many works.

strongest were holding it down while some were bringing up basketfuls of rocks and others were stuffing them into the mouth of the poor thing. They forced the sharp stones down its throat with an iron rod all the way to its stomach. I shuddered at the sight. If I were able to help the sufferer, I would have done it, but what could I do against 20 monsters—the strength of one of them was enough to bring down an entire army of our men. I prayed to the Supreme Being to take pity on the worm man and it did not take long to see that my prayers were answered.

In fact, soon thereafter all the monsters abandoned the sufferer. When I figured that it was safe to approach, I did so. The worm man was stretched out on the ground, barely breathing. His stomach was so full of rocks that they were coming out of his mouth, which was ripped open by the last stone forced in. It made me more tearful than fearful. "Heavens," I cried out, "how can creatures of the same species be so savage to each other?" The words I poured out from my heart made the dying monster open its eyes and seem to recognize my compassion. Its heavy hand reached up to take the cruel stone out of its mouth, but it was too weak. Its hand dropped and its eyes closed again.

A humane sentiment took hold of me and I said to my loyal Froul-brac, "Let's try to take out that stone and, if possible, the others that are killing the poor thing. Maybe a little help will do some good." I wasn't wrong. After a great deal of effort, we got the stone out. The monster opened its eyes again and breathed, or rather sniffed. It was easy to see that if we could dig out his throat it would get back the life it was on the verge of losing. Thus inspired we set to work. Its throat was so big that we could both stick our arms down it at the same time. For eight hours straight we removed the rubble covered in blood and sand. There was no end to it and we started to worry that we would not be able to take out everything that was crammed in. Then nature, clever as always, did better than us. Breathing easier now thanks to our efforts, the monster sneezed so violently that it threw us 30 feet away. Luckily we landed on a bed of moss from where we saw the monster vomiting piles of rocks and sand. He was holding his sides and trying so hard to throw up everything that the caves around us resounded with his retching.

After a good hour of discharge, the worm man slapped his hands on his scaly[240] butt,[241] made a huge leap, dried his face with sand and looked around as if searching for something. He saw us, spanked himself again and jumped over to us.

My natural reaction was to imitate Froul-brac, who ran away as soon as he saw the monster heading for us, but an idea held me back. It is not natural, I thought, that a man be ungrateful for such a vital service as we just did. So, I waited.

"Tumpingand," it said, licking my face[242] with its huge tongue, "don't be afraid. I owe you my life. I was sentenced to death by the cruel Za-ra-ouf for opposing his marriage, which the laws of the state forbid. Without you I would have entered the void. There is nothing in the world that I won't do for you to show my gratitude. Without asking why you are here in this place I will serve you like a slave. That's the rule[243] here when you owe your life to someone. I conform to it with pleasure, especially since you had no reason to rescue me. You risked your life to save mine. Bour-bourouk."[244]

I congratulated myself silently for putting the monster in a position to be beholden to me and I considered how I could put his obedience to good use. Oh daughter, imagine how

---

[240] The skin of the worm men is like a snake except that it is so hard that the Great Mughal thought of making armor of it.

[241] A sign of great joy.

[242] A sign of gratitude.

[243] This is hard to understand and deserves to be explained. It is the law in the realm of the Trifoldaysters to lose your freedom when you owe your life to someone—you become their slave. Rich or influential people pay this off with huge sums. Horace was in this situation, which he explains rather well in a poem that has never been printed, but exists in a manuscript that can be found in all scholars' libraries.

[244] Which means, "I am yours. Command and I will obey."

comforted I was in knowing that not only was he going to help me, but he was ready to second me in my secret plans. And he told me more. He said it would be his great pleasure to take vengeance on Za-ra-ouf. He even added that his justified anger urged him to it; he was set on punishing him. He swore that he himself did not deserve what he got and so it was a matter of honor to overthrow the tyrant, who was hated by everyone for his savagery. He also admitted that the death of the King had been coming for a long time, but he had made himself so imposing that no one had tried to attack him yet. It was different now. By wanting to marry you, my daughter, his crime would weave the web in which he would inevitably perish.

So, it shouldn't surprise you, Nasilaë, (my illustrious father continued), that I got into the palace so easily. The monster became my slave and since he was all-powerful before his disgrace and his family holds almost all the high positions at the moment, he secretly met with his relatives and they conspired together to put Za-ra-ouf's brother on the throne. They will take advantage of his time with you to stick him with the grangard[245] and they promised to help us escape as long as you give the conspirators time to enter your room by keeping the tyrant with you as long as possible. They say it won't be hard for you. He loves you beyond words and you haven't done a thing. It's not hard to make it easy for them. And it's a matter of your freedom and happiness. The barbarian deserves to die because of the outrage that we've suffered and we should be ever so happy that the Heavens have worked in our favor so plainly.

---

[245] Very sharp fork that the worm men use by forcing it into their mouths. It was a very easy death and pretty nice for the soul. The Turks, that sensual, voluptuous nation, have adopted this punishment and they find it very good because when someone is sentenced to death, they die with pleasure.

Nasilaë witnesses a bloody tragedy

I had nothing to say to all this and I promised to do whatever they asked. My father's slave monster came back at the break of day and told us that everything was ready for the plot. Success seemed assured, but the Heavens were looking unfavorably on our attack. Za-ra-ouf was too much in love or had some kind of premonition about his fate: he arrived when they were not expecting him. My father and his slave were talking with the pretender about how they should free me and the clever monster, instead of exploding in anger, snuck away and ordered his guards to come back and catch us. The unlucky conspirator was handed over to the death squad again, which he had now earned twice, and my father was strangled by the tyrant's own hands.

The bloody tragedy took place right next to me. I was so desperate that I tried to kill myself. Za-ra-ouf stopped my hand about to plunge a sword into my breast. Although he tried to make me feel better, I continued to grieve. He could not know how hard it was for me see the death of the one he called the Tumpingand traitor. When he finally realized how inconsolable my grief was, he had the body taken to the mausoleum, thinking that this show of respect would appease me. But his efforts were in vain! The only way to ease my sorrow was to take his life.

While all this was happening, Za-ra-ouf's Council and the people were pressing him to hurry up with my mutilation. He tried to talk me into going to the punishment peaceably and then threatened to force me if I refused. In this situation I knew I had to stall him, so I promised that I would give in if he found two of my species to set an example. My guarantee filled him with joy. He ordered the public tracking and promised extraordinary rewards to his subjects if they brought him the Tumpingands—they had become so rare that I figured I would never be mutilated. I had the tyrant's word and having learned the customs[246] of the country I had no doubt that he would keep his promise to the letter.

While the savage King was working hard to bring his plans to fruition, a public calamity broke out that made the people bitter against him: Falbao showed up. The monsters remembered the fatal effects that his kind always had and that all their precautions were useless. They thought they had to sacrifice everything not to become its prey and they grumbled against their Ruler, saying that his breaking the laws had brought this scourge upon them. Za-ra-ouf was not surprised by the rumors and worked it so well that the basilisk (as they called the loyal dog) was caught. Everything I was told made me very curious to see it and become its master. I wanted to get hold of the animal so I could protect it from the hateful monsters. That was the reason I pretended to have knowledge that I did not have.

The rest of my story you already know, Motacoa, (the Princess of the Amphicleocles continued). You were caught and I awaited your arrival in fear. I thought I was done for when Za-ra-ouf told me that he had finally got hold of the two Tumpingands who would be mutilated with me. In order to make the ceremony as authentic as possible he put me on the throne where I was bound to reign, he said, forever. Some Trifoldayster, jealous of my promotion, had made him suspicious so he hid to see if he was right. He knew your name, which he had learned from the monster who had taken Boldeon. He remembered you. So, I was trembling and recalled the mysterious dream in which you had play such a large part. Your coming proved it was real. I fainted when I recognized you as the one from my dream. When I came to, I was next to that savage Za-ra-ouf.

I don't want to say anything else (Nasilaë said) because the Prince has told you what happened after our fortunate

---

[246] When a Trifoldayster was found to break his word, they considered him despicable and threw him to the toad monsters and became the Troukadors' slave.

meeting. I owe him everything and I will never forget it! Otherwise I would be the most thankless creature on Earth.

Motacoa and family go into hiding

We thanked the beautiful Princess of the Amphicleocles for being kind enough to tell us her story. We admired its singularity and we spent the rest of the day thinking about it. At the break of dawn the next day Boldeon went to see how we could leave the Inner Earth. He came back that evening and told us it was easy if we just went back the same way we came into the monstrous regions. The next day we set out and on the third day we reached Boldeon's house where we took all the necessary precautions to hide ourselves carefully.

Boldeon informed us the next day that my father had learned about Nasildaë's innocence through his experiments and had gone down into the pit of Houzaïl to look for her, but there had been no word from him since then. He said that the chief minister was dead and Ruraos, who had married his daughter, was more powerful than ever. He had killed or exiled everyone who might try to put me back on the throne. Not satisfied with this savagery (our firm friend continued) he made a thorough search for everyone who was attached to the former King.

"This place is not safe for you, Prince," he turned to me. "We all have to go to the other end of the kingdom, live quietly and raise no suspicions about who we are until the time is more favorable. There we can wait for the results of the covert plot I put into action to get you back on the throne. I will tell you later, but when it's time, you will show yourself for who you really are and take back the place that is rightfully yours."

We knew Boldeon too well. He knew too much for us not to do exactly what he said. Three days later we left and when we arrived here the Princess of the Amphicleocles wanted to unite her fate with mine. It was decided that she would return to her kingdom and put me on her throne. But Boldeon, who had been sent on her behalf, said that after the great Lindiagar's departure, the people revolted, reestablished the worship of Fulghane and declared the Princess incapable of ever governing. The cruel turn of events was instigated by the priests who had been chased away. My loving wife was sourly affected by the news because she realized she could not give me the crown that her generous heart had wanted for me. I was very grateful, of course; such sentiments are worthy of admiration and I swore to her that she was more precious to me than all the thrones in the universe.

We lived a calm, easy life until the death of my mother the Queen disturbed our tranquility. We missed her a lot and she deserved it. Ruraos was occupying my throne and, what I had just learned, Lamekis, (Motacoa continued) changed my situation a lot. See, after Boldeon put us there, he stayed incognito at the Court on my behalf. I had just got news from him to keep myself ready to leave at the first sure sign that the party that he had formed for me was in power. I would be on my ancestors' throne soon. That, dear child, (Motacoa told me as he squeezed my knee), is where things stand at the moment for me. It would probably be better not to talk about the important service that I did on the day before bringing you here when I saved your father's life, but it is far too much to your interest not to give it the attention it deserves.

One day as I was coming back with Falbao from fishing, something I did since coming here to hide my identity, I spied the boat you were on, with the others dead or dying. Being curious and humane I hurried to reach you in time. Night was falling and I could barely see things around me and by the time I had waded through the waters it was too late. Your boat was sinking fast and the others were drifting off. I was about to leave when Falbao dove into the sea and brought you back up, Lamekis. I guess you'd been forgotten on the boat. I was glad that I could at least save you and I carried you to my home. The next day I learned in the neighboring town that they had caught some whites and taken them to the King. I was sure that they were the poor folks who had drifted off the night before and my curiosity led me to where they were being held. The majesty of the old man earned my sympathy. I explained to him what happened very simply and imagine my surprise when your wise father thanked me because he spoke my language as well as I did. Just then I was alone with the venerable old man and told him how sorry I was that I could not save his life and that I was not lucky enough to do for him what I had done for you. He interrupted me excitedly and asked me to describe you. Recognizing you from my description he looked up at the sky, screamed,[247] and told me you were his son. He said he could die happy because you were saved. And he seemed so, in fact, and told me about some of his adventures and the persecutions that he had endured at the hands of the savage Semiramis. I was keenly interested in this detail and learned from him how to keep you from falling into the hands of the King by dying your face the color of the people here. He thanked me effusively and left you to my care. I was going to reassure him on the only regret he had in seeing those who were with him die by telling him that only white males were subject to the cruel punishment, but the guards were suspicious of our long conversation and forced me to leave. I have heard nothing since then of your noble father, but it is likely that he suffered his fate. The tyrant was too jealous of the destruction of the whites to pardon him and that is why I told you he was dead. By the Father of Light I hope I'm wrong and he was saved so that he will have some solace one day.

Lamekis and Clemelis

Motacoa finished there and I started crying bitterly. "Don't take it so hard," he said, "there's nothing we can do against the eternal gods. Submission is always the best way to make them well disposed. You have found another father in me and I will never abandon you. Nothing will please me more than to show my constant love for you." In fact, the

---

[247] A way of praying to Vilkonhis.

good-hearted Motacoa kept his word and it is not his fault that I am not the happiest of all men.

A few days later Boldeon came, followed by the most important men of the kingdom. His strategy was a great success. Boldeon had appealed enough to finally assemble the states. Once assembled he told them Nasildaë's story, proved her innocence and boasted about the great, royal qualities of her son, whom he called the legitimate ruler. After this prelude, he boldly asked to have his privileges returned, which had been unjustly stripped away. Following a long deliberation they appointed wise delegates to verify Boldeon's story. They found everything like he said and made their report. Consequently, Motacoa was recognized as the Houcaïs.

He told me this himself and said that of all the wonderful things that had happened to him, to be raised to this highest honor was one of the greatest. I thanked the Heavens for so much goodness and to make myself worthy I became closer and closer to the kind King who was so generous on his throne.

The new Houcaïs was welcomed by the states with sincere and spirited joy. His first act was to promote Boldeon and Lodaï to the highest offices of the empire. The second was to get rid of the barbarous law that banished all whites. The third was to give me an education that would make me chief minister in case the post was vacant.

Of all the subjects I could study, I was mainly attracted to Philosophy. I liked it so much that it took me no time at all to make considerable progress. I devoted myself to it entirely and I spent all my time at it, except for when I was with my kind Sovereign. I was constantly alone in the midst of a brilliant Court. It's even more surprising when you think that there were all kinds of pleasures everywhere. The gentle Houcaïs never grew tired of proving to his beautiful wife his loyalty and passion, but I carefully avoided all pleasures. The farther I went in the study of wisdom, the less I was interested in these dull pleasures. Sometimes I asked myself how you could waste your precious time, which you will never have again, in such empty, frivolous amusements! Isn't it committing your-self to a world that death destroys? If we were born for hea-venly things why do we spend all our time on earthly things?

That was how I thought in that wonderful time and I would be happy if I had kept thinking like that! But alas, we have only one mind to stand up against the myriad of passions that haunt us. Is it any wonder that its voice is so often muf-fled by the blaring commotion, especially once you are un-lucky enough to have let it into your heart?

I chose the loneliest, most secluded place in the palace to do my work. The only break I took was to look up to the Hea-vens sometimes to admire and adore the Creator. Up to then no physical experience had distracted me from the sublime heights—and I thanked the Heavens from the bottom of my heart. In studying man I learned about the different passions that he so often falls prey to and I saw myself as almost pre-destined to know them only in name. Who would have be-lieved that after reaching that age with firm and enlightened sentiments I would have been struck down so easily as I'm about to tell you?

Ah, sovereign Vilkonhis, obviously you allowed it to prove to me that man is nothing and your almighty grandeur has no equal. Love came to trouble my calm, to overthrow my philosophy and cause the tragedies of my life that would last until today.

One day while I was deep in study of an important pas-sage about the principle of man before his creation, I was dis-tracted by a soft, silvery song that struck me to the bottom of my heart. I looked up quickly and saw an open room with two women: the younger was singing while the older was brushing her hair, but from where I was sitting I could not see their fac-es. In all my life I had never dreamed of a woman—the mo-ment had come. I shuddered without knowing why and it de-vastated my heart.

I was embarrassed by what I felt and I knew that it was the beginning of trouble that I had to resist. I lowered my eyes and got back to work, but it was no good. As much as I wanted to, I could not fight the relentless distraction. My mind was a jumble and could not produce a single coherent idea. A powerful magnet was tugging at my eyes. I could do nothing about it—they were naturally drawn to the window. My mind could hold them in check for a little while, and when they slipped away, they saw nothing. Up until then I was still conquering temptation.

But the voice suddenly stopped singing and I could not help wanting to know why. Heavens, what a state I was in! I was blinded by a face more beautiful than the dawn. A young woman fashioned by the Graces was fixing her hair, which was blacker than a crow, around her forehead. The curves of her upraised arm were seductive in their natural beauty. Oh Sinouis, what was happening to me? Why didn't I run? But why run? Was it a crime to admire what the Heavens had created for our pleasure? I stayed there fixed in admiration. My study of morals and my reason tried in vain to tell me that to run away was a victory under such conditions. I was not listening. I gave myself up to the allure of admiring. Ah! It felt too good.

However, the young woman looked over and saw me staring at her. She jumped like she was caught off guard, blushed and ran away. All this happened in an instant. And right afterward my reason took over and despite the charm, perhaps I would have left first, but with what had just happened the excitement that I had almost rid myself of came back to me. I sighed for the loss of my pleasure and I wished it would return. While waiting for it I did not take my eyes off the charming spot where it had appeared.

More than two hours went by without the stranger reappearing. I ended up listening carefully for any movement in the room that might tell me she was still there. She showed up a second time. Was it a premeditated plan to finish me off or simply chance? She was wearing yellow gossamer through which I could see the outline of her body and the color was chosen to make her whiteness stand out. Oh Heavens! I was enraptured by her charms, but I would pay dearly for such

251

pleasures. The stranger left as embarrassed as the first time and I stayed there like a statue in cold blood.

More than eight days went by without her reappearing at the window. I had the patience to stay by mine the whole time hoping that she would show up again. And I was torn apart by my wretched impatience. There was nothing I could do to get her venomous picture out of my heart. There was even less I could do to get that stupid poison of seductive charms out of my head. I struggled in vain, but the harder I fought, the more the wound bled. Nothing could stop it.

Despite Motacoa's serious occupations to organize a group in the kingdom to get the Queen back on the throne of the Amphicleocles, which rightfully belonged to her, despite, I say, how busy he was with these concerns, through his friendship for me he noticed my changing mood and behavior. My present silence made him think that I was exhausted from too much studying, so he encouraged me to find some good company where young people dream all the time of finding new pleasures in order to share them. I would gradually lose the black and melancholic mood that was clouding me. I owed him so much. He explained things so as not to be disobeyed without being disrespectful, so I promised to do what he said. Could I do any less for a Prince to whom I owed so much in so many ways?

But it was always with great sorrow that I left my room, afraid of missing the fervently desired opportunity to see the stranger again. I thought that as soon as I left, she would come to the window and this idea tormented me wherever I went. When I left the Houcaïs, I flew straight to my room and trembled to look at my stranger's window. I saw a hand holding the curtain and I thought I saw a shadow watching from a corner. What went through me? Love makes us clever. I thought that my absence had made her curious and that by hiding myself like her, I would force her to come out. I guessed right. She was obviously worried or interested in my move and wanted to know why. Thinking I was in the back of the room she peeked out to see why I was not there, which was quite unusual, as she told me later. I was free to enjoy looking at her. Though the first sight of her had hit me hard, the second was no different the second time. I was enraptured. What eyes! What lips! Excuse me, Sinouis, but such exclamations are more than justified. It was like she was made to conquer all hearts.

I could not stand still any longer. I got so carried away I became foolish. I showed myself and clapped my hands together, humbling myself in front of her as if she were a divinity. She quickly jumped back, obviously embarrassed at being surprised like that. I was sorry for being brash, but I was not upset. She will see, I told myself, that I love her. My passion will convince her. Maybe it will prove better than the most calculated declaration of love. That's what I thought: Love is perpetual delirium; it is always talking.

Soon I could see that my action was not unsuccessful. Again I saw the shadow of my adorable stranger by the curtain and the hand holding it like the first time. There was no reason to think that this was done out of spite or indifference. No sooner are we lovers than we become actors. I pretended not to be seen. I started talking to myself. I looked up at the sky and prayed aloud to let the beautiful girl respond to my love. Not a word of my monologue was lost. She appeared to be listening carefully, at least as far as I could tell by her quiet, still attitude during the whole time I was talking. I guess I waxed eloquent. It was not possible not to. I was inspired by love, a shrewd teacher—it brought me a long way in a short time.

I received an order from the Houcaïs to go to the Queen's room where they were having a celebration called the Lak-tro-al-dal[248] in order to share the pleasure, which unfortu-

---

[248] There were only three kings who were to have this celebration. Four men, naked as a nail, started out by calling each other rude names and challenging each other. Then a fifth broke in, bigger and stronger, carrying a knurled whip and flogged them until they were furious and streaming with blood. The more they screamed and writhed in pain, the more the onlookers laughed. After this introduc-

nately interrupted the pleasure I preferred to all others. There-fore, I could not stay at my window and get some proof that my tender feelings had been understood.

The celebration was wonderful and gallant. The Court and the people, everyone had a great time except for me, lost in dreams and worried and worse off because I had to hide it out of respect. The Houcaïs was watching me all the time and every time the people cheered he buried a finger in my nose,[249] saying, "Well, isn't that wonderful? Don't you love that look?" and a bunch of other things like that to keep me watching. The King had a way of making his grandeur respected and beloved. Out of kindness he laughed at the most frivolous jokes and out of habit even started to like them. He went out as simply as anyone in his palace, hopping on one leg, and when he was in the street he stopped the passers-by and jumped over their heads, making them bend down, of course,

---

tion the flayed men jumped all together on their punisher and grabbed him wherever they could get hold to tear him apart. He fought until his strength gave out and then fell to the ground. The loser was put on a kind of round stool that was attached to ropes. Every other athlete grabbed a rope end and pulled. The one on the stool was thrown in the air so deftly that he landed on the seat every time. The game lasted about an hour and everyone enjoyed it immensely. It culmi-nated by throwing the loser out the window, under which a huge crowd of people was waiting. It was the height of the party because everyone was ready to catch him and toss him around to one another. The celebration ended by burying him up to his neck and to pay him back for all the trouble he had taken to entertain the court and the people, the King and Queen and all the nobility came and peed on his head. After this the crowd of people ran over each other trying to give him this mark of friendship and respect. According to Strabo the four athletes were not honored so highly, but did they really deserve to be? After the ceremony they put their heads through a specially made board and the people pulled their hair in a friendly way, not stopping until they were entirely bald.

[249] Sign of respect from the King and the greatest contempt for an individual.

so that they would not fall over backward, which happened sometimes.

When the celebration was over the King offered me to Bil-gou-router[250] with the Queen while he did some work with his chief minister, who had got some good news from around the great wall where a whole section had collapsed without anyone knowing why.[251] The event turned out to be opportune because it opened an entrance to the kingdom, which the Houcaïs wanted to take advantage of to put the Queen back on her rightful throne. I saw that the game was going to last a long time and it was a torture for me to think that I was going to lose that time that I could be putting to better use. But on second thought I gave in. What would they think if I refused? Wouldn't the Queen try to find out why? Women are more sensitive than men and cleverer at figuring things out. I cherished my secret and did not want to risk it.

I could have congratulated myself over and over for agreeing to play when I entered the game room. Can you guess, Sinouis, who was there? Oh Heavens, imagine how frenzied I became when I saw my adorable stranger there! She blushed. And I was no less embarrassed. The Queen, who was

---

[250] A royal game that only the nobles could play. It was called Bil-gou-ta-ber-ker and was played like this: Everyone chosen to Bil-gou-router lied down on their bellies in a circle on the ground. Then they let loose the Bil-gou-rout, a fat, wild rat, in the middle. All the chins were touching the ground and the mouths were open so that the rat could save itself in whichever one it chose. The aim was to catch the rat. When it tried to get away there was a slave standing there to whip it and the circle was so tight that there was no way to escape the whip except by running into a mouth. When the Bil-gou-rout was caught, he or she who got lucky stood up and hid it secretly among the players, asking one of them, "Where's the rat?" They had to guess right or do whatever he or she said, usually a song or a kiss. But if he guessed, if it was a man, he had the right to take whichever lady pleased him most into the next room and do what he wanted with her. If it was a lady, she could do the same to a man.
[251] It was caused by an earthquake. See Heinsius, *Treatise on Collapses*, page 13, London edition.

crazy about the game we were about to play, gave us no time to get bothered. We took our places. Mine was facing my charming neighbor. I could look directly at her. God, how happy I was! The Bil-gou-rout was let loose and whipped, made three trips around the circle and finally ran into the Queen's mouth. She snatched it with her teeth and was beside herself in joy. We all saw it as a good, lucky omen and congratulated her. After making a few feints to hide the rat well, the Queen chose me to guess where it was. I had only the stranger on my mind, so how could I have named anyone else? I threw the Bul-gil[252] at her and she caught it looking ashamed, which made everyone laugh. Oh Sinouis, what luck! I had guessed it. I could take her into the next room and talk to her. I could not have behaved better at first, but the second I was alone with her I was like a statue. I did not know what to say and I could not get one word out of my mouth.

Nevertheless, it had to end. The rules of the game granted only four minutes before we had to reappear. No sooner did the Tok-ho-dor[253] ring than the Queen knocked on the door—time's up. I sighed and was angry for wasting such precious time. On leaving I wanted to ask her forgiveness for my trouble and stupidity, but I still had use of my mind only— I could not talk. The stranger smiled and sat back down, giggling at me, which managed to make me even more foolish than ever.

An opportunity lost is lost forever. I had no second chance for the rest of the evening. We were about to stop playing after the three hours were up when the King, coming back with his minister, asked to start over. He took his place, a new Bil-gou-rout was brought out and it took a good thrashing before making its choice. It was great fun, but finally ended up in the chief minister's mouth. We all laughed a lot because his

---

[252] A ball with a string attached so they could pull it back if they were wrong. It was used to keep track of the order because they kept it until they were answered.
[253] Square bell.

mouth was so big that the rat buried itself completely inside and we had all the trouble in the world getting it out. The King and Queen and all the Court watching the game died laughing. Finally the Bil-gou-rout was hidden and my adorable stranger guessed where it was. According to the rules, she had to choose a man and I flattered myself for a minute that she would do me the honor that I did her, but how hard it was—the King got the Bul-gil. I was in a pitiable state, then, without really knowing why. The Prince disappeared with the stranger. The four minutes seemed like a century. How much we suffer when we see the one we love in the hands of another; there is no torture like it!

When the King came back with Clemelis (that was the stranger's name, which was mentioned during her absence) the Queen congratulated her on her choice and I saw a look of satisfaction on his face, which struck me to the core. The Houcaïs sat down next to me and seemed like a totally different man. He asked me kindly if I felt sick. I did not have the strength to answer. The question chilled my blood and I passed out.

I woke up in my room surrounded by all kinds of people and doctors. To get rid of them I said I needed to rest, that that was the only way to get me back on my feet. When they said they did not want me to get sick, I got mad. I had to yell at them to be alone like I wanted.

After they gave in to my wishes and I had blocked my door so I would not be disturbed, I flew to my window. Oh unexpected wonder, unparalleled luck! Clemelis was there! She made a wonderful sign, putting her hands together and then one on her head and the other over her heart to let me know that she had been very worried about my accident. My tongue was untied then. "I am the happiest of men," I told her, "since you are interested in my well-being. I wish I were at your knees to express my deepest and sincerest gratitude."

A sign from Clemelis told me that I did not have to say more. I obeyed right away, punctuating my silence with gestures of love and passion. She looked pleased, tilted her head to the side and looked at me with those eyes…those eyes…Oh Sinouis, I was totally lost. Was any catastrophe greater than mine?

While sharing our feelings I was inexpressibly happy, but Clemelis suddenly went away with a quick sign telling me to do the same. I obeyed grumbling to myself about what was happening. I was really troubled by it, so I stood where I could see but not be seen. Clemelis' window was open and a gentle breeze blew the curtains very slightly. When this happened I could spy all the way to the back of her room and I spent a pretty long time watching to no purpose. But suddenly I saw a man and I knew it was the King. The sight reminded me of the day before. What was I to think? Clemelis had torn herself away from me and obviously had her reasons for dealing with the Houcaïs. I fell into a maelstrom of thoughts.

It was totally natural. Clemelis, the most beautiful girl of the Court, could, of course, have affected the King the same as she did me. The Houcaïs always seemed to love Nasilaë tenderly, but wasn't it possible that this tenderness was worn out? An endless array of thoughts, each more cruel than the last, ran through my brain. I was jealous. I had studied the passions too much not to recognize it. Oh Philosophy, once so dear, what good were you now? If you intended me to be faithful to you, why didn't you come around looking like that adorable Clemelis? I never would have traded you in.

I spent two hours in this cruel state unable to make myself feel better. I tried to recall the signs she had made to me and I shuddered. They could have been ambiguous and the King's visit not. He knew that my room faced Clemelis'; he came by and asked to talk with one of my servants or with me. Without letting on what I was thinking, I decided to figure out his plan, so I called someone to find out after I got back in bed. I had guessed right. The King had asked what I was doing and if I was well enough for him to visit. I sent a message and he came back to my room across the hallway that he had the only key to. If I wasn't so cruelly bent against him, I would have felt very honored. It was a great and sure proof of the friendship that he showed me.

"Lamekis," he said after sitting down, "I have finally learned why you're so listless and distracted. You're in love and if I'm not mistaken, I know with whom. I expect an honest confession from you so that I can help you to be happy. I have been like a father to you and now it's time that you spoke to me like a son. Share your private thoughts with me. I want you to admit it and you will see that it will be for the best."

Instead of trusting these unmistakable signs of kindness, I staunchly denied his assumptions about my melancholy. Two reasons made do this. Firstly, the suspicion I had that the Houcaïs loved Clemelis and a confession like this could be harmful to my love for obvious reasons. The second reason was the false shame I had of refuting my principles that I was once so proud of, but had abandoned so easily. I beat around the bush and blamed my bad moods and bad health. Since the King was only pressing me because he cared about me, when I assured him of what I was saying, he changed the subject and talked about a celebration he wanted to give the Queen and his whole Court. Two days later he was kind enough to amuse me by filling me in on the details, guaranteeing that he would postpone it if I were not feeling well enough to attend. The idea of seeing Clemelis and watching her behavior, in my suspicions about her and the King, made me convince him that I was feeling well enough to revel in my King's glorious celebration, adding with a smile that I was starting to think like a reasonable man and did not want to miss out on the palace pleasures. My speech was well received and put him in the best of moods.

"In honor of this new attitude," he said, "which I like a lot, I want to tell you something that you will be very glad to hear: You have saved the life of the Queen's daughter whom we love a lot and it's only right that she herself give you the thanks you deserve. Until then... Your look of surprise tells me you're curious. And rightly so, I admit, but I have decided not to say more. With a little thought and insight anyone could figure it out, so I imagine it will be easy for you."

After saying this with a cunning smile, the King left and I was as dumbfounded as I had ever been. I had saved the life of the Queen's daughter? But when, good god? And how? (Either my memory was really bad or useless.) And I had to be thanked for it? The girl certainly knew that she had to do it, so why was it taking her so long. How was it that the King knew more than I did? Everything threw me into confusion. One thought led to a thousand more. And yet when the King left Clemelis' room his first words to me were about my presumed passion. What did all this mean? I was lost. Moreover, not long ago Clemelis avoided looking at me and then all of a sudden she kept coming back to the window, looking sweetly at me, making obvious signs. What hidden springs were being set in motion? This was what I thought about.

I was in deep meditation when the charming Clemelis reappeared in the window with an older woman to whom she pointed me out and no doubt talked about me. I was intimidated, surprised and held back my feelings at seeing her again. Every time our eyes met, hers smiled and revealed a well of kindness that could not have astonished me more. Fate was acting and wasting no time to drive me to my destined goal.

Some nobles of the Court, who had been present when I fainted, came to see me and I could not honestly deny them entrance. It was not so much for me as for the Houcaïs that they came. One of the courtiers, a flighty, superficial young man who could not stand still, went over to the window, leaned out for a little while and came back to me congratulating me on having a neighbor who was (he said) the sweetest in the realm. Another, who did stand still and had no idea what the little Monsieur was talking about, asked for a name.

"It's Clemelis," he replied.

"Clemelis," a third one repeated (speaking for me). "How lucky you are! There's no one in the world like her. For me, I would lay a crown at her feet." He raised his voice, went over to the window to be sure to be heard and while pretending to talk to us made the usual declarations of love. I was livid, but I kept quiet. Once begun it was useless to try to change the subject of conversation. After reeling off a bunch of compliments, they went into details, which did not disappoint me.

"We all know that she's a foreigner," the little Monsieur said. "But none of us could find out how the Houcaïs got her under his protection. If we didn't know him so well, we'd imagine that he was under her spell, but his conduct toward her, by giving her to the Queen, makes us to think otherwise. What we can't understand is why they're keeping secret about where she came from. But it doesn't matter," he added like he was speaking to himself, "we'll find out. It can't stay hidden forever. Just like the secret that she keeps about her love life. She's been love struck and there's nothing she can do about it. Even for an expert, however canny they are at playing their game, it doesn't take long to become public. As for me, I love her and I'm cut to the quick. I won't be able to rest until I unravel the mystery, which I'm working on at the moment."

The little Monsieur left it there. The other fool like him took up the conversation and even though he said nothing more or different, he was more than a little helpful in making me hold onto my original suspicions. "Don't torture yourself," he raised his voice, "trying to guess who holds her heart. You've already named him without knowing it."

"What...the King?" the little Monsieur exclaimed.

"Yes, the King," the courtier continued. "I've happened to see him enter or leave her room probably ten times. Even today he went by in the morning and if you want to go on and say that it was nothing and meant nothing, at least you have to admit that it's worth thinking about."

I had been waiting for this semi-proof impatiently and they gave it to me. For some time (they agreed) the King had been going without fail to all the little games when Clemelis played and he had changed, too. This impressed and depressed me. I tried not to show it, but I was so lost and distracted that I was not angry anymore. No doubt they figured they were bothering me and finally took their leave, promising me their friendship, which I gladly would have done without.

Oh Sinouis, think about this new situation and how upset I was after they left. A few days earlier I had been given devoted signs by Clemelis. In 15 minutes I saw them coming from some unknown ploy meant only to make me fall into a trap that I could not understand. I was so deeply disturbed that I resolved to fight against my passion and never again appear at my window unless I was sure to be strong enough for the fight. I resolved and right away started proving to myself how determined I was. I went into another room where I stubbornly waited for the day of the celebration, which I could not get out of after giving my word to the King that I would go.

My behavior brought me an unexpected letter. On the third day an unknown slave came and asked to deliver to me personally a note that had been given to him. It had only a few words.

The Letter of Clemelis

I am worried because I don't see you anymore. I know that you are not so sick that you can't come to the window. What am I think about your enthusiasm followed by such coldness and this strange behavior? I would like to understand it. I dare not. I'm afraid of learning something unpleasant. I am too indebted to you to risk falling out with you. Goodbye.

Instead of delighting me the letter fed my distrust and doubled my troubles. My first reaction was to send the slave back with no answer, but a clever idea stopped me. We owe a certain consideration to women that a well-raised man ought never to forget. I put pen to paper and wrote a response.

The Letter of Lamekis

I can take pride in the kindness mentioned in the note only if it was received with as much gratitude as possible. The behavior that you are pretending to complain about is the nat-

ural result of sensible thoughts. I, too, would like to know and would be less disturbed about an exchange of promises that I don't understand at all. I would be only too happy to have given rise to it; I would commend it, but I won't let improper feelings lead me astray from the respect to a King whom I owe so much and care for so much.

The first draft of my letter was more intelligible and voiced my suspicions, but before sending it I thought it best to be more ambiguous and my note had the effect I was hoping for—Clemelis proved it by the cold looks she gave me when I saw her on the day of the King's celebration. How sensitive she was to the cavalier manner in which I answered her letter! Up until then I thought I was right and even applauded my firmness. I don't love her anymore, I told myself. My reason has pierced the cloud and given me back power over my astonished senses. What could I say? I had never loved so much and I realized that right away.

The celebration lasted for three days and during this time Clemelis looked so beautiful, so wise and so modest that I reproached myself for having been able to suspect her of tricks and intrigue. Her face was all alit with honesty. She often conversed with the King and I even had the chance to follow them into an out-of-the-way grove where I could easily find out, without being noticed, the truth or falsity of my misgivings. But I heard nothing to convince me. Every time the Houcaïs spoke to her, the beautiful girl's eyes lowered and her cheeks blushed, betraying her innocence and modesty. When she smiled, it was with a grace and decency that could only be admired.

When the heart is wounded, good and bad feelings come and go in rapid succession. Before the third day had ended, I was totally wrapped up in beautiful Clemelis and had scolded myself a thousand times for having missed so many favorable opportunities as were offered at a celebration where freedom was given to all. I decided to try to mend my blameworthy behavior.

The Houcaïs provided the means by asking if my attitude and indifference had changed their tune. "You assured me," he said, "that you were more reasonable about having a good time. And yet seeing you up close these last few days I find you dreamy, distracted and melancholic, like a man who is here out of complacency, like you were here just to indulge me. My plan was to keep my word about the matter I mentioned to you, but you haven't looked at all ready to hear me out, so I've left it at that." The King added that I must not be very curious about what he had said: "Either you don't care about anything at all or you hide it better than anyone. I won't humor the one or the other," he laughed, "so, watch out! I'm going to blow you over more than you think."

I answered naturally enough to this new attack and deftly took advantage of it to make the Houcaïs speak. "Lord, I am dreamy and distracted, I agree, but who wouldn't be after what you said to me? My insight is not keen enough to solve unsolvable puzzles. Since I was old enough to live under your laws, I have never strayed. And nothing important has ever happened to me that you were not informed of. How, then, could I save the life of a daughter of the Queen? And where...?"

"Let me break in," the Houcaïs smiled. "Your excuse is well-founded and deserves consideration. Follow me. I don't want to keep you waiting any longer. It's only fair to tell you."

With this he took me by the hand and led me into a room where the Queen was playing Buck, Buck[254] with her ladies, particularly teaming up with Clemelis and another lady whose look struck me to the bottom of my heart. "Lamekis," he told them, "is making me sad. I had decided to keep the secret from him until it was the right time for us, but his worries and sluggishness have made my mind up. I leave him to you," he

---

[254] Only royalty was allowed to play this wonderful game, but by wholly royal kindness the people were allowed to watch. Alas, how fickle is man! This royal game has gone completely out of favor and is almost never played anymore.

told the Queen. "I will take your place and continue your game. Go fill him with the purest joy." With that he left me and the Queen and took his place.

She smiled graciously and said, "Aren't you moved, La-mekis, when you stare at me? I have only one thing to tell you that will make you the happiest of men. Before I explain I would like you to try to guess what it is. You have before you someone very dear. Remember your childhood and that fatal day when you were menaced on the sea and lost this precious treasure."

"Ah!" I shouted, staring at the lady with Clemelis. "I'm seeing...I'm feeling...I know...ah, my dear mother!" I could say no more. My knees gave out from under me. I wanted to jump in the arms of Milkhea. It was her—the Heavens had saved her. But my emotions had wrenched away my strength. She hugged me as hard as she could and called me by the sweet name of "son." I was filled with joy.

The scene was too emotional and very personal to me, but the Queen and Clemelis were watching and seemed to be part of it. I had barely expressed my first reaction when I asked for news of my father. Milkhea suddenly became awk-ward and sad and told me everything. I asked no more questions and there was a moment of silence. I cried as bitterly as if it was the first time I had heard the news.

The Queen interrupted my grief, reminding me that we all must submit to eternal decrees. "Your illustrious father lived too well not to be glorified. Now the Heavens demand acts of gratitude, not grief. You were granted the great favor of seeing your mother again and that should cut off any other emotion." These words dried my tears and the sight of my most venerable mother did indeed fill me with pleasure and I told her this again in my most tender embraces.

Milkhea then told me my father's whole story, which I was only partially aware of, and exactly the way I told you, Sinouis, but when she got to the part of us being cast to sea[255]

---

[255] Part 1.

and on the point of dying of hunger, she stopped. "That's where supreme Providence," she looked up into the sky, "must always be worshipped. Everyone was dying of hunger and misery. I lost my dear daughter and my illustrious spouse was himself on the verge of death. Haronza paid the tribute to nature. A savage mother tried to eat her own daughter. An infant almost died and then, an instant later came back from the everlasting night. Your blood, my son, gave her life! She sucked your wound and the gruesome nourishment saved her."

"What are you saying?" I interjected, looking stunned at Clemelis. "Is that the solution to the puzzle and the thanks that the King alluded to? Could I ever be happier seeing that the Heavens wanted to make me the instrument of their glory and their choice fell upon the one person in the world who seems the worthiest to me?"

"This hugging and kissing that my gratitude has caused," Clemelis broke in blushing, "answers all your questions in the positive. If I hadn't been ordered to hold back my thanks until today, I would have unburdened myself of it the instant I learned that you were my savior."

Her words and grace in saying them brought back all my heart's fire for Clemelis and destroyed all the ideas I had about her complicity with the King. Nothing was more natural than their conversations together. It was easy now to know that they were talking about me. Moreover, this lovely girl had never left my illustrious mother. I had just learned that in her story: she had replaced my sister and Milkhea thought of her as her own daughter whom the Heavens gave her to adopt. In a flash all these thoughts came rushing to me at the same time. Instead of the worry that had eaten away at me for days, my heart was full of pure joy. I expressed it in the liveliest terms. And I did more: I confessed all the feelings that had motivated me. The Queen and my mother made me feel better by saying that the Houcaïs was ready to consent to my happiness. Only Clemelis was silent, but it was a sweet, encouraging silence. How happy I would have been if I could have made the most of Heavens' favors! But alas, are we born to be happy in life?

The King, who soon learned of my love for Clemelis, scolded me a little for hiding it from him. "You know I love you," he said kindly, "and I wouldn't refuse you anything if it would make you happy." I was careful explaining to him my reasons and he was satisfied with my summary. We ended with a formal decision to unite Clemelis and me as soon as possible in sacred bonds. In the meantime I was allowed to see her all the time.

If her adorable charms had made such an impression on me at first sight, her brilliant mind and gentle personality finished it off by making me realize that I was luckiest man in the world. In fact, her admirable qualities were above all possible praise. Oh Heavens, who could have thought that what should have been the source of my happiness, would end up being the cause of our separation? But, Sinouis, allow me to linger a little on this awful moment. It's absolutely necessary under these circumstances to bring everything to light and, if possible, to make me less to blame. That's the result of pride—it does all it can to avoid being blamed.

Boldeon had a son who shared the favors of the Houcaïs. He was so nice to me and was so handsome that I could not help feeling honored to be friends with him. Nevertheless, however close I felt to him, I had hidden until then my love for Clemelis. I felt now I had to be the first to tell him about what would soon become public. He had a right to reproach me and doubt the friendship that I assured him of everyday. Furthermore, he seemed surprised at my confession and talked about the charms of marriage as a hard and heavy load that I would regret sooner or later.

He went on to say that Clemelis was too beautiful to make me happy. "You love her too much. You'll love her even more after you have her. Her delicacy will lead to jealousy and jealousy to the tragedy of your life. Her beauty will lure lovers and you will live in anxiety. As long as her delicacy remains, you will only think about rivals, but as soon as jealousy takes hold, everything will take a turn for the worse. Respect, the foundation of true happiness, will vanish. You will think your spouse is neglecting you in the most important things and when this feeling comes, you will make each other unhappy."

I felt the truth of everything he said, Sinouis, but this cruel attitude was much less born out of friendship than selfishness. Zelimon (the name of this friend) had his reasons for telling me these things. You will soon see why.

Boldeon's return from the kingdom of the Amphicleocles, where he had gone to deal with some business of the Queen, brought some wonderful changes for the Houcaïs. The Queen was recognized as Ruler of the land by means of the skillful minister's ruses; and the conspiracy he had hatched with the subjects who were still loyal to Nasilaë was far more successful than anyone could have imagined. Everyone was happy and the Abdalles showed it by celebrating all the festivals they had for good fortune. I shared the pleasure by getting married to Clemelis. The Houcaïs, the Queen and all the Court attended. Zelimon, my closest friend at the time, served as Absok-cor.[256] The test only made me more confident in my feelings. The next day I was the luckiest man alive.

---

[256] In the kingdom of the Abdalles it was the custom to teach a girl about to be married about the duties that she has to fulfill. He whom the groom chose to indoctrinate his future bride personally attests to her virginity. At sunset on the eve of the wedding day the Ab-sok-cor, who was responsible for their future by imparting the marital duties, went to the virgin's house and showed his authorization to the father, mother or guardian. His authorization was the "shirt of the future" on which was written in red that he was the proxy. When it had been carefully read, they fetched the virgin and handed her over to the Ab-sok-cor, who then shut himself in a dark room with her (a modesty ordained by law so that she not be too ashamed). There, stretched out on a sofa, the future bride listened, but could not speak, to all the nuptial obligations she would enter into. After a long, long speech about the way she had to attract the hugs and kisses of her husband, he asked her if she was pure. She usually answered "yes"

A few months passed in the drunkenness of pleasures, which created a mutual tenderness. The lovely Clemelis was always on my mind. The sweetness of her personality, her seductive ways, everything in her enchanted me; and nothing seemed able to alter my happiness. But how little I knew the world, or better said how little I knew myself! I soon learned through a fateful experience that the happier you believe you are, the more you are on the lookout not to be. The cycles of life, like the seasons of the year, follow one after another. That's what will be proved right now.

The Queen, who was burning with desire to put the crown of the Amphicleocles on the head of her most beloved spouse, sought insistently day after day to make the trip. Eventually the Houcaïs gave in. Orders for the departure were given and Clemelis was appointed to accompany the Queen. For myself, I would stay by the King who would follow them a few days later. This delay was, in fact, political in order to give time to the Queen's subjects to receive her with the requisite solemnity. This cruel, short separation was a dire omen of a much longer one and the dreadful source of all my wanderings.

Clemelis had only just left when an unbearable unrest took hold of my mind. Those rivals whom I did not fear so much when I was in a position to watch their craving for my wife now seemed dangerous and oppressive. It was no good looking in Clemelis' wisdom for an antidote against the fatal poison that was slipping into my heart—nothing could assuage my alarms. Little by little the unrest took control of my worried mind and I could not hide it anymore.

(and that goes for all countries), so the Ab-sok-cor wrote "probably"...and then, after thinking about it, "I have my doubts" to which the virgin was to answer, "Prove it." The chaste author of the story leaves it at that. At the break of day the Ab-sok-cor went to the groom, kissed him and said, "The child sleeps" to which the future husband responded, "So let's go wake her up." Then they went to the temple where they consummated the wedding.

Zelimon saw it. "Well now," he said one day after watching me with pity, "isn't this exactly the state I predicted you would be in? You're jealous and slowly losing it. If this continues, you'll wind up at death's door. And I see no relief for your torment since the cause is not about to disappear. Clemelis is young and her charms are only just blooming. There will be more lovers everyday and consequently more torments for you. Thankfully among all these admirers there's not one who is nice enough, powerful enough or, to be sure, relentless enough in his pursuit to put you in the position of having to question your wife's wisdom. But that's when things will come to a head. There will be no comfort for you then."

Zelimon told me things like that everyday. Instead of reassuring me, he only talked about the fickleness and wickedness of women. His moral philosophy was constantly poisoned by the most detestable traits and outrageous examples. Sometimes it got so bad that I was 20 times on the verge of sneaking away and going alone to verify my mistrust. Only shame held me back. Alas, why didn't it last forever?

The time appointed for the Houcaïs to meet up with the Queen had arrived and he prepared to leave. His entourage was sprightly and gleaming. Every courtier kept adding to the cortege and trying hard to honor his powerful Monarch. Mine was not one of the less noticeable. I even dare say that after the King's it was the best arrayed. The idea of showing up before my dear Clemelis looking nice on the outside to flatter her vanity played a major role in the care I took to manage it. The Queen and her Court were supposed to be in the galleries when we entered. It was a day to get oneself noticed and when you're in love, you try more and more to please.

But baneful fate refused me the consolation that I had sought for so long—I got sick the night before our departure. The teams had already left and the message already sent to the Queen, so when the Houcaïs came to see me alone, he assured me that he wanted to postpone the trip, but he could not do it because of the trouble that he knew a second message would cause the Queen. In spite of my agitation, I was able to show my appreciation of his good intentions. But alas, could I have foreseen that I would soon be so blind. Heavens, is it possible that our reason hangs on by a thread and vanishes at the first shock to our desperate passions. My sickness degenerated into lethargy and I became so weak that I could not travel.

If anything could have distracted me from my devouring melancholy, it was Clemelis' letters in which she expressed her most sincere and tender love. It seemed that this lovely woman foresaw my menacing fate or she spotted the cruel downward spiral in my character caused by jealousy: she gave a faithful account of the effects of her beauty, joked about her victories, ridiculed the admirers and made me want to blush at my ridiculous, misplaced suspicions. But in spite of these honest means to calm me, I could not get over my mistrust: Zelimon was writing me as often as Clemelis. He reeled off camouflaged stories with such skill and malignity that they always seemed to have something to do with what I was thinking and my defiant jealousy would not stop brooding over his words. I waited impatiently for my health to return so that I could watch Clemelis myself. Every minute I imagined different ways to get to the heart of her secrets and my suspicions became so strong that I felt a kind of pleasure when my overheated imagination conjured up proofs to dishonor me. Could the torture have gone further? Yes, of course. The passion drove me to the brink, which I will talk about in time.

I said that Clemelis often wrote to me. Her regularity slowed down the impetuous turmoil that was stirring me up, but I lost it when I was severed from these life-saving letters that were so necessary to me at the time. I pictured thousands of reasons, each one crueler than the last, why Clemelis no longer loved me and was so caught up in her new feelings that she forgot even the least propriety. But I held back the final thought for a few days. A foundation of respect and veneration kept arguing in her favor and prevented me from surrendering to the fires of jealousy that were consuming me. I went from one courtier to another to figure out what was best to do until a letter from Zelimon made my mind up for me. It is too crucial to the events that followed to omit it here. Moreover, you will be able to see the character of this worthless friend. It was written thus:

Letter of Zelimon to Lamekis

> *I would be lying to you, dear Lamekis, if I tried to insinuate that your absence plunges us in sadness and grief— nothing is less true. The Court was never so brilliant and never had so many pleasures. They are endless: what you have seen so far is nothing compared with the present. There's a rumor that the Houcaïs is in love and that the brilliant parties he keeps throwing are aimed at an appreciable, valuable prize. But I'll stop there. Silence is prudent.*
>
> *All our ladies, without exception, are trying to outdo one another in beauty and pleasure. Do you think in this environment that love is lacking? No, Lamekis, it feeds all the courtiers with its sultry flames; it is all we see.*
>
> *The King still loves you a lot. He often says something is missing and it's you he means. You should have received a letter from him the day before yesterday. He is surprised, like everyone, that your sickness drags on. If some hearts are indifferent, we don't bother them. We want you here. We love you and we will be delighted when you come. So, hurry up; it's the best thing that can happen to me.*

The letter was the last word. Without saying anything definitive, didn't it tell me everything? I reread it a hundred times and the more I analyzed it, the more convinced I was that Clemelis was unfaithful. One part in particular plunged my thoughts into the dark depths: *There's a rumor that the Houcaïs is in love and that the brilliant parties he keeps throwing are aimed at an appreciable, valuable prize. But I'll stop there. Silence is prudent.* What should I make of this silence and odd discretion? I decided that in spite of my weakness I would leave and go there "incognito."

While passing through a town where I had to change horses and rest a few hours because of my weakness, I learned

272

that a lady of the Court had left by herself with a man who had met her there. Without thinking I asked for a name. They did not know, but they did say that she was beautiful and their description was so like Clemelis that if I were not sure that she could not leave the Court, I would have thought it was her. When I arrived, I went secretly to Zelimon's rooms. I had to wait a long time for him and when he finally showed up well into the night, he recoiled at the sight of me, looked stunned and turned pale.

"Oh, Lamekis," he said, "what are you doing here? And why all this secrecy in coming? It would have been better if you had announced your journey 15 days ago…" And he shut up as if he had said too much. I urged him to explain, but it was no good. His silence made me desperate and I was so bitter that I went to a room, which had been prepared, with my mind made up to change my lodgings the next day.

As much as I needed to rest, I could not get any. I was totally lost. I did not know what to make of Zelimon's welcome and his behavior. Both were hiding some dark mystery that tormented me. What did it matter whether I announced my arrival? Was there a risk of surprising Clemelis? Oh Heavens, how cruel is uncertainty when a sensitive heart is so troubled! I was being tortured and if it continued, I was in no condition to resist.

I was getting ready to leave Zelimon's house and giving orders to a freedman to find a house for me where I could stay incognito, when my fatal friend came into my room. I was so bitter against him that I continued getting dressed without deigning to answer the usual compliments. He said nothing to me until they came to tell me that the house was ready and I could leave.

"What do you mean by doing this?" he tried to hold me back. "Do you think that I would let you stay anywhere else but here with me?" I answered coldly and tried to go. "No," he said, "I was forced to keep silent out of respect, but since you're reacting so unfairly, I will break it. Go back to bed, Lamekis," Zelimon was more open now, "your situation demands it, then I will tell you what your reckless curiosity wants to know."

The thought of finally learning the truth calmed me down. I obeyed everything he said and went to bed—in fact I needed it. When I was ready to listen, he ordered a slave to wait at the door and let no one enter. After this precaution to be undisturbed, he told me.

Part 7

It only takes the fear of losing such a close, highly valued friend to get me to talk. Remember that you are forcing
me to break my silence and you are demanding sincerity—and
for this I fear for you. After this preamble, I'll start. You are
going to regret this ill-advised confession, but it's too late. I
wish to the Father of Light that I had never known you! I did
not want to have to tell you such cruel things. Your tender,
gullible love brought you here. You have come as a loyal,
loving husband to catch a fickle, faithless wife and, no doubt,
give her proofs of your commitment that she does not deserve.
Poor Lamekis, how sorry I feel for you. Clemelis has been
gone for days. Her trip is a big secret; it is barely allowed to
even think about it. Isn't it too risky to pretend to have discovered the heart of an intrigue that has been carried out with so
much skill and caution? But what am I saying? You don't believe me. Maybe these are only assumptions. There has to be
conclusive proof and I give you only suspicions. Maybe I've
been fooled. That's for you to decide.

(Zelimon's beginning made me tremble to the bottom of
my heart, but I swallowed my emotion fearing that if he saw
it, he would hide some of the details of my tragedy. When he
saw that I was still listening, he continued.)

A few days ago when I was alone with the King, discussing some important business matters, he received a note that
he read with some embarrassment and emotion. I pretended
not to notice and continued working. The messenger reminded
me of one of Clemelis' servants and while he waited for orders
from the Houcaïs, I took time to examine him. The harder I
looked at him, the more convinced I was that I was right. The

idea piqued my curiosity. Your lovely wife had countless opportunities to see the Houcaïs in the Queen's chambers and I could not help being surprised that she had recourse to letters to inform him of menial things. I slyly watched to see if I could shed some light on the old suspicions that I had long ago rejected. The King gave me the chance to verify. He led the servant into a little side room but left the letter on a marble stand that he had leaned on to read it. I skimmed over it as quickly as possible. The note was signed Clemelis and I saw the words "love," "impatient" and "journey," which made me doubt that it was concerning the settlement of some business affair between the King and the charming lady. But I heard the King coming back, so I could not read it all before jumping back to my chair. He was daydreaming for a little while, but soon got back to work. I was sure that Clemelis was mixed up in all this and it did not take long for me to be thoroughly convinced.

Around an hour later I heard a whistle[257] in the lock of the little room and I got up wanting to spare the King the trouble of going to see who was asking to enter, but he ordered me to sit still and to continue working until he came back and he shut the door behind him.

This precaution was suspicious to me. I went to the door and looked through the keyhole to see if I might not be able to see who was shut in there with the King. Chance and diligence were on my side. I caught sight of the Houcaïs presenting his knee to Clemelis to kiss.[258] Then she talked very excitedly to him before the Houcaïs led her away. As much as I tried, I could see no more. I tried to crack open the door as gently as possible, but it was locked from the inside. This other precaution put all kinds of thoughts in my head. Lamekis, in my place wouldn't you have thought the same? But we can fool

---

[257] It was only in the King's rooms that one could whistle. It was a sign of the deepest respect. Before having the honor of speaking with him, you had to whistle; it was a way of asking his permission.

[258] An honor that the kings granted only to princes of their blood or to their favorites.

ourselves, as I already told you. You can't always believe what you see.

I brooded over all this while I pitied the dire fate attached to marriage and I swore to myself that I would never put myself in such a position. When the door opened the King motioned to me to leave. He seemed all astir and I could not fathom why, but I obeyed. The same day he held a secret meeting and when he came out he told us that he would not be seeing us for a few days. Before shutting himself away, he assured us it had to do with some important affairs with his chief minister. Everyone believed him but me. I believed that his behavior held a mystery and that it was a result of his conversation with Clemelis. My eyes were opened too wide not to see clearly and I soon found out that I was not wrong.

I was with the Queen at the gathering that was held after every dinner and even though I should not have expected to meet Clemelis there, I was still as surprised as if I had had no reason to be suspicious. I cleverly found out the reason for her absence: she was a little sick and the Queen told her to stay in her room until she felt completely better. The pretext seemed even more peculiar to me, Lamekis, in that the Queen was in on it. I was completely baffled and I've been hemming and hawing until today. What is it based on? The Houcaïs is still absent or at least nobody has seen him and Clemelis is closed up, they say, in her room. I have nothing else to say. Now it's up to you, Lamekis, if you can, to penetrate this dark mystery. For me, I won't dare say anything more. Oh, what have I done? Haven't I said too much already?

Lamekis uncovers the mystery

I had enough control over myself to hide some of my fury from Zelimon. While he was plunging a dagger into my heart with his cruel assumptions, I mulled over the most terrible revenge: it would be no less than to kill the criminal architects of my dishonor.

My answer to Zelimon was concise. I said that after what he'd just told me, the only solution left for me was to go as far away as possible…forever. The traitor fought shrewdly against this supposed plan, but his reasons to keep me there were spitefully explained!

"How many partners in misfortune do you have?" he asked me. "Does the Court itself have any? If some men, out of brutality instead of honor, have had recourse to violence, what was the effect of their cruel vengeance? The loss of their wealth and universal invective. For unrequited evils the only solution is patience. There are even those that have turned it to their greater benefit. All things considered, though this may not be the most respectable choice, at least it is more certain and less dangerous."

I still feel the loathing I had for his cruel advice, as well as for just being in his presence. We cannot love those who strike such sensible blows. Zelimon started to disgust me and being afraid that I might show it, I pretended that I could no longer live in a place where my honor was torn to shreds. He asked me what I wanted to do. "To flee to the other end of the earth," I answered. "To cut myself off from all mankind and never come back." Alas, I did not know how true these words were. My experience has taught me that I foresaw everything that would happen to me.

When I left Zelimon, I went to hide in the house that I had rented. I waited there for the right time to put my plan of revenge into action. I wanted to catch the Houcaïs with my wife and wash away the stains of my dishonor in their guilty blood. But I did not want to take any risks. It was not easy getting into Clemelis' room because it was not far from the Queen's and from the outside it could be confused with the other ladies' rooms. I had to enter cunningly and be able to recognize it. I was still so weak that sometimes I despaired that I would not be able to accomplish my goal. But fury supplemented strength and was even more formidable in that it reflected and judged calmly the meaningful blows it wanted to deal.

I got into her room disguised as a Bour-rouk,[259] accompanied by a slave whose zeal, bravery and loyalty I could count on. The King's rooms were always open except at ungodly hours, so I was hoping that in my honorable clothes I could infiltrate as far as the wicked woman's room and in case anyone was uneasy or curious about me being there I had some reference letters that I could say would keep me safe around the Queen and since I did not know when I needed to show up, I was trying to find where I would have to go when summoned.

It was lucky for the guilty parties that I did not find them. We got all the way to Clemelis' room, where a surprising solitude prevailed. The single glass-paned closet was locked. I got the idea that she was shut up inside (because jealousy can convince you of the most unlikely things) and I had to get in. With much effort we forced the door and found that everything was set up (I was sure) to confirm my suspicions. In the weal light of a candle burning in a lantern a porphyry portrait[260] became visible, of the Houcaïs, which inflamed my fury so much that I smashed it to pieces.

The expedition, in which I took unusual pleasure, agitated me so much that I felt sick. I flopped onto the sofa next to the table I was leaning on, but as I did so I touched something with my hand. I brought the candle over and saw a paper on which was written a draft of a letter with a number of cor-

---

[259] A kind of hermit who had the right to go everywhere by yelling "ab-da-kak," which means "Glory to the Highest." These characters wore tinplate robes, brown leather caps and wicker sandals; their faces were the color of goose turd; and over everything a cowhide that had been soaked in goat urine served as a coat and gave them an air of majesty, which inspired a great deal of respect.

[260] Painting was not in use in those times. They made portraits in a very singular fashion, seeing that they knew the secret of melting porphyry. When it was in liquid form, after covering the face with putty to catch all the features, they poured the porphyry into the hardened putty, which produced a likeness down to the smallest trait.

279

rections. It was Clemelis' handwriting. I read, or better said deciphered it hungrily.

Clemelis' Letter

> *How could you ever doubt, ingrate, that I love you? I barely knew you and my heart was yours in all its tenderness. That I love you, alas! There has been no moment of my life that wasn't devoted to you. I see you everywhere. I search for you everywhere and I ask everyone I see about you. After this, you ask me if I love you...*

Suspicion can do anything when you are blinded by jealousy! I shook with rage at the sight of such plainly expressed passion. I kept the letter as proof that my grudge was justified and then hid myself in the closet hoping that the traitor would come sooner or later to deliver herself to my righteous fury.

I was wrong. I waited all night and the next day, but no one came. My astonishment was beyond compare. I had no doubt that I was betrayed, but what baffled me was by whom? I had confided my secret to no one. Even my slave did not know what brought me to the place. As for Zelimon, unless he was in on it with Clemelis, which seemed unlikely, no one could have found out. I concluded that my wife was with the Houcaïs in one of his country mansions. There was no way I could find out if that were true, especially if I went there, without putting my plan at risk. It was too important for me to jeopardize it; my role was to wait. I hid myself in another house until Clemelis came back. Everyday I sent my slave to the Court to get immediate information. The treacherous woman, I told myself, cannot stay in the arms of her lover forever. She will come back sooner or later and my vengeance will hound her. In the end she will succumb.

No news of Clemelis came for eight days. I started getting impatient and taking measures to make a new search, but then the slave I used as a messenger showed up out of breath and with ecstatic eyes. I had ordered him to report to me when the Houcaïs or my wife returned. He obviously guessed, since he so often witnessed my worried state, that both were terribly important to me. He informed me that the King had just appeared in public. I trembled with joy. According to my assumptions Clemelis should not be long in coming to the Court. Oh, how dreadful is chance! My conjecture was only too right. She came that very evening.

As soon as I was sure, I went in disguise again to the palace. But I was dismayed and disappointed when I got to her room to find Clemelis surrounded by a crowd of people, saying that something extraordinary had happened. When I heard what it was, I was not surprised; I really should have expected it and thus made provisions. The closet that I had forced open and the broken bust of the King were causing a stir. My wife, who could not understand it, was scared and crying about the violence. The King was informed and came directly to her room to found out more about the unusual event. A rumor was quietly spread around about a secret conspiracy: to the simplest of events in the Courts they attributed the most complicated principles.

The King stayed with Clemelis for more than three hours and then left looking distracted and lost. I took advantage of the moment when the crowd followed him to sneak into my wife's rooms and I jumped into the first place I could hide—it was a wardrobe with a door that opened onto Clemelis' bedroom. I saw her through the keyhole. Could I have been in a better place?

I waited with inexpressible impatience for the calm of night to help my plan. With zenghuis in hand and glued to the door I was listening closely in order to slip into the room just at the right time when all of a sudden I heard a shrill cry that sharpened my attention. I cracked open the door so that I could hear better what was going on. A man was hiding in her room like me and had obviously tried to attack her. I couldn't believe it! It was Zelimon. I knew it at Clemelis' first curses. What did he want? Sinouis, imagine how ready I was. I had just learned that he was a traitor and the most deceitful of all men.

After Clemelis called him all the names he deserved, she commanded him to leave or else she would ruin him. "If it weren't for the extreme respect I have for your father," she added, "the King would know about your aberration right now...You love me, you say? Lovely excuse and nice way to win me over! Until now I thought you were a reasonable man, but I didn't know you. Surely you've lost your mind and the best thing that could happen to you would be to get someplace safe. Leave and don't say anything. You should already be gone."

Instead of leaving, Zelimon asked to speak for a minute, not to make excuses, he said, but to do her an important service that was a matter of life and death. She barely heard my name, but it changed her mind. She pressed him for information about me, what had happened to me and why he knew more than she did.

The question made Zelimon hesitate, all prepared as he was to answer. He cut himself short over and over. First he started off by saying that the love I had for a young Phoenician girl was the reason I stayed away. Right after that he said I was jealous and if it were not for him I would have finished her off. He did not say that he was the one who told me everything I believed. What I found out in all this was that he was a cheat, a seducer and for that I had to get my revenge.

It was different for Clemelis. Not only did she believe everything he said, but she even forgave him, provided that, she said, he give her a faithful account of my plot with the young girl (whom he had invented by saying she had helped me to recover). Zelimon, who was madly in love and therefore thought he was getting lucky, painted me with the blackest colors and told far-fetched tales that were as false as he was. I could not stand it anymore. I burst into the room and in spite of my disguise Clemelis recognized me and held out her arms. I answered her with my zenghuis. Zelimon saw that he was caught in his treachery and tried in vain to escape. Then he stood still like a statue and took the punishment he deserved.

Just as I was feeling satisfied with a legitimate vengeance, a cruel thought poisoned the sweetness. If Clemelis was innocent, I told myself, and the traitor whom I had just punished had the same effect on me in his situation as he had had before in mine, I would be the cruelest, most savage of all men! This idea spawned a thousand regrets. I looked at poor Clemelis; death pallor covered her lovely face. She fell down with her arms outstretched, in the same position she held to embrace me. My eyes swelled with tears at the cruel sight. "Heavens," I cried, "what have I done?" I could say no more. I was so overwhelmed by remorse and grief that I passed out.

When I came back to my senses, I was in chains, in a dark dungeon, surrounded by people trying to wake me up and waiting to make me talk. I had barely opened my eyes when a voice shouted to tell Boldeon. I trembled. Certainly he had to interrogate me. What did I have to say to him? What proof did I have of the dishonor that made me commit the crime? Simple conjectures: a letter that could be interpreted differently, the words of a traitor who, maybe, wasn't one anymore or who could have denied everything with as much gall as he had had to say it in the first place. Far from being in control over things, I was repulsed by them. I would have preferred to die a thousand times on the scaffold than to save myself by admitting such a shameful history. I felt like I was being dishonored twice.

Boldeon came as I was brooding over the tragedy. I was expecting to be buried in the harshest harangue—I was mistaken. He approached me looking sad but gentle. He asked why I was pushed to such violent extremes and what his son could have done to deserve the awful treatment I inflicted on him. "I come here," he said, "less as a father who should demand your condemnation than as a judge trying to find an excuse not to punish you. The King, as upset as he is with you, really wants to know how you can justify yourself. Answer me frankly. Your sincerity will, perhaps, pardon you. As for myself, I can't believe that you committed such cruelty without a reason, extraordinary perhaps, but legitimate. Speak, I'm ready to listen."

I held my silence. Boldeon was surprised and tried all his diplomacy to make me change my mind. After he saw that his efforts were in vain, he got up and warned me gravely to change my attitude or it would spell my certain death. I said as little to his threats as to the promises he had made a minute earlier and he left mumbling about my blindness and the fate I was preparing for myself.

An hour later the door of my prison opened and they threw in the unfortunate slave who had helped me. He had just suffered the gil-gan-gis[261] and they were giving him the customary meal. As soon as he entered he fell at my feet and begged me in a flood of tears to spare him the second assault that they would inflict on him if I refused to speak. "If you knew" he said to me, "everything I just suffered, you would take pity on your poor slave. I'd prefer the cruelest death to torture like this."

I was sorry for him, but my mind was made up. Without answering his plea I ordered him to tell me everything that happened after I passed out. He told me that Clemelis' servants had woken up at the sound of Zelimon's wails after I stabbed him. They ran in with the palace guards and howled so loudly at the sight of the bloodshed that the King, Queen and the whole Court were woken up and crowded into Clemelis' room to see what has going on. The Houcaïs looked furious and swore by his sacred belly[262] to punish the perpetrator with death. Then he was taken aback when he learned from Zelimon, who had regained consciousness, that I was the crim-

---

[261] The interrogation. The people of this country had an extraordinary process: whoever they wanted to make talk they delivered to four torturers who flogged the sufferer with iron-tipped whips and then they served him the most exquisite meal before putting him back to torture until he finally died.

[262] Such a terrible vow for the kings that they could not break it except by royal anointment.

inal whom he had just condemned. The Queen not only supported his outrage, but she swore herself to see me die.

After this they examined Clemelis' wounds and the doctors unanimously agreed that it would take a miracle for her to survive, which incensed everyone's resentment against me. And since the poor slave refused to confess, he was condemned to the gil-gan-gis where he would mercilessly lose his life in the torture of the four,[263] unless I took pity on his unfortunate fate.

Two hours later Boldeon came back. He came to know my final decision and when I persevered in my silence, he declared me condemned. I accepted the sentence without saying a word, surprisingly calm.

The dinner that started the gil-gan-gis was brought to me in the middle of the night and shook my confidence. I couldn't take it, but there was no mercy. If I did not talk, I would go to the four in two hours. The Houcaïs desperately wanted to know why I had committed such violent acts and he believed that the gil-gan-gis was an infallible means to the truth. He had ordered it and no one had tried to intervene for me since everyone was angry. What would have become of me, great Vilkonhis, if you had not taken pity on my misery!

The Goulu-grand-gak[264] was just starting to take off my tunic to deliver me to the four when the grand Tok-ho-dor sounded. At the venerable toll we all lay face down on the ground until the public criers had made their announcement. It did not take long: the Houcaïs and the Queen were going to be anointed so they could cancel their vow against me. I thanked Vilkonhis. The Goulu-grand-gak put my tunic back on me and led me to my cell until they decided my fate.

Boldeon came to see me two hours later. "The royal anointment is done," he exclaimed. "The King is free of his

---

[263] The four torturers appointed to the interrogation.

[264] Chief executioner. He had the privilege of undressing the sufferers and when they were dead, he got their skin, which he soaked in urine and sold at a very high price to be used as clothing for noble ladies.

285

vow and sent me here one last time. You have been pardoned on the condition that you state the real reason that compelled you to try to kill Clemelis and my poor son."

In spite of everything he said to get me to answer, I persevered in my silence. He left boiling with anger. A few days later they came and took me on a very long walk escorted by a lot of guards. When we reached the shores of the sea, two men got in a boat with me and sailed away. In the middle of the sea they stuck me in a barrel and cast me adrift.

Sinouis saves Lamekis

"Heavens," Sinouis interrupted, "what are you saying? Was that really the outcome of the merciful anointment? How did you escape from this great danger?"

I was about to answer him by telling the rest of my story when something cold and slimy rubbed against my body. I turned my head in fright and saw a snake, much bigger than I was, slithering up to me. Then its head, body and tail started coiling up. My animal instinct knew it was a female of the species I looked like under the monstrous spell. I slithered away in disgust and buried myself under a nearby rock. Of course my safeguard was useless; the female in love followed me and when I tried to get out, I was entwined by her awful body and I could think of no way to escape the awful torture.

"Come here, Sinouis," I yelled. "Come here and use all your strength to get me out of this cruel embrace."

"Well, what can I do?" he had flown away and was perched on a dry branch. "Have you forgotten how powerless I am in my sad lot?"

"Ah! You're abandoning me. Can't you at least try to help me? Or are you one of those fickle friends who run away at the very moment when they could be useful?"

Sinouis was obviously hurt by my insinuation and came down without really knowing what he could do for me, but he risked coming all the way up the narrow crevasse in the rock. His eyes, as sad as they were, gave me heart. I made a furious effort and he was not so powerless seeing that he got me free of the bonds encircling me. I was no sooner free than I hurried away as fast as I could from that deadly hole. Sinouis, who did not recognize me and mistook me for the enemy trying to get at him to strangle the sad cries that he was uttering at my fate, flew up on top of a rock. He was so scared that he fell off at the very moment when the snake came out to follow me. What great luck! He delivered me of my implacable enemy. Sinouis barely touched its body:[265] it hissed three times, stretched out, opened its mouth and died in front of us.

The sight was so fascinating to me that I, too, hissed but in joy and Sinouis regained his courage. At that moment I felt everything that my friend must have felt and instead of laughing inside like I had done before, I swore that if the opportunity ever rose again, I would kill my enemy for good.

After talking a little while about our harsh destinies, we agreed to find a different refuge until it pleased the Heavens to end our tragedy. We decided to set out the next night and my plan was to find some house and shrewdly try get some information about where we were and how we might get back to the kingdom of the Abdalles where I could look for the divine woman who would put us back in our original form. If Cleme-lis, I told myself, is still alive, maybe I will find a way to get together with her. A glimmer of hope made me imagine that my vengeance was unjust and it was she who would make me happy again one day.

While waiting to leave, Sinouis urged me to tell how I miraculously escaped from the barrel in the sea. So, I continued my story.

Lamekis and the giant birds

The rolling of the barrel was so violent that my senses were burning up. I called upon the Creator and made for him a sacrifice of the cruel death I was condemned to. They say that

---

[265] See Pliny in his chapter on snakes, Ch. IX, p. 135.

a ray of hope always shines in our soul no matter how desperate we may be. I did not experience it in this situation. I did not try to fool myself at all—I was lost for good and the only consolation I had was the hope of dying quickly to stop my suffering.

It's no use pretending to be strong! We are weak when we see death approaching. An accident happened that not only rattled my apparent surrender, but made me scared of the great danger I was facing: I noticed that water was leaking into my rolling vessel. I sought desperately to fix the new daunting problem and finally, after a hard search, I found where death was slowly entering. It was a hole; I plugged it up with my finger. Every wave rolled me out of place and the water took the opportunity to leak in. What could I do to save myself? "Oh Vilkonhis," I screamed, "why are you holding me in suspense? Finish me off! You swore to; I see it. Is it fun for you to toss me around in despair? I ask you for no favors but to let me die right now. Are you so cruel as to refuse me?"

I finished this plea just as some turbulence, inexpressibly stronger than any before, made me think that my prayers were answered. It was not hard to figure out that an awful storm was driving the waves up to the clouds. I heard a ghastly grinding during the violent jolts. Oh Heavens, how could I endure this terrible time? It was like the universe was shattering. Every minute I thought that the boards of my frail vessel were going to be smashed in. The constant shock of the waves on my barrel was like a blacksmith hammering an anvil. Oh Sinouis, what a state I was in! It was beyond me. And there are situations that are beyond words—I could not describe it to you if I tried.

The dire situation lasted for quite a while. During the long hours I lost my strength. I had stopped thinking about the hole and the barrel was slowly but surely filling up with seawater. Now it was almost half-full. Finally, I was going to die. But then a jolt even more terrible still than all the others smashed my refuge to pieces and left me in open water. An ounce of courage, or better said the approach of death tried in vain to save my life against everything hammering away at it. I floundered and almost sunk to the bottom of the sea. The weight of my body was dragging me down; my mouth and ears were filling with water.

All of a sudden a most unexpected miracle snatched me from my murderous fate. A huge bird lifted me into the air. Its rapid flight and the painful way it was holding me opened my eyes. Oh Heavens, I was tossed from one doomed peril into another! I was as high as the sky and it seemed like all the elements were conspiring against me. Oh Sinouis, can you picture me victimized by such ominous events? And we're not at the end. Really, we've barely just begun!

I crossed an immense space and the bird suddenly swooped down toward some craggy rocks near the sea. How weak and absurd is man! There was no greater risk of falling upon the rocks than over the sea, but I was terribly afraid. At the sight of them my hair stood on end. I was dying a thousand times before I died.[266]

The nature of my punishment soon changed. I had no expectations about the kind of death I was destined for. Why not being eaten alive? The bird had snatched me up as food for its babies, but what babies! Sinouis, our cows are not much bigger. They flapped their wings at their mother's approach and their heads popped out of the nest with open beaks, chirping merrily like the sound of a roaring lion. "So, that's my waiting grave," I screamed and howled. "So be it, but I'm ashamed that the Heavens are so openly savage." As I vomited out these desperate blasphemies, I apparently scared my abductor. Until then I had not opened my mouth. Either I spoke in some strange tongue or my cries had some mysterious influence. Whatever the case, as soon as the words were out of my mouth, the bird dropped me. I was over the nest and fell hard on the little ones who started crowing and cawing.

---

[266] Death is the least of sorrows that we are subject to in this life. Only its approach is terrible and the idea of what will become of the soul after leaving its body.

289

It hurt less than I expected. The little eaglets, (for, I had never seen birds of this species and do not know what else to call them), were so fat and soft that their plentiful plumage preserved me from the invasive cold. Instead of devouring me as I presumed, they closed their beaks, lowered their heads and looked at me in such a way that I could tell they were not used to food like me. The fear of being their prey kept me awake for a while, but finally all the fatigue hit me and as I slowly warmed up next to these animals and lay down in their softness, I started dozing off. I did not try to think about the new danger or form a plan or fight against sleep. I surrendered and slept and I never slept so comfortably and peacefully in any bed.

When I woke up I was fresh as if none of these exhausting experiences had happened. The little eaglets moved to make a more comfortable place for me and I sunk to the bottom of the nest where I got cozy. Now I could think about my present situation and I started believing that the Heavens did not keep me safe through all these harrowing dangers just to kill me. I plucked up courage and thought of how I was going to get out of the refuge, which really was not one for me. I knew that the mother bird would come back and I had to eat something, realizing that it had been a long time and I was worn out.

I was deep in serious thought when the eaglets started up the same racket as before and I knew the mother bird was on her way back, so I hid as best as I could. Indeed, I saw her through the little logs that made up the structure of the nest and I was as astonished and afraid as I was at the first sight of her. She was unbelievably huge, carrying a sheep in her beak that she tore it to pieces with her claws when she came into the nest and gave to her babies to devour in no time at all.

Lucky result of wonderful providence! One of the pieces slipped out of a baby's beak and dropped near me. I was so hungry and it looked so good that I ate it. It was exquisite, really, Sinouis. I had never eaten with such a good appetite.

When the babies were full, the mother flew off and I watched her until she was out of sight. I popped my head through an opening that I had made in the logs and looked around. I shuddered at my situation. The nest was placed on the peak of a rock that was so high and steep that I could see no way of getting down without dying. On one side the sea washed against the rock and on the other was a chain of mountains whose heights were lost in the clouds.

My disappointment was beyond compare. Whichever way I turned I saw only death and despair. I started moaning against destiny again (which was also pretty appalling). Patience can last only so long before it degenerates into fury.

Toward the end of the day, when I was falling asleep, the chirping eaglets warned me of their mother's return. I looked through my little window and saw two birds in view. I figured the second was the papa eagle. He had a kind of multi-colored crown on his head; he was bigger and glided more majestically. On any other occasion I would have admired them carrying their provisions. The male had a cow, whiter than snow, between its talons and the female a calf. They put them down in the nest and outdid each other tearing the meat to pieces. Oh miracle of divine decrees! I was dying of thirst, Sinouis. It was inevitable that the heat devouring me would do what so many perils had failed to do. But the cow's udder, full of milk (obviously this was not one of the eagles' skills), was sliced off completely and lying next to me. I sucked on one of the teats with incomparable relief. This quenched my thirst and I felt so good that I fell back into a priceless sleep.

I spent a few days leading this extraordinary life because I could not figure out how to escape the bizarre prison. My imagination offered me nothing feasible. Ideas came one after another, each less convincing than the one before, until I finally decided that I could hope for nothing but from the Heavens.

One day when I was lost in thought, I suddenly heard noises, awful howling, which shook up the nest and almost knocked it down. I trembled in fear and looked through my window. Two birds, different from my hosts, and even bigger, were attacking the nest with incredible violence. It looked like they wanted to knock it down and grab it. The frantic shocks were steadily weakening the bottom of the nest. In spite of their courage, the mother and father were already covered in blood and could not stop one of the eaglets from plummeting toward the rocks below. Without its wings it would probably not survive the fall. My hosts shrieked, little by little giving ground. Pity and gratitude were stirring in the depths of my heart. I decided to do what I could to prevent the destruction of the refuge that had saved my unlucky life. Whatever way I looked at it, it was true that I owed my life to these eagles. With this in mind I tore out a big stick from the nest, stood halfway out of my hiding place, lifted my arm and whacked one of the enemy birds on the head. I hit it so hard that its eyes popped out of its head and it let go of the nest and plummeted down. Its partner was scared but furious. It stood up high, spread its wings, opened its beak and came at me to punish my brashness and eat me. Another blow from my stick broke its foot and one wing (it had ducked its head just in time). It dragged itself back to me and the battle started over again. It was a fight to the finish. I defended myself wildly but skillfully until I got the upper hand so that it could not sustain the fury of my blows. It took flight screeching and squawking away.

My hosts were astounded by this unexpected help. They looked at me and did not know what to do. Their instinct told them to fly away. The male followed the enemy whom I had just driven off; and the female landed on the ground. I figured that the mother's love was taking her to look for her fallen eaglet. I was not wrong, but I could not see how she found it. Besides the fact that I was so high up that I could barely make out the objects below, I also lost sight of her, so I looked at other things.

Up in the clouds I witnessed a sight that would have enchanted me in any other situation. The male eagle had caught up to his adversary and they were fighting in mid-air. As wounded as he was, the enemy defended himself courageously, which made the outcome of the battle, for a little while, uncertain. As a result of my gratitude and indebtedness, I was scared that the eagle would be defeated (without thinking of the danger that his return might put me in), but I rejoiced (without foreseeing the peril, I say) when I saw the adversary fall. The eagle dove down in pursuit, certainly to finish him off and I could see no more. Their distance and my weak eyesight put an end to the spectacle.

A few moments later I heard the usual sounds of my hosts returning. I went back into my little niche and from my usual vantage point I saw the female carrying the eaglet in her talons. It was all banged up and the mother cried out plaintively, which brought the male to her side and together they made a dreadful concert of howls over the baby lying in the nest. The male watched it sadly. Its foot was broken, its neck twisted and it seemed to be at its end. The female went to the other eaglets, took some of their feathers and tried to make a comfortable bed for the injured one. All the productions of nature are admirable.

I was torn between the desire to heal the eaglet and the fear of being evilly paid for being human. The sad mother was doing all she could to staunch the blood from the injured foot. It was pouring out and steadily weakening the bird. I could not sit still at this touching sight. I poked my head out of the hole and then my arms, hoping to help the sick bird. I was barely all the way out when the parents dropped back and perched on the edge of the nest, stretching their necks and beating their wings while looking at me wide-eyed. Their calmness reassured me. I tore off a piece of my shirt, took a few loose sticks, dried the wound and washed it with my urine. Then I set the bones as best I could by wrapping them all up in bandages. I set the sticks around it so that it would not move and covered it with new bandages to make it as strong and straight as possible.

After doing this, which was watched by the eagles with inexpressible surprise in their eyes, I looked to see if the eaglet's neck might not be fixed. With great luck I managed to do it. As soon as it was in place the bird opened its eyes, flapped its wings and asked, in its usual way, to eat. The mother hurried over, also flapped her wings and showed her joy in every way she knew how. I stepped back and she called the male in their language to come and admire the miracle that saved their baby. The result of all of this was to tear off some pieces of meat, grind them in their beaks and each in turn gave me a little. Afterward the mother watched her baby and the father perched on the nest, keeping an eye on all sides.

I was deep in my niche where I watched everything in strange comfort. In fact, wasn't my hosts' gentleness a good omen of a future less cruel for me?

The male eagle kept watch for a long time and then made a tour of the nest. What a piercing glance! You could compare it to the Father of Light—it penetrated everything. I could not escape it; it stared at me. And my glance made the male more nervous. He started scratching with his feet and clearing out the obstacles between us with his beak. I did not know what to think about this crazy work. I got scared. Could it be, I thought silently, after the service I rendered for him, that he is unthankful enough to devour me? Lovely consequence! As if they had their own way of reasoning. How could I ask for gratitude from these beasts, knowing that it is hard enough to find it among men whose hearts seemed to be better made? There was no comparing them, men would always lose out.

The closer the work got to me, the more worried I got. I could do nothing else but be on my guard. I grabbed my stick, but what was the use of such a precaution? The friendly animal was only trying to show me his gratitude. In fact, as soon as the path was clear for him to approach, he did so shyly, to reassure me. And I was surprised that when he was next to me he lowered his head to the ground, ruffled his feathers, leaned his neck on my knees and sighed sorrowfully. I petted his plumage as a sign of friendship and believed he understood and responded in his way because he gently flapped his wings like a little hungry bird awaiting it meal. But I was wrong. There was a good, solid reason for everything the eagle had just done. How admirable nature is and what we call instinct is almost reason! The bird was wounded and understood by what I had done to his baby that I could heal him. He had come to ask for my help.

I understood when petting him. I felt something wet—it was blood from a wound. I did the same thing with bandages as I had done to the eaglet. I took a shred of my clothing and bandaged the wound after sterilizing it and I searched for more. There was a minor cut on his head that did not look serious enough to do anything but lick it. While I was working on the friendly animal, he did not budge, but when I stopped, he got up, stared at me, beat his wings and with the same solemnity as he had come he went back to the female, who had not quit staring at me during the whole operation. It looked like she understood my purpose by the behavior she soon exhibited.

She and the male spent a little time together, watching me, opening their beaks and singing in a strange way that seemed to mean something. After a few minutes the female got up and came over to me with the same gait as the male. I figured that the visit had the same purpose in view and, indeed, her gullet was hurt. The bandage was harder this time since a beak had taken off a chunk of skin. The wound was wide and I had a great deal of trouble to stop the bleeding. The rest of my shirt was used to bandage it.

After my care, the female returned to the male and together they tore apart some meat. I did not try to imagine what they were planning. Whenever I think about it now I can't help laughing. Can you believe, Sinouis, that they both brought me this meat in their beaks? I took it in my hands and ate it to please them. They examined me very carefully and thought that they were doing me a favor, so they brought more. There was enough to feed 30 men, so I got bolder with the friendly animals, gathered up the flesh they left at my feet, stood up and carried it to the eaglets. They took it out of my hands eagerly, as if I was their parent. The male and female watched me wide-eyed, but kindly let me do it, which showed the justice and bounty of their instinct.

That night we all slept well. At the break of day the two eagles cleaned their nest. That's what woke me up. They threw the babies' feces out onto the rocks, as well as the meat and whatever might detract from the cleanliness. When the babies were all plucked and put in a new place, the male and female came to me, cleaned me up with their beaks, arranged my bedding, mended the little logs, firming them up, and then left me free to do as I pleased. For my part, I practiced my new profession as surgeon. I started with the little eaglet. All was going marvelously; the neck was perfectly in place, the foot was no longer bleeding, the thigh was a little swollen, but all told it seemed that my cures were a grand success.

I put new dressings on the male and female also. It could not have gone better and I thanked the Heavens for that. After everything was taken care of, the male flew away to get the daily provisions, as I soon found out. The female stayed behind, refusing to leave the wounded eaglet. She spent the entire day plucking and petting it in her way. I was not forgotten and if I had feathers, she would have done me the same favor. Lacking that, she nibbled my hands and fingers and sometimes I paid dearly for this favor when she bit a little harder than I could stand.

A little later the male came back carrying several kinds of animals that I did not recognize. The female and he worked at tearing them apart and giving them to their babies to eat. Having become familiar to my hosts, I shared in the latter chore and what was really amazing was that they took the pieces out of my hand unabashedly, especially the wounded eaglet who chirped happily and flapped its wings. Can you believe, Sinouis, that I became such fast friends with these animals that I almost stopped fretting about being with them? The truth is that I had a dream that made me feel better and imagine a way to get out of this slavery, a way as strange as it was daring. I dreamed that the male eagle brought me back to earth in the same way that I had been taken away. When I woke up I pondered over this: the thing seemed impossible, but maybe it was just a matter of trying. The birds were strong and it was very easy for them to do me this service, as timid as I was to risk it.

I thought about it for eight days. The horrible thirst I endured was a real torture. I was withering away every minute. If I did not lap up the blood of the animals brought to the nest, I would have died of rage or madness because the gruesome brew, instead of refreshing me, heated me up too much. I was covered in spots and sores and it was not hard for me to see that if this lasted much longer, I would absolutely have to die.

After battling a long time between hope and fear, I put my foot down and decided to hop on the next trip the male took. I would grab his feet and pull him down to the ground. I had become so friendly with them that he would let me do whatever I wanted. So, after carefully weighing the risks, I found it less dangerous than I had first thought. His feet were so wide that I could stand up on them and if I hugged his two legs like pillars, I would not worry about falling. I tried it right away. It was like it was made on purpose for me and I knew that my project could not fail.

As soon as my mind was made up, a thought struck me. I was attached to these animals and particularly to my little eaglet to the point that the idea of separation truly saddened me. If devouring thirst were not pressing me I would certainly have waited until the little eaglet I was taking care of was completely healed. Our attachment to each other made me imagine that one day I could use him to fly through the air, that it would be easy for me to train him. He was young and loved me; such a thing seemed feasible. But the cursed thirst decided the affair. I had to drink or die. Besides, the food was not to my liking and I was afraid of becoming totally sick one day or even dying from it. Wasn't all this natural? Wasn't I right to make this choice?

A few days before I got the male eagle used to having me on his feet and the night before my departure, I stuck by him as close as I could around the nest. The next day I did not leave him and when he wanted to fly away on his usual hunt, he tried to get rid of me, but I held on tightly and he took off. When the female realized I was flying away she shrieked and came after us. It was lucky that the giant wings of the eagle acted as a screen. The female stretched out her beak and tried to snatch me, but I kept holding on. After a pretty long flight the male eagle swooped down into a forest where he stopped to drink from a fast-flowing river. I, too, wanted to quench my burning thirst. I got off, knelt down and put my lips to the water. Oh Heavens, what pleasure! I took big gulps of the delicious drink. The male and female watched me very cautiously and looked surprised at what I was doing.

I felt so good next to this wonderful river that I could not dream of leaving. I washed my hands and face and felt so refreshed that I undressed and took a bath. I also thought I should wash my clothes since they had become pretty unsavory, but when I undressed, the eagles, watching all this, moved away and started shrieking horribly. Obviously they thought that my clothes were part of me and that somehow I was shedding my skin and withering away. But they were even more astonished when, after I washed my clothes and let them dry on a rock, they saw me in the river up to my neck. Their shrieking got louder and they flew over my head trying to help me and keep me from drowning. I spoke to them like I did in the past and they seemed reassured that I was still alive. I was too used to them and had studied them too much to be mistaken. These friendly animals loved me and the more they showed it, the harder it was for me to have to leave them.

My plan was to wait until they flew off before I got out of the river because I had good reason to fear that they wanted to snatch me up again. But I waited in vain—the male took off and the female stayed. I could tell by her impatience that she wanted to see me get out of the river. Sometimes she flew over me and at other times she went up to my clothes, stretching out her neck, contemplating them, and then she came back to the river's edge to keep me in sight.

A little later I heard a noise in the air that signaled the male's return. I looked up, but was completely flabbergasted. He had the wounded eaglet in his grasp and was bringing it to me. Oh Sinouis, it touched me. I was right in thinking that these friendly animals trusted me to heal their little ones. The mother went off to meet the male as he flew in. I couldn't bear the sight of it. I got out of the water, got dressed and ran to my hosts who backed away just like the first time they saw me in their nest. But they were happy to see me as I always looked. They beat their wings and twittered and chirped, gathered around, nibbled at me and gave me every sign of true affection they knew.

I responded as best I could, which was usually to scratch their necks. I went back to the river figuring that they would bring the eaglet, which was too big for me to carry. Obviously they understood because they followed me. I took two steps in the water and washed the eaglet's wounded foot. I could tell by the movements of the talons after the bath that the foot was recovering and the little bird could actually put pressure on it. I got it to drink, which it liked so much it would not stop. The father and mother stretched out their necks and watched everything I did very carefully.

While I was doing everything I thought I should to make the eaglet feel better, I pondered over my next move. If it were possible, I told myself, to escape from the watchful eyes of the parents and save myself with the eaglet, I could use it to travel comfortably and get my revenge on the savage Houcaïs. The idea tickled my imagination, but how could I do it? The eaglet could still not walk and its wings were still too weak to carry me. I had to forget about it. As for the parents, they kept such a close watch that I could not even think of escaping from their omnipresent gaze. When the female left, the male stayed behind and remained by my side until she came back. They took turns like this well into the night and I did not know what to do. I was completely at a loss.

Looking around distractedly like a man in a quandary, I saw a tree pregnant with fruit. I ran to it, found the fruit delicious and ate with an unusual greed. After this charming meal, I spied some shrubbery to my right that was thick enough to give me an idea. If it were possible, I told myself, to reach it and lure the eaglet over, it would be impossible for the parents, because of their size, to enter. I could hide there, raise the little one until it was healed and big enough to carry me and then do whatever I wanted. The idea did not seem too farfetched, so I tried to put it into action. I headed straight for the shrubs. I do not know if the male was challenging me or if he got fed up with waiting and decided to do something, but he came to me, patted me with his beak, grabbed me in his talons and flew off back to the nest, soon followed by the mother and the eaglet.

I consoled myself with the hope that the opportunity to escape would come again if I wanted. But I was not expecting the diabolical trick that the eagles played on me to keep me there. It was so surprising that I still get bewildered when I think about it. Oh Sinouis, an animal's instinct is perfect! You're going to have real, convincing, unimaginable proof of this.

I felt so good after being by the river and so refreshed from the bath that when I got to the nest I fell asleep, long and deep, during which my hosts were busy at the most extraordinary work you can imagine. Would you believe, Sinouis, that when I woke up I found myself in a cage? Thousands of branches were intertwined around the nest to close it up tightly, making it impossible to leave and even more impossible to enter. The work was so solid that there did not seem any way to pull out even the smallest twig. I sat there startled, just staring around. The eagles were perched on a nearby rock, stretching out their necks and watching me carefully.

A moment of quiet reflection calmed the awful worry I was starting to feel. I have been patient, I told myself, until now. Keep it up until my eaglet is strong enough to fly. He knows me and will obey me. When the time comes, I will find a way out of this prison while the eagles are away. If their instincts made them take such strong measures in fear of me leaving them, then they should be more relaxed and therefore less vigilant around me.

That was my hope, anyway, which consoled me. But even though I could not get over the surprise at my present situation and the logical thought these animals displayed, I would soon know more and better that their minds were also full of memory, analysis and foresight.

Toward the end of the day I saw the male carrying back some big branches in its beak. At first I thought it was to reinforce my prison, but I was surprised to see him bring them to me. The branches were full of the same fruits he had seen me eat so greedily by the river. I received the gift kindly. In spite of my cruel situation, I could not help feeling grateful.

The attention did not stop there. The female, who was there when the male came back, returned a little later with a huge shell in her claws. Oh Vilkonhis, was it you who offered me this gift? Or was the animal's instinct perfected to this point? The big shell was full of water, enough to quench my thirst for several days.

I was in awe of these things when the two eagles shrieked out, lifted a branch that the strength of four men could not have budged, and dove into the nest. I did not know what to think of their unusual alarm, but as I was about to find out it was well founded. Three birds of the species I mentioned earlier appeared in the sky. They were heading straight for the nest and swooped down on it with such a loud, frightening noise that I thought it was going to tip over. My hosts cried out louder and stood tall to resist their powerful enemy. If it weren't for their lucky precaution, we would all be lost. The terrible birds waged a cruel war. Under the circumstances I did the best I could to fight them off. I took my stick and wore myself out beating and stabbing them, but I did not do much harm to them. However, their feet felt the blows and they were forced to fight in mid-air. Then they tried to stand on the branches, but I forced them off and this tired them out. I saw it and was encouraged.

In fact, they were forced to take a break from their attacks because they could not keep it up. They caught their breath on a nearby rock while my hosts labored to twist back in the branches that were torn out. I was amazed at the skillfulness of their work, but this along with the battle seemed to have worn them out. I saw it in their wings—they could no longer hold them up and I knew it was either exhaustion or sickness in them.

So, afraid that they were in no condition to sustain a second attack I was inspired to give them some water to drink. I brought it to them in my cupped hands and after they tasted it they went to the shell and guzzled it down. They looked as fresh as before the battle. Only language was lacking in these animals—their instinct was perfect. Even the eaglets showed signs of courage and sensibility: they helped in the fight by pecking at the incoming enemy, which unsettled them and was not a small contribution to make them retreat.

However, the enemy birds had gone off only to catch their breath. They soon came back. But their mighty efforts would have been no more successful than the first time if help had not arrived. Two more similar birds came and tore at the branches with their tremendous beaks while the others were fighting. In no time at all they breached the nest and the fighting became furious. Soon my poor hosts were covered in blood and fighting hopelessly in a battle that all the pens in the world could not do justice to. The most devoted bravery let loose its fury. Seeing myself useless and unable to help my poor hosts, I had to think about saving myself, without, however, really believing that I could. I slipped to the back of the nest, under the poor eaglets and buried myself so that I might, at least, not have to look death in the face when it came for me.

The battle lasted another two hours before the shrieks died down and silence followed. I risked popping my head up and looking around the nest. I saw nothing but my solitary eaglet, wounded and bloody, and the nest all torn up with parts missing. I left my hiding place to examine the battlefield more closely. It was covered in blood and feathers and as I looked around, what grief, or rather despair I felt when I saw the bodies of my dear hosts on a nearby rock, devoured by the enemies in front of me. "Oh Heavens," I cried frantically, "What is to become of me? Who will take care of me and my dear little eaglet? What miracle will get me down from this steep rock?"

In spite of all the tears I shed, I saw what could happen. I gathered up the plumage and covered the eaglet so that if the enemy returned, they would not take his life and I hid again in my hole until the next day.

The eaglet's cries startled me awake. He was obviously crying because he was hurt or hungry, so I jumped up to comfort myself with the sight of the dear animal. Alas! What a state he was in! He had lost almost all his blood, his wings were dragging, his beak gaping open and his eyes signaled approaching death. I called him by the name I usually used and he turned his head weakly in my direction. His gaze made me start crying. He was cold; I hugged him and did everything possible to warm him up, only trying to pull him through his lethargy.

After holding him in my arms for a long time and noticing that he was slowly recovering, I examined his wounds. They were not so lethal. I washed and bandaged them as best as I could. When this was done I searched for something to give him to eat. Luckily there were the remains of a cow and a few pieces already torn off. I offered them to him. His greatest pain was hunger and when he smelled the meat he flapped his wings in joy and gobbled it up. His appetite boded well: it proved to me that his lethargy did not spell death. In fact, after three days he regained all his strength and the most comforting thing was that he could put pressure on his hurt foot. The bird was a perfect beauty. He was crowned like his father, his wings were as wide as the eye could see and he looked like it would not take long for him to start voyaging in the skies.

The next day I tried to mount him so that he would gradually get used to it. First I fed him, which softened him up and made him as gentle as a lamb. The supply of fruits that my poor hosts had brought me became a great consolation. I rationed them so that I had enough until the day of departure. It happened 15 days later when I was least expecting it. I had got onto my bird's neck as usual when all of a sudden he flew off and left the nest. At first I was scared of his choppy flight. Sometimes he carried me into the clouds and then dove down so rapidly that I shook all over. But I did not have to worry. My eaglet was delighted to be on his own, to let the allure of freedom carry him away and he let me know this by staying in the air as long as he could. He would not let up until it got dark when he finally alit on the summit of a mountain.

I dismounted and kissed him. After so much had gone wrong, could I hope for such good luck? With tears in my eyes I thanked the great Vilkonhis to whom I owed it all. In fact, it was a downright miracle and deserved my eternal gratitude and admiration.

If my misfortune had been such that it could be consoled, it would have been just then—I was free after a cruel enslavement. I had my little friend (that was what I called the eaglet), a priceless treasure whose devotion and affection would do what I wanted. The main thing now was to get my revenge on the Houcaïs and find out if Clemelis had taken part in the cruel punishment that I was sentenced to. My little friend had become a vital part of the project and I was thinking up foolproof ways of reaching my goal. Now I just had to find out where I was and how to get to the kingdom of the Abdalles. It was not a difficult task. Examining my surroundings I saw that I was near a big city. It would be easy for me to get information there and take all necessary precautions to accomplish my plan.

I looked around the nearby woods to find a place to spend the night. An abandoned farm on the edge of the forest looked as safe as it was convenient. My little friend and I set up the best we could. I snuggled under one of his wings and was as comfortable and warm as in any bed. But having something of value naturally brought worries. I was awake for a long time brooding over what would happen to my little friend when I went down to the city. There was no place to lock him up, so I decided that I would chain him by his foot to be sure about him from then on, but I did not have a chain and until I got one, I could not figure out what to do with my precious bird. It certainly was not right to take him to the city with me. I was about to lose the only valuable thing I had, which was ever the more dear since it was due to the grandeur of my suffering. This acute anxiety kept me from sleeping so that by the time it was already day, I still had not decided on the best thing to do.

After pestering my imagination again, I gave myself entirely into the arms of Providence. It had guided me so well up to his point that I had no doubt it would finish its work. While waiting I decided to have my little friend take me to a high tower that I spotted. I mounted him and patted his neck, and pushed him with my hand. I directed him straight to the city. It looked large and full of people; the streets were bustling and the people were dressed so oddly that I knew I had to be far from the kingdom of the Abdalles. This upset me. How was I going to find my way back if my language was different from theirs?

Mulling these things over I alit on the tower. As I looked over the city I was surprised at the number of people staring at me. Every minute the crowd grew bigger, like a swarm of bees. I figured I had been spotted in the air and the strange way I landed on the tower was the cause of the public amazement. It was quite simple, but I was not expecting what was coming. The superstitious people went straight from amazement to superstitious worship. They took me for a divinity.[267]

---

[267] If the ancients had been fortunate enough to have had this story appear in their times, they would not have fallen into the darkness of paganism. It is clear that this passage clears up many obscurities. The allegory of Jupiter on an eagle is nothing but the adventure of Lamekis. The Egyptians, who saw him carried in the skies on his eaglet, took him, as he well said, for a divinity; and that's where the whole fable came from.

There was no doubt considering their behavior: some stretched out their arms, others crawled on the ground and almost all of them howled dreadfully. The eaglet, taken aback at the commotion and the crowd, was constantly on the verge of taking flight out of fear. If he were not so obedient to me, I would not have been able to hold him back. He was not used to seeing so many people. Nevertheless, he slowly got used to it.

The inhabitants of the city were not long satisfied with the outward show of veneration that they believed they owed me. They hurried to the tower and instantly the huge crowd surrounded it. The tower had a wide stairway on the outside made of snail shells on which a score of people set off in a peculiar manner[268] carrying live animals on the ends of sticks, hopping on one foot and singing a song whose constant refrain was kind of marvelous and crazy. At the sight of them the eaglet stretched out his neck, beat his wings like a baby wanting something to eat and then suddenly flew onto the stairway. I did not know what he was thinking, but I soon found out. He was obviously hungry and seeing the meat sticks, he thought the people were humanely coming to bring him breakfast. He jumped on a sheep carried by two men, lifted it up and let out a cry of joy and hunger. One of the men carrying the stick did not want to let go out of superstition and was carried up with the sheep. At the sight of this everyone shouted, which echoed throughout the city. Indeed the spectacle was quite curious and should have given a pretty good idea of my power, if I was considered the instigator of what just happened.

The eaglet went to perch on another tower on the other side of the city where he shredded the sheep. The poor fellow, who had been carried off and was holding on in spite of his fear, dropped off and right away fell on the ground started banging his head and talking in a hard, barbarous language[269]

---

[268] See Semiramis' descent into the catacombs, Part 1.

[269] Strabo claims that it was Hebrew; Scaliger is sure that it was Syrian; for my part, after much research, I found that it was neither and you would have to be crazy to accept everything the scholars say in

that I understood by his gestures,[270] which punctuated every sentence, to be a fervent prayer. Sometimes he turned to my little friend and addressed a few words to him. But the eaglet paid no attention, munching the sheep with an appetite that reminded me that I, too, would soon be imitating him.

I would really have liked to take advantage of the situation to talk with the native, but knowing that I would not be understood kept me from saying a word. I examined him attentively and was pained by his ignorance. I pitied his excitation as much as the cruel condition that this ridiculous pity reduced him to: his forehead was bleeding from all the marks of respect he was showing me and it was possible that he would crack open his skull if it lasted much longer.

With my humanity always needling me, I was touched and dismounted from my little friend. As soon as the stranger saw me, he lay face down on the ground and thrashed around like he was possessed. I ran to him and did my best to lift him up to stop his convulsions, but I could find no other way except to pull him up by his hair as hard as I could. The eaglet, who was watching and obviously thought the poor man wanted a piece of me, ran over and pecked him 20 times with his beak (which would have taken as many lives if he had them) and then threw him off the tower. If I was in real trouble because of this barbarity, I would have been no less impressed to have such a powerful defender at my side. In fact, right after tossing the native over the edge, he came to me and caressed me in his way, rubbing his beak against my face, nibbling me and then lying down as if inviting me to mount him. I was flattered and answered his intelligently expressed desire. When he felt me on him, he beat his wings in joy and went back to get the rest of his sheep as coolly as if nothing had happened.

---

such matters. After reading 20 volumes, I know less about it than before.

[270] The Egyptians put their fingers in their ears and tapped their feet to pray. The Jews inherited from them this impatient way of making their vows to Heaven.

However, what had just happened caused an awful rumble among the people. They kept watching us on the tower and cried out horribly when they saw their fellow citizen thrown off. The way they were gathered around looked like they were holding a high council, as far as I could tell from my vantage point. They ended up with a new committee; I trembled in fear for the delegates. Indeed, as soon as 30 or so of these natives dressed just like the other showed up, my little friend went over to them. I held him by the head and patted him and he understood, I suppose, what I was trying to say. He stopped in his tracks while I continued patting him and I made a sign to the delegates to send one person toward us. Apparently the sign meant the complete opposite among these people because when they saw it they all started hopping up and down and then throwing themselves on the ground, banging their heads with the same sound and beat as a blacksmith's hammer on an anvil. I got furious seeing these ridiculous, cruel marks of respect. The eaglet, too, looked astonished, but seemed to be enjoying it.

"Oh Heavens," I shouted out loud, "can these men, created by you, be so addled-brained?"

No sooner said than these poor men started somersaulting and dancing on their heads. During this display, one of them, an old man as venerable for his white hair as he was absurd for his strange dance, spoke to me in my own language, which made me flinch with both pleasure and horror: pleasure at the relief of being able to talk with him and horror at the awful promises that he made to spill the blood of hundreds of human victims to appease, he said, my wrath.

"Lan-douil-loc,"[271] the old man cried out (still dancing on one foot), "deign to hear our timid voices. From the rising of your son[272] until his setting, we adore you constantly. Your temple is pure and your girls perpetually purified. And now you show yourself today. May your presence heap upon us the

---

[271] Lord of all things.
[272] He thinks Lamekis is the Father of the Sun.

goods that we need! 100 of the most tender, most beautiful boys will be sacrificed on your altar and as long as you are here we will sacrifice the same number every day. Kat-ka-la."[273]

My answer was simple: "Tell these people to go away and stay away." As soon as I said this, the old man ripped out one of his eyes and presented it to me. I turned away at this gruesome offering and the minister took it back. The other people carried a crystal basin and received it ceremoniously, hopping up and down.

When I was alone with the old man, I started with what interested me the most and asked him how to get to the kingdom of the Abdalles, but instead of answering, he danced on his head. I became furious. Never was an old man more absurd and stubborn. It was impossible to be reasonable with him; he just kept jumping.

I decided to wait it out until he got too tired to continue, but his stamina was endless. He hopped and spinned more and more. The eaglet, who was young, obviously found this amusing and he, too, started hopping. I could not help laughing and ended up hopping myself.

At last the damned elder fell backward and I thanked the Heavens. "Can I finally talk with you?" I asked. "Will you answer me and tell me how I can get to the kingdom of the Abdalles?"

"Lan-douil-loc," the old man replied, completely out of breath, "you know everything and you question me!"

"If it was so, I would not be questioning you. In the name of whatever you respect the most, answer me."

"So be it, Lan-douil-loc. You jest, but it doesn't matter. The kingdom of the Abdalles is to your left."

"Is it far?"

"1,000 baldaillak."[274]

---

[273] Have mercy.

[274] Days: measured by the distance a man could walk from sunup to sundown, which was around 20 leagues.

"What is the name of this land," I continued.

"Egypt," the old man answered.

At this word I shuddered. It was my country. I eagerly asked the name of the city and learned it was the capital, the happy residence where my illustrious father showed his grandeur and heroism. His reputation was still held in high esteem, but Semiramis was still alive. Right then and there I formed a plan to avenge the death of my father—I had the perfect opportunity.

My plan had been to tell the elder the truth about my so-called divinity since he was the High Priest and successor of Lamekis, my father. But I did not believe that I would offend the Heavens by staying silent about this and using the ready means to punish the wicked Queen. After learning everything that might prove conducive to my project, I sent the old man back with orders to bring me Semiramis to whom I wanted, I said, to explain my supreme will. No sooner said than done.

Oh Heavens, can the years really bring about such stupendous changes? This Queen, whose ultimate beauty had been the source of so many crimes, looked like a monstrous, living skeleton. Four old men wearing cow heads hopped her forward on a litter. At the sight of her I was enraged.

"Receive the punishment of your crimes," I shouted. "You see the son of an illustrious father whom you killed. Lamekis lives no more, but the Heavens saved me to revenge his angry *manes*." With these words I smacked Semiramis on the head 20 times with a rod and she was knocked senseless. The eaglet, watching me as usual and reading the indignation in my eyes, finished the punishment. He tore her to pieces and if the priests of Serapis (for, that is who they were) had not fled at the first signs of his fury, there is no doubt that they would have been shredded in turn.

I have to admit, Sinouis, that vengeance felt good. I felt like it was an omen of another that I believed justified. The idea of Clemelis, unfaithful and seduced by Motacoa, was still on my mind. However, before losing control of the emotions rising up in me, I wanted to be of some use to my country by

310

opening their eyes to the blindness they suffered under their false gods. The whole city was gathered in the center at the foot of the tower where the scene had just played out. The people were extremely distressed. Before leaving them I wanted to harangue them and expose their ignorance in taking me for a god and use the opportunity to urge them to quit their superstitious ways and demand a legitimate, true worship. With this in mind I got back on the eaglet and gently squeezed my knees while laying my hand on his head. He understood the signs and we alit on a dome from where I could be heard. My plan was as successful as I could have hoped. On my arrival the people gathered from all over the city and I asked the High Priest if he knew my language and I could speak through him.

As soon as the people found out that I was the son of the High Priest Lamekis, they expressed their joy and paid very careful attention to me. I took advantage to explain my views that filled them with such delight that by the end of the day the cult of Serapis and all the false divinities were destroyed. The proofs they gave me left no doubt: they carried all their idols to the square and burned them shouting in joy, which proved the sincerity of their conversion.

And yet the people asked me for a favor that put me in a most difficult situation and was very hard to refuse. They wanted me to instruct them in the new way that I had just opened up. They asked me to be their High Priest, to build the temple to the great Vilkonhis and teach them his laws. Instead of leaving everything behind to answer such a distinguished and flattering honor, I was so preoccupied with my prospective vengeance that I put their offer off for another time, even though it was really the most important of my duties. Oh Vilkonhis, you have punished me for that and I still suffer today. The results of my misfortunes are sure proofs of this. But it is only fair that I atone for such a great crime and receive my punishment with complete and humble deference.

The Egyptians seemed humiliated by my leaving and I could not convince them that I would return soon. They started howling pathetically and the eaglet got so upset he flew off. I was not angry with this because it saved me from my own emotions.

Off to the left we took a break in some woods where I saw trees bursting with fruit. I was famished. I gathered some, ate them and quenched my thirst on the shores of a river. There were some sheep around that fed my little friend—he munched on one that had wandered off. After both of us had had our fill, we got back on our way until we bedded down on the heights of a rock that reached into the clouds.

We traveled like that for 20 days, always keeping to the left following the old man's instructions. Around noon on the 21st day I spied the great peak of the capital of the kingdom of the Abdalles, which could be seen for 30 leagues around. My heart jumped at the sight and trembled with joy...and then with rage. I spent the night in a nearby forest and the next day I went down into a remote part of the dear city to the house of a freedman who owed me his fortune and on whom I could rely.

I was actually welcomed so hardily and amiably that I had no fear in telling him why I had come back. He could not have been more astonished that I had escaped the punishment I was sentenced to and after hearing the story of my adventures he concluded that the Heavens would not have protected me so much without grand and worthy designs. I learned from him that the Houcaïs had come back from the kingdom of the Amphicleocles soon after my banishment. What he said about Clemelis astounded me: she was living in an austere retreat, saw no one, not even the Queen or her closest friends and spent her precious days in constant sadness and lethargy.

I also learned that soon after I left the Houcaïs, the Queen and Boldeon did all they could to get her to marry Zelimon, who had recovered from his wounds, but my wife who was still dear to my heart made herself loud and clear about all the notions they might have about her by affirming that she would never belong to anyone.

Curiously I found out how the Houcaïs was living with her and wondered if it was not possible that this retreat was a wily pretext to have a freer hand. The freedman assured me of the contrary and to leave no doubt in my mind (he said), he offered to conceal me in Clemelis' house for as long as I wanted. It was easy for him because his brother was the steward and his residence was situated so that no one could enter or leave my wife's rooms without him knowing. And the time was ripe because the steward was away on business for the Princess and in the meantime the freedman took care of the household affairs.

I was too jealous and upset to deny such a favorable opportunity. I told the freedman how much his offer pleased me and how much in debt I would be to him if it could support or deny my justifiable suspicions. He promised to get me into his brother's room that very night. I prepared for the affair by arming myself with a zenghuis to use a second time if my jealous assumptions were verified. I still thought that this retreat housed my shame and dishonor and that the Houcaïs possessed the goods that I alone should enjoy. I was acting on the awful, savage way he had me banished from the states after so many previous signs of friendship. I figured it was only love, and a jealous, angry love that could have carried him to such cruel extremes. The young courtiers' speech, the letter I found, the secret meetings between the King and Clemelis and Zelimon's reports—all this roiled in my imagination and bolstered my suspicions. At last a way was open for me to clear up all my doubts; I seized it with jealous avidity.

Before going to Clemelis' rooms, I got a key from the freedman to lock up the eaglet in a big room. I chained him by one foot so that he could not get away and I explained to the freedman that he was the only thing left to me and to take special care of him. I told him what to give him to eat and how to do it so that he would not be eaten at the same time.

In the middle of the night we went to Clemelis' with my heart pounding as we entered. Her light was still on, but I showed nothing in front of the freedman. He left promising that he would come back every morning to receive my orders. The first thing I did was to run to her room and study it carefully so that I could find my way around in the dark if need be.

The next day I carefully examined the exterior. There was only one court separating me from her; our windows faced each other; the same hallway connected both rooms and from the window no one could enter my lovely wife's room without me seeing. I was satisfied with the layout. It seemed to me that I could rest absolutely assured.

When it was day, I hid in ambush to spy on the room to see if someone left. I waited more than two hours without anything happening. Finally the door opened and I recognized Milkhea, my venerable mother whom I loved so much. The sight of her brought tears to my eyes. She was with a woman whom I knew belonged to Clemelis, but she looked very different—she looked sad. I knew that the tears I caused her by my behavior and by the idea that I was dead were the cause of this change and of her dark melancholy. I sighed and sincerely felt pity and affection for her.

And if I was touched by this, Sinouis, imagine what I felt when Clemelis appeared. Oh, how she affected me! Her beauty was preserved in all its brilliance, but her lethargy made her a thousand times more beautiful. She looked sad and dreamy when she walked by and sat on the lawn across from my window. She plucked a few blades of grass absentmindedly, lost deep in thought. Sometimes her beautiful eyes looked up at the sky and seemed tear-soaked. Then she looked back down at the ground and sighed. I could see her mumbling and making forced gestures to her sorrowful lament. I lost my breath, but did not miss one of her movements. Everything was dear and precious to me. Love alone was in control and I was so completely absorbed and delighted by her presence that I could not even think.

Milkhea came with a different girl from the one she had left with. She had a whistling parrot on her finger and brought it to Clemelis, no doubt to distract her from her profound melancholy. Everything is precious when you are in love. My eyes and heart were in step with all her movements: when Clemelis smiled receiving the lovely bird, I smiled with her. She petted it and her reverie vanished for a moment, but how short that moment was! Milkhea and the bird came in vain. Clemelis saw them no more. Her tears got the upper hand and she abandoned herself openly to the raging grief.

Such a touching state affected me and finally made me think of something. It was unlikely that Clemelis was in love with the Houcaïs and that he paid her back so hard. She was too worthy of love for such a passion to be the source of the fatal situation she was prey to. This so clear, so unsuspicious grief could only be born of a love that was thankless or unreliable. Clemelis was too lovable to get into such a situation. So what could all the weeping mean? If it weren't for my cruel suspicions, wouldn't I have thought it was for me?

The following night I snuck stealthily up her window and witnessed the same signs of sorrow. Three whole days of watching did nothing but prove to me how innocent Clemelis was and how guilty I was. I started to recover completely from the jealousy that I found no likely evidence of. I was already getting ready to surprise her, to clear up my suspicions and then show her every sign of my affection. I told the freedman that very day and he applauded my plan. But that would have been too lucky. An unfortunate accident tore apart all my wonderful projects and threw me back into my old feelings.

Oh Heavens, I still cannot think of it without trembling with rage! Put yourself in my place, Sinouis, and you will agree that it was justified. Seeing her actions, like I just told you, on the fourth night I left my room with the intention of knocking softly on Clemelis' window, making myself known and asking to talk with her in secret to explain myself when, on opening my door, I saw someone slip into my wife's room. I stood there dumbfounded. In spite of the dark night I saw clearly enough that it was a man and by his clothes it was no commoner. I had no doubt that it was the King because in the house there was no other man but me. Besides the freedman telling me this, my own investigation had proved it. So who

would have entered the house at such an hour except the powerful Houcaïs or a private lover? They were the same thing
to me. I decided once and for all to be sure that the guilty parties would not escape their just desserts. It was just a matter of
waiting there for the door to open—it was pretty certain that
the lover would leave before the light of day. The wait was
long next to the door with sword in hand. My plan was to first
strike down my rival and then rush to Clemelis to sacrifice her
to my fury.

The longer the stranger stayed inside, the guiltier Clemelis seemed to me. The evidence was too plain for my heart to
even dare to side with the unfaithful and it was almost day and
there was no sign of anything. It was agonizing. My forehead
was covered in a cold sweat. I wanted to strike someone down,
but I could barely hold myself up.

Finally the fatal door opened and what did I see? Clemelis leaning on the same man. I bore down with such strong
vengeance that my sword slid straight through the one I took
as was my rival. A second strike laid him at my feet. I was at
the height of rage, but I saw Clemelis. She was seeing the
stranger out and separating from him so sweetly that it left no
doubt as to my suspicions. Three blows of the zenghuis struck
with jealous fury seemed enough to me to take her guilty life.
After this punishment, which I believed justified, I ran from
Clemelis and back to the freedman's house. I had the key to
both houses so I had no problem leaving the one or entering
the other.

I was plunged in such awful distress that I did not even
think of my eaglet. I really had to be in bad condition for that
because I knew how much the kind animal missed me. The
freedman told me that he had been very sad and was refusing
to eat. I had decided earlier to go back to see him, but at that
instant I could think of nothing but what had just happened. If
my honor seemed to me to be saved, my heart certainly was
not. In spite of so much hatred and spite against Clemelis, I
never stopped loving her for an instant. Deep in my soul

where the cruel thoughts brewed, I saw only too well that this love would end in the grave.

I was drowning in an abyss of regret, remorse and bitter worry when someone knocked at the door louder and louder. I had been caught unawares. Ah! Of course, I told myself, they want to take away my freedom; they want to punish me again for repeating my crime. The idea of this and the savagery of my first punishment rushed upon me so hard and fast that I ran to the room where the eaglet was kept, intending to unlock him, open the windows and fly away together.

The dear animal barely saw me when he started crying out in joy, flapping his wings and showing all the signs of perfect happiness. I waited for a more suitable time to thank him. I heard a dreadful noise and an awful roar. As we escaped out the window I saw a large gathering of people and a body carried by slaves entering the house. Without wanting to know about something that I should not have had anything to do with, I squeezed the eaglet with my knees and we were soon lost in the skies.

Part 8

While my kind little friend let himself be swept away by the charms of his new freedom, bearing me along through the immense space of the skies, I pondered deeply over my latest tragedy. It was not possible to argue with my fate since I myself was its maker. Besides, there should be no remorse when the punishment is justified. To see the woman you love in the arms of another man (for, what I saw was pretty much the same thing or at least I thought so) is a horrible sight for a man with uncommon feelings. I believed Clemelis was guilty and I avenged myself in her blood. So, why was I agonizing? Didn't she bring it on herself?

That's what I was thinking. If I still felt love in my heart for a wicked, villainous woman, my honor stifled these tender feelings by showing her as fickle and unfaithful and the nefarious cause of all the evils I had suffered until then. I could have gone even further in consoling myself by accusing her of having been in collusion with the Houcaïs to get rid of me, to free herself forever of a burdensome spouse who would never have put up with her follies.

From these thoughts I passed on to what would become of me. I was still young and I naturally had a few years before me. How should I use them? The question had barely popped into my head when I thought of the offer made by the Egyptians. How better could I devote the rest of my miserable life than in the service of an immortal Being for the happiness of my country? A superstitious worship had just been abolished with my help. Wasn't that the voice of the Heavens speaking? Shouldn't I be listening? People who are infatuated and prejudiced from birth can be seduced at any time; it would not take much for a number of self-interested priests to do what was needed to reestablish the ruined altars. Wasn't it my bound duty to stop them and finish the work that was so well started? And what glory I would get from it!

The thought of it moved me, made up my mind and pointed the way. I kneed the eaglet and followed my old route, but away from the kingdom of the Abdalles. I guided my little friend's flight in such a way as to keep the ground in sight so I could use the landmarks I noted during my first trip. It worked. After a month I saw Egypt and blessed the Heavens. I went to the capital and alit like the first time on top of the great tower. It was night and I spent it in prayer. Overcome by piety I invoked the great Vilkonhis and prayed ardently that he bless my good intentions.

When it was day and I saw the people moving about, I went down onto the dome. The sight of me caused a general cry of astonishment and joy and in less than an hour all the inhabitants of the capital were gathered around the dome. I spoke to them and asked if they remained faithful to the worship I had preached. I could tell by their silence that something extraordinary had happened during my absence. I urged them to tell me.

An Egyptian who was still faithful to the new doctrine came up on the dome and verified my assumption. As soon as I learned about it the priests who had been chased from their temple paraded down the streets with new fangled gods, howling a frightful cacophony and prophesying dire calamities. "The Nile," they shouted, "will be destroyed. It will return to the earth and bring on the worst famine ever seen." That's all it took to affect these crude people. Uneducated in the science of the Heavens they had fallen back into their old errors. The harm was serious and I groaned, but I decided to do the best I could to help them.

Almost all the hearts and minds of the people were held captive by the recidivist threats of the fanatic priests. I spoke for more than six hours to no avail. The ministers of the false gods had found out about my return and my goal and had run straight to the people to keep them from listening to me. The High Priest was especially outstanding at hurling curses that made their hair stand on end. He steadily influenced them and I recognized sadly that the lie was going to prevail over the truth. A holy horror seized me. Something spectacular needed to happen to regain the trust I had lost by my sudden departure. With no miracles at hand, I had to make do with politics. I lowered the eaglet's head and led him toward the maddened elder, who could not get out of the way. At the sound of my voice the animal swooped down on him and I grabbed him by his once so venerable cap. With one swift blow of they zenghuis, his blasphemies and his life ended.

The example had an effect. The people fell silent and the other troublemaking, rebellious priests ran away and hid, thereby leaving me free to continue haranguing them. I was emotional and persuasive. After three consecutive days of teaching, I was victorious: the great Vilkonhis was worshipped, the idols overthrown and I became the chief minister of the religion.

I did not think the religious principles would be lost by allying them with the state. They needed the support of a sovereign authority to give them a foundation safe from the perpetual assaults that would inevitably come against them. For this I went to the newly elected King. The new doctrine convinced him and he looked on it as the most solid base of the monarchy. I communicated to him the dogma of the religion and he found it so holy and praiseworthy that he publicly declared my doctrine as the true one and the one that every reasonable man should profess. In less than one round of the Sun,[275] Vilkonhis was worshipped throughout Egypt. Superb temples were built and I worked so devotedly that I forgot all my misfortunes.

Religion is a powerful way to make you happy! I spent my days in a wonderful tranquility. The sanctuary was my only delight. There I lived sheltered from anything that might disturb my peace. If I went to the Court, it was less to enjoy the charm of being praised than to have nice conversations

---

[275] The Egyptians counted the year by the revolutions of the Sun.

with the King about the worship that I led. Several years went by in this peaceful state; it seemed that nothing could disrupt it. But what am I saying! Was I made to be happy for long?

One day as I was leaving the King I was stopped by a stranger whose face made me balk. "What's this I see?" I said holding out my arms. "What luck has brought you here?" It was the loyal freedman who had got me into Clemelis' rooms and to whom I owed the ravishing pleasure of punishing a wicked wife. He shook my hand and said that he would answer my questions later. He looked timid, insecure and I saw sadness and confusion in his eyes. He came back with me and when we were alone, he respectfully criticized the tranquility I enjoyed at a time (he said) when I should be gnawed at by regret and remorse. I was hardly expecting such reproaches and I showed my surprise.

He continued, "From what I can tell, you're wrong. I don't know if I should help you or if it'd be better to leave you like this forever. Oh, Lamekis," he clasped his hands together, "how unlucky you are and how little you deserve the calm fate you are enjoying!" He looked up to the Heavens and continued, "How cruel! The innocent suffer and the guilty gloat! Faithful Clemelis..."

"What am I hearing? What are you saying?" I interjected. "Faithful Clemelis? Ach, stop saying these things that remind me of the horrors I've tried to forget and that I've suffered so much for. It's useless to try to manipulate me after I saw her wickedness with my own eyes..."

"Stop, Lamekis," the freedman interrupted in his turn. "Don't make your well-known crimes worse by this masquerade. Your eyes betrayed you. Clemelis is the best behaved, most innocent of all women and I'm ready to prove it to you and answer all the suspicions you might have against her."

I tapped my foot impatiently while listening. My fury enflamed and brought back all the grievances I had against the wicked woman. I did not forget one of them: her meetings with the Houcaïs, her letter to him and their secret rendezvous, her absence from the Court after this so carefully hidden appointment, the Houcaïs caught at ungodly hours in her room, the letter that I had kept, that I showed, my savage punishment by the King to do away with a defiant spouse and finally the man in her room in the middle of the night, seen and killed by me—all this seemed to...did certainly justify me, didn't it? From my outraged heart I spilled out my loathing and threats. "And she's still alive?" I railed. "That villainous wife? My hand betrayed me twice? Well then, let her tremble. I am ready to take my revenge. I'll risk a thousand lives, if I had them, to rip out the heart that was created only to make me the unhappiest of men."

While I was spewing this fire, the freedman kept silent and looked at the ground, but when he saw the heat of my anger die down, he begged me to hear him out. "Although your grievances looked likely," he told me firmly, "they were false. Clemelis has always been faithful to you and no wife is better behaved. You are the only one in the world who dared to suspect her. Did you ever think that all this evidence you allege is really against you and not a piece of it doesn't make you doubly despicable? Listen to me, Lamekis," he saw my impatience at what he was saying, "after what I have to say, you are the master and if you want, you can stay bitter."

The freedman's story

Before starting this justification where the truth is going to get mixed up with jealous suspicions and prejudice, you have to know how I can give it to you. I never had the honor of getting too close to poor Clemelis—she only trusted my brother. If I was given any consideration, it was only because of him; and my loyalty to you made me search this out. I wanted to serve you both, as you will see, but you're going to agree that there's a high, sad price to pay for good intentions.

Remember the day when you trusted me with your complaints against good Clemelis? Do you also remember that I did the best I could to talk you out of those dire impressions that were consuming you and I offered my brother's room for you to clear up your doubts completely? At the time I was only acting on my gut feelings. I had never been close enough to the worthy woman to speak for her behavior, but her favorable reputation spoke to me when I saw you resolved to verify your doubts. Besides, they seemed based on so little that I thought I would be doing you both a great service by giving you the opportunity to see for yourself and stop all the worries that seemed to me to be only in your head. Therefore, I asked for a secret meeting with Clemelis through one of her servants, assuring her that it was of the utmost importance. I thought it best to meet during the night, hoping to hide her from you and give you a nice surprise. She agreed.

I told Clemelis about your return and she did not take the news well. That's why I stayed so long in her room. After recovering from a weak spell, she urged me to take her to you. I tried in vain to make her understand that it was better for me to see you first and warn you so that I could shatter your suspicions. She would not hear of it. Her impatience drove her on, beyond my wise caution. I had to obey. She was so emotional and weak that she had to lean on my arm to leave the room and we were so scared…

"Heavens," I gasped wildly, "what are you telling me? Can it be…"

The freedman did not give me time to finish: Yes, Sir. It was me you struck down at your feet. Our cries woke up the whole house and they went to get help. They put Clemelis to bed and the doctors took care of her. As for me, whom they thought dead because I gave no sign of life, they carried me back home. After a few days I got better and learned that you had escaped with your wonderful bird, but knowing this was no comfort to me since you would be arrested in no time. The Houcaïs was informed as soon as you attacked and to prevent any future attacks, he decided to take your life. They looked long and hard for you and when I felt better, I had to deal with all this cruel information.

When Clemelis was barely able to talk, she sent for me. Her wounds took longer to heal than mine and her weakness did not go away, maybe never will. She was curious and eager to know what had become of you and if I knew why you continued to act so violently against a wife who loved only you. I told her everything that you had told me, particularly the grievances you kept repeating.

When I finished she said, "What are you telling me? Oh crooked, cheating Zelimon, what did we ever do to you for you to turn on us so cruelly? And Lamekis, my dear husband, who I will always love and whose hardheartedness I will forgive, I hope you will learn of all the wicked tricks that have been played against us! You will come back someday soon to give me the joy that I only feel when I'm in your arms."

As the freedman paused to take a breath I stammered quickly, which presaged the sorrow I was on the verge of suffering, "So then, she told you about the horrible tricks used to ruin the two of us?"

"Alas, lord!" he continued, "You will learn them soon enough."

"Go on! Continue!" I urged. "If it's about Zelimon, I can feel my fate. I knew him too well not to expect the most wicked designs from him." And the freedman told me what Clemelis told him:

Clemelis and Zelimon

A few days after I had to leave my beloved husband, I received an anonymous letter that told me that he was being unfaithful to me and that he had been living with an incredibly beautiful Phoenician woman for a long time. Without any consideration for his benefactor, the King, he preferred this woman to me. This news made only a slight impression on me—I always hated this kind of gossip too much to believe any of it.

The first letter I received from my husband was full of affection and assurance of his loyalty and dissipated the faint clouds of suspicion that my delicate heart let form. I did not even think of asking his opinion about it, since it would have looked like I was challenging his love—even the shadow of

324

suspicion was too offensive to let my dear husband see it. As long as I was getting letters from him, I forgot all about that other fatal letter, but as soon as his letters stopped coming, my soul was mortally wounded. Before becoming suspicious, however, I took it upon myself to wait. Maybe, I told myself, the delay is only due to his forgetfulness and not to his indifference. The first letter will put an end to all my worries and calm me down. How hard it was! I waited in vain. Meanwhile I believed he had forgotten me and I was dying of sorrow.

I said that I believed he had forgotten me because I had no doubt that my husband was in a position to write. The King had come back and was receiving letters regularly from him, as well as other members of the Court from time to time. Zelimon, who had his own reasons for letting me know about this, was cruel enough to show me the ones he got from Lamekis at the Queen's residence and to brag about his close friendship with him. And he often looked at me compassionately, which surprised me. When I caught him looking, he changed and looked stressed and mysterious, which surprised me even more and troubled me.

This happened so often that I finally decided to know why he looked at me like this. I had him sent for in the morning. When he came and I questioned him on the matter, he looked embarrassed, which again increased my curiosity. After much coaxing, he finally confessed that his intimate friendship with my husband was difficult for him when it came to the unfair treatment of me. He broke off everything he said in such a way that he told me nothing, which was supposed to make me guess that it was all because my husband was reluctant to leave the Phoenician woman whom he loved. Imagine how overwhelmed I was with grief. It crushed me so cruelly that I decide to put an end to the painful situation by going to find my husband and doing all I could to win his heart again. Otherwise I would become the unhappiest woman in the world.

I spoke to the Queen about my plan to go find my husband without telling her why. I pretended that my worries were due to an uncomfortable feeling I could not shake. She kindly agreed, as long as I got the King's permission. Afraid of losing time, I wrote to him through a servant of mine to beg him to grant me an audience that very day because otherwise I would have been forced to wait for him to come to the Queen's rooms, which was not supposed to happen for two days. The Houcaïs was kind enough to let me come to see him. While I was there, he did his best to hold me back or better said he wanted to know why I was leaving. He found out so much and was so sympathetic with my troubling secrets that I confessed everything. He was kind enough to console me. He promised me his help to win back the heart I believed was lost and granted me permission to leave, along with the promise that he would hide my departure from everyone so that Lamekis, who was corresponding with the Court, would not find out about my intentions. I took cruel pleasure in discovering for myself my husband's intrigue and scolding him when he least expected it.

(While the freedman was giving me these details, I suddenly remembered two incidents that could more than a little justify Clemelis in my eyes. The first: the audience with the Houcaïs that now seemed so natural, but that Zelimon had made out to be so guilty. The second: the meeting of the young woman in the town where I passed through on the way to the Court, whose description was like Clemelis. But I did not want to interrupt the freedman; my curiosity was in a hurry. And so he continued.)

What was I to think (Clemelis cried in sorrow) when I got to the kingdom of the Abdalles and Lamekis was not there. I figured he had been told about my arrival in spite of all the precautions taken and had fled at my approach. In the hope of his return I stayed a little while in the country and investigated so carefully that I finally learned that he had gone to the Court. No sooner did I confirm the information than I left to go back. But imagine the trouble and fear I felt on my return when I saw my closet forced open and the mess caused by some furious rage. What could this mean? The Houcaïs, whom I informed, came to my room and was as surprised as I was. He told me that the mystery bothered him even more than if he found out that there was a plot against him. Then, he gave such perfect orders for my safety and protection that I could stay and sleep in my room.

My constant worry, which had kept me from sleeping for so long, had finally given way to a deep sleep that made me very happy after such a long deprivation. But it was interrupted by the filthiest adventure you can imagine. I felt someone kissing my hand and I awoke with a start. This unexpected audacity was followed by the most spirited declarations of love...It was Zelimon...

(I interrupted the freedman here. "I know about this. I saw it with my own eyes. What happened after? After my fury, what did Clemelis make of the inhuman, savage treatment I was given?"

"She had no part in the cruel events," the freedman replied. Her almost fatal wounds kept her in bed and you were banished without her knowing.")

How many tears did I shed (she continued) when I learned how savagely they treated my husband, even though he was unworthy of my pity because of his fury against me! I surrendered to despair. I asked to retire from the Court. In spite of all the advice given to me, I did not want to live in a place where everything that was dearest to me in the world was treated so inhumanely. The Queen tried in vain to make me understand that as long as he was alive, my life was in danger, but nothing could dissuade me. I withdrew into this house where I plan to spend the rest of my life without seeing anyone so that I can lament all my misfortunes in peace.

I was not here long before I was exposed to the persecutions of that traitorous Zelimon. He still loved me and was so hopelessly, uncontrollably in love that he did not even fear my living husband. He used all his influence to get me to marry him. His father Boldeon came to see me, to propose him to me, using all his persuasive skill to get me to make him happy. Fancy that! How foolish! I stood up against all his assaults.

Zelimon became desperate when he could not win me over, so he decided to kidnap me. He had bribed one of my people to sneak him into my house during the night, but your brother's bravery saved me from this horrid business. I complained bitterly to the King. Zelimon was exiled and before leaving he got such a strong reprimand and such precise instructions not to badger me anymore that I have not heard from him since.

Lamekis in Egypt

"Well, Sir," the freedman continued, "that's what poor Clemelis told me. Then she asked me to do all I could to try to find out where in the world you might be, assuring me that after a year of searching she herself would go look for you. I was so touched by how sorry she was and by her fervent desire to see you again that I left the next day to carry out her impatient wishes. Since that time I have crossed the seas, wandered from one kingdom to the next, everywhere mentioning you in the hope that your great, famous name would sooner or later root you out. As you see, my hope was not in vain. I heard about you living in distant lands, so what did I have to lose? The whole Earth is full of your heroic deeds in the amazing revolution affected by your divine genius in Egypt. I hastened here and saw you, Lamekis, and flattered myself that my good intentions would affect you as I expected."

If it were possible for me to cry a torrent of tears, my devastated heart, pricked by such true and sincere details, would have done so. I clearly saw my injustice and my crimes. I was repeatedly on the verge of agreeing with him and admitting them all and going to ask for forgiveness. But the power that pride has over a man who is jealous of his reputation held me back. What will posterity say, I asked myself, of such a confession? These real, true crimes with unknown motives will seem mysterious in the future, evidence of determination and grandeur...as long as the cause stays unknown. But how I will be buried in hatred and scorn if they are found out!

However the desire to see Clemelis, who had become infinitely more precious to me since I knew she was innocent, (for, I had seen that the passionate letter that had bothered me so much was an answer to me), got the better of my proud thoughts. I assured the freedman that my plan was to go very soon to join her and sincerely ask forgiveness at her feet for all my offenses. In anticipation, I in turn gave him the details of what had happened to me, looking for some sympathy for my weaknesses, or better said my furies. Before leaving Egypt, I had to resign the High Priesthood to the King. According to the laws I myself had set up, it was not allowed to a married man, so I had to renounce it forever for Clemelis. Besides this important duty, my gratitude for so many good things in Egypt required all kinds of considerations from me. I was so venerated and always treated so kindly that I would have been the most ungrateful of all men if I left without the unanimous consent of the people. It was not easy to get. I was loved and thought of as the spiritual father of the country. Didn't that deserve consideration?

The freedman agreed and was quick to broach the dilemma. We decided that he would go ahead of me to inform Clemelis about everything and that I would wait in Egypt for news from him. I wrote a long letter to my adorable wife in which I assured her, without going into detail, that I had never stopped loving her for an instant and that I was waiting for her to write to me herself to forgive me and let me come and swear my eternal gratitude at her feet.

After he left with the letter, I went to the King and to make especially sure that I would get his approval to leave, I made an honest and natural confession of the reasons for my request. Not only did he accept it, but he even wanted to help me by designing the plan I should follow so as not to be held back. He was as wise as he was intelligent. I began by naming a High Priest of the kingdom as adjunct to take over for me in case of sickness or death. The nomination was received with great applause by the Egyptians. It was easy then to leave when I wanted to on the pretext of sickness and, supposing that the events of my life forced me to return, I would be restored to honor in Egypt where I could peacefully spend the rest of my life.

Three months had already passed without any news from Clemelis. I was living in lethargy and cruel impatience. I had calculated the time for the freedman to get there and the time I should have received some mail from him—it had been more than enough. Sometimes I would say aloud, "Oh Heavens, what can be the cause of such a delay? Does Clemelis not want to see me? Have I become so hated by her that she won't hear me out? But the freedman would tell me. He wouldn't leave me in this harrowing uncertainty." Sometimes I thought that the loyal man got into some accident and that my dear wife was ignorant of my repentance, continuing to live in her remorse. At other times jealousy came back into the control that it had tyrannized me with for so long. But my mind, which had banished it, was able to resist all the motives that its powerless voice put forth; they were just feeble impressions and when they came, it took only a moment of reflection to wipe them out entirely.

One day when I was bothered by this cruel uncertainty and shocked by all the tragedies in my life, I heard a commotion break out in the capital, which made me shudder to the depths of my being. I was leaving to find out the cause of the terrible hubbub when one of the priests from the temple ran in scared, completely out of sorts and said, "Oh Holy Minister, the altars of the great Vilkonhis are smashed, the temple is about to collapse, the priests of Serapis have triumphed and the people are in revolt, sacrificing to a new god."

"What's this I hear? Just Heavens…" I could not say any more. I left and ran to the temple and up into the galleries. Oh Sinouis, what do you think I saw? The eaglet was flying around ridden by one of the priests of idolatry who was haranguing the people, seducing them, leading them astray. I tried to shout out, but it was no use. The fire of rebellion consumed all their hearts. A natural wonder had made them shake off the good yoke—see, a drought had dried up the Nile for several days and it was being called a punishment for their infidelity. The priests of all the gods of Egypt, on the same day, at the same hour, sparked the revolution and the fury in their eyes got stronger when they pronounced their oracles. Everyone bent; everyone obeyed; and I was grieved to see the worship destroyed and all my projects overthrown in an instant.

The King sought for me everywhere to give me advice to save myself from the public fury. To save his throne he was forced to capitulate to the revolution and consent to my death. The Egyptians were crowding around the temple, howling out, trying to break in and would not stop until they had me in their hands to tear me to pieces.

The one whom the King had sent to me found his way through a secret corridor that connected the palace to the temple. But instead of yielding to his advice I mounted the temple's guerluche.[276] There was one last urgent hope left to me. The eaglet knew me too well not to come when I called. They must have surprised him during the night for him to let the priest now riding him get on. Since I had come back to Egypt I had left the good bird free, putting it in a forest near the temple that the people held sacred. I often went to see him there and never imagined that anyone would be so bold as to take him. And he had never left the place except for a few times when he came to surprise me at the window of my room to give me signs of his affection. In short, I trusted his loyalty and put all my faith in it at the moment.

It was not in vain. The bird, with its keen, piercing eyes, barely glimpsed me on the guerluche when it beat its wings, stretched out its neck, stopped a moment as if to make sure and then descended toward me. The priest who was riding him certainly guessed his intention and did all he could to prevent it, but the animal was stronger and came to perch on the guerluche, showing me in his way how happy he was to be with

---

[276] A kind of weathervane made from a dried out steer whose rear end was positioned so that the wind always blew up its butt, which was quite helpful in preserving it whole for a long time.

me again. But the priest, desperate at seeing his plans take a turn for the worse, screeched at me to go away or else he would throw me off the guerluche. I answered him sternly that he had better get off my bird or else he would be eaten. And to show him that his threats did not intimidate me, I grabbed the eaglet and jumped on his neck. The priest of Serapis, who was not expecting this bold move, raised his zenghuis to strike me. I grabbed his arm and we struggled—him to stab me and me to disarm him. During the fight the eaglet flew up and sliced through the air with unparalleled speed.

Nothing bolsters courage as much as fear of danger. The danger that threatened me gave me new strength, but the man I was dealing with had so much already that he got his arm free, raised his sword and brought it down with such force that it would have taken a thousand lives if I had them. Even though I dodged the blow, it was still fatal: it fell straight down on the back of the eaglet. I became so furious then and shook the priest so violently that he was thrown off the eaglet and plummeted down. As soon as the poor bird noticed it, he swooped to the ground on top of my enemy and tore him to shreds.

But what was the use, what good was my righteous vengeance? My lovable eaglet was wounded. The blow had gone so deep that seeing it put shivers down my spine. He moaned and caressed me in his way, showing me in his eyes the cruel torment he was suffering. I gave him as much care and comfort as I could, but he languished, wasted away before my very eyes. Oh Sinouis, how alarmed I was! Before the end of the day my dear eaglet closed his eyes, laid his head on my knees and opened his beak; he closed it again with hiccups that presaged his near death. I cried buckets then and my laments could have moved rocks. My little friend cracked open his eyes from time to time and seemed to share in my grief. So, what can I tell you? Savage death came to take away my partner in so many misfortunes. My little friend, my dear friend stretched out his legs, flapped his wings and pressed his head against me to say goodbye. Forgive me for crying when I think of this baleful memory; I still cannot think of him without getting choked up. Yes, dear bird, if we can see each other again in another life, if the perfect instinct you were blessed with earned you a different fate and rendered you immortal, I will never forget the tender affection that you had for me and I will enjoy telling you that I never forgot you.

Heavens, can it be that we are given so few days and they are run through like that? After the death of my dear, little friend I was dejected; I could do nothing. I spent two turns of the Sun with my arms crossed, tears in eyes, not able to make any decision. It seemed that an empty hope kept me in that fatal place, promising to bring my eaglet back to life. I stared at him. The slightest wind that ruffled his feathers convinced me that he was regaining his senses. I kissed him, called him my pet names and begged him to show me some sign of affection like he had always done before. Alas, I was fooling myself! The eaglet was no more. The evidence was all too certain: he started decaying and in spite of my love for him, I had to get away or else make up my mind to perish alongside him.

Never should a sensible man be attached to anything in life—that way he will avoid some of the grief and desolation in getting through it. Depriving ourselves of goods that we become attached to is much more sensible than the pleasure we feel in acquiring them. I was proof of this: at every step, at every moment I missed my little friend. He was not only a faithful companion, but also a nice and gentle aide. With him I went from one land to another without feeling any danger. Without him I was vulnerable to fatigue and countless other dangers.

In fact, how many had I been through in Egypt? The Priests of Serapis had given such strict orders to arrest me that if it wasn't for you, Sinouis, I would be lost. Your generous pity defended me against a mob that was ready to crush me. Since that time you have not left me. Your compassionate friendship, on the pretext of having business in the kingdom of the Abdalles, made you leave your home to follow me and save me from the patent dangers I faced.

Lamekis gets revenge

You know the rest. Through your personal experience and with your own eyes you know that I was predestined for the most extraordinary adventures. Do you remember that before relating my story I told you how bad luck always followed me? Alas! Why are you so devoted? Why haven't you left me? You have suffered through so much wandering and today you are in this grim situation—you have every right to reproach me.

I had barely finished speaking when Sinouis screamed and flew over to me saying that he was doomed. I saw what he saw: a hunter with his bow drawn and ready for the fatal shot. I hissed in fear and slithered as fast as I could to escape a certain death. Since the owl could fly, he escaped the deadly peril, but his lethargy brought him to perch on a rock and it did not take long for the enemy to get him in his sights. He fell back on the other side of the rock and I saw him no more.

I was seized by rage at this new tragedy. What did I have more precious to me than Sinouis? I decided to avenge his death and I snuck up unseen on the barbarian who had killed him. My head was poised and my venomous tongue was ready to lash out. I was calculating, so to speak, the strike that would punish the cruel murderer of my dear friend, when the sound I made slipping beneath his arm made him jump back and scream at the sight of me. But what a surprise and what rage I felt when I recognized the hunter as the traitorous Zelimon. The villain, the false friend, the savage architect of all the tragedies burying me. I struck out and reached him. I grabbed onto his leg and like ivy I wrapped around his body.

"The Heavens have finally delivered you to my wrath," I cried out. "I am Lamekis. Prepare to get the punishment you deserve. A quick death is a too easy revenge for all your wickedness. I want to follow you everywhere. My monstrous embrace will bring you to the brink of death a thousand times everyday—a death that you earned a thousand times. Your life now depends on mine. You can get rid of me by taking my miserable life with the sword, but remember that I'm watching you and I have good eyesight. If I see you make the slightest effort to kill me, I will bite you a thousand times in the heart, which will kill you before me."

Zelimon shuddered in horror and fright at my words. At least the punishment fit the crime. He started crying like a coward and begged for mercy.

"No, no," I went on, "I won't change my mind. Besides, you can go wherever you want as long as I'm with you...everywhere."

While he was thinking bitterly of his hard fate, I silently thanked the great Vilkonhis for his supreme bounty. Indeed, could it be any more supreme? If he had punished me by keeping me away from what was most dearest to me, at least he gave me the opportunity to take vengeance on the wicked architect of all the evils I suffered. Besides, couldn't I hope that this new guide would get me back my original shape by taking me to Clemelis? I had to find a faithful woman. After everything I said about my respectable wife could I doubt that she would perform this miracle? My confidence in Zelimon was well founded. He had never stopped loving her and it was only natural to think that he kept her in sight and knew where she was.

I asked him. "Tell me, you worst traitor of all traitors, what has happened to Clemelis because of your wicked love for her?" At this question I felt the traitorous Zelimon tremble. He hesitated to answer. "Speak," I squeezed him hard enough to make him lose color. "Speak or I'll torture you worse than you ever dreamed of."

"Well," he sighed bitterly, "I will tell you, Lamekis, but my confession will do nothing except trigger more of these horrors you threaten me with."

"Do it. Tell me." I was furious. "You can say nothing to surprise me. I know you too well to be naïve. I know that you are capable of the most dreadful wickedness."

Zelimon was trembling as he sat at the base of a tree. He had asked my permission because he could not stand up any longer. After breathing heavily he told me of the beginning of his love for Clemelis. He had loved her long before I married her and had done all he could to stop our union. After this he ran through all the suspicions I talked about and got to his reckless entrance into Clemelis' room by bribing one of her servants. He confessed that his exile only inflamed his passion and made him more determined to get her at any price. To force an opportunity he had again bribed one of Clemelis' servants. Oh these despicable acts deserve the worse punishments! The poor lady had informed Zelimon of the freedman's arrival and the joy that her mistress felt after talking with him. And Zelimon continued.

Zelimon's story

I was no sooner informed of your wife's emotions since the freedman's arrival than I decided to learn the reason at any price. For this I went secretly to this man and used every means possible to wheedle him into trusting me. But it was no use! His loyalty and discretion were invincible and annoyed me. The more care he took to hide from me what seemed to be of great interest to my love, the deeper I dug. I had recourse to the only way I could get what I wanted—violence.

I had the freedman kidnapped in the middle of the night. It was done so carefully that they did not make the slightest noise in bringing him to me. I kept him in a cellar where he caved in to torture and told me what I wanted to know. I was delighted to learn that Clemelis was waiting for you. I thought long and hard about how to satisfy my long-suffering love. Afraid that the freedman might ruin my plans if I let him go, that he might complain of how violently I treated him, I killed him with my own hands. Only our first crime counts—I had been used to it for a long time. But before sending him to the grave, I made him write a letter to Clemelis that would complete my plan. With it there was no doubt that I would succeed.

I told the bribed slave about my plan to enter Clemelis' room in the middle of the night pretending to be her husband...

("What!" I was beside myself as I untangled the knot of this intrigue. "Villain! You would have gone so far as to dishonor me in the flesh?")

I won't (the traitor continued) hide anything from you. That was the only means I had to get her to forgive me. I would have done anything to save myself. The slave tried in vain to tell me what would come of this. I was going to die for love or die trying to win it. The next night was planned for the final touch. Toward the end of the day I had a stranger bring the letter that I had forced the freedman to write to Clemelis. It went something like this:

Zelimon's Letter to Clemelis

Lamekis has just arrived. He is burning with desire to atone for his crimes at your feet. He begs you to order one of your servants to open the door when she hears him knock three times. He also asks that his coming be kept secret for important reasons that he will tell you about. And to avoid any surprises he would like your room to stay in the dark. He is so ravished by the desire to see the wife whom he loves that he cannot find the words to express it.

Signed, Zinouk-bour, the humblest of your slaves.

Clemelis was not only overcome with pleasure on receiving the letter, but also thought she could ruin my plans by the enthusiasm she felt to see you again, Lamekis. She wanted to go to the freedman's house right away and get a foretaste of your hugs and kisses. If it weren't for the bribed servant, she would have done it, but my crony talked her out of it by cleverly making her fear upsetting you. So, she held her desires at bay and waited for me as I advised.

I went to her house toward the middle of the night, knocked three times and the door was opened. The servant led me into Clemelis' room. The lovely woman ran up to me, threw her arms around me…her happy emotions…

Zelimon's death

"Wretch," I cut in and hit and bit over and over again until he lay senseless on the ground. "Take the punishment for a crime that a million lives like yours cannot atone for." I was at the height of rage and did all I could to tear him to pieces, but by a surprising marvel, I could not rip his flesh apart. His skin was as hard as his heart.[277] My fury was even more terrible after the traitor's story that I thought dishonored my return. My outraged love could no longer dream about the woman whom I had pined and suffered for, for so long.

In spite of Dehahal's oracle, I finally saw myself condemned to be a snake for the rest of my life. It was too cruel and truly worth every ounce of my despair.

But just as I realized that Zelimon was gone forever, I regretted his death. Indeed, my recklessness was too much. I had just taken away the only way for me to find out the most important details of the matter, however humiliating they might be for me. And however right I was to tell myself that I was surely dishonored, certain circumstances might make it more or less serious. I still had to find out if my gullible wife was ignorant of her crowning infamy, in which case she would be less guilty even though my insult would be no less bloody. I still boiled with desire to know if the villainous architect of my misfortune had told her or if he continued to take advantage of her gullibility. Carried away by anger, I also thought about the desire to punish the wretched servant who had sold

---

[277] Zelimon wore a cuirass. It was javelin-proof and became the model for the metal mail-armor which replaced it.

herself for these criminal attacks. Never was a mortal burdened by so many horrors at the same time. I had to be a snake not to collapse under their weight.

I spent several days in such cruel despair that I tried the best I could to put an end to my unlucky destiny. There were all kinds of things I did, but in vain. With my transformation, the Heavens had given me such a tough skin that it was impossible for me to take my own life, as miserable as it was to me. I could not leave Zelimon's corpse; I came and went like a madman. There was not a moment that I did not give it new bites. Just to look at it inflamed my bitterness, but I could not go away.

Then some woodcutters chanced upon the corpse, examined it carefully and after showing signs that they recognized it, they cried out at the sight. Slipping under a nearby rock I watched everything they did and listened to every word they said. The peasants talked about it and sometimes talked very reasonably. Finally after a lot of talking and shouting about Zelimon's death, from which they could easily see the cause, one of them took off to go (he said) to the next village to inform the family and relatives. After he left, the rest of them discussed the accident confidentially.

"It's a punishment, this sudden death!" the eldest said. "Zelimon didn't fear the Heavens. He was mean and hard on his inferiors and would just about kill them over the littlest thing. Since our great King exiled him," the good man continued, "he hasn't stopped tormenting and torturing us with whatever grief is eating away at him. I don't know the reason, but..."

"Oh!" one of the peasants interjected, "I'll bet trik-&-bak[278] that I know. And to prove it to you," he slapped his hand on the rock he was sitting on, "I'll tell you what happened to me over these past few days and then judge for yourself if I'm wrong to brag about knowing so much." The woodcutters gathered around and the peasant told his story.

---

[278] My wares and woman.

The woodcutter's story

Around a month ago I was rudely awakened out of a sound sleep by Zelimon himself. He was carrying a dark lantern and he was all sweating, like he'd been running. He told me to get up and follow him and take my tools with me. "I know you can keep a secret," he said to me on the road. "That's why I chose you to help me and I'll pay you well for it. But if you ever dare to open your mouth, your disobedience will cost you your life." There was nothing to say to that.

He brought me down into a deep cellar where I worked for him for a few days to set up a room and he helped me every night. We furnished it with the best of his furniture and after four days it had everything it needed. We spent the same time getting the doors in good condition: had to put on locks and bolts whose size would make you shiver. I was surprised sometimes myself. Of course he wants to lock somebody up in here, I told myself, somebody who did something bad to him and that somebody must be somebody important because he's going out of his way to make it comfortable. Really, except for being free, it was crawling with everything you could want in life. It was a real delight.

I really would've liked to know what it was all about, so I mentioned something about it once, but he turned on me full of gall and vinegar, so I never brought it up again.

When everything was like he wanted, he sent me back, reminding me to keep it a secret with the same threats he used the first time. I've been careful about it because he wouldn't go easy on me. And now you know as much as me and that's plenty.

Lamekis finds the underground prison

The peasant's story made a strong impression on me. Without quite figuring out what particular interest I took in the story, I decided right then and there to clear up such an interesting mystery. Thus, when the woodcutters left, I slithered into Zelimon's clothes. They are surely going to take his body away from here, I said to myself, and they will not notice me. They will carry it back to his house and when I am there, it will not be hard for me to get to the mysterious dungeon. A certain something burned inside me with a fervent desire not only to try, but to succeed in this project.

I waited impatiently for 15 minutes when they should have come back, but they did not. Halfway through the night nobody showed up. I was starting to despair when I heard Zelimon's people coming at the break of day. Of course it was them—they had brought a tou-kam-bouk[279] on a wagon to put their master's body in. The mourners walked in front of the convoy followed by a large number of people howling frightfully.

As soon as they arrived they formed a circle around the dead man. Then everyone became silent. Each of the heads of the funeral ceremony came up one after another to ask, according to custom,[280] if he was dead, why he had died and what his last wishes were. The corpse did not budge at any of these questions. After the gift ceremony,[281] they put him into the tou-kam-bouk...and me with him. The wagon, dragged by slaves,[282] took off, like an arrow out of a crossbow, on a relay race. In under an hour we got to the castle whose majesty and grandeur astonished me.

After the mourning ceremonies, they hung the tou-kam-bouk in the room where Zelimon lived, as was the usual cus-

---

[279] A curious coffin. It was a kind of deep barrel in which they put the corpse upright and then filled it with herbs and spices to preserve it.

[280] When an Abdallese paid nature's tribute, they took off his shoes and put his feet in water. Then they dressed him in a very expensive tunic before everyone came in to ask the questions that this note is written for.

[281] The gifts were a thimble, a needle, thread and scissors to mend his clothes in case they were torn on the road.

[282] The slaves not only had to drag their master to the tomb, but also leave behind one of their limbs, like a head, arm or leg.

tom.[283] When night fell and the Guer-ma-ka[284] were sleeping, I poked my head out of the barrel to see how I might get down. Afraid of hurting myself I dropped onto one of the Guer-ma-ka who woke up with a start and was so scared at the sight of me that she died on the spot, which embarrassed me a little because of the glory[285] that I got for her.

I went down the stairs to find out where the cellar windows were and I slipped through the first one I found. By the weak light I thought that chance had chosen the one I was so eager to find, but instead of finding myself, like I pretended at first, in the room I had been told about, I was only in the hallway leading to it. Some hanging lamps illuminated the passage and after a rather long journey in the subterranean cellar I came to a door that looked like it might be the one I wanted, but there was no way for me to get through it. It was closed so tightly that it was impossible, however hard I tried, to slide through. While I was examining it, I heard a faint moaning that made me listen more carefully. Heavens, I thought I recognized the voice. It sounded like Clemelis. My heart beat faster and I tried to listen, but it was no good. The thick door was an invincible obstacle. I was furious and sank into deep meditation.

How could she, I asked myself, be in this dark dungeon? I must be mistaken. What mask did Zelimon wear to get her to follow him into such a dreary place? Or did he kidnap her in the middle of a crowd in the bustling city? Either Clemelis is the unluckiest of all women or the most villainous. But why this suspicion? Don't I know how traitorous Zelimon is? His

---

[283] They tied the rope to a hook in the ceiling specifically installed for this. So that the dead not be disturbed, they rocked it constantly and it was considered very humane to help with this work, a proof of respect for the deceased.

[284] Women who got drunk to make the dead laugh. Only nobles were granted this honor.

[285] That of dying a violent death among the Abdallese. They said it was proof that the sun needed them and had chosen them to accompany its course.

behavior is detestable. Isn't this just another cruel outcome of his wicked ways? Let's wait to judge until things are better cleared up. Haven't I learned from experience now? After what I thought were well-founded suspicions, Clemelis was found innocent. Isn't it likely that the same appearances here will find the same solutions? If my poor wife was faithful to me when she thought I was dead for sure, shouldn't I only presume that when she learns of my fate she will keep her loyalty that she knows too well was jealously suspected by me? These thoughts reassured me and tempered the story that Zelimon had told just before his death. Love was on Clemelis' side; it had always ruled my heart.

The harder it was for me to get in, the harder I tried. I found no other way but to dig and try to open up a passage under the door. It was long and tricky work, even though I was a snake I had kept the same senses of touch and smell like when I was a man and they and my feelings were suffering. There's no use changing states; we always keep the same prejudices.

I spent two days at this painful labor and was almost ready to give up when I glimpsed a light. It was about time. My sapped energy regained its vigor then and finally got me into that place that had become so important to me. First I looked around, searching for the cause of all the pain and effort. A bed with the curtains drawn gave me hope that my desires would be answered. If I followed through on my first move, I would have gone there right away. But alas! I got hold of myself and stayed back. What fright would my monstrous appearance cause? Wouldn't I freeze the blood in her veins, supposing it was my dear wife in the bed? A snake of my size was a dreadful sight. I could barely look at myself, so how would she react? But I was bent on resolving my suspicions. In the end I found no way more natural than to slide deftly into the bed next to the wall and from this hiding place see who was there. I slithered over, but for nothing—it was empty. Soon I heard moaning again, coming from a closet and I knew my speculations were not idle. It was Clemelis. I saw her come back into the room. In spite of the sadness and depression in which she was sunk, she still had all the grace that distinguished her above all other women.

Oh Heavens, how hard it was for me just to look at her! She wept bitterly and whispered sweet words that struck my heart: I was the reason for her tears—she was calling upon me for help, promising she had always been faithful and tender in her love for me and without any explanation I had every reason to believe that my honor was safe from the horrible stains that the traitorous Zelimon had hinted at.

The charm of recovering such a lovely wife had blurred all my thoughts and I could not think straight. But a few minutes later I did and was cast into dire straits. My transformation should have stopped on meeting a chaste and loyal woman. I was with Clemelis, but I was still a snake. Heavens, what was going to become of me after that! My senses slowly chilled; the fire went out in me; and I completely lost the good feeling.

I mentioned that I had slid into Clemelis' bed. Obviously the spell that was meant to give me back my original form needed her to touch me! In any case, clearing my head, I found myself again as I used to be, but completely naked except for a snakeskin belt. My first reaction was to thank the Heavens for this singular favor bestowed on me; my second was to gaze upon my Clemelis. I was transported by the purest joy. What had just happened to me proved her wisdom and fidelity. I started running around her room to express all the feelings inside me, but alas, my tragedy was not over. Clemelis was gone. I could not understand what new miracle had made her disappear like that. It was like some fatal destiny was constantly opposing our reunion.

So, my joy was short-lived. When I knew for sure that my lovely wife had vanished, I struggled in vain to untangle the mystery that had taken her away from me. Everything was so tightly sealed that except for imagining a transformation like mine, I could not figure out how she could have left in a normal way. The thought threw me back into sorrow. "Oh Heavens," I shouted, "when will you stop persecuting me?"

Really, could my fate have been any more deplorable? I saw myself again in the grip of an awful death, imprisoned naked as the palm of my hand, with no food to prolong my wretched life. What was to become of me? And what did the Heavens have in store? Imagining the worst finally got to me. I breathed faster and heavier and felt like I was suffocating until I broke down and cried bitter tears, which helped to comfort me.

I spent three days and nights in this awful state. Toward the end of the fourth, I heard the door open. I raised my head, anxious to see who was paying me a visit. For a minute I thought it might be Clemelis, but what a surprise when I saw in the open door none other than Sinouis, the erstwhile owl whom I thought was dead. He was chained up like a wild beast and followed by a troop of culambis,[286] but what really threw me for a loop was that he still had his owl's beak. As soon as he saw me, he cried out in joy and astonishment, lifted his arms (weighed down by irons) and tried to come closer. I went up to him instead.

"What's this? I've found you again, my dear Sinouis" I hugged him tightly. "I thought you were dead. I cried so hard for you." The culambis gave us no time to talk. They ran in, slapped heavy irons on me and left without saying why I was being treated so inhumanely. Everything that happened to me was so extraordinary and so unlikely that I was less surprised at it than I should have been. But then again, Sinouis was taking up all my attention.

We stared at each other for a long time without saying anything. Finally he broke the silence to ask me how I came to be locked up in the place. I told him everything that had hap-

---

[286] Archers or guards who arrested and watched over criminals. They were allowed to have only one eye and hung the other around their neck: that was the mark of their office. When they arrested someone, they slapped him and said, "Long live liberty." When it comes to informing a curious reader, we can never be too explicit.

345

pened to me since our separation, but instead of making him feel better, it made him cry.

"Oh Lamekis, what are we destined for? What do all these trials and tribulations mean? Will we always be struggling? Is there no end?" He sighed heavily and told me what had happened to him.

Sinouis, the hunter and the cellar

After you saw me shot by an arrow, Lamekis, I fell into a lake that was behind the rock. It saved my life. A fisherman in his bark was casting his nets and I fell right next to him. He lifted me out of the water and gave me to his little boy as a toy to dry up his baby tears. The boy pulled out the arrow and in the course of torturing me woke me up. But the cruel kid made me pay dearly for the favor. He started his fun by ripping out my feathers one by one and every time I yelped in pain he busted a gut laughing. If I had any strength left in me, I would have pecked his face off, but I could barely breathe. He did not stop plucking me until I was completely bare in his hands.

I do not know what the wicked little kid had in mind by putting me in such a state, but I was getting anxious for him to stop torturing me when he started blowing on a little stove and telling the fisherman that he was going to roast me and eat me for lunch. And he really did lay me out on the coals, but the extreme pain gave me strength. I shrieked and made a lucky jump that landed me in the lake.

When the little boy saw this, he started shrieking himself and begging his father with tears to get his lunch back for him. He did his best to come after me, but as weak as I was, I swam off fast enough that they could not catch me. But I got out of one danger only to face another. Hundreds of different kinds of fish were chasing me in the water and doing their best to devour me. The fact that there were so many of them slowed them down and warded off the evil because their fighting over the prey prolonged my death. No sooner did one of them get a hold of my foot than another jumped and made it let go. This

346

merry-go-round lasted quite a while and exhausted me to the point of almost giving up.

A dog came to quench its thirst at the shore and saw me—it changed the form of my punishment. I looked like an appetizing snack, so it started swimming straight toward me, snatched me up and carried me back to shore. It put me down and stared, probably trying to figure out if I would make a good or bad meal. It was already licking me and nudging me with its nose to sink its teeth into my tastiest part when it turned its head at the sound of a voice shouting "tok-brifs,"[287] which saved my life. The dog's master had a bow and arrows and was no doubt hunting around the lake. He came up to me, looked at me and stepped back with his hand on the dog's head, saying "Bah!" I thought I might get out of it and in fact the dog followed its master without thinking twice.

It turned back to look at me a few times, but I did not let it bother me until it suddenly sprinted back and stood over me slobbering, ready to snatch me up and gobble me down in some corner without its master knowing. I was so scared that I screamed out "tok-brifs, tok-brifs!" The dog stopped and the master, who was 30 feet away, turned around to see where the voice came from. The dog came and went a few times, wanting to plunder me, but when I found that I could talk, I did so every time my life was in danger—it was too easy to pass up.

However, the hunter got really worried and could not figure out where the "tok-brifs" kept coming from, so he finally came back to his dog and me and very soon noticed where the voice came from. When he was sure that it was coming from me, he recoiled in fear and surprise and in a trembling voice asked me the reason for such an extraordinary phenomenon. I came up with an idea that I thought perfect for my

---

[287] "Hold on." Almost all the scholars acknowledge the author's accuracy and mildness in interpreting this word. However, one respected scholar today explains it very differently. He says that *tok* means tuna and *brifs* fresh and therefore this means "fresh tuna," which does not seem likely. The scholar apparently loves this fish and wants to bring it up whenever he has the opportunity.

current situation: I said that I had been raised by a great philosopher who wanted me to talk and who had found the means to teach me. My answer reassured the hunter who thought our meeting was so special that he lifted me up, put me in his hat and covered me with his handkerchief, saying that he was going to make me the happiest bird on earth. I did not think I should respond to this and even less that I should talk so much, afraid of getting into more trouble. It was enough that I had found a way to save my life—as unlucky as it was, I was not ready to lose it. This might seem hard to believe, Lamekis, but I admit my weakness: I was never able to stay cool in the face of death.

The hunter carried me to a nearby manor, gave me something to eat, cleaned my wounds and took such great care of me that after a few days I was in perfect health. Even my feathers were starting to grow back and it did not take long before I looked like one of the best-dressed owls of the country. I found myself so much better off compared with where I was before (except for worrying about what became of you, Lamekis), that I fed their good feelings toward me by talking sometimes, without, however, being too intelligent, afraid that the marvel might make them think too much. My behavior was successful. In the hope of making me talk, he did all he could for me. I was treated like the most valuable bird in the world.

Every time my master left, he locked me up in a cage and took every precaution that I would not fly away. One day when it took him longer than usual to return, he came back with a man whose voice I recognized as the villainous Zelimon, whom you mentioned so often, the architect of your disgrace. If I had as much strength as I had righteous indignation, your revenge would have been accomplished—I would have torn him to pieces.

The hunter was his servant, as I could tell by their conversation, and told him everything about his valuable find. "It's a real present to give the Queen," he said. "No bird of his species has ever spoken before, especially with so much intelligence. It's a sure way to get back in her good graces."

"I agree," Zelimon said, "but that makes 20 times I've hid here to witness what you're telling me and I haven't been able to see it for myself. I'm certainly not going to risk taking it out unless I'm absolutely sure."

What I'd just heard hit me hard—I felt a strong desire to change my fate. I thought it would be a lot better to belong to the Queen than to this nameless hunter. With this in mind I thought I should talk and did so. The few words I pronounced were so perfect for what was just said that Zelimon was beside himself.

"Let's not talk about the Queen for the moment," he said lifting up my cage, "this may be too precious to give to anyone but the love of my heart. You know how crazy I am about that adorable woman; how I have sighed after her for so long; whom my passion has put in irons. You know how far I've gone so far. Well, here's a good way to be seen in a gentler light. This bird will entertain her in her prison and maybe even do something better. I've given this cruel woman some time to come around to my point of view. I gave her my word. But I don't want to miss any opportunity that might fulfill my desires in a good way. After that, if I use the rights that I've got in kidnapping her, she'll have only herself to blame and I'll have nothing to criticize myself for."

Saying this, which he did not seem too confident in even though he pretended to be, Zelimon took me into his room, grabbed some big keys from a closet, lifted a trap door and went down a stairway lit by hanging lamps. I did not know what to think of all this. We threaded through cellar after cellar until he finally stopped at an iron door. He opened it and we entered a magnificently furnished apartment.

There were several rooms that we crossed without meeting anyone, but in the last one, Lamekis, I saw her—that lovely Clemelis, the object of your desires! I was sure of it because her name was called and I recognized her from all your descriptions. She received Zelimon's gift with tears. She did not see it as a diversion, but as an omen that her misfortunes would continue. She spit out all kinds of bitter complaints, called her abductor all the names he deserved and swore that she would kill him herself if he dared to show up again.

In spite of the traitor's cruelty, he obeyed and left, but before locking the door he told her that he would do as she said until the agreed upon day and after that, he too, would be respected. Clemelis did not deign to answer; she kept sinking deeper in sorrow.

The bitter situation reminded me of mine and I got depressed. "Oh Heavens," I said, forgetting all about the fact that Clemelis was there, "could it be that you take pleasure in bringing nothing but unhappiness?" Although your respectable wife should have expected to hear me speak since Zelimon had warned her of it, still she cried out in astonishment and fear. "Don't worry," I told her, "if destiny is hunting you down, you're not the only prey. Lamekis, your loyal husband, is disastrous proof of this…"

"Lamekis?" Clemelis stared at me with fright in her eyes. "How…what do you know about his fate?"

"Stay calm, Clemelis," I said in response.

"Ah! I'm out of control," she dropped on a pile of sheets. "You're far too shocking to overcome my fear. I'm not used to such wonders. Who are you that you know me so well? Please, fast, put a stop to this cruel uncertainty. That's the only way to help me."

I quickly told her who I was and as soon as I said I was your close friend she asked me, trembling, how I had miraculously changed my form and where I had last seen you. I told her in full everything she wanted to know. She listened carefully, which proved her love for you and her surprise. But when I came to your transformation, she clasped her hands together, stared at the sky and stayed in this position for so long that I thought she had turned to stone. I called out to her until she finally responded by crying. She choked on her tears for more than an hour without being able to say a word.

A truly compassionate soul forgets its own misfortunes to lament those of another. I used all my energy to comfort lovely Clemelis. To succeed I got her to hope that the Heavens would bring you back to her some day and that you were beholden to her for the end of your metamorphosis and unhappiness. The idea seemed to calm her down. "Oh, if his happiness depends on my faithfulness to him, Lamekis will stop being a snake some day. The Heavens have protected my virtue until now, in spite of the terrible, tempting assaults that I've had to endure. I believe it's still pure."

"It's for sure," I said. "Take comfort, Clemelis, let's both take comfort. The great Dehahal promised Lamekis and me that we would get our original forms back. He is too great and too respectable to debase himself to fool us."

Clemelis and I spent three whole days telling each other everything that happened to us. Since I can assume, Lamekis, (Sinouis went on) that you didn't know what happened after Zelimon's detestable deed when he got into your wife's room under your name, seeing that the story you confessed to me was interrupted when you killed him, I'll tell you what followed. I'll do my best to tell it like she did. Pretend it's Clemelis talking.

(In spite of the proofs of my lovely wife's virtue, the idea of this made me turn pale. "Well," I said in a broken voice, "what miracle snatched her from that wretch's arms?"

"That's what you want to know?" Sinouis asked. "Don't be scared. Your honor is in wise hands...too wise to take it away.")

Clemelis continues her story

In spite of the wonderful sensation I had when I kissed my husband, I suddenly felt a certain repugnance that did not seem natural to me. My elation gradually subsided and something secretly opposed the passion I was feeling. To answer it, I had to resort to that art of imposture that puts emotional masks on the outside that we do not really feel on the inside.

At first I was the most ungrateful being in the world. I thought that what I felt about my husband was resentment, but it was really a premonition. The colder I became, the more the one who seemed to be my husband assured me of his love. All of a sudden I found myself so distraught that I my knees gave way. I had to lie to hide my frigidity. I said that I was feeling bad and I pretended to faint. I needed some time to breathe and ponder over the cause of the strange state I was in. I tried not to appear too obvious.

And my so-called spouse, believing that I had fainted, dashed off and came back a moment later carrying a torch and a bottle full of an elixir that was surely meant to revive me. I opened my eyes just a little, hoping that the sight of him would bring back my fading emotions. I thought I had not opened them enough because I did not recognize the face that I kept so well guarded in my heart. I stared and screamed at the same time. "Ach! Wretch!" I recognized Zelimon and jumped up in anger. "So that's your wicked, evil game. Watch out now, I could kill you, which should have happened a long time ago."

The traitor, being caught and discovered, dropped his torch and it went out. I started screaming so loudly that everyone came running. Zelimon got scared of being arrested and fled, finally ridding me of his awful presence.

I asked so many questions of my servants that I ended up finding the villainous slave who had betrayed me. I kicked her out with all the fuss she deserved and to avoid running any future risks, I decide to never go to bed without locking myself in. After Zelimon's two bold attempts, I could not be too careful. I complained again to the King and if it weren't for Boldeon I would have been avenged, but he was pardoned in this case on the condition that he never set foot in the Court again.

Several months passed without a word about him. I fooled myself that I would never again have to worry about him, but one night I was awoken from a deep sleep by a terrible sound at my door. I jumped out of bed, ran to the windows and shouted as loudly as I could, but it was useless. He had taken careful measures that I not be helped. The door of my room burst open and Zelimon stood there, sword in hand, ordering his followers to take me away. After a long trip he brought me into this underground room where he told me that same night that I would be locked in until I fulfilled his passion.

Oh wise friend of my worthy husband, (Clemelis cried a river of tears), can you imagine what became of me after this detestable attack. I spent my days and nights in grief, rage and despair. As these emotions slowly abated and I fell sick, the traitorous abductor got scared that I would die and swore awful vows that he would never resort to violence, which promise held my worries and fears at bay. My sickness did not get worse. I slowly got over it and in spite of myself I started living the life that was given me, that I would have cut short a thousand times if it weren't for the hope of seeing my beloved husband again.

Since this time my abductor did not dare to force himself on me, but a few days ago he seemed a little less respectful. When I complained to him, he was adamant that in the end I would have to answer to his consuming passion since there was nothing to hold him back. In spite of my tears, prayers and threats, he told me to make up my mind to satisfy him, swearing that in a month he would resort to violence.

So, Sinouis, that's where I am. You can see how just my tears are. I see only death as a means of escaping the awful destiny that the Heavens have apparently condemned me to without appeal.

Sinouis goes to the Court

Clemelis had just finished talking when we heard the horrible noise of locks and bolts announcing Zelimon's entrance. Clemelis trembled. "Oh Sinouis, what's going to become of me? The tyrant is surely coming to unleash the rest of his brutality. The time has come for me to prepare myself. So, do we see now that the Heavens never protect the innocent?"

The door opened, but instead of Zelimon, it was the hunter. "Don't worry, Clemelis," he approached respectfully. "Your fate will change in a short time. I would like to free you at this very moment, but you would only be put in more danger. If I weren't afraid of risking your precious life, I would instantly open the doors of this hateful prison, but acting on my incredible compassion for you would kill us both or at least put us under Zelimon's cruel control forever. I have seen too many of his inhuman acts to doubt it. My plan is the surest. I'm going to the Court to inform the King of your imprisonment and the brutality you are suffering. His sovereign order will break your chains and take revenge on your cruel enemy. I'm tired of obeying a tyrant whose crimes I hate. I will confess them and be protected from his wrath. The unforgivable way he's been using me, the tyrannical way he's just taken away the priceless treasure that I thought would make my fortune, has finally made up my mind. This bird was meant for the Queen and I brought it to him for that. I won't say anymore, Clemelis. Before long you will have reason to thank me, but while you're waiting, remember not to say anything about it to the tyrant. He is too preoccupied with you to even think about the bird. I'm going to put back the keys I stole. I'll say no more; time is of the essence."

This said, the hunter put me back in my cage. My first reaction was to scream; my second stopped me. Nothing could be better for Clemelis and me than the decision this man made. It was easy to see that it was purely out of self-interest, but whatever the motive only great good could come from it. I was going to the Court to belong to the Queen. And even though the hunter might change his mind and not speak about Clemelis in fear of punishment, I would be there and I could talk. Thinking about this made it easier for me to separate from Clemelis—it was only to be better reunited later.

Never had anyone made a trip so fast. The hunter was in a hurry to get there. I could see the worry in his eyes and I saw him constantly looking back, thinking that at any moment the formidable Zelimon would be on his tail. All his worries stopped when we got to the Court. The next day he went to the Brouk-chailloc[288] and the day after he was presented to the Queen, as he wanted. His present was too well received for him to suffer the least delay. The Queen was enchanted when they told her how well I talked. The Houcaïs was there jumping up and down. They put me in a magnificent cage and I was celebrated throughout the Court.[289] They were waiting impatiently for me to talk. I myself was waiting for the hunter to talk, still hoping that he would tell everything about Clemelis and especially how Zelimon was abusing her. He was obviously debating it. I thought I should start, so I spread my wings, stretched out my neck, rose up on my feet, stared the King in the face and cried out, "Oh Houcaïs, Queen and Nobles of the Court, listen to me, I'm going to speak." At these words everyone stuck out their tongues[290] and paid close attention to me.

The hunter and everyone else were not a little taken aback by the way I told of Clemelis' kidnapping by Zelimon. I left nothing out. The Houcaïs got extremely angry, drank down his fury in three straight cups[291] and immediately gave orders to free Clemelis.

---

[288] The first lady-in-waiting to whom you had to give a present to get an audience with the Queen. The present was important and could be only one of three things: a soft-roed herring, a tin comb or a pair of pewter earrings. The hunter gave her a tin comb.

[289] A way of expressing satisfaction.

[290] The original says "Fla-ri-crok-dol-ki-kan-gran-douil-guerlache," which literally means "each let their tongue fall out." In fact, that is the real sense of it because the note says that when they wanted to pay very close attention, they let their tongues fall out to show they were listening carefully and well-raised people took great care to hold their hand under it to catch the drool. Noble women had the right to play around with the tip of their tongue like the Gauls do with their fans.

[291] The sign of violent anger was to drink and it was from these people's customs that we got the polite way of talking by inviting a

After calming down from his boiling anger, he turned to Boldeon and whispered to him that he had better get to the gilgan-gis because I was surely a Grouil-grou-gran[292] and it was impossible for me to be so intelligent without the Bar-bu-fou[293] being mixed up in it. I shuddered at his words. Afraid of the impending punishment, I asked to speak with the King: I whistled and he stuck out his tongue to listen to me. I was about to tell him about my adventures and all about yours, too, Lamekis, when a wonder, which seemed dreadful to the whole Court but quite nice to me, terrified the crowd around me. All of a sudden my bones cracked with a horrible clicking sound; instead of wings my old arms popped out and my legs were down there in place of a bird's feet. The transformation happened so suddenly that in no time at all I was back to my old self, just like you see me today. It was a good thing my cage was big otherwise I would have been crippled for the rest of my life. Unfortunately my nose was too crowded to come out and stayed like you see it—an owl's beak. It's pretty tragic, but I hope that the great Dehahal will get it out. He is too great and respectable not to do me this favor.

The Houcaïs and the Court were astonished at the wondrous change that had just happened to me. It was unanimously agreed that I was a Grouil-grou-gran and it was useless for me to defend my humanness. The order was given to send me here until my death. The Queen, who thought the prank was unforgivable, demanded that I be imprisoned here because in my story I emphasized how deep it was, hoping to heighten the horror and to illicit more and more sympathy for Clemelis' imprisonment. The reason why she chose this for me was that since it was so deep, I would be less of a threat

---

guest to drink: Monsieur, Madame, Mademoiselle, etc., let's swallow our pain; I forgive you; let's go, I swallow my pain. Grotius, however, who loved dinner parties, never spoke like this any more than Cicero, Aristotle, Virgil, Tacitus, etc., which becomes very awkward.
[292] Sorcerer.
[293] Devil.

and seeing that I was possessed by the Bar-bu-fou, they could not take too many precautions.

Whatever the case may be, they imprisoned me here like you see, but they probably won't leave me here for long if they continue to think I'm a Grouil-grou-gran because, Lamekis, you know the law. There's no appeal—after the gil-gangis I'll have to die. And that will be the end of all my adventures. Oh Vilkonhis, why did you pull me out of the chaos just to make me so miserable?

Zelimon unearthed

Sinouis finished up there and started crying like a suckling calf. I did my best to comfort him. "You and I are in the same situation," I said, "we're on the same run and the Heavens are tired of our bad luck: they gave us back our old shapes and reunited us. That's a sure sign that things are about to change. For myself, I have nothing but thanks to give as far as I can tell by what you just told me. I figure that Clemelis is back at the Court."

"Don't kid yourself," a voice came out of the closet. "All chained up as I am, Clemelis is still my slave and she won't get out of it until I am free."

We trembled at these words. Who could have spoken them? I got up to find out. In spite of the weight of my chains, I dragged myself to the closet and what a shock! It was Zelimon whom I thought I had taken revenge on, whom I had bitten so many times and whom I thought was reduced to dust. Oh Heavens, always what you least expect, you neglect to anticipate. But what was I saying? Oh great Vilkonhis, aren't you omnipotent? And when you decide on a miracle, who are we to doubt it?

In spite of my growing rage at the sight of the traitor who kept giving me so much trouble, I thought I should hide it to try to find out what air Clemelis was breathing.

"I'll tell you about it," he continued, "but it will do you no good. I'll say nothing you want to hear. But it's different for the adventure that kept me alive. It will upset you and that's good enough for me tell it.

"Know, then, that I pretended to die, but I didn't. I saw the awful risk I was taking, but I had to try. I was very lucky to be wearing the cuirass otherwise your rage would have completely annihilated me. All this surprises you, but it's nothing compare to what came next. Stick out your tongue, Lamekis, I'm going to strike you with blows as deadly as you thought you'd struck me. I heard everything and judging by the story of your Sinouis, you were thinking that Clemelis had not given in to my advances. Don't believe it, Lamekis. I possessed the treasure that you are so jealous of. I admit that it was to you that she gave in, but what does it matter? I enjoyed it all the same. Don't be fooled by assurances to the contrary—a woman would never confess such deeds. That's the truth. Believe it if you want."

The way the villain told me this so succinctly affected me and threw me in a rage. "Well, Sinouis," I turned to him, "what am I think of your story?"

"That Zelimon is a wretch," he replied, "worthy of the most horrible punishments. He knows very well that he has to die and his black soul wants to drag down all his enemies in its wake. Could it be that you still dare to doubt the wisdom of your most respectable wife? After getting back your original form? Isn't this decisive and convincing proof in her favor?"

There was nothing to say to that and it calmed me down, but it did not remove the worries I had about Clemelis' fate. Zelimon seemed so wicked and not so very scared of death that I had reason to believe that he would die without ever saying what he did with her. Sinouis felt likewise and the traitor did not stop telling me the same thing.

Later we learned from him how he had dealt with the orders that the Houcaïs pronounced against him. He said everything could devastate us. One of his people had met the fleeing hunter and had informed him right away. He said he had no doubt that the servant had met with Clemelis, was won over and was going to tell everything at the Court. Considering what might come up, the first thing he did was to check on Clemelis, transfer her that very night from her prison to another and hide himself at a reliable friend's house. But since he was a wretch, his friend was like him and to get in good with the King he gave him up to an officer sent from the Court to arrest him. He was sure that he was going to die, so he swore and blasphemed to high heaven that Clemelis and us would all die with him.

If we were at all able to take revenge on this villain, we would have killed him on the spot. But we were chained in such a way that it was impossible for us to follow our instinct.

The orders from the Court should have arrived any day to decide our fate. They finally came and we were taken to the capital to be handed over to the law for our trial. Zelimon was pardoned on behalf of his father's rank and the urgent appeals of his friends. They let him go on the condition that he bring Clemelis to the Queen and he acquiesced when he learned that Sinouis and I were bound to die in spite of our innocence. We were foreigners. That was enough for everyone to abandon us. Besides, to save the villainous Zelimon we had to be found guilty. All they had to do was to declare us Grouil-grou-gran and possessed by the Bar-bu-fou; there was no pardon and we had no hope.

Sinouis and I waited in a dungeon until they took us out to give us the gil-gan-gis and so to torture. We were helping each other to resign to the divine decrees when the officer who was transferring us came up and was very polite, which was a good omen for us. "Don't worry," he said, "on my word you have a strong lawyer in Clemelis. She brought the Queen along to ask the King to pardon you. He promised to grant it provided that you prove that you are innocent of being Grouil-grou-gran."

We breathed easier at this good news. "Praise be to Vilkonhis," Sinouis shouted. "If we're going to appear before the Houcaïs, we have nothing to fear. Innocence will glory and crime will grumble."

"Clemelis is alive and free," I said, "that's enough for me. I have nothing more to fear."

We were transferred to a room that was as pleasant as the last was glum. "Wait here for new orders," the officer said. "If the King wasn't sunk in melancholy, you would appear before him today, but it shouldn't be long. While waiting, pray to the Heavens to take away the cause of the King's grief."

I asked the gentleman if it wasn't indiscrete to fill us in on the reasons for the Houcaïs' affliction. "They're quite reasonable," he said to me. "No one better than you knows Falbao, the wonderful dog who was given to the King, who saved his life so many times and has never left his side..."

"Wait!" I interjected. "Has some sinister accident befallen him?" I was as desperate and grief-stricken as the King. Besides the fact that I, too, loved this tender dog, I knew how he felt because of what happened to my friendly animal[294] and how sore these kinds of losses are.

"Thank the Heavens," the officer continued, "that Falbao is not dead. The Houcaïs would die himself. No, Lamekis, he lives, but has lately fallen into a lethargy that they fear is the beginning of the end. The King has summoned all the doctors of the kingdom, but not a one of them so far has been able to heal him. All agree on the cause of the sickness (it's lethargy), but no one can cure it. Only one, an Ethiopian, guarantees that the skin of a snake from the South Pole can cure him. But at the same time he agrees on how difficult it would be to get it and that has caused the King great worry and fear. The Court, who loves him, shares his fright, but no one now is willing to prove his respect and affection at the price of his blood."

---

[294] The little eaglet. After printing this book the author got some news of this amiable animal from the Intelligence to whom we owe this wonderful story. It will be communicated to the public later, only after a second appearance of the spirit. While waiting we can tell the reader that the eaglet did not die as was reported. The translator, who resorted to the erudition of a critic for this passage, misconstrued it, causing this gross error. We will strive to amend it later.

While the officer was telling us all this, I had an idea that turned out to be fruitful. I remembered, when I was changed into a snake and cast onto Earth, that I was near one of the poles, but I could not remember which one it was. The affliction of my transformation had erased part of my memory. Nevertheless, I was risking nothing by offering to heal Falbao. My snake's skin still hung onto my body and was so extraordinary that it might have the necessary power for the cure. I told the officer my idea and he thought it feasible. We left to report it, telling ourselves that if I healed Falbao, I would rise from the depths of misfortune to the heights of favor. Sinouis felt the same and broke laughing hilariously at the idea of seeing a near end to his misfortunes. "So!" he cried out. "I'll still be able to enjoy life? Ah, Lamekis, is there any greater good? Isn't the grave frightening? And so, can I imagine that I will see my home again after being gone for so long? Oh father and mother, will you recognize your poor son? Won't his dreadful owl's beak scare you?" This thought saddened him for a moment, but the next melted his sadness. Never were we so weak and so attached to life: I had waged war on it and he accepted in good faith.

I was expecting to see Clemelis again at any moment. The idea of delighting in her yearned-for presence enraptured me. At last she appeared. How could I describe how I felt? She was accompanied by Milkhea. Our reunion was long; hugs and kisses exchanged with laughter and tears again and again—we could not stop. "Oh my dear husband, is it really you at last?"

"Oh my dear Clemelis, you've been given back to me! Are you faithful to me?"

"Oh my son!"

"Oh my mother!"

"How happy we are!" Those were the only things we could find to say. Our emotions did the rest. There was no end to our outpourings.

Lodaï, the chief minister, who held the highest rank in the empire with Boldeon, came to put some order in our reunion. He hugged me tightly and after showing me his joy at seeing me again, he took me aside and asked me if I was really sure that my snake's skin was powerful enough to heal Falbao. I answered him that even without being totally certain, I had a lot of faith in it. "If the cure is as strong as your trust in it," he said, "by saving yourself, you'll save everyone. Falbao is a lot worse this evening. The Houcaïs is in tears and the whole Court is suffering. We shouldn't wait any longer to cure him. The Monarch wants me to take you to his room. He still thinks you're a Grouil-grou-gran, but he pardons you on behalf of the Queen, Clemelis and all those concerned with your fate. As for your Sinouis, he will obey the law: if he doesn't prove his innocence, I fear for his fate. His owl's beak is decisive. I don't know how he will be able to defend himself against an accusation with such convincing proofs. As a friend I advise you to abandon him. The King wants it and between us, he's right."

Sinouis did not miss a word of our conversation and screamed out in fear of his imminent arrest. He ran up to Lodaï. "Really," he cried, "truly, honestly and sincerely, I'm not a Grouil-grou-gran. If my poor nose is guilty, cut it off. I'm ready for the most heinous punishments."

Lodaï motioned for him to leave. "He was a Grouil-grou-gran when he dropped out of his mother's belly and he will be one when he drops into the grave. This unlucky friendship has plunged you into tragedy and you will only be really happy when he has suffered the severity of the law."[295]

The minister was obstinate in his opinion and did not give me time to respond. He led me straight to the Houcaïs. I pitied him in his present state: he was crying bucketfuls and clasping Falbao tightly in his arms. Falbao's dying eyes presaged his near future. The King motioned me to approach, put one hand on my knee and showed me Falbao with the other. The Queen and the whole Court encouraged me. I did the same and whistled at the King. He gave me permission to

---

[295] It consisted of swallowing your guts while still alive.

speak, so I asked if I could touch Falbao. It was granted. I put my hand on the friendly animal's head. His eyes opened and stared fixedly at me; he wagged his tail and showed that he recognized me. The Houcaïs was surprised and said aloud that the reaction boded well—it had been a long time since he had done as much. But if this surprised him, it was nothing compared to what happened next. Falbao, who had stopped staring at me, suddenly lifted his head, stuck his nose out and sniffed me all over. Then even more suddenly he got up and jumped on me. I was almost thrown backward.

The King cried out in joy, "Ha! Falbao is saved!"

I had no doubt that my snake's skin was the secret cause of the marvel. With this in mind I took off my clothes and stood there naked. The wonderful dog no sooner saw the skin than he grabbed it with his teeth and greedily gobbled it up.

The Queen and the ladies, who took a strange pleasure in this spectacle, all asked me at the same time how I came to possess such a precious, miraculous treasure and if it was easy to find skins with virtues like this. The Houcaïs, in his joy at seeing Falbao back on his feet (his bowing and jumping proved his total recovery), cried out that he owed his life to me and he would grant me anything I asked.

"Two things," I answered instantly. "The pardon of a friend accused of being a Grouil-grou-gran, but is not; and the punishment of that wicked Zelimon." They were both granted. Besides this the Houcaïs named me his chief Bilthou-car[296] and I was greeted as such right away.

---

[296] The superintendant of all illness in the kingdom. One of his primary responsibilities, because it's what he wore, was to be in charge of the hair of everyone who died, which produced enormous revenues. Strabo very rightly pointed out the significant blunder of Aristotle in his *On Hair*, Ch. 2, page 357, where he says that "houil-choul" means hairless and adds that "graf-jak" signifies head, meaning hairless head, which the Egyptian author never claimed and never said that in the kingdom of the Abdalles the superintendants were bald. Aristotle held this opinion against all other scholars.

Before leaving the King to go into the room assigned to me, I begged him to allow Sinouis to defend himself in his presence and before the whole Court. It was granted. They sent for him and barely had he entered the room when Falbao jumped on him and ripped away his owl's beak. The King spanked himself at this sight and we all did the same, but an even more wondrous event froze us all in terror. The owl's beak that Falbao had thrown on the ground immediately started spinning around, stretching out and growing taller until there suddenly appeared before us the figure of a man.

"Greetings, Houcaïs. Greetings, Lamekis. Scealgalis be praised forever. I am the philosopher Dehahal (I had already recognized him), come to announce to you a never-ending happiness. Lamekis would have been granted immortality if he had asked to forgive his cruel enemy Zelimon. Know, then," he turned to me, *that there is more glory in forgiving than in punishing.*" With that he disappeared.

We were all flabbergasted by this wonder when Boldeon entered and threw himself at my feet. "Oh Lamekis," he cried, "have pity on my poor son. Give him back his original form and after that you can do what you want with him."

I did not understand what he was saying. Later we learned that Zelimon had been transformed into an owl, the most hideous kind you can imagine. In spite of Dehahal's advice, I held onto my bitterness and secretly rejoiced. I decided that if the Heavens made me master of the traitor's fate, I would never turn him back to the way he was before.

Conclusion

Oh you mortals, for whom I tried to write my story, forever bless the Creator of the Universe and thank him with me for all the graces that he gave me. I have ruled this great kingdom for a long time and my rule has been mild and peaceful. I wage war to make a lasting peace. Without pretending to have the mysterious marks of a great politician, my works have proved that those of my predecessors were but shadows of mine. The kingdom of the Abdalles under my ministry has become an ocean that all the other seas and rivers of the Earth empty into. Without using violence I brought down pride, suppressed reckless opulence, cut off useless members and uprooted forever the shrubs of future rebellion. Under my reign the Kings of the Abdalles have truly become Kings. Blessed be the Almighty forever. It is he who has performed these miracles. I am only lucky to be his instrument and I will be glorified forever for this.

APPENDIX

Preface to Part 3

The welcome that the public has given to the first two parts of this work makes me hope that the rest will be received with the same gratitude. The design is so new and the fiction so extraordinarily elaborate that I can confidently assume that it will receive the same honor.

I will not take the time here to answer a number of letters that have been written on the matter, for example that they see a hidden purpose that I never dreamed of. A number of people who have done me the honor of reading my book have spent their time paying attention only to this. I can say with the utmost sincerity that my works are as virtuous as they are entertaining and I have always kept my writings far from that dangerous venom that some books are infected with only to slip in some ambiguous reference to the state or religion. Anything like this is absolutely foreign to my way of thinking. I respected everything that is forbidden. A few critics will no doubt take issue with this statement, but I do not think my reputation will change. I would rather be praised for simplicity than make a name for myself among those detestable conspiracies whose only satisfaction is in this frivolous benefit. Peace is on the side of a subject who is submissive to the civil laws; anxiety belongs to those other minds that rear up only to get famous for kicking against authority.

But let's get back to Part 3. I think I should advise the readers to skip the notes the first time through. The subject itself is so abstract and calls for so much attention that it should be read through without stopping. I will advise them, too, that one reading will not be enough to understand the matters that are dealt with.

Everything here is mystery and secret. It is only with constant attention that one can manage to find the key. If any reader is fortunate enough to succeed, I beg them to please communicate it to me—I lost it a long time ago and would be ever so happy to find it again.

I think I should also state that this work bears the sacred talisman of the most mysterious cabal. If my readers wish to take me at my word, they will never leave their houses without this wonderful book in their hands. It will keep them from harm, bestow wealth, prevent unwanted or unpredictable accidents, give spirit to those without any and tone down those with too much. But its greatest attribute is to give peace to the soul and a lot of money when there is real need. It is an incontestable fact and cannot be doubted.

Although these benefits are great, they are nothing compared with what it can do for the fair sex. All women, no matter what their social status or virtue, whether they be young or old, married, widowed or virgins, are promised that if they read this Part of the book and what follows with a mind free of all prejudices on May 9 at three in the morning all their desires will come true before the end of the year. By reading this book, an ugly girl will become beautiful, a blonde will become a bedazzling brunette and a brunette will become a blinding blonde. It is impossible for me here to list all the goods that can come from a careful reading, but my guarantee is as positive and certain as it is true that the notes adorning this work are taken from our best authors and without them this work would be missing something essential. Can anything be more valuable? I will let the learned decide.

Preface to Part 5

Let's be reasonable, dear reader. I've got you hooked and I'm delighted. In what spirit are you going to read my book? If you truly do me justice, I will be as happy as the Grand Turk. That's because my goal has been to entertain you and I will surely entertain you, whatever your bias may be. The last four parts are not ridiculous, I have to admit, and that should be enough for you to like them. Between us I will confess that they please me immensely. But don't say a word about it. They will spread it around that I am conceited and truthfully that is not true. Just know that here is one of my most sensible works. It is lively, interesting, nice, funny, critical and has all the seductive qualities of novelty. It is a well, an abyss of treasures. Hope, dear reader, with me that I live long enough to produce many more works like this and above all do not forget to give me the praise I well deserve. Do not stop publishing my talent, my grace and my inspired inventions. Do not let an ignorant, jealous gang say anything bitter against me without going unpunished for it. Like a new Don Quixote, defend me at the crossroads as the nicest, most entertaining author. And don't forget to tell about all the good things I have done for you. My fertile imagination will find ways to be thankful. My heart is an ocean of gratitude—just dive in and you will be soaked in gratitude and generosity. To see me, to love me and to want to please me is really all the same thing. God knows it, as well as everyone who knows me. I am the wildest monk in Paris, I'll brag, and there's nothing to say.

Since I am the most considerate of all men and the most thoughtful, I have worked this fifth part so that you, dear reader, will not forget too much from the previous ones due to the lapse of time. You are going to be comfortable and gobble up all the sweet pages I have prepared for you. You are so lucky. Everyone else should be jealous!

I was going to say thank you here to a beautiful Dame who was kind enough to give a detailed portrait of me in her work called *La Princesse Laponoise*[*] where I am called Chevalier Frisquer. She depicted me with all my talents in a brilliant court. But I am waiting for the results and the role I must play in the second part of the same work, which I've been told about. Her brilliant and enchanting pen is going to spread gracefully the natural good qualities. I will make up my mind after reading the work so that my thanks will be equal to its praises and so that I in turn can do justice to her who so rightfully sang them. I am always infinitely grateful to those who want to show me as I am. I have so much to gain from being famous that I suffer with pleasure and without blushing when they say all the good things about me that I deserve. The only fear I have is that they will not say enough. My modesty (one of my strongest points) hides so many things that I am sometimes ashamed of giving it too much power. I lose too much from it, really, and that cannot be excused.

---

[*] [The Lapland Princess] published in 1738 by Louise Cavelier Lévesque.

Preface to Part 8

I am too grateful to the kindness that the public has honored me with not to give them an exact account of the state of my productions. If it were only up to me, this would have been done long ago. Jealous as I am of my words, I have tried to do this.

I printed the last four parts *La Païanne* and the last four parts of *Lamekis* in Holland and I am just now printing the next of *Mentor à la mode* and *Mémoires posthumes* and several other works. I hope that some of these writings will appear before the end of the year. I will, of course, neglect nothing in the future to make myself worthy of the kind affection with which my first works were received and I am not embarrassed to say that I owe it more to the public's indulgence than to my own ability.

It seems to me that the first maxim of an honest man is to be blameless and never hedge the truth.

I will take this opportunity, if I may, to thank the German author who set and printed the first four parts of *La Païanne*, which came out in my name. They tell me it was in Herstal, a few leagues away from Liege. If he had had the kindness to warn me, I would have sent the outline of the work and I would have been the first to help him, if he thought me capable. I have a special respect for this nation and generally for all foreigners. I hope I don't have to prove it on every occasion.

Since I am putting this Preface in *Lamekis*, I naturally have to say something about this work as well. If I had not started out so seriously, I would have much good to say about it, but the serious entails the truth and it is a real bore for self-esteem. The best thing I can do for myself is to wait for the public's opinion. If I were in its place, I would not pretend to say that either the author is crazy or he is very likely going to be soon. If this confession is not honorable, at least it is clever. There are many things they attribute to madness but it is a different story for those who call themselves reasonable and want to be so in spite of all common sense. We give them no quarter and truthfully we are right.

Afterword

At 650 pages and with numerous interwoven plots, *Lamekis, ou Les Voyages extraordinaires d'un Égyptien dans la terre intérieure; avec la découverte de l'Île des Sylphides*, by Charles de Fieux, Chevalier de Mouhy, is a forgotten but rather unusual and even original novel. Set in the distant past, the characters move from ancient Egypt through a number of fantastic countries in a series of adventures reminiscent of Lucian's *True History* or, more probably, Galland's translation of the *Thousand and One Nights* (1704-17).

The very complicated narrative follows very generally the adventures of Lamekis and consists of a number of different plots and subplots set in a mythical past, which may be reduced to five basic narratives. The novel begins with the title character's father and his adventures as a high priest in Egypt. We are then introduced to the intertwined stories of two exiles from the neighboring North African kingdoms of Abdalles and Amphicleocles—Princess Nasildaë and Prince Motacoa—who have been banished to the underground world and who befriend Lamekis after the death of his parents.[297] The third narr-

---

[297] This appears to be a consistent and inexplicable error of Fitting's, found both in this extract from his book and in his earlier, slightly more substantial 1993 essay, "Imagination, Textual Play, and the Fantastic in Mouhy's Lamékis," in *Eighteenth-Century Fiction*, Vol. 5: Iss. 4, (http://digitalcommons.mcmaster.ca/ecf/vol5/iss4/1). Prince Motacoa of the Abdalles was married to Princess Nasilaë of the Amphicleocles. Princess *Nasildaë*, Motacoa's mother (also known as Queen Hildaë), died soon after their marriage in the Inner Earth. After Motacoa saved Lamekis from the sinking boat/raft, he spent the next 10 years of his life with Motacoa and Nasilaë. Since he was ten years old when his father was banished and put out to sea, Motacoa and Nasilaë were more surrogate parents than friends. Motacoa him-

ative follows Lamekis to the now joined kingdoms of Abdalles and Amphicleocles and tell of his terrible jealousy; while the fourth describes Lamekis's exile, including his celestial voyage to the Island of the Sylphs. A fifth and concluding narrative relates his return to Abdalles and Amphicleocles. The novel also includes an account of its composition, beginning with a preface in which Mouhy explains that he was told this story by a mysterious Armenian.

At the same time, there are a number of elements in *Lamekis* that destabilize traditional narrative by introducing imaginative and fantastic elements into the actual narration of the story. Halfway through the novel, there is a lengthy scene in which the author is visited by various characters from the novel, who now complain to him about his inaccuracies. They are followed by the philosopher Dehahal—a character from the Island of the Sylphs who had tried unsuccessfully to convince Lamekis to undergo a ritual of purification, and who again urges de Mouhy to undergo this same initiation. After he declines, the author awakes in his bed clutching a mysterious

---

self places his rescue of Lamekis in chronological succession following his marriage to Nasilaë and the death of his mother, Nasildaë (cf. p 253). Fitting's work on *Lamekis* must be used with caution. Until such time as further research is generated or existing sources translated, Fitting's remains the only commentary on *Lamekis* available in English. Readers may also wish to consult F.C. Green's two articles on Mouhy—far more positive than Fitting allows in his reading of them: "The Chevalier de Mouhy, an Eighteenth-Century French Novelist" in *Modern Philology*, Vol. 22, No. 3 (Feb., 1925), pp. 225-237, which is a general outline of Mouhy's life, and "A Forgotten Novel of Manners of the Eighteenth Century: *La Paysanne Parvenue* by Le Chevalier de Mouhy" in *The Modern Language Review*, Vol. 18, No. 3 (Jul., 1923), pp. 309-316, a positive reading of Mouhy's most successful novel. And whilst Mouhy's *Lamekis* receives only a brief but positive notation, Edward D. Seeber's "Sylphs and Other Elemental Beings in French Literature since Le Comte de Gabalis (1670)" in *PMLA*, Vol. 59, No. 1 (Mar., 1944), pp. 71-83, is a fascinating piece of work. (Ed.)

manuscript that defies all attempts at translation until, six months later, his pen—on its own—starts to translate the conclusion to *Lamekis.*

In a more comic mode, there are also numerous depictions of strange and exotic customs that take the reader from the fantastic to a kind of delirium of textual play and vivid imaginings. As a manifestation of the king's grandeur, for instance, no one is allowed to look at him, nor speak to him, nor even breathe in his presence. (This leads to a number of amusing and ridiculous situations, although the interdiction against breathing in the king's presence is softened by the practice of putting a finger in one's mouth.) Given these restrictions, communications are rather complicated, although various stratagems have been devised to deal with this situation. At one crucial moment, the king takes off his left shoe and hands it to the eldest of his councilors. This signifies that he is to be carried at once to the temple. There the king acknowledges the gravity of the situation by dropping a brass ball, which signals that his subjects are allowed to breathe and indeed to look at him. This is such an exceptional event that most of his subjects have never seen their king before; that opportunity comes once in a lifetime, when the king is installed. Moreover, the king is provided with a number of brass balls with specific instructions inscribed on them, which he throws to various ministers according to the situation.

These examples are only a small sample of the ludicrous ceremonies in the novel, which seem to lack any purpose other than the exercise of the author's imaginative abilities. These weird rituals and observances are certainly not a model of some better way of doing things (as such descriptions would be read in the utopian novel), and any satirical purpose is overwhelmed by the bizarre description. Other types of fantastic customs include ritual punishments (of which the most terrible is to be tickled to death by the priestesses) and outlandish royal games, such as the Bil-gou-router,[298] in which the king and a chosen few lie with their heads in a circle into which a large rat is placed. The winner is decided when the rat hides in someone's mouth.

In terms of the frequent classification of *Lamekis* as an underground novel, three episodes in particular may explain Charles Georges Thomas Garnier's original designation, although none of them goes beyond the depiction of caverns and subterranean temples. The first involves Lamekis's father, the high priest of a secretive, monotheistic religion in Egypt. When the Queen demands to be initiated into its mysteries, he disguises her as a man, and they descend into a city hidden beneath the temple. But there is little description of this underground city, and this setting is quickly abandoned.

The second underground setting is the most interesting, for its depiction of a race of giant and intelligent worm creatures. This is the story of Motacoa, who, in a ritual probably taken from Sinbad's fourth voyage, is lowered with his mother into a bottomless pit and left for dead. Here, in an underground cave world, a number of adventures befall them as they battle various fantastic underground creatures.

Finally, the third subterranean episode is similar to the first: in Paris, when the author begins to think of abandoning the novel, he is visited by a large black dog that one night leads him through the Paris catacombs to an underground temple; there on the walls, in a series of murals, is the story of Lamekis. Again, this does not really constitute a subterranean world.

While *Lamekis* should not really be classified as a novel set in a subterranean world, the imagination that the author demonstrates goes beyond the fantastic inventions of any of his predecessors, and it merits inclusion here, even if it is only remotely connected to our concerns. Nonetheless, this is the

---

[298] The correct name is "Bil-gou-ta-ber-ker." "Bil-gou-router" is defined in the text as the actual playing of the game, not the name of the game. (Ed.)

most extreme case of mistakenly labeling a novel as subterranean. It probably happened when Garnier, wanting to include the novel in his 1789 collection *Voyages imaginaires, songes, visions et romans cabalistiques*, because of its many fantastic elements, had to find a category in which to put it, and then chose the "Voyages to the Underground" section since it did not fit in anywhere else.

Here is how Garnier describes this category in the introduction to volume 19 (actually the introduction to Ludvig Holberg's *Niels Klim's Underground Travels*): "After having taken our readers to the seven planets and having traveled the Heavens with them, we are now going to take them into the bowels of the Earth where they will again be pleasantly surprised to discover a new world, as well as the kinds of beings who live there."

At the beginning of volume 20, Garnier introduces *Lamekis* as follows: "Again we are taking the reader to the inside of the Earth. But this is not a new world that we are visiting, but only the retreat of the wise, where the faithful devotees of Serapis, in order to celebrate the mysteries of their religion, sought to find a place hidden from prying eyes. Nonetheless extraordinary things happen in this secret part of our globe, and the fertile imagination of the author is given free rein in the various adventures which take place there."

Once this decision was made, later readers such as Camille Flammarion and Régis Messac simply continued to call it a subterranean work. In this case, however, because the novel has never been reprinted since its appearance in Garnier's collection, it was not easily accessible, and later critics continued to repeat this description without really knowing what was in the novel.

Peter Fittting

377

SF & FANTASY

Guy d'Armen. *Doc Ardan: The City of Gold and Lepers*
G.-J. Arnaud. *The Ice Company*
Cyprien Bérard. *The Vampire Lord Ruthwen*
Aloysius Bertrand. *Gaspard de la Nuit*
Richard Bessière. *The Gardens of the Apocalypse*
Félix Bodin. *The Novel of the Future*
André Caroff. *The Terror of Madame Atomos*
Didier de Chousy. *Ignis*
Captain Danrit. *Undersea Odyssey*
C. I. Defontenay. *Star (Psi Cassiopeia)*
Charles Derennes. *The People of the Pole*
Georges Dodds (anthologist). *The Missing Link*
Harry Dickson. *The Heir of Dracula*
Jules Dornay. *Lord Ruthven Begins*
Sâr Dubnotal *vs. Jack the Ripper*
Alexandre Dumas. *The Return of Lord Ruthven*
J.-C. Dunyach. *The Night Orchid; The Thieves of Silence*
Henri Duvernois. *The Man Who Found Himself*
Achille Eyraud. *Voyage to Venus*
Henri Falk. *The Age of Lead*
Paul Féval. *Anne of the Isles; Knightshade; Revenants; Vampire City; The Vampire Countess; The Wandering Jew's Daughter*
Paul Féval, *fils. Felifax, the Tiger-Man*
Charles de Fieux. *Lamékis*
Arnould Galopin. *Doctor Omega*
G.L. Gick. *Harry Dickson and the Werewolf of Rutherford Grange*
Nathalie Henneberg. *The Green Gods*
V. Hugo, P. Foucher & P. Meurice. *The Hunchback of Notre-Dame*
Michel Jeury. *Chronolysis*
Octave Joncquel & Theo Varlet. *The Martian Epic*
Gérard Klein. *The Mote in Time's Eye*
Jean de La Hire. *Enter the Nyctalope; The Nyctalope on Mars; The Nyctalope vs. Lucifer*
André Laurie. *Spiridon*
Gabriel de Lautrec. *The Vengeance of the Oval Portrait*
Georges Le Faure & Henri de Graffigny. *The Extraordinary Adventures of a Russian Scientist Across the Solar System* (2 vols.)
Gustave Le Rouge. *The Vampires of Mars*

Jules Lermina. *Mysteryville; Panic in Paris; To-Ho and the Gold Destroyers; The Secret of Zippelius*
Jean-Marc & Randy Lofficier. *Edgar Allan Poe on Mars; The Katrina Protocol; Pacifica; Robonocchio; Tales of the Shadowmen 1-7*
Xavier Mauméjean. *The League of Heroes*
John-Antoine Nau. *Enemy Force*
Marie Nizet. *Captain Vampire*
C. Nodier, A. Beraud & Toussaint-Merle. *Frankenstein*
Henri de Parville. *An Inhabitant of the Planet Mars*
J. Polidori, C. Nodier, E. Scribe. *Lord Ruthven the Vampire*
P.-A. Ponson du Terrail. *The Vampire and the Devil's Son*
Maurice Renard. *The Blue Peril; Doctor Lerne; The Doctored Man; A Man Among the Microbes; The Master of Light*
Albert Robida. *The Adventures of Saturnin Farandoul; The Clock of the Centuries; Chalet in the Sky*
J.-H. Rosny Aîné. *Helgvor of the Blue River; The Givreuse Enigma; The Mysterious Force; The Navigators of Space; Vamireh; The World of the Variants; The Young Vampire*
Han Ryner. *The Superhumans*
Brian Stableford. *The New Faust at the Tragicomique;The Empire of the Necromancers (The Shadow of Frankenstein; Frankenstein and the Vampire Countess; Frankenstein in London); Sherlock Holmes & The Vampires of Eternity; The Stones of Camelot; The Wayward Muse.* (anthologist) *The Germans on Venus; News from the Moon; The Supreme Progress; The World Above the World*
Jacques Spitz. *The Eye of Purgatory*
Kurt Steiner. *Ortog*
Eugène Thébault. *Radio-Terror*
Villiers de l'Isle-Adam. *The Scaffold; The Vampire Soul*
Philippe Ward. *Artahe*
Philippe Ward & Sylvie Miller. *The Song of Montségur*

MYSTERIES & THRILLERS

M. Allain & P. Souvestre. *The Daughter of Fantômas*
A. Anicet-Bourgeois, Lucien Dabril. *Rocambole*
A. Bisson & G. Livet. *Nick Carter vs. Fantômas*
V. Darlay & H. de Gorsse. *Lupin vs. Holmes: The Stage Play*
Paul Féval. *Gentlemen of the Night; John Devil; The Black Coats ('Salem Street; The Invisible Weapon; The Parisian Jungle; The Companions of the Treasure; Heart of Steel; The Cadet Gang)*

Emile Gaboriau. *Monsieur Lecoq*
Steve Leadley. *Sherlock Holmes: The Circle of Blood*
Maurice Leblanc. *Arsène Lupin vs. Countess Cagliostro; Lupin vs. Holmes (The Blonde Phantom; The Hollow Needle)*
Gaston Leroux. *Chéri-Bibi; The Phantom of the Opera; Rouletabille & the Mystery of the Yellow Room*
William Patrick Maynard. *The Terror of Fu Manchu*
Frank J. Morlock. *Sherlock Holmes: The Grand Horizontals*
P. de Wattyne & Y. Walter. *Sherlock Holmes vs. Fantômas*
David White. *Fantômas in America*

SCREENPLAYS

Mike Baron. *The Iron Triangle*
Emma Bull & Will Shetterly. *Nightspeeder; War for the Oaks*
Gerry Conway & Roy Thomas. *Doc Dynamo*
Steve Englehart. *Majorca*
James Hudnall. *The Devastator*
Jean-Marc & Randy Lofficier. *Royal Flush*
J.-M. & R. Lofficier & Marc Agapit. *Despair*
Andrew Paquette. *Peripheral Vision*
R. Thomas, J. Hendler & L. Sprague de Camp. *Rivers of Time*

NON-FICTION

Stephen R. Bissette. *Blur 1-5; Green Mountain Cinema 1; Teen Angels & New Mutants*
Win Scott Eckert. *Crossovers* (2 vols.)
Jean-Marc & Randy Lofficier. *Shadowmen* (2 vols.)
Randy Lofficier. *Over Here*

ART BOOKS

Jean-Pierre Normand. *Science Fiction Illustrations*
Raven Okeefe. *Raven's L'il Critters*
Randy Lofficier & Raven OKeefe. *If Your Possum Go Daylight...*
Daniele Serra. *Illusions*

HEXAGON COMICS

Franco Frescura & Luciano Bernasconi. *Wampus*
Franco Frescura & Giorgio Trevisan. *CLASH*
L. Bernasconi, J.-M. Lofficier & Juan Roncagliolo Berger. *Phenix*
Claude Legrand, J.-M. Lofficier & L. Bernasconi. *Kabur*
Franco Oneta. *Zembla*
L. Buffolente, Lofficier & J.-J. Dzialowski. *Strangers: Homicron*
Danilo Grossi. *Strangers: Jaydee*
Claude Legrand & Luciano Bernasconi. *Strangers: Starlock*